PENGUIN  CLASSICS

THE BOOK OF THE CITY OF LADIES

CHRISTINE DE PIZAN was one of the most remarkable and respected literary figures in the courts of medieval Europe, the more so for being the only professional woman writer of her time. She was born in Venice in 1364, but while still a child her family left Italy and went to the Court of Charles V of France, where her father, Tommaso da Pizzano, was court physician and astrologer. When she was fifteen years old she married the young nobleman and courtier Etienne de Castel. Her happiness was marred first by the death of Charles V in 1380, which led to the demotion of Tommaso da Pizzano, and then by the illness and death of the latter only a few years later. In 1390 Etienne de Castel also died, leaving his young widow with three children, her mother and a niece to support. Around 1399 Christine de Pizan turned to writing as a living and soon secured an enviable reputation for her lyric poetry. She went on to write with great success on moral issues; two of her major concerns were the need for peace and the role of women in society, but she also wrote with authority on public affairs and the art of government, as well as producing a highly acclaimed biography of Charles V. Her output was vast and she incorporated many autobiographical details into her poetry, making it an invaluable record of medieval life. Much of her work survives in lavishly illuminated manuscripts, for she enjoyed influential patronage throughout her career. The outbreak of civil war in France prompted her to take refuge in a convent in 1418, where she remained until her death some time around 1430.

ROSALIND BROWN-GRANT took her BA and Ph.D. at the University of Manchester and is now Lecturer in French at the University of Leeds, where she specializes in medieval literature. She has published numerous articles on Christine de Pizan and is the author of *Reading Beyond Gender: Christine de Pizan and the Moral Defence of Women*.

PENGUIN BOOKS

Published by the Penguin Group
Penguin Books Ltd, 80 Strand, London WC2R 0RL, England
Penguin Putnam Inc., 375 Hudson Street, New York, New York 10014, USA
Penguin Books Australia Ltd, 250 Camberwell Road, Camberwell, Victoria 3124, Australia
Penguin Books Canada Ltd, 10 Alcorn Avenue, Toronto, Ontario, Canada M4V 3B2
Penguin Books India (P) Ltd, 11 Community Centre, Panchsheel Park, New Delhi – 110 017, India
Penguin Books (NZ) Ltd, Cnr Rosedale and Airborne Roads, Albany, Auckland, New Zealand
Penguin Books (South Africa) (Pty) Ltd, 24 Sturdee Avenue, Rosebank 2196, South Africa

Penguin Books Ltd, Registered Offices: 80 Strand, London WC2R 0RL, England

www.penguin.com

Published in Penguin Books 1999

035

Introduction, Notes and Translation copyright © Rosalind Brown-Grant, 1999
All rights reserved

The moral right of the translator has been asserted

Set in 10/12.5 pt Monotype Garamond
Typeset by Rowland Phototypesetting Ltd, Bury St Edmunds, Suffolk

Printed and bound in Great Britain by Clays Ltd, Elcograf S.p.A.

ISBN-13: 978-0-140-44689-0

www.greenpenguin.co.uk

CHRISTINE DE PIZAN

The Book of the
City of Ladies

Translated and with an introduction and notes by
ROSALIND BROWN-GRANT

PENGUIN BOOKS

ACKNOWLEDGEMENTS

I would like to thank various friends and colleagues for kindly giving me their help and advice: Roy Gibson, Eric Hicks, Angus Kennedy and James Laidlaw. I am particularly grateful to Milly Nettleton for her invaluable help with the layout of the typescript and to Steve Rigby for his constant willingness to comment on drafts of the text, essay and glossary. The above are, of course, absolved of all responsibility for what follows.

CONTENTS

PART II

Here begins the second part of the Book of the City of Ladies *which recounts how and by whom the houses and buildings were constructed inside the enclosure walls and how the City was filled with inhabitants.*

PART III

Here begins the third part of the Book of the City of
Ladies, *which explains how and by whom the high turrets of
the towers were finished off, and which noble ladies were
chosen to dwell in the great palaces and lofty keeps.*

INTRODUCTION

Virginia Woolf famously remarked that the most vital ingredient of
literary creativity was neither genius nor inspiration, but quite simply 'a
room of one's own'. To her mind, authors could not produce anything
of value if they had no place in which to cut themselves off from the
cares and duties of their daily existence so as to dedicate themselves to
their writing. In Woolf's opinion, it was for this reason that fewer women
than men appear in the canon of famous authors, particularly in the
period prior to 1700. Being financially dependent on men and bearing
almost exclusive responsibility for the household, women had few opportunities to shut themselves away from the rest of the world and to create
works of art. Moreover, for Woolf, this lack of a tradition of women
writers itself acted as a further brake on the female imagination. Unlike
male authors, who always had literary forefathers against whom to
measure themselves, prospective female authors were unable to 'think
back through their mothers' in order to assert their ideological and
aesthetic independence from them.[1]

Yet the work of recent feminist scholars suggests that Woolf may
have been too pessimistic in her assessment of the obstacles confronting
female creativity in the pre-modern period. Thanks to their endeavours,
a lost literature by women of previous generations is now starting to be
recovered. For the Middle Ages in particular, a period which Woolf
dismissed as being one of the least productive for female writers, an
authoritative body of evidence now exists which suggests that women
could frequently overcome the obstacles which, to Woolf, appeared to
be insurmountable.[2]

Christine de Pizan (*c.* 1364–1430), an Italian by birth who lived most of her life in France and wrote exclusively in French, was one such medieval woman who managed to find a 'room of her own'.[3] Unique amongst female authors in the Middle Ages, most of whom (such as Hildegard of Bingen) were nuns in established orders, Christine was the first to earn her living exclusively from her pen. She produced many works across a wide range of genres: from interventions in literary debates to courtesy manuals, from lyric poetry to treatises on chivalry, and from biographies of kings to books of pious devotion.[4] Yet Christine was not only a groundbreaking author in terms of her personal career. She was also the first woman in the Middle Ages to confront head-on the tradition of literary misogyny or anti-feminism that pervaded her culture.[5]

Christine composed a number of texts in defence of women, the most important of which is *Le Livre de la Cité des Dames* (*The Book of the City of Ladies*) (1405).[6] This text, which was well received in France during Christine's own lifetime and was later translated into both Flemish (in 1475) and English (in 1521), is probably the most familiar of all her works to modern readers. The *City of Ladies* belongs to the genre of the biographical catalogue, a genre established in classical antiquity which celebrated the lives of famous men and women.[7] Christine's catalogue of illustrious heroines appears within the framework of an allegorical dream-vision in which she herself is the chief protagonist. This vision comes to her one day as she sits in her study reading Matheolus's *Lamentations*, a thirteenth-century tirade against marriage in which the author vilifies women for making men's lives a misery.[8] The misogynist portrait which he paints of womankind as depraved and malicious creatures so shocks and depresses Christine that she falls into a state of despair at being a member of such a sex.

At this point in Christine's dream-vision, three personified Virtues – Reason, Rectitude and Justice – come to correct the negative view of women that she has absorbed from her study of Matheolus. They inform Christine that she has been chosen by God to write a book which will refute, point by point, the misogynists' accusations against womankind. This book will be like a city, one which is designed to house virtuous ladies and to protect them from anti-feminist attack. The Virtues then go on to provide Christine with examples of past and present heroines who will form the foundations, walls and towers of this allegorical City of Ladies. In Part I, Reason gives her examples of women, mostly pagans, who were famous for their soldierly courage, artistry or inventiveness; in Part II, Rectitude supplies Christine with stories of pagan, Hebrew and Christian ladies who were renowned for their prophetic gifts, exemplary chastity or devotion to their loved ones and fellow countrymen; in Part III, Justice recounts the lives of female saints who were crowned with glory for their steadfastness in the face of martyrdom or for their unfailing devotion to God. Christine's major source for Parts I and II of the *City of Ladies* is the *De Claris Mulieribus (Concerning Famous Women)* (*c.* 1375), a catalogue of women by the Tuscan author Boccaccio, which she may have read in its French translation, the *Des Cleres et Nobles Femmes*. For Part III of her text, Christine is heavily indebted to the *Miroir historial* (1333), Jean de Vignay's French translation of the historical sections of Vincent of Beauvais's vast encyclopedia, the *Speculum Maius* (begun after 1240). Through her examples of distinguished women, Christine seeks to prove in the *City of Ladies* that the female sex has played a crucial part in human civilization, artistically, politically and spiritually. Her aim is thus two-fold: both to refute the misogynist equation of womankind with sinfulness and to instil a sense of self-worth in her female readers.

In claiming that women can match men in terms of their military prowess, leadership, ingenuity and intelligence, Christine may seem to anticipate some of the key tenets of twentieth-century feminism. However, unlike modern feminists, Christine stopped well short of demanding for her sisters the equality of opportunity or access to education which would have enabled them to realize their potential. Although the heroines of the *City of Ladies* demonstrate that women have the innate capacity to be warriors and teachers, orators and artists, Christine does not recommend that her female contemporaries should actually pursue such careers. Indeed, in the sequel to her catalogue of women, *Le Livre des Trois Vertus (The Book of the Three Virtues,* also known as *The Treasure of the City of Ladies)* (1405), Christine's ambitions for her contemporaries seem to be even more modest. In this later text, which is a courtesy book for women offering them moral teachings and pragmatic advice about how they should dress, speak and behave, Christine instructs her female readers to accept their lot with patience and to submit to male control, be it that of their husbands or their fathers. Far from inciting her contemporaries to resist the limitations placed on them by society, she recommends traditional virtues to them: tolerance and humility to wives, modesty and obedience to virgins, and courage and dignity to widows.

Not surprisingly, this contradiction between the pioneering role which Christine created for herself as a professional writer and the restricted roles as daughters, wives and mothers which she outlined for other women, has led some twentieth-century critics to question whether she really deserves to be thought of as a 'mother to think back through'.[9] However, it would be anachronistic to apply modern standards to Christine's ideas about the position of women which, inevitably, differ radically from our own. If we are to evaluate the true nature of her achievement as a defender of women in the early fifteenth century, we must put Christine back into her proper historical context and read the *City of Ladies* in the light of the intellectual resources that were available to her at that time.

What then were the dominant medieval ideas about women which Christine had to refute in order to mount a successful defence of her sex?

The Middle Ages inherited a tradition of anti-feminism from two different sources: Judaeo-Christian theology and the medical science of classical antiquity.[10] From the Book of Genesis, medieval theologians took the idea that Eve – rather than Adam – was the one chiefly responsible for Original Sin entering the world. As a result, God had punished her and all other women by making her subject to her husband and inflicting upon her the pains of childbirth. This condemnation of the entire female sex on the basis of Eve's sin was buttressed by the teachings of Saint Paul. According to the apostle, women should keep silent in church and should cover their heads when praying in remembrance of the shame brought upon humankind by Eve's transgression (I Corinthians 11: 5–13). Misogynist clerics also had at their disposal other key passages of the Bible, such as the descriptions of the harlot in Proverbs 7: 10–12 and of the wicked woman in Ecclesiasticus 25: 23–6, which inveighed against female vices such as disobedience, garrulity, treachery and lasciviousness. Even the undoubtedly virtuous example of the Virgin Mary was not enough to counter totally this negative view of women. Although, for medieval theologians, Mary's conception of Christ had made possible the salvation of our individual souls in the next world, her virtue still did not remove women's guilt for their part in the Fall. Women's punishment, in the form of subjection to their husbands, thus remained firmly in place in this world.

From Greek scientific thinkers such as Aristotle and Galen, medieval medicine derived a view of the female as a defective male.[11] This opinion was based on the theory of the four elements which make up all living things: earth, fire, water and air. Each of these elements has a related quality: coldness, heat, moisture and dryness. Whilst man was thought to be dominated by heat and dryness, woman was supposed to be ruled by coldness and moisture. Since medieval thinkers believed that heat was the primary instrument of nature, they concluded that man was superior to woman, being the warmer of the two sexes. Moreover, this lack of heat in woman meant that her body and mind were unstable. For example, it was feared that she was in danger of going mad if her animal-like womb, which wandered at will due to the coldness of her body, ever strayed up into her head. Menstruation too was taken as a sign that, unlike man, woman was too cold and feeble to regulate internally the amount of toxic humours in her body. Medieval philosophers such as Isidore of Seville, a theologian writing in the seventh century AD, reinforced these scientific views of the differences between the sexes by using pseudo-etymological reasoning. In order to prove that females were a lesser species than males, Isidore claimed that man, *vir* in Latin, was so-called because of his natural affinity with strength, *virtus*, whereas the word for woman, *mulier*, came from the adjective meaning softer or weaker, *mollier*, which was itself derived from the noun for weakness, *mollitie*.[12]

These two traditions bequeathed to the medieval world a view of women as the moral, intellectual and physical inferiors of men. Literary texts in the Middle Ages echoed many of these theological and scientific ideas about the female sex and indeed often drew directly on biblical and classical sources for their anti-feminist inspiration. Matheolus's satirical attack on women and marriage, which Christine cites at the beginning of the *City of Ladies*, was by no means an isolated case. Short moralizing treatises known as *dits* endlessly rehashed the arguments against womankind, using animal similes to compare women to the most dangerous and venomous of beasts, such as bears and snakes, and showing how the traditional female vices of gossiping and backbiting destroyed good relations between men.[13] Another popular genre which helped to reinforce misogynist stereotypes was that of mythography, which involved extracting Christian messages from stories of classical mythology. For instance, in the *Ovide Moralisé*, an anonymous fourteenth-century work based on tales from Ovid's *Metamorphoses*, when a male figure such as Icarus is represented as being guilty of hubris in flying too close to the sun, this is interpreted allegorically as the human soul's refusal to humble itself before God. However, when a female figure such as Venus is condemned for being guilty of sensuality, this is read not only as an allegorical account of the frailty of the human soul in general but also as literal evidence of the duplicitous and fickle nature of the female sex.

The *fabliaux*, the genre of short comic tales, also represent women differently from men. *Fabliaux* writers tended to criticize male characters as individual members of a particular social group, mocking peasants for their stupidity in letting themselves be duped or condemning priests for their lascivious pursuit of women. Female characters, on the other hand, were invariably treated as representatives of their sex, not as individuals.[14] Thus, if a peasant woman or a bourgeois wife cuckolded her husband or cheated him of his money, the author usually appended a moral in which, even if he had to express a sneaking admiration for the woman's cunning, he would none the less warn all men to be on their guard against such a treacherous and two-faced sex.

Even medieval romance, a genre which put forward a much more elevated view of womankind than that found in the *fabliaux*, was not immune from misogynist influence.[15] Though certain romance authors presented adulterous queens such as Isolde and Guinevere as tragic heroines whose doomed passion for their lovers commands the reader's sympathy, other authors were less lenient in their treatment of women. One of the stock anti-feminist stereotypes circulated in medieval romance was that of the 'Potiphar's wife', a stereotype derived from the Bible. In the Old Testament, this character is a high-born lady who tries to seduce

Joseph, her husband's servant, and then, when unsuccessful, spitefully denounces him to her husband for attempting to rape her. Heldris de Cornuälles, author of the thirteenth-century French romance the *Roman de Silence*, for example, pulls no punches in condemning the 'Potiphar's wife' of his text. Here, it is a queen, Eufeme, who tries to avenge herself on Silence, a young knight in her husband's service, whom she has been unable to seduce. When it is revealed that the innocent Silence is in fact a girl dressed up as a knight, Eufeme's husband, King Ebain, punishes his wife for her treachery and has her put to death whilst the narrator adds his own scathing remarks about the unreliable and corrupt nature of woman.

The most infamous work in terms of its treatment of women was the *Roman de la Rose* (*The Romance of the Rose*), a text which became the supreme literary authority in the medieval anti-feminist canon. This vast allegorical narrative was first begun around 1240 by Guillaume de Lorris but was greatly expanded around 1275 by Jean de Meun who, for this reason, was regarded in the Middle Ages as the more important author of the two. The *Rose* tells of a young man's quest for a lady, symbolized by a rosebud, in which he is aided and abetted by personified figures such as the Friend, who instructs him in the art of seduction, the Old Woman, who guards the rose, and Genius, Nature's chaplain, who encourages the lover to consummate his desire for the lady in the interests of perpetuating the human species. The *Rose* rehearses many familiar commonplaces of classical literary misogyny, including Ovid's ironic advice in his *Art of Love* on how to catch women who, despite appearing chaste, are in fact all too willing to be caught.[16] It also repeats many key arguments from classical misogamous or anti-marriage texts, such as the view expressed by the Greek writer Theophrastus in his *Aureolus* that wives neglect their husbands and have eyes only for their lovers.[17] Because of the great prestige which the *Rose* enjoyed throughout the late-thirteenth and fourteenth centuries, it was with this text that Christine had to engage most actively and critically throughout her works in defence of women.

Literary misogyny in the medieval period was not confined to secular works but was also a staple ingredient of religious texts. Christian doctrine stated that, on the Day of Judgement, men and women alike would be treated according to their individual just deserts. However, as in the *fabliaux*, preachers tended to criticize men for failing to live up to the ideals of their particular occupations whereas women were condemned as an entire sex for their garrulity and lechery. Moreover, where both sexes were at fault, as for example in the case of adultery, preachers tended to hold women responsible for attracting men in the first place, rather than apportioning equal blame to both parties.

Even in hagiography, which provided examples of women who *were* moral and virtuous, male and female saints were not treated identically. For both sexes, sanctity was achieved as the soul struggled to liberate itself from the temptations of the flesh. However, for women, but not for men, this process was primarily defined in sexual terms. Whereas men could attain sainthood through a wide variety of roles, for example through their eloquence as preachers or their asceticism as hermits, the typical roles reserved for women were those of virgin-martyr or repentant prostitute.[18] In the former scenario, a beautiful young maiden, such as Saint Margaret, would find herself under attack from a lustful pagan emperor who wanted to seduce her and force her to worship idols. Her only response would be to protect her virginity at all costs, even if it entailed the most horrific forms of physical torture. In the latter scenario, the whore who converted to Christianity, such as Saint Mary the Egyptian, would suffer terrible torments leading to the loss of her beauty as penance for the sensual pleasures she had supposedly enjoyed as a sinner. As in preachers' sermons, hagiographical texts thus tended to represent women as a sex whose corporeality was more problematic than that of men. Unlike their male counterparts, women were deemed to reach the ranks of God's chosen saints only by overcoming the obstacle of their innate sexual attractiveness.

How then could a writer such as Christine begin to take issue with a set of ideas that had so thoroughly permeated every area of medieval thought? The misogynists' position was not entirely unassailable: their chief weakness lay in their heavy reliance on previous sources for their ideas. As was common practice for all writers in the Middle Ages, anti feminist authors proved their erudition principally by recycling the acknowledged authorities on a topic. It is thus hardly surprising that misogynist opinions gained such currency in medieval culture given that they were derived from the very weightiest sources, such as Aristotle and the Bible. However, the misogynists were in fact forced to quote *selectively*, citing the bad things that their favourite authorities said about women and leaving aside the good.[19] And good things there certainly were. Whether in scripture or in history, illustrious members of the female sex were not lacking. Far from it: for every sinful Eve or Jezebel, there was an heroic Judith or an Esther; for every lustful Clytemnestra or Jocasta, there was a valiant Penthesilea or an Andromache. In theology, the early Fathers of the Church might have condemned Eve as the instigator of the Fall but they had also argued that, since she was made from Adam's rib and not his foot, God had intended her to be her husband's cherished helpmeet, not his downtrodden slave. Moreover, no less an authority than Saint Augustine himself had argued that men and women were equal in their rationality. Even in scientific thought, women's supposed physical and mental inferiority might disqualify them from public office, but it also meant that they were deemed to be more affectionate than men, particularly towards children.[20] By turning the misogynists' method of selective quotation against them, a pro-woman writer could therefore cite exactly the same authorities as they did whilst taking the good said of women and leaving out the bad. In practice, however, very few male authors took up this option, one notable exception being the early thirteenth-century Italian author Albertano of Brescia.[21] As Christine herself observed, it was only when a woman put pen to paper that a more positive view of the female sex would emerge. What then were the circumstances which led to Christine's being the first woman to do precisely that?

Christine had gone to live in what was to become her adopted country of France in 1368 when her father, Tommaso da Pizzano (whom she referred to as Thomas de Pizan), accepted the position of physician and astrologer at the court of King Charles V. Along with her two brothers, Paolo and Aghinolfo, Christine spent a comfortable childhood in Paris. Unusually for girls of her social rank, most of whom were taught to read French but almost certainly not to write it, she was encouraged by her father to do both, despite opposition from her mother, who preferred her to spend her time on more traditional female pursuits, such as spinning. Christine read widely in the vernacular and probably acquired some knowledge of Latin as well. In 1380, at the age of fifteen, she was given in marriage to Etienne de Castel, a royal secretary. By her own account, the union was a happy one, producing three children. Yet, within the space of ten years, she was to lose both her father and her husband, two events which forced her to adopt a lifestyle for which her previous privileged existence had scarcely prepared her.

Christine did not become a professional writer immediately on becoming head of her household. Rather, it is thought that, in order to provide for her children, as well as for her elderly mother and a niece who had been placed in her care, she worked for a number of years as a copyist for the various manuscript workshops which flourished in Paris. However, from 1399, Christine began to compose her own literary works. Her aim was to make a living for herself by writing books that would appeal to the tastes of the royal princes at the Valois court, such as Louis, Duke of Orleans, brother of King Charles VI (who had succeeded their father, Charles V, in 1380). These early works, which were mostly lyric poetry, were well received by her aristocratic audience. She built quickly on this initial success and began not only to write more serious texts, such as an account of the role of Fortune in human affairs, *Le Livre de la Mutation de Fortune* (*The Book of the Mutation of Fortune*) (1403), but also to receive commissions from her noble patrons for political and moral works, such as a biography of the late king for his brother Philip, Duke of Burgundy, *Le Livre des Fais et des Bonnes Meurs du Sage Roy Charles V* (*The Book of the Deeds and Good Character of King Charles V the Wise*) (1404).

Yet Christine was also concerned throughout these initial years of her career with matters which struck a personal chord with her: the defence of women against the misogynist claim that the female sex was, in every respect, inferior to the male. *The City of Ladies* undoubtedly formed the cornerstone of Christine's critique of misogyny, but it was not an isolated work in her literary output. As early as the *Epistre au dieu d'Amours* (*The Letter of the God of Love*) (1399), Christine complained of men's behaviour towards women. Using Cupid as her mouthpiece in this text, she accuses knights of failing in their chivalric duty to protect women, claiming that they go around slandering ladies' good names after having tried unsuccessfully to seduce them. She similarly attacks authors such as Ovid and Jean de Meun for condemning the entire female sex as unfaithful and unstable purely on the basis of a few bad examples. Adopting a rhetorical strategy which she would apply more systematically in the *City of Ladies*, Christine here counters these negative views by citing examples of virtuous women of the past, such as Penelope, Dido and Medea, whom she presents as a credit to their sex. In the *Epistre Othea* (*The Letter of Othea to Hector*) (*c.*1400), a courtesy book which provides young knights with lessons in good behaviour and in spiritual conduct culled from pagan tales of classical mythology, Christine also gives the lie to misogynist stereotypes. Unlike the author of the *Ovide Moralisé*, who often draws an anti-feminist moral from his tales of female characters, Christine interprets her stories in the *Letter of Othea* exclusively for their general relevance to the human soul, irrespective of the sex of the person portrayed in them.

Christine's main challenge to anti-feminism before she wrote the *City of Ladies* was contained in a series of letters on the subject of Jean de Meun's *Rose* which she exchanged between 1400 and 1402 with other leading intellectual figures of her day: Jean de Montreuil, Provost of Lille; Gontier Col, first secretary and notary to King Charles VI; and his brother Pierre Col, canon of Paris and Tournay. For her opponents, the *Rose* was a work of the highest literary merit, a moral text which skilfully satirized and condemned the pursuit of sensual love. In Christine's opinion, by contrast, the *Rose* was a pernicious text, the work of an immoral and foul-mouthed author whose views of women were vicious and vitriolic in the extreme. She took particular exception to the way in which its male characters, such as Friend and Genius, attack women for their supposed lasciviousness, fickleness and inability to keep secrets whilst counselling the would-be lover to continue pursuing his lady by any means necessary, even by trickery or physical force. Christine also condemned the *Rose* for the way in which it portrays female characters, such as the debauched and unprincipled Old Woman who is supposed to act as the lady's chaperone but instead gives the lover access to her mistress in exchange for a bribe. However, Christine's main criticism of Jean de Meun's text was that it presented an un-Christian view of relations between the sexes, one based on mutual mistrust and antagonism rather than on love and charity. To her mind, the *Rose*'s talk of the traps and snares which men need in order to catch their sexual prey encouraged its male readers to think of women as somehow less than human, as almost bestial. Instead, Christine sought to prove misogynists such as Jean de Meun wrong by arguing that what unites men and women as human beings – their rationality and possession of a soul – is more important than what divides them as sexes.

At the heart of Christine's defence of women, both in her letters on the *Rose* and in the *City of Ladies*, was her profound conviction that it is a *human* – and not a specifically *female* – trait to be prone to sin. However, she also believed that if men and women are alike as sinners, they are equally capable of adopting rational forms of behaviour and of making informed moral choices. It is here, in defending women by replying to the misogynists' assault on female virtue, rather than in demanding the same rights for both sexes, that Christine's brand of feminism in the *City of Ladies* differs most markedly from that of the twentieth century. Instead of campaigning for causes which would have been completely unthinkable in her day, such as universal suffrage or equal opportunities, Christine focused on what she saw as the single, most crucial issue: proving to misogynists and to women themselves that neither virtue nor vice is the prerogative of one sex to the exclusion of the other. Moreover, unlike those modern feminists who exhort women to valorize sexual difference and to celebrate female sexuality,[22] Christine was in flight from the body in favour of the spirit. This is because, in her day, it was the misogynist tradition in all its manifestations – scientific, theological and literary – which aligned the female sex with corporeality and sensuality in order to justify their claims about women's social, juridical and psychological inferiority to men.

How then did Christine create the necessary authority for herself in the *City of Ladies* to attack the accepted truths of her age? What examples and arguments could she take from the misogynists' sources in her efforts to beat them at their own game? How were Christine's illustrious heroines meant to inspire her female readers to pursue virtue in their actual daily lives?

The prologue of the *City of Ladies* opens with a secular version of the Annunciation as recounted in Luke 1:38.[23] On being informed by the three Virtues that God has chosen her to build a city in which all virtuous women would be invited to dwell, Christine accepts her mission with humility. Echoing the Virgin Mary's reply to the angel Gabriel, she states: 'Behold your handmaiden, ready to do your bidding. I will obey your every command, so be it unto me according to your word' (I.7). Christine uses this rather bold comparison between herself and the Virgin Mary as a rhetorical device to help her out of the acute dilemma that she faced both as author and as champion of her sex. Being the first woman to raise her voice against the misogynist tradition, Christine certainly had originality on her side. Yet, in being original, she necessarily lacked the authority which a male writer such as Jean de Meun enjoyed by following in the footsteps of an Ovid or a Theophrastus. In the absence of a prestigious female forerunner whose arguments she could cite as a precedent, Christine turned to the most obvious and unchallengeable source of womanly authority that was available to her: the Virgin Mary. Since Mary's exceptional status as a virgin mother means that she is an impossible model for other women to follow, this choice may seem rather surprising on Christine's part. However, it is Mary's qualities of meekness and mildness which – even anti-feminists had to concede – women *are* capable of imitating, on which Christine draws in her prologue. In allying herself with Mary as a humble creature who has been chosen to perform a difficult task, Christine also alludes to the biblical commonplace by which God elects 'the weak things of the world to confound the things which are mighty' (I Corinthians 1:27). Women's very meekness thus becomes the most potent weapon in their armoury which they can wield against their misogynist enemies. In the *City of Ladies*, Christine exploits the rhetorical charge of this argument to the full, claiming that if women have been weak in might, they have been strong in right. As Reason declares to Christine:

Out of the goodness and simplicity of their hearts, women have trusted in God and have patiently endured the countless verbal and written assaults that have been unjustly and shamelessly launched upon them. Now, however, it is time for them to be delivered out of the hands of Pharaoh (I.3).

Christine reinforces this paradoxical idea that women are empowered by their own powerlessness by adding a strong legalistic flavour to her text.[24] This particular rhetorical strategy is introduced in the prologue of the *City of Ladies* where Reason cites a proverb which states that 'even the most undeserving case will win if there is no one to testify against it' (I.3). Christine thus contrasts the moral rectitude of womankind with the unscrupulousness of anti-feminists by conjuring up the image of a court-room in which women are being tried *in absentia* as the misogynist plaintiff launches accusations at an empty dock. The *City of Ladies* is Christine's opportunity to put the case for the defence and throughout the text there are innumerable references to 'slander', 'proofs' and 'evidence'. The dialogues between Christine and the three Virtues frequently take the form of a cross-examination in which, ironically, she plays the part of devil's advocate. No sooner does Christine herself put forward the case for the misogynists than her argument is summarily dismissed by Reason, Rectitude or Justice, all of whom deliver their counter-arguments with the oratorical flourishes of a lawyer. For example, Christine quotes the opinion of the Roman orator, Cato, who asserts that 'if woman hadn't been created, man would converse with the gods'. In her reply, Reason points out that it is precisely thanks to a woman, the Virgin Mary, that Christ was born, not simply to redeem the sin of Adam and Eve but also to save humankind from worshipping those pagan gods whom Christians regard as devils. Reason sums up by sarcastically agreeing with Cato that 'it's definitely true to say that men would be conversing with the gods of hell if Mary had not come into the world!' (I.9).

Christine also calls upon a further rhetorical strategy with which to boost her authority. By using the building of a city as the key metaphor of her text, she exploits its multiple connotations.[25] Firstly, this image connects Christine's text to Saint Augustine's influential treatise the *City of God*, in which the city represents the Christian faithful both on earth and in heaven. Christine explicitly alludes to this text towards the end of the *City of Ladies* when she declares, '*Gloriosa dicta sunt de te, civitas Dei*' (III.18), and she follows Augustine's lead in using the city as a symbol of the ideal community held together by its common pursuit of virtue. In Christine's case, however, her city is populated by female warriors, good wives and saintly women. Secondly, Christine's use of the symbol of the city underpins one of the central arguments of her text, namely that women have contributed to the moral and spiritual development of civilization as epitomized by the urban community.[26] She thus cites women such as Nicostrata and Isis for their vital role as city-builders or law-givers (I.33 and I.36 respectively). Finally, the image of a walled and turreted city is frequently used in medieval literature as a symbol of defence and, more specifically, of defence of one's chastity. In Jean de Meun's *Rose*, for example, the chastity of the lady is represented as a fortress in which Jealousy, the allegorical figure who personifies her self-restraint, has locked her up in order to protect her virtue. When the lover finally consummates his desire for the lady, he does so by killing Jealousy and storming the fortress itself. The *Rose* thus implies that, despite putting up a fight, women in fact collude with the loss of their own virtue, a suggestion which was one of the mainstays of misogynist thought. Christine explicitly rejects this view in Part II of the *City of Ladies*, where Rectitude refutes the charge that women take pleasure in being raped (II.44–6). Moreover, the whole of her text is as much an impregnable fortress of female virtue as it is a community. As Christine exclaims at the end of Part III:

Most honourable ladies, praise be to God: the construction of our city is finally at an end. All of you who love virtue, glory and a fine reputation can now be lodged in great splendour inside its walls, not just women of the past but also those of the present and the future, for this city has been founded and built to accommodate all deserving women (III.19).

Yet all of Christine's efforts to give her text authority would have come to nothing if she had not been able to derive the bulk of her pro-woman material from well-known and authoritative sources. To be sure, she does sometimes quote from her own experience in the *City of Ladies*, for example when she attacks the misogynist claim that women are prone to gluttony or avarice by stating that she knows plenty of abstemious and generous women whose example disproves these charges (I.10 and II.66 respectively). However, Christine was well aware that the oral testimony of one woman would not be enough to outweigh the written testimony of countless male authors. The only way that she could offer a persuasive defence of her sex was by showing that selective quotation was a game that two could play. Christine therefore plunders the misogynists' favourite scriptural and classical authorities in order to come up with a mass of examples that support her thesis against theirs. For instance, she counters their theological trump card, Eve, with more positive models of Old Testament women: Judith, the brave and resourceful widow who kills Holofernes, the general who besieged the city of the Jews (II.31); Esther, the valiant queen who saves her people from persecution (II.32); and Susanna, the chaste wife who is ready to be stoned to death rather than submit to the lecherous advances of two corrupt priests (II.37). Moreover, unlike her main source, Boccaccio, whose catalogue barely touches on contemporary women, Christine brings her series of heroines right up to date, citing the queens and princesses of France in tones just as favourable as those she employs in her portraits of Biblical heroines (I.13, II.68).

Christine's selectiveness towards her sources even extends to modifying them, where necessary, in order to highlight the good rather than the bad qualities of her heroines.[27] For example, Boccaccio's version of the story of Medea, the Greek princess and sorceress, tells how, when Medea runs away from her father's court with her lover Jason, she kills her younger brother and scatters his dismembered body along the road in order to distract her father from pursuing her. Not surprisingly, in the *City of Ladies*, Christine omits all mention of this brutal act, emphasizing instead how Medea uses her expertise in sorcery to help Jason win his quest for the Golden Fleece and how she shows exemplary fidelity to him, even when he eventually abandons her for another woman (I.32, II.56). Christine also takes liberties with her sources in those cases where she feels the need to clarify or justify an aspect of her heroines' behaviour which might otherwise appear to be blameworthy. For instance, she is at pains to explain why the Babylonian queen Semiramis, whose story is the first 'stone' to be laid in the foundations of the City of Ladies, decided to marry her own son, Ninus, after the death of her husband.[28] In an attempt to absolve her heroine for committing an act which would have offended medieval sensibilities, Christine has Reason cite Semiramis's own political rationale:

firstly, she wanted no other crowned lady to share her empire with her, as would have been the case if her son had married another woman; and secondly, in her opinion, no other man than her son was worthy of her (I.15).

However, in her eagerness to exonerate the queen still further, Christine also feels honour-bound to add a rather more speculative explanation. Reason thus also claims that Semiramis was so proud and honourable that 'if she *had* thought she was doing anything wrong or that she might be subject to criticism for her actions, she would have refrained from doing as she did'(I.15).

Not content simply to cite examples from classical and scriptural authorities which counter those of her misogynist opponents, Christine demonstrates that whole arguments from one set of sources can be played off against those from another. For example, she refutes the scientific view that woman is a defective male by citing the theological commonplace that not only was Eve born in a nobler place than Adam, since she was formed in paradise and he outside, but also that the actual matter from which she was made, a rib, was nobler than the earth from which he was created (I.9). In the *City of Ladies*, Christine even manages to make positive capital for women out of some of the anti-feminists' opinions. For instance, she accepts the fact that the female sex is not as physically strong as the male, but she rejects the misogynist deduction that women therefore also have weaker minds. On the contrary, she claims that women are in fact morally *advantaged* by being physically frailer than men on the grounds that what Nature takes away with one hand, she gives on the other. As Reason declares:

if Nature decided not to endow women with a powerful physique, she none the less made up for it by giving them a most virtuous disposition: that of loving God and being fearful of disobeying His commandments (I.14).

In putting the case for women against the misogynists' accusations, Christine also seeks to empower her female readers by persuading them that, as members of the human race rather than of some lesser species, they too have the moral capacity to shun vice and pursue virtue. Indeed, they themselves have a duty to realize this potential and so refute anti-feminist slanders through their own praiseworthy actions. Addressing her audience directly, Christine exclaims:

My ladies, see how these men assail you on all sides and accuse you of every vice imaginable. Prove them all wrong by showing how principled you are and refute the criticisms they make of you by behaving morally (III.19).

Yet, given the restrictions which their own society placed on them, could Christine's contemporaries actually be expected to imitate her heroines of the pagan or Judaeo-Christian past by becoming teachers or artists, let alone warriors or political leaders?

Christine's answer to this problem is to present her heroines as role models whose moral *qualities*, rather than their literal *deeds*, are offered to her readers for emulation. Instead of being encouraged to harden their bodies for battle like the Amazons of Part I or to suffer the pains of physical torment like the martyrs of Part III, Christine's audience are meant instead to imitate the resourcefulness of the former and the steadfastness of the latter. And it is the women of Part II who provide the readers of the *City of Ladies* with the clue as to how this should be done. These wives, mothers and daughters of past and present themselves perform deeds which 'translate' into their own domestic sphere of influence the qualities shown by warriors and by saints in the public and spiritual domains.

A classic instance of this process of 'translation' at work is provided by those examples of women who used language to benefit humankind in a variety of different domains. Thus, in Part I, Reason celebrates the fact that, in the public sphere, pagan women such as Nicostrata invented the alphabet and facilitated learning and communication between people (I.33), whilst others, such as Isis, devised written laws which replaced barbarism with order (I.36). Then, in Part II, Rectitude transposes women's use of language for the good of human civilization into moral and domestic terms. For example, she commends Antonia for persuading her husband Belisarius to accept the difficult military mission which the king has given him (II.29), praises the Sabine women for begging their husbands and fathers to call off their battle with each other (II.33) and applauds Veturia for imploring her son, Marcius (Coriolanus), to spare the city of Rome (II.34). In Part III, Justice exults in the deeds of those women whose language performs the spiritual function of rescuing the souls of unbelievers from damnation. Virgin-martyrs such as Saint Martina (III.6) are kept alive by God precisely in order to convert as many people as possible through their preaching. In the case of Saint Christine, the martyr miraculously continues to speak and to proselytize even after having had her tongue cut out (III.10).

The women of Christine's medieval audience would obviously be unable to establish new laws or to convert pagans to Christianity like the heroines of Parts I and III of the *City of Ladies*. Nevertheless, they could still be expected to emulate the women of Part II who 'translated' this moral use of language into virtuous deeds such as offering words of comfort and advice to their loved ones. Christine's concept of role models as moral exemplars therefore has nothing in common with that of modern feminism, with its emphasis on female pioneers striving to break down the bastions of male power and privilege. However, her aim was not to demand reform of the social order but rather to show how the qualities exhibited by extraordinary women in the past could also be demonstrated by women of the present acting in their more ordinary roles of daughter, wife and mother. It was, after all, in this private domain that the women of Christine's day could in fact aspire to playing an influential role in medieval society.

After 1405, when she had finished writing the *City of Ladies* and its sequel, the *Three Virtues*, Christine turned her attention back towards wider political concerns. As the king, Charles VI, became increasingly subject to bouts of madness and the royal princes battled for control of the crown, France began to slide inexorably towards a state of civil war. Christine initially responded to this state of affairs by writing treatises in favour of peace and stability in the body politic. However, she became an increasingly marginalized figure in Parisian political circles and, after 1418, she is thought to have withdrawn altogether from the court and taken refuge at the convent of Poissy outside Paris, where her daughter was a nun.

Yet, towards the very end of her life, Christine took up her pen one last time in defence of women. This time it was to add her weight in support of Joan of Arc, the maiden-warrior, as leader of the French troops against the English enemy. In the *Ditié de Jehanne d'Arc* (*The Poem of Joan of Arc*) (1429), Christine presents the Maid of Orleans as the embodiment of all the virtues that she had extolled in the women of the *City of Ladies*: like the Amazons, Joan is valiant and brave; like the Virgin Mary, she is chaste and pure; and like the heroines of the Old Testament, she is a saviour sent by God to rescue her people in their darkest hour. Fortunately, Christine appears not to have lived to see the Maid suffer her terrible end at the stake two years later. It is the Joan covered in glory from her victory at Orleans and from her part in the coronation of Charles VII at Rheims cathedral who thus provides a most fitting final chapter for Christine's celebration of women.

Christine de Pizan's achievement as a defender of her sex lies not in her anticipation of the strategies which later feminists would employ, but rather in her critical engagement with the dominant ideology of her own day. Though many of her arguments in favour of women, such as her stress on the moral equality of male and female, have been superseded by other ideological and pragmatic concerns, they none the less commanded a great deal of authority in their own time. We need to pay Christine's critique of misogyny the respect it deserves and to see it as a dialogue with the society and culture of the late Middle Ages, rather than judging it by the standards of the late twentieth century. Christine's voice in defence of women is utterly different from our own, but it was in its time a dissenting voice and one which spoke out to its audience with as much urgency and vigour as that of any modern feminist.

NOTES

1. Virginia Woolf, *A Room of One's Own* (Harmondsworth: Penguin, 1928), 76.
2. See, for instance, Peter Dronke, *Women Writers of the Middle Ages* (Cambridge: Cambridge University Press, 1984); Katharina M. Wilson, *Medieval Women Writers* (Manchester: Manchester University Press, 1984); and Carolyne Larrington, *Women and Writing in Medieval Europe: A Sourcebook* (London and New York: Routledge, 1995).
3. For standard studies of the life and works of Christine de Pizan, see Enid

McLeod, *The Order of the Rose: The Life and Ideas of Christine de Pizan* (London: Chatto & Windus, 1976); and Charity Cannon Willard, *Christine de Pizan: Her Life and Works* (New York: Persea Books, 1984).

4. For an anthology of Christine's works translated into English, see Charity Cannon Willard, ed., *The Writings of Christine de Pizan* (New York: Persea Books, 1994).

5. For an excellent sourcebook of works in the misogynist tradition, see Alcuin Blamires, ed., *Woman Defamed and Woman Defended: An Anthology of Medieval Texts* (Oxford: Clarendon Press, 1992).

6. For editions of Christine's works, see the bibliography below.

7. See Glenda K. McLeod, *Virtue and Venom: Catalogues of Women from Antiquity to the Renaissance* (Ann Arbor: University of Michigan Press, 1991).

8. For editions of works by Matheolus and other authors cited in this introduction, see the bibliography below.

9. See, for example, Sheila Delany, '"Mothers to think back through": Who are they? The ambiguous case of Christine de Pizan', in her *Medieval Literary Politics: Shapes of Ideology* (Manchester: Manchester University Press, 1990), 88–103.

10. See Ian Maclean, *The Renaissance Notion of Woman: A Study in the Fortunes of Scholasticism and Medical Science in European Intellectual Life* (Cambridge: Cambridge University Press, 1980); and for a succinct account of medieval ideas on women, S. H. Rigby, *English Society in the Later Middle Ages: Class, Status and Gender* (London: Macmillan, 1995), 246–52.

11. See Vern L. Bullough, 'Medieval medical and scientific views of women', *Viator* 4 (1973), 485–501; and Claude Thomasset, 'The Nature of Woman' in Christiane Klapisch-Zuber, ed., *A History of Women: Silences of the Middle Ages* (Cambridge, Mass. and London: Belknap Press, 1992), 43–69.

12. See Blamires, *Woman Defamed*, 43–5.

13. See *Three Medieval Views of Women: 'La Contenance des Fames', 'Le Bien des Fames', 'Le Blasme des Fames'*, Gloria K. Fiero, Wendy Pfeffer and Mathé Allain, eds. and trans. (New Haven and London: Yale University Press, 1989).

14. Norris J. Lacy, 'Fabliau women', *Romance Notes* 25 (1985), 318–27.

15. See Joan M. Ferrante, *Woman as Image in Medieval Literature: From the Twelfth Century to Dante* (New York: Columbia University Press, 1975); and Penny Schine Gold, *The Lady and the Virgin: Image, Attitude and Experience in Twelfth-Century France* (Chicago and London: University of Chicago Press, 1985).

16. For extracts from Ovid, see Blamires, *Woman Defamed*, 17–25.

17. For extracts from Theophrastus, see Blamires, *Woman Defamed*, 70–2. See also Katharina M. Wilson and Elizabeth M. Makowski, *Wykked Wyves and the Woes of Marriage: Misogamous Literature from Juvenal to Chaucer* (Albany: State University of New York Press, 1990).

18. See Elizabeth Robertson, 'The corporeality of female sanctity in *The Life of Saint Margaret*', in Renate Blumenfeld-Kosinski and Timea Szell, eds., *Images of Sainthood in Medieval Europe* (Ithaca: Cornell University Press, 1991), 268–87; and *The Lady as Saint: A Collection of French Hagiographic Romances of the Thirteenth Century*, Brigitte Cazelles, trans. (Philadelphia: University of Pennsylvania Press, 1991).

19. See R. Howard Bloch, 'Medieval misogyny', *Representations* 20 (1987), 1–24.

20. See Maclean, *The Renaissance Notion of Woman*.

21. Albertano's *Book of Consolation and Advice* (1246) is a debate between the impetuous Melibeus, who wants to avenge himself on his enemies, and his sensible wife, Prudentia, who counsels him not to take any rash action. In the course of their dialogue, Prudentia refutes many of the misogynist arguments which her husband initially uses in order to belittle her advice before eventually winning him over to her point of view. For extracts from this text in English translation, see Blamires, *Woman Defamed*, 237–42.

22. This type of modern feminist theory is most closely associated with French thinkers such as Julia Kristeva, Hélène Cixous and Luce Irigaray. For an introduction to their work, see Elaine Marks and Isabelle de Courtivron, *New French Feminisms: An Anthology* (New York: Harvester Wheatsheaf, 1981); and Toril Moi, *Sexual/Textual Politics: Feminist Literary Theory* (London: Methuen, 1985).

23. See V. A. Kolve, 'The Annunciation to Christine: authorial empowerment in the *Book of the City of Ladies*' in Brendan Cassidy, ed., *Iconography at the Crossroads: Papers from the Colloquium Sponsored by the Index of Christian Art, Princeton University, 23–24 March 1990* (Princeton: Princeton University Press, 1993), 171–96.

24. Maureen Cheney Curnow, ' "La pioche d'inquisicion": legal-judicial content and style in Christine de Pizan's *Livre de la Cité des Dames*' in Earl Jeffrey Richards *et al.*, eds., *Reinterpreting Christine de Pizan* (Athens, Georgia: University of Georgia Press, 1992), 157–72.

25. Sandra L. Hindman, 'With ink and mortar: Christine de Pizan's *Cité des Dames*: an art essay', *Feminist Studies* 10 (1984), 457–84.

26. See Rosalind Brown-Grant, *Reading Beyond Gender: Christine de Pizan and the Moral Defence of Women* (Cambridge: Cambridge University Press, 1999).

27. See Patricia A. Phillippy, 'Establishing authority: Boccaccio's *De Claris Mulieribus* and Christine de Pizan's *Cité des Dames*', *Romanic Review* 77 (1986), 167–93.

28. Liliane Dulac, 'Un mythe didactique chez Christine de Pizan: Sémiramis ou la veuve héroïque (du *De Claris Mulieribus* à la *Cité des Dames*)', *Mélanges de philologie romane offerts à Charles Camproux* (Montpellier: Centre d'Etudes Occitanes, 1978), 315–43.

·TRANSLATOR'S NOTE

My primary aim in translating Christine de Pizan's *City of Ladies* has been to make this fifteenth-century Middle French text as readable as possible for a modern audience. Christine was writing at a time when intellectuals in France were trying to increase the prestige of the vernacular because they felt that it was inferior to Latin. They therefore attempted to replicate the complexities of Latin syntax in French and frequently used linked pairs of synonyms or near-synonyms in the hope that two French words would express all the nuances that they thought a single word in Latin could do. In line with many of her contemporaries, Christine's syntax in the *City of Ladies* is often tortuous and she rarely gives just one word when two or three could be used. These features of writing in this period do not make for easy reading, nor do they make literal translation desirable. In the interests of readability, I have altered Christine's word order considerably and shortened her sentences. Groups of near-synonyms have been respected but I have dealt with pairs of exact synonyms in different ways, depending on grammar and context. Where two verbs are strictly identical in meaning and would be completely redundant in English, I have tended to reduce them down to one: for example, '*ars*' and '*bruslé*' have become simply 'burnt'. Where Christine has two identical nouns, I have often changed one of them into an adjective which reinforces the other noun: for instance, '*congié*' and '*licence*' have been translated as 'express permission'. I have, however, attempted to remain faithful to the legalistic style of her original text and to render as much of its polemical tone as possible.

One important feature of Christine's style in the *City of Ladies* deserves a special mention here as it touches on the key issue of gender. When she wants to make a particular point about men as opposed to humankind in general, Christine is careful to distinguish between, on the one hand, the specific term '*les hommes*', meaning simply the male sex, and, on the other hand, generic terms such as '*les gens*', which refer to both sexes, or sex-neutral terms such as '*la personne*', which can indicate either sex. Moreover, Christine is equally concerned not to subsume the female pronoun '*elles*' under the male pronoun '*ils*' in those cases where she wants to highlight the moral equality of men and women, as in, for example, the pursuit of virtue. In this respect, if in few others, she is ahead of her time in anticipating many of the arguments that modern feminist linguistics has raised about sexist language. I have therefore endeavoured to respect Christine's usage throughout and have used 'people', 'humankind' and 'humanity' as generic terms, 'person' and 'individual' as sex-neutral terms, and 'men' exclusively to refer to males. Where Christine differentiates between male and female pronouns, I have done the same, and in those cases where a sex-neutral pronoun is appropriate, I have given either 'he or she' or 'they', depending on the context.

I have followed Maureen Cheney Curnow, who edited the *City of Ladies* in 1975, in taking Bibliothèque Nationale, f. fr. 607 as my base manuscript. Christine herself closely supervised the execution of this text and of the three miniatures which illustrate each of its three parts. Ms 607 is a deluxe item, forming part of a collection of Christine's works which she presented after 1405 to one of her noble patrons, John, Duke of Berry. Like Curnow, I have also consulted British Library, Harley 4431 as a control. This manuscript, which contains a later version of the *City of Ladies*, was part of a lavishly illustrated collected volume of her works modelled on that previously given to the duke, which Christine offered to the queen, Isabeau of Bavaria, after 1410.

As a catalogue of famous women, the *City of Ladies* contains literally hundreds of references to places, people and other works. I have therefore provided the reader with additional information and explanations at the end of the text in two different forms: a substantial glossary, which can be consulted at the reader's leisure; and notes on biblical references and aspects of medieval culture, which have been kept to a minimum so as not to interfere unduly with the reader's enjoyment of the work. There is also a bibliography which gives details of editions and translations of both Christine's primary works and those of her medieval counterparts. This bibliography also offers a selection of secondary studies of the *City of Ladies* as well as suggestions for further reading on its historical and literary background.

*The Book of the
City of Ladies*

PART I

1. *Here begins the* Book of the City of Ladies, *the first chapter of which explains why and for what purpose the book was written.*

One day, I was sitting in my study surrounded by many books of different kinds, for it has long been my habit to engage in the pursuit of knowledge. My mind had grown weary as I had spent the day struggling with the weighty tomes of various authors whom I had been studying for some time. I looked up from my book and decided that, for once, I would put aside these difficult texts and find instead something amusing and easy to read from the works of the poets. As I searched around for some little book, I happened to chance upon a work which did not belong to me but was amongst a pile of others that had been placed in my safe-keeping. I opened it up and saw from the title that it was by Matheolus. With a smile, I made my choice. Although I had never read it, I knew that, unlike many other works, this one was said to be written in praise of women. Yet I had scarcely begun to read it when my dear mother called me down to supper, for it was time to eat. I put the book to one side, resolving to go back to it the following day.

The next morning, seated once more in my study as is my usual custom, I remembered my previous desire to have a look at this book by Matheolus. I picked it up again and read on a little. But, seeing the kind of immoral language and ideas it contained, the content seemed to me likely to appeal only to those who enjoy reading works of slander and to be of no use whatsoever to anyone who wished to pursue virtue or to improve their moral standards. I therefore leafed through it, read the ending, and decided to switch to some more worthy and profitable work. Yet, having looked at this book, which I considered to be of no authority, an extraordinary thought became planted in my mind which made me wonder why on earth it was that so many men, both clerks and others, have said and continue to say and write such awful, damning things about women and their ways. I was at a loss as to how to explain it. It is not just a handful of writers who do this, nor only this Matheolus whose book is neither regarded as authoritative nor intended to be taken seriously. It is all manner of philosophers, poets and orators too numerous to mention, who all seem to speak with one voice and are unanimous in their view that female nature is wholly given up to vice.

As I mulled these ideas over in my mind again and again, I began to examine myself and my own behaviour as an example of womankind. In order to judge in all fairness and without prejudice whether what so many famous men have said about us is true, I also thought about other women I know, the many princesses and countless ladies of all different social ranks who have shared their private and personal thoughts with me. No matter which way I looked at it and no matter how much I turned the question over in my mind, I could find no evidence from my own experience to bear out such a negative view of female nature and habits. Even so, given that I could scarcely find a moral work by any author which didn't devote some chapter or paragraph to attacking the female sex, I had to accept their unfavourable opinion of women since it was unlikely that so many learned men, who seemed to be endowed with such great intelligence and insight into all things, could possibly have lied on so many different occasions. It was on the basis of this one simple argument that I was forced to conclude that, although my understanding was too crude and ill-informed to recognize the great flaws in myself and other women, these men had to be in the right. Thus I preferred to give more weight to what others said than to trust my own judgement and experience.

I dwelt on these thoughts at such length that it was as if I had sunk into a deep trance. My mind became flooded with an endless stream of names as I recalled all the authors who had written on this subject. I came to the conclusion that God had surely created a vile thing when He created woman. Indeed, I was astounded that such a fine craftsman could have wished to make such an appalling object which, as these writers would have it, is like a vessel in which all the sin and evil of the world has been collected and preserved. This thought inspired such a great sense of disgust and sadness in me that I began to despise myself and the whole of my sex as an aberration in nature.

With a deep sigh, I called out to God: 'Oh Lord, how can this be? Unless I commit an error of faith, I cannot doubt that you, in your infinite wisdom and perfect goodness, could make anything that wasn't good. Didn't you yourself create woman especially and then endow her with all the qualities that you wished her to have? How could you possibly have made a mistake in anything? Yet here stand women not simply accused, but already judged, sentenced and condemned! I just cannot understand this contradiction. If it is true, dear Lord God, that women are guilty of such horrors as so many men seem to say, and as you yourself have said that the testimony of two or more witnesses is conclusive,[1] how can I doubt their word? Oh God, why wasn't I born a male so that my every desire would be to serve you, to do right in all things, and to be as perfect a creature as man claims to be? Since you chose not to show such grace to me, please pardon and forgive me, dear Lord, if I fail to serve you as well as I should, for the servant who receives fewer rewards from his lord is less obligated to him in his service.'

Sick at heart, in my lament to God I uttered these and many other foolish words since I thought myself very unfortunate that He had given me a female form.

2. *Christine tells how three ladies appeared to her, and how the first of them spoke to her and comforted her in her distress.*

Sunk in these unhappy thoughts, my head bowed as if in shame and my eyes full of tears, I sat slumped against the arm of my chair with my cheek resting on my hand. All of a sudden, I saw a beam of light, like the rays of the sun, shine down into my lap. Since it was too dark at that time of day for the sun to come into my study, I woke with a start as if from a deep sleep. I looked up to see where the light had come from and all at once saw before me three ladies, crowned and of majestic appearance, whose faces shone with a brightness that lit up me and everything else in the place. As you can imagine, I was full of amazement that they had managed to enter a room whose doors and windows were all closed. Terrified at the thought that it might be some kind of apparition come to tempt me, I quickly made the sign of the cross on my forehead.

With a smile on her face, the lady who stood at the front of the three addressed me first: 'My dear daughter, don't be afraid, for we have not come to do you any harm, but rather, out of pity on your distress, we are here to comfort you. Our aim is to help you get rid of those misconceptions which have clouded your mind and made you reject what you know and believe in fact to be the truth just because so many other people have come out with the opposite opinion. You're acting like that fool in the joke who falls asleep in the mill and whose friends play a trick on him by dressing him up in women's clothing. When he wakes up, they manage to convince him that he is a woman despite all evidence to the contrary! My dear girl, what has happened to your sense? Have you forgotten that it is in the furnace that gold is refined, increasing in value the more it is beaten and fashioned into different shapes? Don't you know that it's the very finest things which are the subject of the most intense discussion? Now, if you turn your mind to the very highest realm of all, the realm of abstract ideas, think for a moment whether or not those philosophers whose views against women you've been citing have ever been proven wrong. In fact, they are all constantly correcting each other's opinions, as you yourself should know from reading Aristotle's *Metaphysics* where he discusses and refutes both their views and those of Plato and other philosophers. Don't forget the Doctors of the Church either, and Saint Augustine in particular, who all took issue with Aristotle himself on certain matters, even though he is considered to be the greatest of all authorities on both moral and natural philosophy. You seem to have accepted the philosophers' views as articles of faith and thus as irrefutable on every point.

'As for the poets you mention, you must realize that they sometimes wrote in the manner of fables which you have to take as saying the opposite of what they appear to say. You should therefore read such texts according to the grammatical rule of *antiphrasis*,[2] which consists of interpreting something that is negative in a positive light, or vice versa. My advice to you is to read those passages where they criticize women

8

in this way and to turn them to your advantage, no matter what the author's original intention was. It could be that Matheolus is also meant to be read like this because there are some passages in his book which, if taken literally, are just out-and-out heresy. As for what these authors – not just Matheolus but also the more authoritative writer of the *Romance of the Rose* – say about the God-given, holy state of matrimony, experience should tell you that they are completely wrong when they say that marriage is insufferable thanks to women. What husband ever gave his wife the power over him to utter the kind of insults and obscenities which these authors claim that women do? Believe me, despite what you've read in books, you've never actually *seen* such a thing because it's all a pack of outrageous lies. My dear friend, I have to say that it is your naivety which has led you to take what they come out with as the truth. Return to your senses and stop worrying your head about such foolishness. Let me tell you that those who speak ill of women do more harm to themselves than they do to the women they actually slander.'

3. *Christine recounts how the lady who had spoken to her told her who she was, what her function and purpose was, and how she prophesied that Christine would build a city with the help of the three ladies.*

On receiving these words from the distinguished lady, I didn't know which of my senses was the more struck by what she said: whether it was my ears as I took in her stirring words, or my eyes as I admired her great beauty and dress, her noble bearing and face. It was the same for the other ladies too; my gaze darted back and forth from one to the other since they were all so alike that you could hardly tell them apart. All except for the third lady, who was no less imposing than the other two. This lady had such a stern face that whoever glanced into her eyes, no matter how brazen they were, would feel afraid of committing some misdeed since she seemed to threaten punishment to all wrongdoers. Out of respect for the ladies' noble appearance, I stood up before them but was far too dumbfounded to utter a single word. I was extremely curious to know who they were and would have dearly loved to dare ask them their names, where they were from, why they had come, and what the priceless symbols were that each of them held like a sceptre in her right hand. Yet I didn't think myself worthy to put these questions to such honourable ladies as these, so I held my tongue and carried on gazing at them. Though still frightened, I was also in part reassured, for the lady's words had already begun to assuage my fears.

Presently, the wise lady who had addressed me first seemed to read my mind and began to answer my unspoken questions with these words: 'My dear daughter, you should know that it is by the grace of God, who foresees and ordains all things, that we, celestial creatures though we may be, have been sent down to earth in order to restore order and justice to those institutions which we ourselves have set up at God's command. All three of us are His daughters, for it was He who created us. My task is to bring back men and women when they drift away from the straight and narrow. Should they go astray but yet have the sense to know me when they see me, I come to them in spirit and speak to their conscience, instructing them in the error of their ways and showing them how exactly it is that they have done wrong. Then I teach them to follow the correct road and to avoid doing what is undesirable. Because it is my role to light their way to the true path and to teach both men and women to acknowledge their flaws and weaknesses, you see me here holding up a shining mirror like a sceptre in my right hand. You can be sure that whoever looks into this mirror, no matter who they may be, will see themselves as they truly are, such is its great power. Not for nothing is it encrusted with precious stones, as you can see. With the help of this mirror, I can determine the nature, quantity and essence of all things and can take full measure of them. Without this mirror, nothing can come to good. Since you obviously want to know what function my two sisters perform, each of them will shortly speak to you in turn and will add her weight to my words by giving you a clear explanation of both her name and her powers.

'First, however, I will tell you exactly why we are here. I want you to know that, as we do nothing without good reason, our appearance here today has a definite purpose. Though we do not attempt to be known in all places, since not everyone strives to acquaint themselves with us, we have none the less come to visit you, our dear friend. Because you have long desired to acquire true knowledge by dedicating yourself to your studies, which have cut you off from the rest of the world, we are now here to comfort you in your sad and dejected state. It is your own efforts that have won you this reward. You will soon see clearly why it is that your heart and mind have been so troubled.

'Yet we also have a further, more important reason for coming to visit you, which we'll now go on to tell you about. Our wish is to prevent others from falling into the same error as you and to ensure that, in future, all worthy ladies and valiant women are protected from those who have attacked them. The female sex has been left defenceless for a long time now, like an orchard without a wall, and bereft of a champion to take up arms in order to protect it. Indeed, this is because those trusty knights who should by right defend women have been negligent in their duty and lacking in vigilance, leaving womankind open to attack from all sides. It's no wonder that women have been the losers in this war against them since the envious slanderers and vicious traitors who criticize them have been allowed to aim all manner of weapons at their defenceless targets. Even the strongest city will fall if there is no one to defend it, and even the most undeserving case will win if there is no one to testify against it. Out of the goodness and simplicity of their hearts, women have trusted in God and have patiently endured the countless verbal and written assaults that have been unjustly and shamelessly launched upon them. Now, however, it is time for them to be delivered out of the hands of Pharaoh.[3] For this reason, we three ladies whom you see before you have been moved by pity to tell you that you are to construct a building in the shape of a walled city, sturdy and impregnable. This has been decreed by God, who has chosen you to do this with our help and guidance. Only ladies who are of good reputation and worthy of praise will be admitted into this city. To those lacking in virtue, its gates will remain forever closed.'

4. How, before the lady revealed her name, she spoke at greater length about the city which Christine was destined to build, and explained that she was entrusted with the task of helping her to construct the enclosure and external walls.

'So you see, my dear daughter, that you alone of all women have been granted the honour of building the City of Ladies. In order to lay the foundations, you shall draw fresh water from us three as from a clear spring. We will bring you building materials which will be stronger and more durable than solid, uncemented marble. Your city will be unparalleled in splendour and will last for all eternity.

'Haven't you read that King Tros founded the city of Troy with the help of Apollo, Minerva and Neptune, whom the people of that time believed to be gods? Haven't you also heard of Cadmus, who created the city of Thebes at the gods' command? Yet, in the course of time, even these cities fell into ruin and decay. However, in the manner of a true sibyl, I prophesy to you that this city which you're going to build with our help will never fall or be taken. Rather, it will prosper always, in spite of its enemies who are racked by envy. Though it may be attacked on many sides, it will never be lost or defeated.

'In the past, as the history books tell you, certain courageous ladies who refused the yoke of servitude founded and established the realm of Amazonia. For many years afterwards, this realm was maintained under the rule of various queens, all of whom were noble ladies chosen by the women themselves, and who governed well and wisely, making every effort to keep their country safe. These women were very strong and powerful, having extended their rule over many of the lands of the east and having subjugated to their will all the neighbouring countries. They were feared by everyone, even the Greeks, who were the bravest nation in the world at that time. None the less, even the Amazons' power began to crumble in due course, as is the way with all earthly rulers. Now, the only trace that is left of that proud realm is its name.

'By contrast, the city which you're going to build will be much more powerful than these. As has been decided amongst the three of us, it is my task to help you begin by giving you tough, indestructible cement which you will need to set the mighty foundations and to support the great walls that you must raise all around. These walls should have huge high towers, solid bastions surrounded by moats, and outer forts with both natural and manmade defences. This is what a powerful city must have in order to resist attack. On our advice, you will sink these foundations deep in order to make them as secure as possible, and you will construct such high walls that the city inside will be safe from assault. Dear Christine, I have now told you all about why we have come. However, in order to convince you to give greater weight to my words, I'm going to reveal my name to you. The very sound of it should reassure you that, if you follow my instructions, you will find me to be an infallible guide to you in all your endeavours. I am called Lady Reason, so rest assured that you are in good hands. For the moment, I will say no more.'

5. Christine tells how the second lady gave her name, explained what her role was, and revealed how she would help Christine to lay out the buildings of the City of Ladies.

When the first lady had finished, and before I could say anything, the second lady began to speak: 'My name is Rectitude and I dwell in heaven more than on earth. However, like a shining ray of light sent down by God, I bring with me the message of His goodness. When I visit those who are just, I encourage them to do good in all things, to strive as far as possible to give each person his or her due, to speak and preserve the truth, to protect the rights of the poor and the innocent, to refrain from stealing from others, and to uphold the good name of those who are wrongfully accused. I am the shield and defender of those who serve God and I help to prevent the wicked from abusing their power. I make sure that those who are industrious and charitable are rewarded for their efforts. Through me, God reveals His secrets to those He loves, and it is I who am their advocate in heaven. This splendid rule that you see me holding in my right hand like a sceptre is the yardstick of truth which separates right from wrong and distinguishes between good and evil. Whoever follows my yardstick cannot go astray. It is the rod of peace, used by the just who rally to its cause, and which also strikes down those who do evil. What more can I tell you? With this rule, whose powers are infinite, all things are measured out. As far as you are concerned, this rule will help you to plan the city which you have been commissioned to build. You'll have good need of it in order to lay out the interior of the city and to build its high temples, palaces and houses, its roads, squares and marketplaces; in fact, everything that is needed to accommodate its inhabitants. It is in this capacity that I have come to help you. Don't be put off by the vast circumference of the enclosure walls. With the help of God and us three, you will build the city, covering the whole area with beautiful buildings and houses and leaving no space unfilled.'

6. *Christine tells how the third lady revealed her name and outlined what her role was, then explained that she would help to finish off the high turrets of the towers and palaces and would bring Christine a queen for her city accompanied by a host of noble ladies.*

Next, it was the turn of the third lady to speak: 'My dear friend Christine, I am Justice, the most beloved of God's daughters since my being arises directly from His own. I live in heaven, on earth, and in hell: in heaven I exalt the glory of the saints and the blessed spirits; on earth I divide up and allot to each person their share of the good or bad that each has done; and in hell I punish the wicked. I am ineluctable and immovable, having neither friend nor enemy who can overcome my will either by pity or by cruelty. My task is purely and simply to judge and repay everyone according to their just deserts. It is I who keep things in order, since without me nothing remains stable. I am part of God and God is part of me: in effect, we amount to the same thing. Whoever follows me cannot go wrong, since my way is the true way. First and foremost, I teach all men and women who are of sound judgement and who believe in me to look into and correct themselves, to do as they would be done by, to apportion goods without showing favouritism, to speak the truth, to avoid and detest falsehood, and to shun all forms of vice. This vessel of pure gold that you see me holding in my right hand is like a measuring cup, given to me by God my father, which I use to share out to each person exactly what he or she deserves. It is engraved with the *fleur de lys* of the Holy Trinity and, since it never gives out wrong measure, there are no grounds for anyone to complain about their lot. Mortal men have their own measuring cups which they claim to have derived from mine, but their judgement is never accurate as they always give out too much to some and too little to others.

'I could tell you even more about my powers and my function but for now let me just say that, of all the Virtues, I am the most important since they all culminate in me. We three ladies whom you see before you are one and the same, in the sense that one cannot act independently of the others. What the first lady decides, the second one puts into effect and then I, the third one, bring all to completion. I have been chosen by the three of us to help you finish off your city, my task being to construct the high turrets of the great towers, houses and palaces which will all be covered in bright gold. I will not only fill the city full of worthy ladies for you but I will also bring you their noble queen who shall be revered and honoured above all the other great ladies present. Before I hand you the keys to your finished city, I will need your help to fortify it and make it safe with strong gates that will be brought down for you from heaven.'

7. *Christine tells how she replied to the three ladies.*

Once I finished listening to the words spoken by the three ladies, which had commanded my complete attention and had totally dispelled the dismay that I had been feeling before their arrival, I threw myself fully face down in front of them, not just on to my knees, out of respect for their noble status. Kissing the ground they stood on, I adored them as if they were great goddesses, praising them with these words: 'Oh noble and worthy ladies, light of the heavens and of the earth, fountains of paradise bringing joy to the blessed, how is it that you have deigned to come down from your lofty seats and shining thrones to visit me, a simple and ignorant scholar, in my dark and gloomy retreat? How could one ever thank you enough for such graciousness? The sweet rain and dew of your words have already sunk into my arid mind, refreshing and replenishing my thoughts which are now ready to take seed and to put forth new shoots which will bear fruit of great virtue and delicious flavour. But what have I done to be chosen to undertake the task of building a new city on earth that you have just described to me? I am no Saint Thomas the Apostle who, by the grace of God, created a fine palace in the heavens for the king of India. Nor does my poor brain have any idea of art or geometry, let alone of the theory and practice of construction. Even if I could learn the rudiments of these things, my weak female body would hardly be strong enough for such an undertaking. Yet, honoured ladies, though I'm still daunted by the prospect of this extraordinary task, I know that nothing is impossible for God. Nor should I be afraid that anything which was undertaken with your help and advice could not be brought to a satisfactory conclusion. I therefore thank both God and you with all my heart for having entrusted me with such a noble task, one which I accept with great pleasure. Behold your handmaiden, ready to do your bidding. I will obey your every command, so be it unto me according to your word.'[4]

8. *Christine explains how Reason instructed her and helped her to begin digging up the ground in order to lay the foundations.*

Lady Reason replied to my words, saying: 'Stand up now, daughter, and without further delay let us make our way to the Field of Letters. There we will build the City of Ladies on flat, fertile ground, where fruits of all kinds flourish and fresh streams flow, a place where every good thing grows in abundance. Take the spade of your intelligence and dig deep to make a great trench all around where you see the line I have traced. I'll help to carry away the hods of earth on my shoulders.'

Obeying her instructions, I jumped to my feet: thanks to the three ladies, my body felt much stronger and lighter than before. She took the lead and I followed on behind. When we came to the spot she had described, I began to excavate and dig out the earth with the spade of my intelligence, just as she had directed me to do. The first fruit of my labours was this: 'My lady, I'm remembering that image of gold being refined in the furnace that you used before to symbolize the way many male writers have launched a full-scale attack on the ways of women. I take this image to mean that the more women are criticized, the more it redounds to their glory. But please tell me exactly what it is that makes so many different authors slander women in their writings because, if I understand you correctly, they are wrong to do so. Is it Nature that makes them do this? Or, if it is out of hatred, how can you explain it?'

Reason answered my questions, saying: 'My dear daughter, in order to help you see more clearly how things stand, let me carry away this first load of earth. I can tell you that, far from making them slander women, Nature does the complete opposite. There is no stronger or closer bond in the world than that which Nature, in accordance with God's wishes, creates between man and woman. Rather, there are many other different reasons which explain why men have attacked women in the past and continue to do so, including those authors whose works you have already mentioned. Some of those who criticized women did so with good intentions: they wanted to rescue men who had already fallen into the clutches of depraved and corrupt women or to prevent others from suffering the same fate, and to encourage men generally to avoid leading a lustful and sinful existence. They therefore attacked all women in order to persuade men to regard the entire sex as an abomination.'

'My lady,' I said, 'forgive me for interrupting you. Were they right to do so, since they were acting with good intentions? Isn't it true that one's actions are judged by one's intentions?'

'You're wrong, my dear girl,' she replied, 'because there is no excuse for plain ignorance. If I killed you with good intentions and out of stupidity, would I be in the right? Those who have acted in this way, whoever they may be, have abused their power. Attacking one party in the belief that you are benefiting a third party is unfair. So is criticizing the nature of all women, which is completely unjustified, as I will prove to you by analogy. Condemning all women in order to help some misguided men get over their foolish behaviour is tantamount to denouncing fire, which is a vital and beneficial element, just because some people are burnt by it, or to cursing water just because some people are drowned in it. You could apply the same reasoning to all manner of things which can be put to either good or bad use. In none of these cases should you blame the thing in itself if foolish people use it unwisely. You yourself have made these points elsewhere in your writings. Those who subscribe to these opinions, whether in good or bad faith, have overstepped the mark in order to make their point. It's like somebody cutting up the whole piece of cloth in order to make himself a huge coat simply because it's not going to cost him anything and no one is going to object. It thus stops anyone else from using the material. If instead, as you yourself have rightly remarked, these writers had tried to find ways to save men from indulging in vice and from frequenting debauched women by attacking only the morals and the habits of those who were evidently guilty of such behaviour, I freely admit that they would have produced texts which were extremely useful. It's true that there's nothing worse than a woman who is dissolute and depraved: she's like a monster, a creature going against its own nature, which is to be timid, meek and pure. I can assure you that those writers who condemn the entire female sex for being sinful, when in fact there are so many women who are extremely virtuous, are not acting with my approval. They've committed a grave error, as do all those who subscribe to their views. So let us throw out these horrible, ugly, misshapen stones from your work as they have no place in your beautiful city.

'Other men have criticized women for different reasons: some because they are themselves steeped in sin, some because of a bodily impediment, some out of sheer envy, and some quite simply because they naturally take delight in slandering others. There are also some who do so because they like to flaunt their erudition: they have come across these views in books and so like to quote the authors whom they have read.

'Those who criticize the female sex because they are inherently sinful are men who have wasted their youth on dissolute behaviour and who have had affairs with many different women. These men have therefore acquired cunning through their many experiences and have grown old without repenting of their sins. Indeed, they look back with nostalgia on the appalling way they used to carry on when they were younger. Now that old age has finally caught up with them and the spirit is still willing but the flesh has grown weak, they are full of regret when they see that, for them, the "good old days" are over and they can merely watch as younger men take over from where they have had to leave off. The only way they can release their frustration is to attack women and to try to stop others from enjoying the pleasures that they themselves used to take. You very often see old men such as these going around saying vile and disgusting things, as in the case of your Matheolus, who freely admits that he is just an impotent old man who would still like to satisfy his desires. He's an excellent example to illustrate my point as he's typical of many other similar cases.

'Yet, thank goodness, not all old men are full of depravity and rotten to the core like a leper. There are many other fine, decent ones whose wisdom and virtue have been nourished by me and whose words reflect their good character, since they speak in an honourable and sober fashion. Such men detest all kinds of wrongdoing and slander. Thus, rather than attacking and defaming individual sinners, male or female, they condemn all sins in general. Their advice to others is to avoid vice, pursue virtue and stick to the straight and narrow.

'Those men who have attacked women because of their own bodily impediments, such as impotence or a deformed limb, are all bitter and twisted in the mind. The only pleasure they have to compensate for their incapacity is to slander the female sex since it is women who bring such joy to other men. That way they are convinced that they can put others off enjoying what they themselves have never had.

'Those men who have slandered the opposite sex out of envy have usually known women who were cleverer and more virtuous than they are. Out of bitterness and spite, envious men such as these are driven to attack all women, thinking that they can thereby undermine these individuals' good reputation and excellent character, as in the case of the author of *On Philosophy* whose name I've forgotten. In this book, he goes to great lengths to argue that men should on no account praise women and that those who do so are betraying the title of his book: their doctrine is no longer "philosophy" but "philofolly". However, I can assure you that it is definitely he who is the arch-exponent of "philofolly" because of all the false reasoning and erroneous conclusions he comes out with in his book.

'As for those men who are slanderous by nature, it's not surprising if they criticize women, given that they attack everyone indiscriminately. You can take it from me that any man who wilfully slanders the female sex does so because he has an evil mind, since he's going against both reason and nature. Against reason, because he is lacking in gratitude and failing to acknowledge all the good and indispensable things that woman has done for him both in the past and still today, much more than he can ever repay her for. Against nature, in that even the birds and the beasts naturally love their mate, the female of the species. So man acts in a most unnatural way when he, a rational being, fails to love woman.

'Finally, there are those who dabble in literature and delight in mimicking even the very finest works written by authors who are greatly superior to them. They think themselves to be beyond reproach since they are merely repeating what others have already said. Believe me, this is how they set about making their defamatory remarks. Some of them scribble down any old nonsense, verse without rhyme or reason, in which they discuss the ways of women, or princes, or whoever it might be, when it is they themselves, whose habits leave much to be desired, who are most in need of moral self-improvement. Yet the common folk, who are as ignorant as they are, think that it's the best thing they've ever read.'

9. How Christine dug over the earth: in other words, the questions which she put to Reason and the answers she received from her.

'Now that I have prepared and set out this great task for you, you should carry on the task of digging up the ground, following the line which I have laid down.'

In obedience to Reason's wishes, I set to with all my might, saying, 'My lady, why is it that Ovid, who is considered to be the greatest of poets (though others, myself included, think that Virgil is more worthy of that accolade, if you don't mind my saying so), made so many derogatory remarks about women in his writings, such as the *Art of Love*, the *Remedies of Love* and other works?'

Reason replied: 'Ovid was a man very well versed in the theory and practice of writing poetry and his fine mind allowed him to excel in everything he wrote. However, his body was given over to all kinds of worldliness and vices of the flesh: he had affairs with many women, since he had no sense of moderation and showed no loyalty to any particular one. Throughout his youth, he behaved like this only to end up with the reward he richly deserved: he lost not just his good name and his possessions, but even some parts of his body! Because he was so licentious, both in the way he carried on and in the encouragement he gave to others to do the same, he was finally sent into exile. Even when he was brought back from banishment by some of his followers, who were influential young men of Rome, he couldn't help himself from falling into exactly the same pattern as before. So finally he was castrated and deprived of his organs because of his immorality. He's another good example of what I was telling you about just now: once he realized that he could no longer indulge in the same kind of pleasures as before, he began to attack women with his sly remarks in an attempt to make others despise them too.'

'My lady, your words certainly ring true. However, I've seen another book by an Italian writer called Cecco d'Ascoli who, if I remember correctly, comes from the Marches or Tuscany. In this work, he says some extraordinarily unpleasant things which are worse than anything else I've ever read and which shouldn't be repeated by anybody with any sense.'

Reason's response was: 'My dear girl, don't be surprised if Cecco d'Ascoli slandered the whole of womankind since he hated and despised them all. Being unspeakably wicked, he tried to make all other men share his nasty opinion about women. He too got what he deserved: thanks to his heretical views, he suffered a shameful death at the stake.'

'My lady, I've also come across another little book in Latin, called *On the Secrets of Women*, which states that the female body is inherently flawed and defective in many of its functions.'[5]

Reason replied, 'You shouldn't need any other evidence than that of your own body to realize that this book is a complete fabrication and stuffed with lies. Though some may attribute the book to Aristotle, it is unthinkable that a philosopher as great as he would have produced such outrageous nonsense. Any woman who reads it can see that, since certain things it says are the complete opposite of her own experience, she can safely assume that the rest of the book is equally unreliable. Incidentally, do you remember the part at the beginning where he claims that one of the popes excommunicated any man found either reading the book out loud to a woman or giving it to her to read for herself?'

'Yes, my lady, I do remember that passage.'

'Do you know what evil motive drove him to put such vile words at the front of his book for gullible, foolish men to read?'

'No, my lady, you'll have to tell me.'

'It was because he didn't want women to get hold of his book and read it or have someone else read it to them for fear that if they did, they would pour scorn on it and would recognize it for the utter rubbish that it is. By this ruse, he thought he could trick the men who wanted to read his text.'

'My lady, amongst the other things he said, I seem to remember that, after going on at great length about female children being the result of some weakness or deficiency in the mother's womb, he claimed that Nature herself is ashamed when she sees that she has created such an imperfect being.'

'Well, my dear Christine, surely it's obvious that those who come out with this opinion are totally misguided and irrational? How can Nature, who is God's handmaiden, be more powerful than her own master from whom she derives her authority in the first place? It is God almighty who, at the very core of His being, nurtured the idea of creating man and woman. When He put His divine wish into action and made Adam from the clay of the fields of Damascus, He took him to dwell in the earthly paradise, which has always been the noblest place on this lowly earth. There He put Adam to sleep and created the body of woman from one of his ribs. This was a sign that she was meant to be his companion standing at his side, whom he would love as if they were one flesh, and not his servant lying at his feet. If the Divine Craftsman Himself wasn't ashamed to create the female form, why should Nature be? It really is the height of stupidity to claim otherwise. Moreover, how was she created? I'm not sure if you realize this, but it was in God's image.[6] How can anybody dare to speak ill of something which bears such a noble imprint? There are, however, some who are foolish enough to maintain that when God made man in His image, this means His physical body. Yet this is not the case, for at that time God had not yet adopted a human form, so it has to be understood to mean the soul, which is immaterial intellect and which will resemble God until the end of time. He endowed both male and female with this soul, which He

22

made equally noble and virtuous in the two sexes. Whilst we're still on the subject of how the human body was formed, woman was created by the very finest of craftsmen. And where exactly was she made? Why, in the earthly paradise. What from? Was it from coarse matter? No, it was from the finest material that had yet been invented by God: from the body of man himself.'

'My lady, from what you've told me, I can see that woman is a very noble creature. Yet, all the same, wasn't it Cicero who said that man should not be subject to woman and that he who did so abased himself because it is wrong to be subject to one who is your inferior?'

Reason answered, 'It is he or she who is the more virtuous who is the superior being: human superiority or inferiority is not determined by sexual difference but by the degree to which one has perfected one's nature and morals. Thus, happy is he who serves the Virgin Mary, for she is exalted even above the angels.'

'My lady, it was one of the Catos, the one who was a great orator, who declared that if woman hadn't been created, man would converse with the gods.'

Reason's reply was: 'Now you see an example of someone who was supposed to be very wise coming out with something very foolish. It is because of woman that man sits side by side with God. As for those who state that it is thanks to a woman, the lady Eve, that man was expelled from paradise, my answer to them would be that man has gained far more through Mary than he ever lost through Eve. Humankind has now become one with God, which never would have happened if Eve hadn't sinned. Both men and women should praise this fault of Eve's since it is because of her that such an honour has been bestowed on them. If human nature is fallen, due to the actions of one of God's creatures, it has been redeemed by the Creator Himself. As for conversing with the gods if womankind hadn't been invented, as this Cato claims, his words were truer than he knew. Being a pagan, he and those of his faith believed that both heaven and hell were ruled by the gods. But the ones in hell are what we call devils. So it's definitely true to say that men would be conversing with the gods of hell if Mary had not come into the world!'

10. *More questions and answers on this subject.*

'It was also this Cato Uticensis who said that a woman who is attractive to a man is like a rose which is lovely to look at but hides its sharp thorns underneath.'[7]

Reason replied: 'Once again, he was wiser than he knew, this Cato, because every decent, upright woman who leads a virtuous life is, and should be, one of the loveliest things to behold. Yet the thorn represents both her fear of doing wrong and her contrition, which are lodged deep in the heart of such a woman and make her reserved, cautious and prudent in order to protect herself.'

'My lady, is it true what certain authors have said about women being by nature gluttonous and prone to overindulgence?'

'My dear girl, you must have often heard the saying, "What is in our nature cannot be taken away." It would be very surprising if they *were* naturally so inclined when in fact so few of them ever actually frequent taverns and other such establishments which sell rich and intoxicating fare. It is extremely rare to find women in these places: not from shame, as some might suggest, but rather, in my opinion, because they are naturally disposed to avoid them altogether. Even if women *were* given over to gluttony and yet managed to restrain their appetites out of a sense of shame, they should be praised for showing such virtue and strength of character. As we're on this subject, don't you remember that on a feast day a little while ago you were talking outside your house with your neighbour, a respectable young lady. You saw a man coming out of a tavern who said to his friend: "I've just spent so much in the inn that my wife won't have any wine to drink today." You called him over and asked him why she wouldn't do so. He replied: "My lady, it's because every time I come home from the tavern she asks me how much I've spent. If it's more than twelve deniers,[8] she makes up for this cost by refraining from drinking herself. Her view is that we don't earn enough for the two of us to be able to indulge ourselves so heavily."'

'My lady,' I replied, 'I remember this incident very well.'

Reason then said to me: 'With many examples such as these, you can see that women are inherently sober creatures and that those who aren't go against their own nature. There is no worse vice in women than gluttony, because whoever is gluttonous is susceptible to all kinds of other vices too. Instead, it's well known that women flock to churches in great numbers to listen to sermons, to make their confessions and to say their daily prayers.'

'My lady, you're quite right,' I said, 'but some writers make out that, in fact, women go to church all dressed and made up in order to show themselves off to men and find themselves lovers.'

Her reply was: 'That might be true, my dear friend, if it was only pretty young girls who went to church. But, if you notice, for every young woman that you see, there are twenty or thirty old women attending services and dressed in plain, modest clothes. Moreover, women are not just pious but also charitable. After all, who is it that visits the sick and attends to their needs? Who gives aid to the poor? Who goes to the hospitals? Who helps bury the dead? To my mind, these are the tasks that women perform and which are like milestones on the road that leads to God.'

'My lady, you've put it very clearly. Yet, there is another author who has said that women are by nature weak-minded and childish, which explains why they get on so well with children and why children like being with them.'

She replied, 'My dear daughter, if you look carefully at the nature of a child, you will see that it is instinctively attracted to kindness and gentleness. And what could be kinder or gentler than a respectable woman? It's truly wicked of people to try to turn something which is good and praiseworthy in a woman – her tenderness – into something bad and blameworthy. Women love children because they're acting not out of ignorance but rather a natural instinct to be gentle. And if being gentle therefore means that they are childlike, so much the better for them. Remember the story the gospels tell about what Jesus Christ said to his apostles when they were arguing amongst themselves as to who would be the greatest of them all? He called a child to him and laid his hand on its head saying, "I tell you that he who is humble and meek like a child will be the greatest among you, for he who abases himself will be exalted whereas he who exalts himself will be abased." '[9]

'My lady, men have made a great deal of mileage out of mocking women because of a Latin proverb which says that "God made woman to weep, talk and spin".[10]

Reason's reply was: 'My dear Christine, this is absolutely true, though it's not meant to be a criticism, despite what some might claim. It's a fine thing that God endowed women with such qualities because many have been saved thanks to their tears, words and distaffs. In answer to those who have attacked women for weeping, I would say that if Jesus Christ, who could read directly into human hearts and minds, had thought that women only wept because they were weak or simple-minded, he would never have lowered himself in his majesty to let fall tears from his own saintly eyes out of compassion at the sight of Martha and Mary Magdalene weeping for their dead brother, the leper,[11] whom he brought back to life. Indeed, God has showered women with so many favours precisely because He has been moved by their weeping. Far from despising Mary Magdalene's tears, He appreciated them so much that He forgave her all her sins. It is thanks to her weeping that she is now living in heavenly glory.

'Nor did God scorn the tears of the widow who wept for her only son as he was being laid in the ground. When Christ saw her weeping, his compassion gushed forth like a fountain of mercy at the sight of her tears. Asking her, "Woman, why are you crying?", he straightaway brought back her child from the dead.[12] The Holy Scriptures tell of so many other miracles which God has performed in the past and still does perform for the sake of a woman's tears. Indeed, the tears shed by a pious woman have often been the cause of her own salvation or that of those for whom she has been praying. Take the example of Saint Augustine, the holy Father of the Church, who was converted to Christianity by his mother's weeping. The good lady never stopped crying and praying to God to shine the light of faith into the unbelieving heart of her heathen son. Because of her persistence, Saint Ambrose, whom she used to implore to pray to God to save her son, was moved to say: "Woman, I believe that your tears will surely not be shed in vain." Blessed Ambrose, you didn't dismiss a woman's tears as trivial. What one should say to anybody coming out with this opinion is that it was thanks to the tears of a woman that Saint Augustine, this holy luminary, now shines his light down from the altar and illuminates the whole of

Christendom. So men really should have nothing more to say on this point.

'God similarly endowed women with speech, thank the Lord, for if He hadn't done so, they would all have remained dumb. But let's go back to that proverb, which somebody has obviously just cobbled together to get at women. If women's speech had been as unreliable and worthless as some maintain, Our Lord Jesus Christ would never have allowed news of such a glorious miracle as his resurrection to be announced first by a woman, as he told the blessed Magdalene to do when he appeared to her first on Easter day and sent her to inform Peter and the other apostles. Praise be to God for having bestowed so many gifts and favours on women by wishing them to become the bearers of such great glad tidings.'

I said to Reason, 'My lady, these envious men would all be reduced to silence if they could see the truth of the matter. I've just remembered something that makes me smile, something silly which I've heard men and even foolish preachers say about Christ appearing first to a woman because he knew she couldn't keep her mouth shut and so the news of his resurrection would spread all the faster.'

Reason replied, 'My dear daughter, you're quite right to say that it's only fools who have come out with this view. They're not just criticizing women but also going so far as to suggest that Jesus Christ blasphemed when he said that such a perfect and holy mystery could be revealed by a vice. I don't know how men can dare say such a thing. Even if they're only joking, they shouldn't do so at the Lord's expense.

'To get back to your first point: it was a fine thing that the woman from Canaan should have been such a talker since she never stopped shrieking and shouting out to Christ as he went through the streets of Jerusalem, begging him to have pity on her and cure her sick daughter.[13] And what did Our Lord do, he who has always been an endless fountain of mercy and who shows compassion at the least little word spoken truly from the heart? He seemed to take delight in the unending flow of words and prayers pouring out of this woman's mouth. Why? Because he wanted to test her constancy. When he used harsh words to compare her to a dog for not being of the Christian faith, she did not flinch but rather replied most intelligently, saying: "Lord, that is absolutely true, but little dogs feed off the crumbs which fall from the master's table." What a wise woman! Who taught you to speak like that? You won your case thanks to the modest words which you spoke from a pure heart. This was made clear when Christ turned to his apostles, declaring that nowhere in the whole of Israel had he ever come across such faith as in this woman, and then granted her request. One cannot praise highly enough this honour shown to women which the envious seek to denigrate, when one sees that Jesus Christ found greater faith in the heart of a poor little heathen woman than in all the bishops, princes and priests, not to mention the whole of the Jewish race who claimed to be God's chosen people.

'The Samaritan woman is another example of one whose persuasive words redounded to her glory when she went to the well to draw water and met Christ who was sitting there all dejected.[14] Blessed was this noble body in which God chose to manifest Himself, deigning to pour forth such words of comfort from His holy mouth into this little female sinner who was not even a Christian. That was clear proof that He does not despise the female sex. How many of our great bishops today would condescend to speak to such a humble little woman, even if her salvation was at stake?

'The woman who was listening to one of Jesus's sermons was no less wise in her speech when she was set alight by his holy words.[15] She is a good example of that saying that women can't keep quiet, since she covered herself in glory for jumping up and shouting out, "Blessed be the womb that bore you and the breasts which fed you!"

'My dear, sweet friend, you can now surely see that God gave women the power of speech so that they might serve Him. They shouldn't therefore be criticized for something which has done so much good and so little harm, since women's words rarely hurt anyone.

'As for spinning, God made this into women's natural domain, and it is an activity which is essential for serving Him and for the good of all rational beings. Without it, the world would be in a vile state. So it's the height of wickedness to reproach women for something for which they should be thanked, honoured and praised.'

11. *Christine asks Reason why women aren't allowed in courts of law, and Reason's reply.*

'Most honourable and worthy lady, your excellent arguments have satisfied my curiosity in so many areas. Yet, if you don't mind, I'd like you to explain to me why women are allowed neither to present a case at a trial, nor bear witness, nor pass sentence since some men have claimed that it's all because of some woman or other who behaved badly in a court of law.'

'My dear daughter, that whole ridiculous story is a malicious fabrication. However, if you wanted to know the causes and reasons behind everything, you would never get to the end of it. Even Aristotle, though he explained many things in his *Problemata* and *Categories*, was not equal to the task. But, dear Christine, to come back to your question, you might as well ask why God didn't command men to perform women's tasks and women those of men. In answer, one could say that just as a wise and prudent lord organizes his household into different domains and operates a strict division of labour amongst his workforce, so God created man and woman to serve Him in different ways and to help and comfort one another, according to a similar division of labour. To this end, He endowed each sex with the qualities and attributes which they need to perform the tasks for which they are cut out, even though sometimes humankind fails to respect these distinctions. God gave men strong, powerful bodies to stride about and to speak boldly, which explains why it is men who learn the law and maintain the rule of justice. In those instances where someone refuses to uphold the law which has been established by right, men must enforce it through the use of arms and physical strength, which women clearly could not do. Even though God has often endowed many women with great intelligence, it would not be right for them to abandon their customary modesty and to go about bringing cases before a court, as there are already enough men to do so. Why send three men to carry a burden which two can manage quite comfortably?

'However, if there are those who maintain that women aren't *intelligent* enough to learn the law, I would contradict them by citing numerous examples of women of both the past and the present who were great philosophers and who excelled in many disciplines which are much more difficult than simply learning the laws and the statutes of men. I'll tell you more about these women in a moment. Moreover, in reply to those who think that women are lacking in the ability to govern wisely or to establish good customs, I'll give you examples from history of several worthy ladies who mastered these arts. To give you a better idea of what I'm saying, I'll even cite you a few women from your own time who were widowed and whose competence in organizing and managing their households after their husbands' deaths attests to the fact that an intelligent woman can succeed in any domain.'

12. *About the Empress Nicaula.*

'Tell me, if you can, whether you have ever read about a king who was more skilled in politics, statesmanship and justice and who maintained a more magnificent court than the great Empress Nicaula? The many different vast and extensive lands which she held under her dominion were ruled by the famous kings known as pharaohs, from whom she herself was descended. However, it was this lady who first established laws and good customs in her realm, thus putting end once and for all to the primitive ways of the people in the countries under her control, even to the savage habits of the bestial Ethiopians. Those authors who have written about Nicaula praise her in particular for the way in which she brought civilization to her subjects. She was the heir of the pharaohs, inheriting a huge territory which included the kingdoms of Arabia, Ethiopia, Egypt and the island of Meroë, a long, broad stretch of land, which was extremely fertile, located in the middle of the Nile. She governed all of her territory with exemplary skill. What more can I tell you about this lady? Nicaula was so wise and so powerful that even the Holy Scriptures speak of her great abilities. She herself established just laws by which to rule her people. In nobility and wealth, she surpassed almost any man who ever lived. She was extremely well versed in both the arts and the sciences and was so proud that she never condescended to take a husband nor wanted any man to be at her side.'

13. *About a queen of France called Fredegunde, and other French queens and princesses.*

'I could give you many examples of women of the distant past who governed well, and what I will now go on to tell you about also illustrates my point. In France lived Queen Fredegunde, wife of King Chilperic. Although this lady was unnaturally cruel for a woman, she none the less ruled over the kingdom of France most wisely after her husband's death. At that time, the country was in grave danger, since her young son Clotar was the only surviving heir to the throne. The barons were fiercely divided as to who should rule and war had already broken out in the country. This lady never let her child out of her arms as she called the barons together and told them: "My lords, behold your king. Don't forget that we French have always been renowned for our loyalty, so don't betray this boy just because he's a child. God willing, he will grow up and, when he comes of age, he will remember those who supported him and will reward them for their loyalty, provided you do not commit the sinful error of disinheriting him. You can also be sure that I, for my part, will show my gratitude to those who stick by me and I guarantee that they shall want for nothing in the future." In this way, the queen appeased the barons and, by her skilful handling of power, managed to save her son from his enemies. She even brought him up herself and crowned him with her own hands. All this would have been impossible if she had been lacking in prudence.

'I could tell you a similar story about the wise and noble Queen Blanche, the mother of Saint Louis, whose goodness was infinite. She ruled the kingdom of France with such skill and care until her son was old enough to accede to the throne, that no man could have done better. Even when he was grown up, she proved herself so worthy that she remained at the head of his advisors and nothing was decided without her consent. She even followed her son into battle.

'There are so many others I could tell you about but lack of space prevents me. However, whilst we're on the subject of queens of France, we don't need to go too far back into history. In your childhood, you yourself knew Queen Jeanne, wife of Charles IV. If you can recall her, think about all the good things which she is remembered for having done: both the fine way in which she ran her court and exercised justice and the virtuous manner in which she lived her own life. Of no prince has it ever been said that he maintained the rule of law and safeguarded his lands and powers better than this lady did.

'Her noble daughter, who was married to the duke of Orleans, the son of King Philip, was just like her mother in this respect. Throughout her long widowhood, she upheld justice in her lands so steadfastly that no one could have done better.

'The same could be said of Queen Blanche, the late wife of King John, who retained control of her lands and enforced law and order.

'And what about the brave and good duchess of Anjou, daughter of Saint Charles of Blois, Duke of Brittany, and late wife of the duke of Anjou, the younger brother of wise King Charles V, who became king of Sicily? This lady certainly ruled her lands and territories, both in Provence and elsewhere, with the strictest justice, keeping them intact for her noble children until they came of age. One cannot praise highly enough this lady in whom all virtues abounded. In her youth, she not only surpassed all other ladies in beauty, but was also as chaste as she was wise. In her later life, she proved herself to be supremely prudent in the way she governed, for her strength and fortitude were unfailing. After the death of her husband in Italy, the whole of Provence rebelled against her and her noble children. By using both force and gentleness, this lady succeeded in regaining the loyalty and obedience of her subjects and henceforth ruled Provence with such perfect fairness that no further murmurs or complaints were ever heard against her rule.

'I could cite you so many more examples of other French ladies who, in their widowhood, governed their territories and conducted themselves with supreme skill. Take that great landowner who is still alive, the countess of La Marche who is also countess of Vendôme and Castres. What can one say about her powers of government? Isn't it true that she has constantly sought to master the art of upholding justice? She applies herself most diligently and intelligently to this task. What more can I tell you? I assure you that the same can be said of a whole host of widowed ladies of high, middle and low rank who, if you looked at them closely, have been able to maintain their lands in just as good a state as their husbands did when they were alive, and who are as much loved by their subjects. Whether men like it or not, there is no doubt that there are countless women who fit this description. Though some women are undeniably silly, there are many others who have more intelligence, sensitivity and shrewdness than a whole group of men put together. If these women's husbands trusted them or had as much sense as their wives, they would be much better off.

'Yet, if women generally do not pass sentence or adjudicate in legal cases, this should not displease them, as it means that they are less physically and mentally bowed down with responsibilities. Though these tasks have to be done in order to punish the wicked and to dispense justice to all, the men who perform them must sometimes wish that they were no more learned than their mothers. Even if they all try to acquit themselves well of their duties, God knows that the punishment for those who fail to do so is very great.'

14. More discussion and debate between Christine and Reason.

'My lady, you have truly spoken well, and your words are like music to my ears. Yet, despite what we've said about intelligence, it's undeniable that women are by nature fearful creatures, having weak, frail bodies and lacking in physical strength. Men have therefore argued that it is these things that make the female sex inferior and of lesser value. To their minds, if a person's body is defective in some way, this undermines and diminishes that person's moral qualities and thus it follows that he or she is less worthy of praise.'

Reason's reply was, 'My dear daughter, this is a false conclusion which is completely untenable. It is definitely the case that when Nature fails to make a body which is as perfect as others she has created, be it in shape or beauty, or in some strength or power of limb, she very often compensates for it by giving that body some greater quality than the one she has taken away. Here's an example: it's often said that the great philosopher Aristotle was very ugly, with one eye lower than the other and a deformed face. Yet, if he was physically misshapen, Nature certainly made up for it by endowing him with extraordinary intellectual powers, as is attested by his own writings. Having this extra intelligence was worth far more to him than having a body as beautiful as that of Absalom.

'The same can be said of the emperor Alexander the Great, who was extremely short, ugly and sickly, and yet, as is well known, he had tremendous courage in his soul. This is also true of many others. Believe me, my dear friend, it doesn't necessarily follow that a fine, strong body makes for a brave and courageous heart. Courage comes from a natural, vital force which is a gift from God that He allows Nature to implant in some rational beings more than in others. This force resides in the mind and the heart, not in the bodily strength of one's limbs. You very often see men who are well built and strong yet pathetic and cowardly, but others who are small and physically weak yet brave and tough. This applies equally to other moral qualities. As far as bravery and physical strength are concerned, neither God nor Nature has done the female sex a disservice by depriving it of these attributes. Rather, women are lucky to be deficient in this respect because they are at least spared from committing and being punished for the acts of appalling cruelty, the murders and terrible violent deeds which men who are equipped with the necessary strength have performed in the past and still do today. It probably would have been better for such men if their souls *had* spent their pilgrimage through this mortal life inside the weak body of a woman. To return to what I was saying, I am convinced that if Nature decided not to endow women with a powerful physique, she none the less made up for it by giving them a most virtuous disposition: that of loving God and being fearful of disobeying His commandments. Women who don't act like this are going against their own nature.

'However, dear Christine, you should note that God clearly wished to prove to men that, just because *all* women are not as physically strong and courageous as men generally are, this does not mean that the entire female sex is lacking in such qualities. There are in fact several women who have displayed the necessary courage, strength and bravery to undertake and accomplish extraordinary deeds which match those achieved by the great conquerors and knights mentioned in books. I'll shortly give you an example of such a woman.

'My dear daughter and beloved friend, I've now prepared a trench for you which is good and wide, and have emptied it of earth which I have

34

carried away in great loads on my shoulders. It's now time for you to place inside the trench some heavy, solid stones which will form the foundations of the walls for the City of Ladies. So take the trowel of your pen and get ready to set to with vigour on the building work. Here is a good, strong stone which I want you to lay as the first of your city's foundations. Don't you know that Nature herself used astrological signs to predict that it should be placed here in this work? Step back a little now and let me put it into position for you.'

15. *About Queen Semiramis.*

'Semiramis was a truly heroic woman who excelled in the practice and pursuit of arms. Because of her great military prowess, the people of the time – who were all pagans – said that she was so invincible both on land and sea that she must be the sister of the great god Jupiter and the daughter of the old god Saturn whom they regarded as the rulers of these two domains. This lady was married to King Ninus, who named the city of Nineveh after himself. With the help of his wife Semiramis, who rode into battle at his side, this fine lord conquered the mighty city of Babylon, the vast land of Assyria and many other countries.

'When Semiramis was still quite young, it so happened that her husband Ninus was killed by an arrow during an assault on a city. Once he had been buried with all due ceremony as befitted a king, his wife didn't lay down her arms but rather took them up with renewed vigour and seized the reins of power over the kingdoms and territories that she and her husband had conquered together in battle. She gained full control over these lands, thanks to her military skills, and likewise accomplished so many other marvellous deeds that no man could match her in strength and ability. This supremely courageous lady had no fear of pain and was undaunted by anything. Semiramis confronted any type of danger with such courage that she crushed all her enemies who thought that, once she was widowed, they could overthrow her in the lands which she had conquered. However, she had such a fearsome reputation as a warrior that she not only kept all the lands she had already taken but even added others to her empire. Accompanied by vast numbers of troops, she attacked Ethiopia with such force that she defeated it completely. From there she set off with a huge army to conquer India, a country on which no one had ever dared wage war. She attacked this nation so ruthlessly that it fell entirely into her hands. To keep the tale short, she then went on to attack still more countries so that, in the end, the whole of the East came under her control. Thanks to these magnificent and mighty conquests, Semiramis was able to rebuild and fortify the city of Babylon which had been founded by Nimrod and the giants on the plains of Shinar. Though the city was already powerful and fiercely protected, she strengthened it still further with more defences and deep moats all around.

'One time, Semiramis was sitting in her room surrounded by her handmaidens, who were busy combing her hair, when news suddenly came that one of her territories had rebelled against her. She jumped up immediately and swore on her kingdom that the half of her hair which had not yet been plaited would remain loose until she could avenge this outrage and take the country back into her control. Without further delay, she ordered huge numbers of her troops to prepare for battle and attacked the rebels with such ferocity and might that they submitted once more to her rule. These rebels and all her other subjects were so intimidated by her that none ever dared to revolt against her again. In memory of this great and noble deed, an enormous bronze statue of her, richly decorated in gold, was erected on a massive pillar in the middle of Babylon. This statue, which stood for many years, depicted a princess holding a sword in her hand with only one side of her hair plaited. Queen Semiramis founded and built several new cities and fortresses, and performed so many other notable feats that no man has ever been commemorated in the history books for having as much courage and for doing as many marvellous things as she did.

'It's true that some authors have criticized Semiramis – and rightly so, if she had been a Christian – for having married her own son whom she had borne to her husband, the lord Ninus. Yet she had two main reasons for doing so: firstly, she wanted no other crowned lady to share her empire with her, as would have been the case if her son had married another woman; and secondly, in her opinion, no other man than her son was worthy of her. This terrible transgression of hers can partly be excused by the fact that, at that time, there was no written law: people observed only the law of nature whereby they were free to do as they pleased without fear of committing a sin. There's no doubt that, since she was so proud and honourable, if she *had* thought she was doing anything wrong or that she might be subject to criticism for her actions, she would have refrained from doing as she did.

'The first foundation stone of our city is now in place, but we must follow it up with many more stones in order to raise high the walls of the building.'

16. *About the Amazons.*

'There is a country near the land of Europe which lies on the Ocean, that great sea that covers the whole world. This place is called Scythia, or the land of the Scythians. It once happened that, in the course of a war, all the noblest male inhabitants of this country were killed. When their womenfolk saw that they had lost all their husbands, brothers and male relatives, and that only very young boys and old men were left, they took courage and called together a great council of women, resolving that, henceforth, they would lead the country themselves, free from male control. They issued an edict which forbade any man from entering their territory, but decided that, in order to ensure the survival of their race, they would go into neighbouring countries at certain times of the year and return thereafter to their own land. If they gave birth to male children, they would send them away to be with their fathers, but the female children they would bring up themselves. In order to uphold this law, they chose two of the highest-born ladies to be queens, one of whom was called Lampheto and the other Marpasia. No sooner was this done than they expelled all the men who were left in the country. Next, they took up arms, women and girls together, and waged war on their enemies, laying waste to their lands with fire and sword and crushing all opposition until none remained. In short, they wreaked full revenge for their husbands' deaths.

'This is how the women of Scythia began to bear arms. They were later known as the Amazons, a name which means "they who have had a breast removed". It was their custom that, by a technique known only to this race of women, the most noble of them would have the left breast burnt off at a very early age in order to free them up to carry a shield. Those young girls who were of non-noble birth would lose the right breast so that they could more easily handle a bow. They took such pleasure in the pursuit of arms that they greatly expanded their territory by the use of force, thus spreading their fame far and wide. To get back to what I was saying, the two queens Lampheto and Marpasia each led a great army into various countries and were so successful that they conquered a large part of Europe and the region of Asia, subjugating many kingdoms to their rule. They founded many towns and cities including the Asian city of Ephesus, which has long been justly renowned. Of these two queens, it was Marpasia who died first in battle and who was replaced by a young daughter of hers, a beautiful and noble maiden called Synoppe. This girl was so proud that she chose never to sleep with a man, preferring instead to remain a virgin until her death. Her only love and sole pleasure in life was the pursuit of arms: she never tired of going into battle and seizing new lands. She also avenged her mother's death fully by putting to the sword the entire enemy population and laying waste to their whole country, adding it to the others which she went on to conquer.'

17. About the Amazon queen, Thamiris.

'As you will now go on to hear, the state founded by the Amazons flourished for a very long time, with a whole succession of valiant ladies becoming queen. Since it would be tedious to tell you all their names, I'll limit myself to the most famous individuals.

'One of the Amazon queens was the noble Thamiris, who was as brave as she was wise. Thanks to her intelligence, cunning and military prowess, she defeated and captured Cyrus, a great and powerful king of Persia who had performed many marvellous feats, including the conquest of the mighty Babylon and a large part of the whole world. Having vanquished so many countries, Cyrus decided to attack the realm of the Amazons in an attempt to bring them too under his control. Once this wise queen had been informed by her spies that Cyrus was advancing towards her with an army big enough to defeat the entire world, she realized that there was no way to beat his troops by force and that she would have to use guile. So, like the battle-hardened leader she was, on learning that, as she had intended, Cyrus had now come well inside her territory having met no opposition, Thamiris ordered all her ladies to put on their armour and cleverly sent them off to set up strategic ambushes in the mountains and forests through which Cyrus would have to pass.

'Hidden from view, Thamiris and her army waited for Cyrus and his men to move into the narrow passages and gullies between the trees and rocks where he had to pick his way. At the key moment, she had her horns sounded, taking Cyrus completely by surprise. To his dismay, he found his army attacked on all sides by ladies who were hurling down great piles of rocks to crush them. Because of the difficult terrain, his men could neither advance nor retreat: if they tried to go forwards or backwards, they were ambushed and killed as soon as they emerged at either end of the passages. All were crushed and slain, except Cyrus and his barons, who were taken prisoner by order of the queen. When the massacre was over, Thamiris had them brought before her pavilion, which she had ordered to be put up before the fighting began. She was so full of anger at Cyrus for having killed one of her beloved sons whom she had sent to his court that she decided to show no mercy. She had all his barons decapitated in front of him, saying: "Cyrus, you who were so cruel and bloodthirsty from killing other men, can now finally drink your fill." Thereupon she had his head cut off and thrown into a barrel in which all the blood of his barons had been collected.

'My sweet daughter and dear friend, I'm reminding you of these things because they are relevant to what we've been discussing, even though you are already familiar with them. Indeed, you yourself have recounted these stories elsewhere in your *Book of the Mutation of Fortune* and *Letter of Othea to Hector*. I'll now go on to tell you some more.'

18. *How the mighty Hercules and his companion Theseus came*
from Greece to attack the Amazons with a great army and fleet of
ships, and how the two maidens Menalippe and Hippolyta brought
them down, horses and all, in a big heap.

'What else shall I tell you about them? The ladies of Amazonia were so
successful in warfare that they were feared and respected by all other
nations. Their reputation for being invincible and their unquenchable
thirst for conquering new lands which led them to lay waste any country
which refused to surrender to them, spread even as far as the distant
land of Greece. This made the Greeks very afraid that the Amazons
would one day attempt to use force against them.

'Then living in Greece at the very height of his powers was the great
and mighty Hercules. In his day, he performed more feats of strength
than any mortal man whose deeds are recorded in the history books,
fighting with giants, lions, snakes and terrifying monsters, and beating
them all. In short, the only man who ever matched him for strength was
the magnificent Samson. Hercules was of the opinion that the Greeks
shouldn't wait for the Amazons to come to them but would be much
better advised to invade them first instead. In order to execute this plan,
he ordered ships to be made ready for war and gathered together a large
group of young noblemen to go and attack the Amazons in numbers.
When Theseus, the good and valiant king of Athens, heard what was
happening, he declared that they wouldn't go without him. He joined
forces with Hercules and they sailed off with a huge army towards the
land of the Amazons. When they were just off the coast, Hercules,
despite his extraordinary strength and bravery and the fact that he had
so many troops with him, did not dare to moor the ships and disembark
during the daytime as he knew just how fierce and courageous the
Amazons were. This would be an almost unbelievable thing to say were
it not that so many history books have recounted how this man, who
could not be beaten by any creature alive, was extremely wary of these
women's strength. He and his army therefore waited until nightfall when,
at that hour when all living things are fast asleep, they leapt out of their
ships and ran ashore. They swept through towns, setting fire to everything

and killing all those who were caught unawares and had no time to defend themselves. The news about what had happened spread like wildfire and, as soon as they could, the brave Amazons rushed over themselves to pick up their weapons and to head down in great waves to attack the enemy's ships.

'The queen of the Amazons at that time was called Orithyia, a very valiant lady who had conquered many lands. She was the mother of the good Queen Penthesilea, about whom I'll tell you more later. Orithyia had succeeded the courageous Queen Antiope who had ruled the Amazons and governed the country with superb military skill, achieving many great things in her time. Orithyia soon heard the news that the Greeks, entirely unprovoked, had landed like a pack of thieves in the night and were going around killing everyone. As you can imagine, she was livid with rage, and vowed that they would regret having made her so angry. Cursing her enemy, whom she didn't fear in the least, she immediately called her troops together for battle. You should have seen the ladies as they dashed about for their arms and lined up at their queen's side. By daybreak, all her battalions were ready.

'Two of the strongest and most courageous maidens, the finest and most valiant of all the Amazons, Menalippe and Hippolyta, who were closely related to the queen, decided not to wait for her order once they heard that her plan was to get all her ladies together and order them into battle formation. Instead, as quickly as they could, they threw on their arms and, with lances at the ready and shields of tough elephant hide slung round their necks, they headed off on their swift chargers directly towards the port. Boiling with the most terrible rage and fury, they lowered their lances and aimed straight for the leaders of the Greek army: Menalippe against Hercules and Hippolyta against Theseus. Despite the great strength, bravery and courage of their enemies, the women's anger soon bore fruit as each of them struck against her adversary with such power that the two knights were brought down, horses and all, in a big heap. The women too fell from their horses, but they immediately recovered themselves and attacked the knights with their swords.

'How can one praise these maidens highly enough for having brought down, completely unaided, two of the most valiant knights who ever lived? The story would be almost impossible to believe if so many reliable authors had not made mention of it in their works. Those writers who were themselves clearly amazed by the story attempted to find excuses for Hercules in particular, given his exceptional physical strength, claiming that he only fell because his horse stumbled on the impact of the blow, adding that he would never have been brought down if he had been on foot. These two knights were completely shamefaced to have been knocked off their horses by the two maidens. Although the women continued to fight long and hard with their swords in a drawn-out battle, they were eventually beaten by the two knights, which is hardly surprising given that there were no two other heroes like them in the whole world.

'Hercules and Theseus were so highly gratified at having taken the two maidens prisoner that they wouldn't have exchanged them for the wealth of an entire city. They returned to their ship to disarm and refresh themselves, for they were only too aware that the battle had been a hard one to win. The two knights treated their captives with the greatest of honour and, once the ladies had disarmed and revealed themselves in all their true splendour and beauty, they were even more delighted. As they feasted their eyes on the two ladies, it seemed to them that they had never won a prize which gave them greater pleasure.

'When Queen Orithyia heard that the two maidens had been captured, she advanced towards the Greeks with a huge army. She was deeply distressed by what had happened but, out of fear that more harm would come to the two prisoners if she attacked the Greeks, she called a halt and sent a couple of her baronesses to parley with the enemy and to tell them that whatever ransom they demanded for the return of the girls, she would pay it. Hercules and Theseus received the two messengers with great respect and courteously replied that if the queen chose to make peace with them and promise that she and her ladies would never wage war on the Greeks but would be their allies, they would make a reciprocal pact with her. As for the ransom, they were prepared to surrender the two women and keep only their arms as a token and reminder of the victory that they had won over them. Since Orithyia's only concern was to have the two maidens whom she loved dearly returned safely to her, she was obliged to agree to the Greeks' demands. Once all the negotiations were done and the terms accepted by both parties, the queen arrived unarmed to celebrate the peace treaty with a feast, accompanied by a whole host of ladies and girls who were more beautifully arrayed than any the Greeks had ever seen. This feast took place amidst much happiness and joy.

'Yet Theseus was extremely reluctant to let Hippolyta go as he had already fallen deeply in love with her. He therefore begged Hercules to ask Orithyia to allow him to marry Hippolyta and take her back to Greece with him, a request to which the queen gave her consent. After a magnificent wedding feast, the Greeks left for home with Hippolyta at Theseus's side. She later bore him a son called Hippolytus who became a famous knight of exemplary prowess and skill. When the people of Greece learnt that peace had been made with the Amazons, they were overjoyed because there was no other race in the world whom they feared more.'

19. *About Queen Penthesilea and how she went to the rescue of the city of Troy.*

'This Queen Orithyia lived for a long time and died at a fine old age, having kept the realm of Amazonia in a flourishing state and expanded its dominion. The Amazons crowned as her successor her own daughter, the brave Penthesilea, who surpassed all others in intelligence, courage, prowess and virtue. She too was forever eager to take up arms and fight, increasing the Amazons' power further than ever before in her relentless pursuit of territory. She was so feared by her enemies that none dared approach her and so proud that she never slept with a man but preferred to remain a virgin all her life.

'It was during her reign that the terrible war between the Greeks and the Trojans broke out. Because of the name that the great Hector had made for himself as the finest, bravest and most highly skilled knight in the world, Penthesilea, who was naturally drawn to him since they shared the same qualities, heard so much about him that she began to love him with a pure and noble heart and desired above all else to go and see him. In order to fulfil this wish, she left her country with a great host of noble ladies and maidens all expert in the arts of war and richly armed, setting off to the city of Troy which lay a great distance away. However, distances always seem shorter when one's heart is filled with a strong desire.

'Unfortunately, when Penthesilea arrived in Troy, it was already too late: she discovered that Hector had been killed by Achilles during a battle in which the flower of Trojan chivalry had been wiped out. Penthesilea was received with all honours by the Trojans – King Priam, Queen Hecuba and all the barons – yet she was inconsolable and heartbroken to find that Hector was dead. The king and queen, who never left off grieving for the death of their son, offered to show her his body since they had been unable to let her see him alive. They took her to the temple where his tomb had been prepared, truly the very noblest and finest sepulchre that has ever been recorded in the history books. There, in a beautiful, sumptuous chapel all decorated with gold and precious stones, sat the embalmed and robed body of Hector on a throne in front of the main altar dedicated to the gods. He appeared to be more alive than dead as he brandished a naked sword in his hand and his haughty face still seemed to be throwing out a challenge to the Greeks. He was draped in a long, full garment which was woven with fine gold and trimmed and embroidered with jewels. This garment came down to the floor, covering the lower half of his body, which lay completely immersed in a precious balm that gave off a most delicious scent. The Trojans worshipped this body, bathed in the dazzling light of hundreds of candles, as if it were one of their gods. A costlier tomb surely never was seen. Here they brought Queen Penthesilea, who no sooner glimpsed the body through the open chapel door than she fell on her knees in front of Hector and greeted him as if he were still alive. She then went up close towards him and gazed deeply on his face. Through her tears she cried out: "O flower of chivalry, the very epitome and pinnacle of bravery: who can dare to call themselves valiant or even strap on a sword now that the finest and most shining example of knighthood has gone? Alas, cursed be the day that he whose vile hand deprived the world of its greatest treasure was ever born! Most noble prince, why was Fortune so contrary as to prevent me from being by your side when this traitor was plotting your downfall? This never would have happened because I would not have allowed it. If your killer were still alive, I would surely avenge your death and thus extinguish the great sorrow and anger which are burning up my heart as I see you lifeless before me and unable to speak to me, as was my only desire. Yet, since Fortune decreed that it should be so and I can do nothing to gainsay her, I swear by the very highest gods of our faith and solemnly promise you, my dear lord, that as long as I have breath in my body I will make the Greeks pay for your death." As she knelt before the corpse, Penthesilea's words reached the great crowd of barons, knights and ladies who were all gathered there and moved them to tears. She could barely drag herself away from the tomb but, finally, she kissed his hand that was holding the sword and took her leave, saying: "Most excellent knight, what must you have been like when you were alive, given that the mere image of you in death is so full of majesty!"

'Weeping tender tears, she left his side. As soon as she could, she put on her armour and, with her army of noble ladies, dashed out of the city to attack the Greeks who were holding Troy in a state of siege. To make a brief tale of it, she and her army set to with such vigour that, if she had lived longer, no Greek would ever again have set foot in Greece. She struck down and nearly killed Pyrrhus, Achilles's son, who was a very fine soldier. It was only with great difficulty that his men were able to rescue him and drag him, half-dead, back to safety. Thinking that he was unlikely to survive, the Greeks were distraught, for he had been their greatest hope. If Penthesilea felt hatred for the father, she certainly didn't spare the son.

'In short, though Penthesilea performed the most extraordinary feats, she finally succumbed after having spent several days with her army in the thick of battle. When the Greeks were at their lowest ebb, Pyrrhus, who had recovered from his wounds but was overcome with shame and sorrow that she had done him such grievous harm, ordered his valiant men to concentrate solely on surrounding Penthesilea and separating her from her companions. He wanted to kill her with his own hands and would pay a handsome reward to anyone who managed to trap her. Pyrrhus's men took a long time to do his bidding because Penthesilea dealt out such fearsome blows that they were extremely afraid of approaching her. However, in the end, after an enormous amount of effort on their part, they finally managed to encircle her one day and isolate her from her ladies. The Greeks attacked the other Amazons so fiercely that they were powerless to help their queen and Penthesilea herself was exhausted after having accomplished more in that time than even Hector himself could have done. Despite the astonishing strength with which she defended herself, the Greeks were able to smash all her weapons and tear off a good part of her helmet. When Pyrrhus saw her bare blonde head, he struck her such a blow that he split her whole skull in two. Thus died the great and good Penthesilea, a huge loss both to the Trojans and to her own countrywomen, who were immediately plunged into grief, which was understandable since from that day forth the Amazons never knew any other queen to rival her. With heavy hearts, they carried her dead body back home.

'So, you have now heard how the realm of Amazonia was founded and how it lasted for over eight hundred years. You can work this out by checking in the history books for the length of time it took from the beginning of their reign up to when Alexander the Great conquered the entire world, at which point they were still reckoned to be a powerful nation. The accounts of his exploits tell how he went to their country and was received by the queen and her ladies. Alexander lived a long time after the destruction of Troy and more than four hundred years after the founding of Rome, which itself postdated the fall of Troy by a great deal. So, if you make the effort to compare these histories and calculate the timescale involved, you will see that the reign of the Amazons was extremely long-lived. You'll also realize that, of all the kingdoms that lasted this long, there is none that could boast such a large number of illustrious rulers who accomplished such extraordinary deeds as this great nation could of its queens and ladies.'

20. *About Zenobia, Queen of Palmyria.*

'The Amazons were not the only example of courageous womanhood: no less famous was the valiant Zenobia, Queen of Palmyria, a lady of very noble blood who was descended from the Ptolemies, kings of Egypt. It was clear from this lady's infancy that she was full of valour and had a leaning towards the pursuit of arms. As soon as she had developed enough physical strength, it was impossible to stop her from leaving the safety of the city, with its palaces and royal chambers, to go roaming through the woods and forests where, armed with her sword and spears, she would spend hours tracking down wild animals. From chasing stags and does she moved on to hunting lions, bears and all manner of ferocious beasts which she fearlessly attacked and magnificently brought down. Come rain or shine, this lady thought nothing of sleeping on the hard ground amongst the trees, and she had no fear of anything. She took similar delight in picking her way through forests, climbing mountains and running through valleys in pursuit of her prey. This maiden had no interest in physical love and held out for a long time against taking a husband since she wished to remain a virgin all her life. However, under pressure from her parents, she eventually married the king of Palmyria. The noble Zenobia had an extremely beautiful face and body but she paid no attention to her looks. Fortune was kindly enough disposed towards her to give her a husband who was of a similar bent to herself.

'This king, who was a very worthy knight, had the ambition to lead an army to conquer the whole of the East and all the surrounding empires. At that time, Valerian, the emperor of Rome, had been taken prisoner by Sapor, king of the Persians. The king of Palmyria therefore gathered together a great army, accompanied by Zenobia, who was more interested in taking up arms to fight at her husband's side and sharing with him all the physical hardships which his military campaign would entail, than worrying about how to keep herself beautiful. The king, whose name was Odenaethus, ordered Herod, one of his sons by a previous wife, to lead part of his army in an advance approach on the Persian ruler Sapor, who was currently occupying Mesopotamia. He then commanded another section of the army under Zenobia to attack Sapor from one side whilst he would move in from the other side with the remaining troops. His instructions were followed to the letter. What can I tell you? The outcome of this episode, which you can find in the history books, was that Zenobia set to with such vigour, leading a bold and fierce attack, that she won several battles against this king of Persia and secured the final victory over him. Thanks to her bravery, she subjugated the whole of Mesopotamia to her husband's rule. In the end, she laid siege to Sapor's stronghold and succeeded in capturing both him and his concubines, seizing his enormous wealth in the process.

'After these triumphs, her husband was killed by one of his relatives in an attempt to usurp the throne. However, nothing more came of it as this brave lady stopped the would-be usurper in his tracks and showed her courage and wisdom by taking control of the empire into her safekeeping until her children, who were still very young, could come of age. She had herself crowned empress, taking up the reins of power with skill and ability and governing with such good sense and military prowess that neither Gallienus nor, after him, Claudius, who were both emperors of Rome and had placed a substantial part of the East under Roman control, dared to raise a hand against her. The same can be said of the Egyptians, the Arabs and the Armenians, all of whom were so wary of her strength and reputation for taking firm action that they were happy just to keep their borders intact. This lady conducted herself so wisely that she was not only held in great esteem by her princes but also loved and obeyed by her subjects, and feared and respected by her knights. Indeed, when she went to war, as was often the case, she would never address her troops unless she was fully armed and helmeted. Moreover, in battle she would not allow herself to be carried in a litter, as was the usual custom for rulers at that time, but insisted on riding a lively steed, sometimes even going on ahead of her troops in disguise so as to spy on her enemies.

'This heroic lady Zenobia surpassed all the knights of her time in her supreme mastery of the skills of warfare. She also outshone all other ladies in her noble and virtuous personal habits because she was renowned for her extreme sobriety. None the less, she sometimes organized great feasts and gatherings for her barons and for foreign visitors, offering them every luxury imaginable and showering them with handsome and costly gifts. She knew exactly how to win the affection and goodwill of the most eminent people. Furthermore, she was completely chaste: not only did she refuse to have anything more to do with men after her husband's death, but even with him she consented to intercourse purely for the purposes of having children, making this apparent by sleeping alone when she was pregnant. In order to ensure that all aspects of her public appearance matched the virtue of her personal morals, she would not allow anyone who was dissolute or debauched to frequent her court and would only look favourably on those whose lives were virtuous and upright. Zenobia honoured her courtiers according to their goodness, valour and morality, not their wealth or birth, and she was particularly fond of those who were very sober in their ways or who were experienced knights. Her lifestyle was very opulent and regal: she spent money freely and maintained a magnificent court, as was the custom of the Persians, who generally lived in the most lavish style of all royalty. She ate off plates decorated with gold and precious stones and dressed in luxurious robes. She amassed a large treasury both from her own fortune and from the revenues which she had raised without imposing an excessive burden on her people. However, she also gave much of it away to those whom she thought deserving of it, thus outdoing all other princes in her generosity and splendour.

'In addition to these virtues, her greatest accomplishment was her knowledge of the arts, which I'll now mention briefly to you. Zenobia was well schooled in works written in Egyptian and her own tongue, diligently taking up her books whenever she had the time. Her chosen teacher was Longinus, the philosopher, who initiated her into his discipline. She knew Latin and Greek and wrote a very elegant abridged history of contemporary events in each of these languages. She also wanted her children, whom she had brought up very strictly, to receive a similar education to her own. So tell me, my dear Christine, if you have ever read about or known any prince or knight who was more perfectly endowed with all the virtues than she was?'

21. *About the noble Queen Artemisia.*

'Shall we dedicate any less space to Artemisia, the most noble and virtuous queen of Caria, than to these other valiant ladies? This lady, who was the widow of King Mausolus, so dearly loved her husband that on his death she left half her heart with him, so to speak, enshrining her feelings for all the world to see. But I'll tell you more about that at the right time and place. She was left with many lands to govern but was not in the least troubled by this as she had all the right qualities needed to rule a country, being honest, sober in manner and politically astute. Moreover, she was a very courageous warrior and so well versed in the art of warfare that she achieved several victories which further enhanced the glorious reputation that she had won for herself. Not only did she govern the state wisely during her widowhood, she also took up arms on two particularly important occasions: the first being to defend her country; and the second to honour an alliance and oath of fealty which she had sworn.

'The first of these occasions arose after the death of her husband, Mausolus, when the people of Rhodes, whose lands adjoined her own, were consumed with envy at the sight of a mere woman on the Carian throne. In the hope of usurping her and seizing her lands, they decided to attack her with a huge army and fleet of ships, heading for the city of Halicarnassus perched high above the sea on an outcrop called Icaria, which was naturally well defended. In addition, this city has two harbours, one of which is cleverly hidden inside the town with a very narrow entrance which could be used for going in and out of the palace without being seen either from outside or from inside the city itself, whilst the other harbour lies alongside the perimeter walls. When the brave and wise Artemisia learnt from her spies that the enemy were approaching, she ordered great numbers of her troops to arm themselves for battle. Before she left, she also instructed the inhabitants of the city, as well as some of her most faithful and trusted courtiers whom she had specially chosen for this purpose, to perform a certain task when they received an agreed signal from her. They were to make welcoming signs to the people from Rhodes and to call down to them from the walls and tell them that they wanted to surrender the city to them. The plan then was that they would do their utmost to persuade the unsuspecting Rhodians to leave their ships and to reassemble in the marketplace inside the city. Once she had delivered her orders, Artemisia and her army crept out of the narrow harbour and made for the open sea without her enemies even noticing. On giving her signal and receiving an answering one from the city that the enemy were now all gathered inside, she stole back through the main harbour and took possession of the enemy's ships. She then burst into the city at the head of her army and attacked the

Rhodians so fiercely on all sides that soon every one of them was overcome and killed. Victory was hers.

'However, Artemisia's bravery went one step further: she and her army took the enemy's ships and set sail for Rhodes, making the sign of victory as if they were returning triumphant to their homeland. When the Rhodians saw them, thinking that it was their compatriots, they were overjoyed as they let them into port. As Artemisia entered the harbour, she ordered her men to take control of the waterfront whilst she headed straight for the palace where she then captured and killed all the royal princes. That's how this lady defeated the people of Rhodes, who were completely unprepared for her attack, taking command of the city and, not long after, of the whole island itself. Having subjugated the Rhodians and fixed the tribute that they would pay to her, she left a garrison of her own trusty soldiers to defend the place and set off for home. Before she left, she had two bronze statues put up inside the city: one of Artemisia herself depicted as the victor and the other of the city of Rhodes portrayed as the vanquished foe.

'The other most famous deed of all those that she accomplished was when Xerxes, King of Persia, had attacked the Lacedaemonians, occupying the country with a great army of horsemen and foot soldiers and flanking the shore with a fleet of ships big enough to destroy the whole of Greece. The Greeks, who had signed an alliance treaty with Queen Artemisia, called on her for help. She responded not simply by sending troops but, like the brave warrior she was, she herself set out at the head of a huge army. The queen more than fulfilled her duty to attack Xerxes by putting him completely to rout. After defeating him on land, she took to the sea once more and attacked his flagship as soon as it came into range just off the coast of the city of Salamis. As the battle raged, the valiant Artemisia stood shoulder to shoulder with the chief barons and generals of her army, urging them on to ever greater deeds and shouting words of encouragement: "Forward, my brave knights and brothers-in-arms; victory is in our sights! Cover yourselves in glory and my riches will be yours!" In short, she fought so well that she crushed Xerxes as thoroughly on sea as she had done on land. The dishonourable king then took to his heels and fled, despite the fact that, as many historians have pointed out, he had such a massive army with him that wherever they passed through, the springs and rivers in the area soon dried up. Thus this heroic lady won a magnificent triumph and returned home to her country resplendent in the glorious crown of victory.'

22. *About Lilia, mother of the valiant knight Theodoric.*

'Although the noble lady Lilia did not herself go into battle, she is no less deserving of praise for her courage in persuading her son, Theodoric, a very valiant knight, to return to combat, as you shall now hear. In his time, this Theodoric was one of the most powerful princes at the court of the emperor of Constantinople. He was very handsome and highly skilled in the military arts. Moreover, thanks to the fine upbringing and moral precepts which he had received from his mother, he was both upright and exemplary in his behaviour.

'It so happened that a prince called Odoacer once attacked the Romans in the hope of destroying both them and the whole land of Italy, if he could. In response to a request for help from the Romans, the emperor of Constantinople sent Theodoric, whom he considered to be the finest of his knights, together with a great army. In the course of the battle against Odoacer, the tide of fortune turned against Theodoric who, out of fear for his life, had to flee the scene of battle and make for the city of Ravenna. When his brave, wise mother, who had been watching the conflict closely, saw her son turn tail, her sorrow knew no bounds since, to her mind, a knight could commit no greater sin than to run from battle. Her noble instincts made her put aside all motherly compassion as she would have preferred to see her son die a valiant death than cover himself in such shame. She ran directly to him and implored him not to dishonour himself in this way but instead to rally his troops once more and return to the battlefield. However, as her words appeared to be having no effect on him, she fell into a great rage and lifted up her skirts, saying: "My dear son, there is no place left for you to hide except my womb, so you should climb back up inside immediately!" Theodoric was so shamefaced that he turned on his heel, gathered his troops together and went back to fight. His mother's words had inflamed him with such shame that he put all his efforts into defeating his enemies and killing Odoacer. The whole of Italy, which had been facing destruction, was now saved by this lady's good sense. Indeed, in my view, it is to the mother rather than to the son that the honour of this victory should go.'

23. More about Queen Fredegunde.

'Coming back to Queen Fredegunde of France, whom I mentioned to you before, she too was supremely valiant in battle. Remember that I told you earlier how her husband Chilperic died, leaving her a widow with her son Clotar still at her breast and the country in the throes of war. At this point, she addressed her barons, saying, "My lords, don't be alarmed at the fact that our enemies are here in great numbers to attack us. I have come up with a plan for beating them, if you will only put your trust in me. Putting aside my womanly timidity, I will strengthen my heart with manly courage and rouse you and your soldiers to acts of great valour, all for the sake of this tender, young prince. I will go ahead of you with him in my arms and you will follow on behind. Whatever I tell your high constable to do, I will expect you to do the same." The barons replied that they would obey her every command.

'She ordered her troops to line up carefully behind her as she rode out with her son in her arms, followed by the barons and with the battalions of knights positioned behind them. They made their way towards the enemy until nightfall, whereupon they headed into a forest. There the high constable cut off a great bough from a tree and all the others followed suit. The knights draped their horses from head to foot in may foliage and hung little bells on many of them as if they were animals going out to pasture. Flanking each other closely, they rode on towards the enemy camp, holding up large may branches in their hands. The valiant queen kept out in front, exhorting the others on to battle with promises and cajoling words, and still holding the little prince in her arms. Behind her rode the barons, who were filled with compassion at this sight, and were more resolved than ever to do their duty. When they judged that they were now close enough to the enemy, they called a halt and stood still without making a sound.

'As dawn began to break, those who were keeping watch at the enemy camp caught sight of them and said to each other, "What an extraordinary thing! Last night there was no sign of a wood or a forest nearby but now look at this great thicket of trees here!" When the others saw this sight, they agreed that the wood must have been there all along and that they had been too stupid to notice it, since they were at a loss to explain it otherwise. That it could be nothing other than a wood seemed to be proved by the fact that they could hear the bells of the horses and other livestock grazing inside. As they were having this discussion, never for a moment dreaming that it might all be a trick, the queen's troops suddenly threw down their branches and what the enemy had taken for trees turned out to be knights in full armour. They hurled themselves at the enemy with such swiftness that their opponents had no time to pick up their weapons as they were all still abed. The troops ran through the entire camp, capturing and killing everyone. They thus secured victory, thanks to the cleverness of Queen Fredegunde.'

24. *About the virgin Camilla.*

'I could tell you much more about such fine, brave women as these, and Camilla is no less worthy than any I've already mentioned. This Camilla was the daughter of Metabus, the venerable king of the Volscians. Her mother died giving birth to her and, soon after, her father was overthrown by his own subjects who had rebelled against him. He was in such danger that he was forced to flee for his life, taking nothing else with him but his beloved daughter Camilla. When he came to a great river which he would have to swim across, he was thrown into despair for he could see no way of taking his daughter with him. However, after a few moments' reflection, the idea came to him of going and breaking off big pieces of bark from the nearby trees and putting them together to make a little boat. He placed the child inside it and strapped it to his arm with some sturdy vines of ivy. He then went into the water and swam across, dragging the little boat behind him, until both he and his daughter arrived safely on the other side. The king made his home in the woods as he was too afraid of being spotted by his enemies to go anywhere else. He fed Camilla with the milk of wild deer until she had grown a little bigger and stronger, and he used the skins of wild animals he had killed as clothing and bedding for himself and his daughter.

'When she was in her early teens, Camilla took to chasing and killing animals with a slingshot. She ran so swiftly after them that she was fleeter than a hare. She carried on these pursuits until she was an adult, by which time she had become extraordinarily hardy and brave. Having learnt from her father the wrong that his subjects had done to him, she felt enough confidence in her strength and courage to leave his side and take up arms. To keep the tale short, her valiant efforts in battle were so successful that, with the help of some of her kinsmen, she managed to win the country back for her father. Even then, she didn't give up her military activities until she had won a glorious reputation for herself. Moreover, she was so proud that she refused to take a husband or even to sleep with a man. This lady Camilla remained a virgin all her life, and it was she who came to Turnus's aid when Aeneas landed in Italy, as the history books inform us.'

25. About Queen Berenice of Cappadocia.

'There was once a queen of Cappadocia called Berenice, a courageous lady of very noble stock who was the daughter of the great King Mithradates, who ruled over a large part of the East, and the wife of King Ariarathes of Cappadocia. This lady was left a widow, whereupon one of her late husband's brothers began to wage war on her in the hope of disinheriting her and her children. In the course of this conflict, the uncle killed two of his nephews, Berenice's sons, in battle. This terrible blow caused her to fly into such a rage that she lost all of her natural womanly timidity. Throwing on armour and attacking her brother-in-law with a huge army, she fought so hard that, in the end, she killed him with her own hands, driving a chariot over his dead body and winning victory for herself.'

26. *About the brave Cloelia.*

'The noble Roman lady Cloelia was as brave as she was wise, though it was not in the arena of war or battle that she distinguished herself. She and some other high-born virgins of Rome were sent as hostages to a certain king, who had been an enemy of the Romans, in order to fulfil the terms of a treaty that he had made with her countrymen. After having initially accepted her fate, Cloelia soon fell to thinking that it was a stain on the honour of the city of Rome to consent to sending all these virgins to be kept prisoner by a foreign king. She therefore plucked up enough courage to trick those who were guarding them with promises and entreaties and to steal away in the night with her companions. They walked on together until they reached the banks of the River Tiber, where Cloelia found a horse that was grazing in a meadow nearby. Though she had never before ridden a horse, she jumped up on to this animal's back. Unafraid and undaunted by the deep water, she had one of her companions sit behind her as she rode across to the other side, coming back to ferry all the others over one by one in the same fashion until they were all safe and sound. Cloelia then led them back to Rome where she returned them to their families.

'She was greatly honoured by the Romans for her courage; even the king who had taken her as a hostage paid homage to her bravery and was highly amused by her exploit. The Romans decided that, in order to preserve the memory of her deed for posterity, they would have a statue made of her. This statue, which depicted a maiden astride a horse, was put up on a tall plinth at the side of the road that led to the temple, where it remained for a very long time.

'The foundations of our city are now complete. Let us move on to our next task, which is to erect a high enclosure wall the whole way round.'

27. Christine asks Reason if God has ever blessed a woman's mind with knowledge of the highest branches of learning, and Reason's reply.

Having listened to what Reason said, I answered, 'My lady, God truly performed wonders by endowing these women you've just been telling me about with such extraordinary powers. But, if you don't mind, please tell me if, amongst all the other favours He has shown to women, God ever chose to honour any of them with great intelligence and knowledge. Do they indeed have an aptitude for learning? I'd really like to know why it is that men claim women to be so slow-witted.'

Reason's reply was: 'Christine, from what I've already told you, it should be obvious that the opposite of what they say is true. To make the point more clearly for you, I'll give you some conclusive examples. I repeat – and don't doubt my word – that if it were the custom to send little girls to school and to teach them all sorts of different subjects there, as one does with little boys, they would grasp and learn the difficulties of all the arts and sciences just as easily as the boys do. Indeed, this is often the case because, as I mentioned to you before, although women may have weaker and less agile bodies than men, which prevents them from doing certain tasks, their minds are in fact sharper and more receptive when they do apply themselves.'

'My lady, what are you saying? If you please, I'd be grateful if you would expand on this point. No man would ever accept this argument if it couldn't be proved, because they would say that men generally know so much more than women.'

She replied, 'Do you know why it is that women know less than men?'

'No, my lady, you'll have to enlighten me.'

'It's because they are less exposed to a wide variety of experiences since they have to stay at home all day to look after the household. There's nothing like a whole range of different experiences and activities for expanding the mind of any rational creature.'

'So, my lady, if they have able minds which can learn and absorb as much as those of men, why don't they therefore know more?'

'The answer, my dear girl, is that it's not necessary for the public good for women to go around doing what men are supposed to do, as I informed you earlier. It's quite adequate that they perform the tasks for which they are fitted. As for this idea that experience tells us that women's intelligence is inferior to that of men simply because we see that those around us generally know less than men do, let's take the example of male peasants living in remote countryside or high mountains. You could give me plenty of names of places where the men are so backward that they seem no better than beasts. Yet, there's no doubt that Nature made them as perfect in mind and body as the cleverest and most learned men to be found in towns and cities. All this comes down to their lack of education, though don't forget what I said before about some men and women being more naturally endowed with intelligence than others. I'll now go on to prove to you that the female sex is just as clever as the male sex, by giving you some examples of women who had fine minds and were extremely erudite.'

28. *Reason begins to speak about ladies who were blessed with great learning, starting with the noble maiden Cornificia.*

'The parents of the noble maiden Cornificia used a clever trick to send her to school along with her brother Cornificius when they were both young children. This little girl applied her extraordinary intelligence so well to her studies that she began to take a real delight in learning. It would have been extremely difficult to stifle this talent in her, for she refused all normal female occupations in order to devote herself to her books. After much dedication, she soon became an excellent and learned poet not solely in the field of poetry itself but also in philosophy, which she just drank in as if it were mother's milk. She was so motivated to excel in all the different disciplines that she soon outshone her brother, himself no mean poet, in all branches of scholarship.

'Moreover, she was not content simply to study the theoretical side of learning but wished to put her own knowledge into practice. Taking up her pen, she composed several distinguished works which, at the time of Saint Gregory, were held in great esteem, as he himself indicates in his writings. The great Italian author Boccaccio says of Cornificia in his book: "What a great honour it is for a woman to put aside all feminine things and to devote her mind to studying the works of the greatest scholars." He confirms what I've been telling you when he goes on to say that those women who have no confidence in their own intellectual abilities act as if they were born in the backwoods and had no concept of what is right and moral, letting themselves be discouraged and saying that they're fit for nothing but fussing over men and bearing and bringing up children. God has given every woman a good brain which she could put to good use, if she so chose, in all the domains in which the most learned and renowned men excel. If women wished to study, they are no more excluded from doing so than men are, and could easily put in the necessary effort to acquire a good name for themselves just as the most distinguished of men delight in doing. My dear daughter, see how Boccaccio himself echoes what I've been saying and note how much he approves of learning in a woman and praises them for it.'

29. *About Proba the Roman.*

'Proba, a Christian lady of Rome married to Adelphus, was equally brilliant. This lady had such a fine mind and so dedicated herself to learning that she excelled in the seven liberal arts[16] and became a remarkable poet. She devoted much time to studying works of poetry, especially those of Virgil, which she learnt entirely off by heart. After having read through these texts with particularly close attention and having pored at length over their meaning, the idea came to her of reworking parts of them in order to put Holy Scripture and stories from the Old Testament into elegant and complex verse. The writer Boccaccio says of her project: "Not only was it admirable that the mind of a woman should have conceived of doing such a thing, but it was even more splendid that she put her idea into action." Fired with enthusiasm, Proba threw herself into bringing her task to completion. She worked her way through the writings of Virgil, his *Bucolics, Georgics* and *Aeneid*, sometimes borrowing entire passages from her sources, and at other times only short extracts. With marvellous skill and artistry, she composed whole stanzas from her source material and then reorganized and linked them together, all the while respecting the rules, conventions, structure and metre of the Latin original and without making a single mistake. The completed text was such a magnificent piece of work that no man could have done better. Her book began with the story of creation and then continued with stories from the Old and New Testaments, right up to the account of the Apostles receiving the Holy Spirit. Her reworkings of Virgil corresponded so closely to the Scriptures that whoever was unaware of how it was really written would have taken Virgil for a prophet, if not for one of the Evangelists.

'Boccaccio was so impressed by Proba's efforts that he declared her to be worthy of the highest accolades for having demonstrated such a full knowledge of the divine works of Holy Scripture, which is very rare, even amongst many of the theologians and clerks of today. It was this lady's wish that her book, the fruit of her labours, should be called the *Cento*. Though this work could have taken a man his whole lifetime to complete, she in fact went on to write several other fine and notable books. One of these, a poem based on the writings and verse of the poet Homer, was also called the *Cento* because it consisted of a hundred stanzas. So, in praise of this lady, we can sum up by saying that she not only knew Latin but had an excellent knowledge of Greek as well. As Boccaccio himself asserts, it should give women great delight to hear about Proba and her achievements.'

30. *About Sappho, who was an extremely fine poet and philosopher.*

'No less learned than Proba was Sappho, a maiden from the city of Mytilene. This Sappho was physically very beautiful, and also charming in her speech, manner and bearing. However, the finest of her attributes was her superb intellect, for she was a great expert in many different arts and sciences. Moreover, she was not only familiar with the writings and treatises of others but was herself an author who composed many new works. The poet Boccaccio pays tribute to her, describing her in these delightful terms: "Sappho, spurred on by her fine mind and burning desire, devoted herself to her studies and rose above the common, ignorant herd, making her home on the heights of Mount Parnassus; in other words, at the summit of knowledge itself. Through her extraordinary boldness and daring, she won the good will of the Muses; that is, she immersed herself in the arts and sciences. She thus made her way through the lush forest full of laurels, may trees, delicious-scented flowers of different hues and sweet-smelling herbs which is the place where Grammar, Logic, Geometry, Arithmetic, and noble Rhetoric dwell.[17] She travelled down this path until she eventually came to the deep cave of Apollo, god of knowledge, where she found the bubbling waters of the spring of Castalia. There she took up a plectrum and played lovely tunes on the harp with the nymphs leading the dance; that is to say, she learnt the art of musical chords as well as the rules of harmonics."

'This description of Sappho by Boccaccio should be understood to refer to the depth of her learning and to the great erudition of her works which, as the Ancients themselves pointed out, are so complex that even the most intelligent and educated men have difficulty in grasping their meaning. Her books, which are exquisitely written and still popular today, offer an excellent model for those of later generations who want to perfect the art of writing verse. She invented many new forms of song and poetry, including lays, sorrowful complaints, strange love laments and other poems inspired by different emotions which are beautifully wrought and are now called Sapphic poems in her honour. On the subject of this lady's works, Horace recalls that a book of her verse was found under the pillow of the great philosopher Plato, Aristotle's teacher, when he died.

'To cut a long story short, Sappho was so famous for her learning that her native city decided to dedicate a prominent bronze statue to her in order to honour her and record her achievements for posterity. She earned herself a place amongst the greatest poets whose glory, according to Boccaccio, far outshines the mitres of bishops, the coronets and crowns of kings and even the palm wreaths and laurel garlands of those who are victorious in battle. I could give you many more examples of brilliant women, such as the Greek woman Leontium, an excellent philosopher, who dared to put forward clearly reasoned arguments against Theophrastus, a thinker who was highly regarded in his own time.'

31. *About the maiden Manto.*

'You can take it from me that if women have been able to learn and gain mastery of the sciences, they are equally capable of excelling in the arts, as you'll soon find out. According to the ancient beliefs of the pagans, people used to try and see what the future would bring by interpreting the patterns made by birds in flight, by the flames of a fire, and by the entrails of dead animals. This was regarded as a proper art or science and was held in great esteem. One maiden who was a particularly skilful mistress of this art was the daughter of Tiresias, high priest of the city of Thebes – or bishop, as we would say now – because priests of these pagan faiths were allowed to marry.

'This lady, who was called Manto, flourished during the reign of Oedipus, King of Thebes. Being gifted and intelligent, she acquired a complete knowledge of pyromancy, the art of divining the future from fire. This art was invented a very long time ago by the Chaldaeans, though others claim that it was Nimrod the giant who discovered it. In her time, there was no man alive who could outdo Manto in interpreting the significance of the movements, colours and sounds made by the flames of a burning fire. She was also adept at reading the shapes made by the veins of animals, the gullets of horses and the entrails of beasts. Her powers were so great that many believed she could conjure up the spirits and make them tell her all that she wanted to know. It was during this lady's lifetime that the city of Thebes was destroyed because of a quarrel between King Oedipus's sons. She therefore went to live in Asia where she had a temple to Apollo built which subsequently became very famous. She later died in Italy where, in her honour, a city was named after her. This city of Mantua, which was the birthplace of the poet Virgil, is still there to this day.'

32. About Medea, and another queen named Circe.

'Medea, who is mentioned in many history books, was no less skilled or knowledgeable than this Manto. An extremely beautiful lady with a tall, slim body and a very lovely face, Medea was the daughter of Aeëtes, King of Colchis, and his wife Perse. In learning she surpassed all other women, for she knew the properties of every plant and what spells they could be used for. Indeed, no art had been invented that she hadn't mastered. Intoning a song that she alone knew, Medea could make the sky go cloudy and black, draw the wind out of the dark caverns in the depths of the earth, stir up storms, cause rivers to stop flowing, brew up all kinds of poisons, create fire out of nowhere to burn whatever she wished, and perform many other marvels besides. It was she whose powers of sorcery helped Jason to win the Golden Fleece.

Like Medea, Circe too was a queen. Her island lay off the coast of Italy. This lady was so well versed in the art of casting spells that there was nothing she couldn't do in this domain. She knew how to make up a potion that could turn men into wild animals or birds. This is borne out in the story of Ulysses, who was returning home to Greece after the destruction of Troy when Fortune whipped up a storm and tossed his ships through the boiling seas until he came to the harbour of the city ruled by this Queen Circe. Since the wily Ulysses had no wish to land on this island without first asking the queen's express permission, he sent some of his knights to her to ask if she would allow him to come ashore. Unfortunately, Circe thought they had come to harm her and so gave his men this potion to drink which immediately turned them into swine. Ulysses lost no time in going to see her and making her change them back again into their proper form. A similar tale is told about Diomedes, another Greek prince, who, on arriving in Circe's harbour, saw all his men changed into birds, the form which they still have today. These uncommonly large and fierce creatures, which are very different in shape from other birds, are known by the inhabitants of the region as "the birds of Diomedes".'

33. *Christine asks Reason if any woman has ever invented new forms of knowledge.*

I, Christine, on hearing Reason's words, took up this matter and said to her, 'My lady, I can clearly see that you are able to cite an endless number of women who were highly skilled in the arts and sciences. However, I'd like to ask you if you know of any woman who was ingenious, or creative, or clever enough to invent any new useful and important branches of knowledge which did not previously exist. It's surely less difficult to learn and follow a subject which has already been invented than it is to discover something new and unknown by oneself.'

Reason replied, 'Believe me, many crucial and worthy arts and sciences have been discovered thanks to the ingenuity and cleverness of women, both in the theoretical sciences which are expressed through the written word, and in the technical crafts which take the form of manual tasks and trades. I'll now give you a whole set of examples.

'First of all, I'll tell you about the noble Nicostrata, whom the Italians called Carmentis. This lady was the daughter of the king of Arcadia whose name was Pallas. She was extraordinarily intelligent and endowed by God with special intellectual gifts, having such a vast knowledge of Greek literature and being able to write so wisely, elegantly and with such eloquence that the poets of the time claimed in their verse that she was loved by the god Mercury. They similarly thought that her son, who was in his day equally renowned for his intelligence, was the offspring of this god, rather than of her husband. Because of various upheavals that occurred in her native land, Nicostrata, accompanied by her son and a whole host of other people who wanted to go with her, set off for Italy in a large fleet of ships and sailed up the River Tiber. It was here that she went ashore and climbed up a great hill which she named Mount Palatine after her father. On this hill, where the city of Rome was subsequently founded, she, her son and her followers built themselves a castle. As she found the indigenous population to be very primitive, she laid down a set of rules for them to observe and encouraged them to live a rational and just existence. Thus it was she who first established laws in this country that was to become so famous for developing a legal system from which all known laws would be derived.

'Amongst all the other attributes that this lady possessed, Nicostrata was particularly blessed with the gift of divine inspiration and prophecy. She was thus able to predict that her adopted country would one day rise above all others to become the most magnificent and glorious realm on earth. To her mind, therefore, it would not be fitting for this country which would outshine and conquer the rest of the world to use an inferior and crude set of alphabetical letters which had originated in a foreign country. Moreover, Nicostrata wished to transmit her own wisdom and learning to future generations in a suitable form. She therefore set her mind to inventing a new set of letters which were completely different from those used in other nations. What she created was the ABC – the Latin alphabet – as well as the rules for constructing words, the distinction between vowels and consonants and the bases of the science of grammar. She gave this knowledge and this alphabet to the people, in the hope that they would become universally known. It was truly no small or insignificant branch of knowledge that this lady invented, nor should she receive only paltry thanks for it. This ingenious science proved so useful and brought so much good into the world that one can honestly say that no nobler discovery was ever made.

'The Italians were not lacking in gratitude for this great gift, and rightly so, since they heralded it as such a marvellous invention that they venerated her more highly than any man, worshipping Nicostrata/ Carmentis like a goddess in her own lifetime. When she died, they built a temple dedicated to her memory, situated at the foot of the hill where she had made her home. In order to preserve her fame for posterity, they borrowed various terms from the science she had invented and even used her own name to designate certain objects. In honour of the science of Latin that she had invented, the people of the country called themselves Latins. Furthermore, because *ita* in Latin is the most important affirmative term in that language, being the equivalent of *oui* in French, they did not stop at calling their own realm the land of the Latins, but went so far as to use the name Italy to refer to the whole country beyond their immediate borders, which is a vast area comprising many different regions and kingdoms. From this lady's name, Carmentis, they also derived the Latin word *carmen*, meaning "song". Even the Romans, who came a long time after her, called one of the gates of the city the *Porta Carmentalis*. These names have not been changed since and are still the same today, no matter how the fortunes of the Romans have fared or which mighty emperor was in power.

'My dear Christine, what more could you ask for? Could any mortal man be said to have done anything so splendid? But don't think that she's the only example of a woman who invented many new branches of learning . . .'

34. *About Minerva, who invented countless sciences, including the art of making arms from iron and steel.*

'Minerva, as you yourself have noted elsewhere, was a maiden from Greece who was also known as Pallas. This girl was so supremely intelligent that her contemporaries foolishly declared her to be a goddess come down from the heavens, since they had no idea who her parents were and she performed deeds that had never been done before. As Boccaccio himself points out, the fact that they knew so little about her origins meant that they were all the more astonished at her great wisdom, which surpassed that of every other woman of her time. She employed her skilfulness and her immense ingenuity not just in one domain but in many. First of all, she used her brilliance to invent various Greek letters called characters which can be used to write down a maximum number of ideas in a minimum number of words. This wonderfully clever invention is still used by the Greeks today. She also invented numbers and developed ways of using them to count and perform quick calculations. In short, she was so ingenious that she created many arts and techniques that had not previously been discovered, including the art of making wool and cloth. It was she who first had the idea of shearing sheep and developing the whole process of untangling, combing and carding the wool with various instruments, cleaning it, breaking down the fibres on metal spikes and spinning it on the distaff, whilst also inventing the tools needed for weaving it into cloth and making it into fine fabric.

'Likewise, she discovered how to make oil from pressing olives and how to extract the juice from other sorts of fruit.

'Likewise, she invented the art of building carts and chariots in order to carry things more easily from one place to another.

'Likewise, an invention of this lady's which was all the more marvellous for being such an unlikely thing for a woman to think of, was the art of forging armour for knights to protect themselves in battle and weapons of iron and steel for them to fight with. She taught this art first to the people of Athens, whom she also instructed in how to organize themselves into armies and battalions and to fight in serried ranks.

'Likewise, she invented flutes, pipes, trumpets and other wind instruments.

'This lady was not only extraordinarily intelligent but also supremely chaste, remaining a virgin all her life. It was because of her exemplary chastity that the poets claimed in their fables that she struggled long and hard with Vulcan, the god of fire, but finally overcame and defeated him. This story can be interpreted to mean that she conquered the passions and desires of the flesh which so vigorously assail the body when one is young. The Athenians held this girl in the highest esteem, worshipping her as if she were a deity and calling her the goddess of arms and warfare because she was the first to invent these arts. She was also known as the goddess of wisdom, thanks to her great intelligence.

'After her death, the people of Athens built a temple dedicated to her, in which they placed a statue representing wisdom and warfare in the likeness of a girl. This statue had terrible fierce eyes to symbolize both the duty of a knight to enforce justice and the inscrutability of the thoughts of a wise man. The statue had a helmet on its head, to suggest the idea that a knight must be hardened in battle and have unfailing courage, and that the plans of a wise man should be shrouded in secrecy. It was also dressed in chainmail, to represent the power of the estate of knighthood as well as the foresight of a wise man who arms himself against the vicissitudes of Fortune. The statue held a great spear or lance as an emblem of the fact that a knight must be the rod of justice and that a wise man launches his attacks from a safe distance. Round the statue's neck hung a shield or buckler of crystal, meaning that a knight must always be vigilant and ready to defend the country and the people and that a wise man has a clear understanding of all things. In the centre of this shield was the image of the head of a serpent known as a Gorgon, to suggest the idea that a knight must be cunning and stalk his enemies like a snake whilst a wise man must be wary of all the harm that others might do to him. To guard the statue, they placed next to it a night bird – an owl – to signify that a knight must be prepared, if needs be, to protect the country both day and night, and that a wise man must be alert at all times to do what is right. This lady Minerva was greatly revered for a long time and her fame spread to many other countries, where they also dedicated temples to her. Even centuries later, when the Romans were at the height of their powers, they incorporated her image into their pantheon of gods.'

35. About Queen Ceres, who invented agriculture and many other arts.

'Ceres was queen of the Sicilians in very ancient times. Thanks to her great ingenuity, it was she who was responsible for inventing both the science and the techniques of agriculture as well as all the necessary tools. She taught her subjects how to round up and tame their cattle and train them to take the yoke. Ceres also invented the plough, showing her people how to use the blade to dig and slice through the soil, and all the other skills needed for this task. Next she taught them how to scatter the seed on the ground and to cover it over. Once the seed had taken root and grown into shoots, she revealed to them how to cut the sheaves and thresh them with a flail in order to separate the wheat from the chaff. Ceres then demonstrated to them how to grind the grain between heavy stones and to construct mills, going on to show them how to prepare flour and make it into bread. Thus this lady encouraged men who had been living like beasts off acorns, wild grasses, apples and holly berries to eat a more noble diet.

'Ceres didn't stop there: she gathered together her people, who at that time were used to wandering about like animals making their temporary homes in woods or moorlands, into large groups and taught them how to build proper towns and cities and to live in communities. She thereby brought humankind out of its primitive state and introduced it to a more civilized and rational way of life. The poets wrote a fable about Ceres which tells how her daughter was abducted by Pluto, god of the under-world. Because of her great knowledge and all the good that she had brought into the world, the people of the time venerated her, calling her the goddess of corn.'

36. *About Isis, who discovered the art of making gardens and growing plants.*

'Thanks to her extensive knowledge of horticulture, Isis was not only queen of Egypt but also the highly revered goddess of the Egyptians. The fables tell how Isis was loved by Jupiter, who turned her into a cow and then back into her original form, all of which is an allegory of her great learning, as you yourself have pointed out in your *Letter of Othea to Hector*. For the benefit of the Egyptians, she also invented certain types of characters to represent their language which could be used to write down ideas in a concise way.

'Isis was the daughter of Inachos, king of the Greeks, and sister of Phoroneus, who was a very wise man. It so happened that this lady and her brother left Greece for Egypt and it was there that she showed the people many different things, including how to create gardens, grow plants and graft cuttings of one species on to another. She also set up a number of fine and decent laws which she encouraged the Egyptians to live by, since up until then they had been in a very primitive state without a properly established system of justice. In short, Isis did so much for them that they honoured her with great ceremony both in her own lifetime and after her death. Her fame spread throughout the world, with temples and oratories consecrated to her springing up all over. Even when Rome was at its peak, the Romans erected a temple in her honour where they performed great sacrifices and solemn rites observing the same customs which the Egyptians used to worship her.

'This noble lady's husband was named Apis, whom the pagans mis-takenly believed to be the son of the god Jupiter and of Niobe, daughter of Phoroneus. The ancient historians and poets make great mention of this man.'

37. *About all the great good that these ladies have brought into the world.*

'My lady, I'm delighted to hear from your lips that so much good has been brought into the world thanks to the intelligence of women. Yet there are still those men who go around claiming that women know nothing of any worth. It's also a common way to mock someone for saying something foolish by telling them that they're thinking like a woman. On the whole, men seem to hold the view that women have never done anything for humankind but bear children and spin wool.'

Reason's reply was: 'Now can you understand the terrible ingratitude of those men who say such things? It's as if they're enjoying all the benefits without having any idea of where they come from or whom they should thank for them. You can clearly see how God, who does nothing without good cause, wanted to show men that they should no more denigrate the female sex than they should their own sex. He chose to endow women's minds with the capacity not simply to learn and grasp all kinds of knowledge but also to invent new ones by themselves, discovering sciences which have done more good and have been more useful to humanity than any others. Just take the example of Carmentis, whom I told you about before. Her invention of the Latin alphabet pleased God so much that He wished it to replace the Hebrew and Greek alphabets which had been so prestigious. It was by His will that the alphabet spread throughout most of Europe, a vast expanse of land, where it is used in countless books and volumes in all disciplines which recall and preserve for ever the glorious deeds of men and the marvellous workings of God, in addition to all the arts and sciences. But don't let it be said that I'm telling you these things out of bias: these are the words of Boccaccio himself and thus the truth of them is indisputable.

'One could sum up by saying that the good things that this Carmentis has done are truly infinite, since it is thanks to her that men have been brought out of their ignorant state and become civilized, even if they themselves have not acknowledged this fact. Thanks to her, men possess the art of encoding their thoughts and wishes into secret messages which they can send all over the world. They have the means to make their desires known and understood by others, and they have access to knowledge of past and present events as well as to some aspects of the future. Moreover, thanks to this lady's invention, men can draw up treaties and strike up friendships with people in faraway places; through their correspondence back and forth, they can get to know each other without ever meeting face to face. In short, it is impossible to count up all the advantages that the invention of the alphabet has brought: it is writing which allows us to describe and to know God's will, to understand celestial matters, the sea, the earth, all individuals and all objects. I ask you, then, was there ever a man who did more good than this?'

38. More on the same topic.

'One might also ask if any man ever did as much for the benefit of humankind as this noble Queen Ceres, whom I was telling you about before. Who could ever deserve more praise than she who led men, who were no better than savage primitives, out of the woods where they were roaming like wild beasts without any laws, and instead took them to dwell in towns and cities and taught them how to live a law-abiding existence? It was she who introduced men to far better nourishment than their previous diet of acorns and wild apples, giving them wheat and corn which makes their bodies more beautiful, their complexions clearer and their limbs stronger and more supple. This is much more suitable and substantial food for human beings to eat. It was she who showed men how to clear the land which was full of thistles, thorns, scrubby bushes and wild trees, and to plough the earth and sow seed by which means agriculture became a sophisticated rather than a crude process and could be used for the common good of all. It was she who enriched humankind by turning coarse primitives into civilized citizens and by transforming men's minds from being lazy, unformed and shrouded in ignorance to being capable of more suitable meditations and of the contemplation of higher matters. Finally, it was she who sent men out into the fields to work the land, men whose efforts sustain the towns and cities and provide for those inhabitants who are freed up to perform other tasks which are essential for human existence.

'Isis is a similar example in terms of horticulture. Who could ever match the enormous benefits which she brought into the world when she discovered how to grow trees which bear fine fruit and to cultivate other excellent herbs which are so suitable for a human diet?

'Minerva too used her wisdom to endow human beings with many vital things such as woollen clothing, instead of the animal pelts which were all there was previously to wear. For the benefit of humankind, she invented carts and chariots to relieve men of the burden of carrying their possessions from place to place in their arms. Not to mention, my dear Christine, what she gave to noblemen and knights when she taught them the art and skill of making armour to give their bodies greater protection in battle, armour which was stronger, more practical and much finer than the leather hides which they had had to put on in the past.'

I answered Reason, saying, 'Indeed, my lady, from what you're telling me I've now realized the full extent to which those men who attack women have failed to express their gratitude and acknowledgement. They have absolutely no grounds for criticizing women: it's not just that every man who is born of woman receives so much from her, but also that there is truly no end to the great gifts which she has so generously showered on him. Those clerks who slander women, attacking them either verbally or in their writings, really should shut their mouths once and for all. They and all those who subscribe to their views should bow their heads in shame for having dared to come out with such things, considering that the reality is utterly different from what they've claimed. Indeed, they owe a huge debt of thanks to this noble lady Carmentis, for having used her fine mind to instruct them like a teacher with her pupils – a fact which they can't deny – and to endow them with the knowledge that they themselves hold in the highest regard, which is the noble Latin alphabet.

'But what about all the many noblemen and knights who go against their duty by launching their sweeping attacks on women? They too should hold their tongues, given that all their skills in bearing arms and fighting in organized ranks, of which they're so inordinately proud, have come down to them from a woman. More generally, does any man who eats bread and lives in a civilized fashion in a well-ordered city or who cultivates the land have the right to slander and criticize women, as so many of them do, seeing all that has been done for them? Certainly not. It is women like Minerva, Ceres and Isis who have brought them so many advantages which they will always be able to live off and which will for ever enhance their daily existence. Are these things to be taken lightly? I think not, my lady, for it seems to me that the teachings of Aristotle, which have so greatly enriched human knowledge and are rightly held in such high esteem, put together with all those of every other philosopher who ever lived, are not worth anything like as much to humankind as the deeds performed by these ladies, thanks to their great ingenuity.'

Reason replied to me, 'These ladies were not the only ones to do so much good. There have been many others, some of whom I'll now go on to tell you about.'

39. *About the maiden Arachne, who invented the arts of dyeing wool and of weaving fine tapestries, as well as the art of growing flax and making it into cloth.*

'Truth to tell, God chose to provide the world with endless useful and important techniques through the efforts of these women and of many others, too. One such example is an Asian maiden named Arachne, daughter of Idmonius of Colophon. Being extraordinarily resourceful and clever, this Arachne was the first person to create the arts of dyeing wool in different colours and of producing what we would call fine tapestries from weaving pictures on cloth to make them look like paintings. Indeed, she mastered every aspect of the art of weaving. There was even a fable about Arachne which tells how she was turned into a spider by the goddess Pallas whom she had dared to challenge.

'Arachne also invented another notable art, for it was she who discovered how to use flax and hemp; from growing, harvesting and stripping the plants, to soaking and combing out the fibres in order to spin them on a distaff and make cloth from them. These techniques have all benefited humankind enormously, despite the fact that some men scorn women for performing such activities. Arachne was also responsible for developing the art of making nets, traps and snares with which to catch fish and fowl. She similarly invented the whole art of fishing and of trapping fierce, wild animals in nets as well as rabbits, hares and birds. All of these skills were unknown before she came along. In my view, this woman did no small service to humanity, which has since derived great pleasure and profit from her inventions.

'Even so, certain writers, including Boccaccio, who is our source on these matters, maintain that the world was a better place before human beings learnt more sophisticated ways and simply lived off acorns and holly berries and dressed in animal skins. With all due respect to him and to those other authors who claim that the world has been harmed by these inventions which enable people to live more comfortable lives and eat a healthier diet, I would say that in fact we are all the more beholden to God for having bestowed these great gifts and favours upon us. If human beings misuse the inventions which the Creator enjoined them to use properly and which He made for the benefit of men and women alike, this is not because the things in themselves are not good and invaluable when used correctly and wisely. Rather, it is because those who misuse them are wicked and perverse in the first place. The life of Jesus Christ himself proves my point, for he used bread, fish, wine, linen and dyed cloth, along with many other indispensable things, which he never would have done if it had been better to live off acorns and holly berries. Moreover, he conferred a great honour on Ceres for her invention of bread by choosing to present his noble body to men and women for them to eat in the form of bread according to the rite of Holy Communion.'

40. About Pamphile, who discovered the art of gathering silk from worms, dyeing the thread and making it into cloth.

'On the subject of great sciences invented by women which are extremely beneficial to humanity, we should not forget the one invented by the noble Pamphile, who came from Greece. This lady was highly skilled in various arts and took such delight in experimenting and discovering new things that it was she who first invented the art of creating silk. Using her great ingenuity and perceptiveness, she noticed that the worms which lived on the branches of the local trees naturally produced silk. Picking the lovely cocoons that she had watched the worms making and pulling the threads together, she tried dyeing them various different colours to see if they would take. After she had thoroughly tested this process and seen how good the results were, she took the dyed thread and wove it into silken cloth. The science brought into the world by this lady has proved to be a most wonderful and useful invention, one which has spread to all countries. In order to serve and glorify God, silk is used to make all manner of robes and vestments worn by prelates during divine service. It is also used by emperors, kings and princes, and even by the whole population of certain countries where they have no wool but an abundance of silkworms.'

41. *About Thamaris, who was a supremely gifted painter, as well as another great artist called Irene, and Marcia the Roman.*

'What more can I say to prove to you that women are just as capable of learning arts and sciences as they are of inventing new ones? Believe me when I tell you that once they have learnt something, women are very quick to put their knowledge into action and to achieve great things. This is certainly true in the case of a woman called Thamaris, whose mastery of the art of painting was such that there was none to touch her while she was alive. Boccaccio says about her that she was the daughter of the painter Micon, and that she was born at the time of the ninetieth Olympiad. This was the name given to a feast day on which various games took place: whoever won was allowed to ask for whatever they wanted, within reason. These games and festivities were held in honour of the god Jupiter every sixth year, with four complete years in between each set of games. It was Hercules who first organized the event and they calculated their calendar from the first year that it was inaugurated, just as Christians do from the birth of Jesus Christ.

'This Thamaris put aside all usual womanly tasks and devoted herself to learning her father's craft. She applied herself so well that, during the reign of Archelaos over the Macedonians, the Ephesians commissioned

Thamaris to paint a picture of the goddess Diana whom they worshipped. For a long time afterwards, this picture was held in very high esteem, as befitted a work of such great artistry, and was only displayed on feast days in honour of Diana. It was preserved for many years as a marvellous testament to this lady's skill and has ensured that even today her brilliance has not been forgotten.

'Irene was another woman from Greece, who excelled herself in the art of painting to the point of surpassing all others of her time. She was a pupil of a painter called Cratinus, who was a master in his field, yet she became such a great expert that she completely outshone her teacher. Her contemporaries were amazed by her achievement and chose to commemorate Irene by dedicating a statue to her of a girl in the act of painting. They reserved an honourable place for this statue in a gallery of other figures which depicted the greatest past masters in a variety of disciplines. This was in accordance with a custom which the ancients had of revering those who outdid all others in a particular domain, be it in wisdom, strength, beauty or some other attribute, preserving their names for posterity by erecting statues to them in prominent places.

'Marcia the Roman was a virgin who lived an exemplary life full of great virtue and morality. She too was another fine craftswoman in the art of painting, achieving such excellence in her field that she outstripped all men, including Dionysius and Sopolis who were thought to be the best artists in the world at that time. To put it briefly, she attained the very pinnacle of perfection in her field, according to the most authoritative sources. In order to leave behind her an indelible record of her expertise, one of this Marcia's most notable works was a brilliantly executed self-portrait done with the aid of a mirror which was so lifelike that anyone who saw it thought it was real. For many years, this picture was greatly treasured and pointed out to other craftsmen as a supreme specimen of their art.'

I then said to Reason: 'My lady, it is clear from these examples that those who were wise were held in much higher esteem in the past than nowadays and that the sciences themselves were much more highly thought of then than they are now. However, to go back to what you were saying about women who excelled in the art of painting, I know a woman called Anastasia working today who is so good at painting decorative borders and background landscapes for miniatures that there is no craftsman who can match her in the whole of Paris, even though that's where the finest in the world can be found. Only Anastasia can execute such delicate floral motifs and tiny details and she is so well regarded that she is entrusted with finishing off even the most expensive and priceless of books. I know all this from my own experience as she has done some work for me which has been ranked amongst the finest creations of the greatest masters.'

Reason replied, 'I can well believe it, my dear Christine. Anyone who wanted could cite plentiful examples of exceptional women in the world today: it's simply a matter of looking for them. Whilst we're on this subject, I'll tell you about another Roman woman.'

42. *About Sempronia of Rome.*

'This Sempronia of Rome was a remarkably beautiful woman. Yet, not only did she eclipse all other women in the loveliness of her face and body, she also outclassed all others in the brilliance of her mind. Her phenomenal intelligence meant there was no discipline, no matter how difficult it was either intellectually or practically, that she couldn't immediately pick up and master. Thanks to her great dexterity, she could perform any practical task and her excellent memory allowed her to repeat anything she ever heard, even the lengthiest of stories. Sempronia knew both Latin and Greek, which she could write so beautifully that it was a marvel to read.

'Likewise, her speech, her way of expressing herself and her bearing were delightfully elegant and engaging, and she could use her words and gestures to persuade anyone to do her bidding. She took great pleasure in being able to change others' moods at will, making the most downcast of people feel joyful and happy or, conversely, causing others to feel sad, tearful or angry. Sempronia was also capable of exhorting men to perform all types of deeds which needed either tremendous courage or physical strength. If she wished, she could make all who heard her follow her there and then. On top of all this, she spoke in such sweet tones and conducted herself in such a courtly manner that those around her never tired of looking at her or of listening to her. She had an exquisite singing voice and could play any stringed instrument perfectly, winning all competitions. In short, in all activities that the human mind has ever invented, she was highly skilled and supremely competent.'

43. *Christine asks Reason if women are naturally endowed with good judgement, and Reason replies to her question.*

I, Christine, came back to Reason, saying: 'My lady, it is now clear to me that God has truly made women's minds sharp enough to learn, understand and retain any form of knowledge. Praise be to Him for this! However, I'm always surprised at how many people you see whose minds are very quick to pick up and grasp all that they are shown and who are mentally agile and clever enough to master any discipline they please, attaining great learning through their dedication to their studies, but yet seem to lack judgement when it comes to their personal morals and public behaviour. This is true even of some of the most famous and erudite scholars. There's no doubt that knowledge of the sciences should help inculcate moral values. So, if you please, my lady, I'd be keen to know whether women's minds, which both you and my own experience have proved to me to be capable of understanding the most complex matters in sciences and other disciplines, are just as proficient at learning the lessons which good judgement teaches us. In other words, can women distinguish between what is the right and the wrong thing to do? Can they modify their current behaviour on the basis of past experience? Can they use the example of the present to anticipate how they should conduct themselves in the future? In my view, this is what good judgement consists of.'

Reason replied: 'You're quite right, my dear girl. Yet don't forget that this faculty that you're talking about is inherent in both men and women, and that some are more generously endowed with it than others. Note too that good judgement does not come from learning, though learning can help perfect it in those who are naturally that way inclined, since, as you know, two forces moving in the same direction are stronger and more powerful than a single force moving on its own. Therefore, in my opinion, anyone who has naturally good judgement or good sense and who also manages to attain learning is thoroughly deserving of praise. But, as you yourself have pointed out, some have one but not the other: one is a gift from God and is an innate quality, whereas the other is only acquired after much study. Both, however, are good.

'There are those who would maintain that it is better to have good judgement and no learning than to have great learning but bad judgement. This is a highly controversial proposition that raises all sorts of questions. You could say that the best person is the one who contributes most to the common good. In that case, it's undeniable that learned individuals help others most by sharing their knowledge with them, no matter how much good judgement they might possess. This is because individuals' faculty of judgement only lasts as long as their lifetime: when they die, it does, too. On the other hand, learning which has been acquired endures for ever, in that the good reputation of those who possess it never dies and they can teach their knowledge to others as well as pass it on in books for future generations to discover. Their learning does not therefore die with them, as I can prove to you by the example of Aristotle and all the others who first brought the sciences into the world. This type of acquired knowledge has been more beneficial to humankind than all the good judgement shown by those figures of the past who had no learning, even though many of them used their good sense to govern and administer their empires and kingdoms most wisely. The fact is, these deeds are transient and vanish with time, whereas learning is indestructible.

'However, I'm going to set these matters aside for others to resolve since they are not strictly relevant to our task of building the city. Instead, let's go back to what you originally asked me about whether women naturally have good judgement. On this question, I can give you a firm "yes". You should be able to gather this not just from what I've already told you but also from observing the way in which women generally go about doing their traditionally female duties. If you care to look closely, you'll discover that for the most part women prove themselves to be extremely attentive, diligent and meticulous in running a household and seeing to everything as best they can. Sometimes, those women who have lazy husbands annoy them by giving the impression that they are nagging them, telling them what to do and trying to be the voice of authority in the house; though husbands like this are just putting a bad slant on what most wives do with all good intentions. The next part of what I have to say will be largely derived from the "Epistle of Solomon"[18] which talks about good wives such as these.'

44. The 'Epistle of Solomon' from the Book of Proverbs.

'Whoever finds a valiant woman, one of sound judgement, will be a husband who lacks for nothing. Her fame spreads far and wide and her husband puts his faith in her for she brings him nothing but good and prosperity at all times. She looks for and acquires wool, in other words she sets her maid servants a worthy task to keep them gainfully employed and her household well stocked, and she herself lends a hand. She is like the ship of a merchant which brings all good things to shore and provides the bread. She rewards those who deserve it and they are her intimate friends. In her house, there is plenty to eat, even for the servants. She weighs up the price of a piece of land before buying it and she uses her good sense to plant the vines which will keep the household in wine. Full of courage and resolve, she girds her loins with strength and toughens up her arms with continuous hard work. Even in the dark of night, the light of her labours still shines through. She toils at the heavy tasks yet doesn't neglect women's work either, for she does her fair share. She extends a helping hand to the poor and brings them comfort in their suffering. By her efforts, the house is protected against the cold and the snow and her servants' clothing is lined. She dresses herself in silk and purple: that is, in integrity and splendour. Her husband too cuts an honourable figure when he is seated in the top ranks with the most venerable people in the land. She makes fine linen cloth, which she sells, and wraps herself in strength and glory. For this, she will have everlasting joy. Words of wisdom spring from her lips and her tongue is ruled by gentleness. She makes sure that the household is fully provided for and does not eat the bread of idleness. Her children's behaviour shows that she is their mother and their actions reveal her tender care. Her husband's fine appearance does her credit. She governs her daughters in all matters, even when they are fully grown. She despises the trappings of glory and the transience of beauty. Such a woman will fear the Lord and be praised, and He will reward her for her labours as they attest to her virtue far and wide.'

45. *About Gaia Cirilla.*

'On the subject of what the "Epistle of Solomon" says about women of good judgement, we should not forget that noble queen, Gaia Cirilla. This lady, who was from Rome or Tuscany, married Tarquin, king of the Romans. She was both very prudent in her behaviour and extremely virtuous, being endowed with great good sense, loyalty and kindness. Gaia was esteemed above all women for managing her household well and seeing attentively to everything. Even though she was a queen and thus had no need to work with her hands, she delighted in always using her time profitably on some task or other. She hated being idle and thus would keep herself constantly occupied, making the ladies and girls who served her at court do likewise. She knew how to distinguish between the different qualities of wool and how to make both fine and coarse cloth, spending her days at what was regarded as a most honourable occupation at that time. For this reason, the noble lady was praised throughout the world: she was held in the highest regard and her reputation was greatly enhanced. In order to preserve glorious Gaia's memory for posterity, the Romans, whose power increased enormously after her lifetime, established and long maintained a certain custom at their daughters' weddings. According to this custom, when the bride first crossed the threshold of the bridegroom's house, she was asked what she wanted her name to be and she would reply "Gaia", to signify that she would do her very best to emulate this lady in her actions and deeds.'

46. *About the good sense and cleverness of Queen Dido.*

'As you yourself pointed out earlier, good judgement consists of weighing up carefully what you wish to do and working out how to do it. To prove to you that women are perfectly able to think in this way, even about the most important matters, I'll give you a few examples of some high-born ladies, the first of whom is Dido. As I'll go on to tell you, this Dido, whose name was originally Elissa, revealed her good sense through her actions. She founded and built a city in Africa called Carthage and was its queen and ruler. It was in the way that she established the city and acquired the land on which it was built that she demonstrated her great courage, nobility and virtue, qualities which are indispensable to anyone who wishes to act prudently.

'This lady was descended from the Phoenicians, who came from the remotest regions of Egypt to settle in Syria where they founded and built several fine towns and cities. Amongst these people was a king named Agenor, who was a direct ancestor of Dido's father. This king, who was called Belus, ruled over Phoenicia and conquered the kingdom of Cyprus. He had only two children: a son, Pygmalion, and a daughter, Dido.

'On his deathbed, Belus ordered his barons to honour his children and be loyal to them, making them swear an oath that they would do so. Once the king was dead, they crowned his son Pygmalion and married the beautiful Elissa to a duke named Acerbas Sychaea, or Sychaeus, who was the most powerful lord in the country after the king. This Sychaeus was a high priest in the temple dedicated to Hercules, whom they worshipped, as well as being an extremely wealthy man. He and his wife loved each other very deeply and led a happy life together. But King Pygmalion was an evil man, the cruellest and most envious person you ever saw, whose greed knew no bounds. Elissa, his sister, was all too aware of what he was like. Seeing how rich her husband was and how well known for his fabulous wealth, she advised Sychaeus to be on his guard against the king and to put his treasure in a safe place where her brother couldn't lay his hands on it. Sychaeus followed his wife's advice but failed to watch his own back against possible attack from the king as she had told him to do. Thus it happened that, one day, the king had him killed in order to steal his great riches from him. Elissa was so distraught at his death that she nearly died of grief. For a long time, she gave herself over to weeping and wailing for the loss of her beloved lord, cursing her brute of a brother for having ordered his murder. However, the wicked king, whose wishes had been thwarted since he had only managed to recover a tiny part of Sychaeus's wealth, bore a deep grudge against his sister, whom he suspected of having hidden it all away.

'Realizing that her own life was in danger, Elissa's good sense told her to leave her native land and live elsewhere. Her mind made up, she carefully considered all that she needed to do and then steeled herself to put her plans into effect. This lady knew very well that the king did not enjoy the full support of his barons or his subjects because of his great cruelty and the excessive burdens he imposed on them. She therefore rallied to her cause some of the princes, townspeople and even the peasants. Having sworn them to secrecy, she outlined her plans to them in such persuasive terms that they declared their loyalty to her and agreed to go with her.

'As quickly and as quietly as she could, Elissa had her ship prepared. In the dead of night, she set sail with all her treasure and her many followers aboard, urging the sailors to make the ship go as fast as possible. Yet this lady's cleverness didn't end there. Knowing that her brother would send his men after her as soon as he learnt of her flight, she had great chests, trunks and boxes secretly filled up with heavy, worthless objects to make it look as if they contained treasure. The idea was that she would give these chests and boxes to her brother's men if they would only leave her alone and let her continue on her course. It all happened just as she planned, for they had not long been at sea when a whole host of the king's men came racing after her to stop her. In measured tones, she pointed out to them that as she was only setting out on a pilgrimage, they should allow her to sail on unhindered. However, seeing that they remained unconvinced by her explanation, she declared that if it was her treasure her brother was after, she would be prepared to give it to him, even though he had no right to interfere with her wishes. The king's men, who knew that this was his sole desire, forced her to part with it as that way they could do the king's bidding and she could appease her brother. With a sad face, as if it cost her dear, the lady made them load up all the chests and boxes on to their ships. Thinking that they had done well and that the king would be delighted with the news, his men immediately went on their way.

'Uttering not a single word of protest, the queen's only thoughts were of setting sail once more. They journeyed on, by day and night, until they came to the island of Cyprus, where they stopped for a short while to refresh themselves. As soon as she had made her sacrifices to the gods, the lady went back to the ship, taking with her the priest from the temple of Jupiter and his family. This priest had predicted that a lady would come from the land of the Phoenicians and that he would leave his country to join her. Casting off again, they left the island of Crete behind them and passed the island of Sicily on their right. They sailed along the whole length of the coast of Massylia until they finally arrived in Africa, where they landed. No sooner had they docked than the people living there rushed down to see the ship and to find out where those aboard were from.

'When they saw the lady and realized that she and her people had come in peace, they went and brought them food in abundance. Elissa talked to them in a very friendly way, explaining to them that she had heard such good things about their country that she wished to make her home there, if they had no objections. They replied that they were happy for her to do so. Insisting that she didn't want to establish a large colony on this foreign soil, the lady asked them to sell her a piece of land by the coast which was no bigger than what could be covered by the hide of a cow. Here she would build some dwellings for herself and her people. They granted her wishes and, as soon as the terms of the deal had been agreed upon, her cleverness and good sense came to the fore. Taking the cowhide, the lady had it cut into the tiniest strips possible, which were then tied together to form a rope. This rope was laid out on the ground by the seashore where it enclosed a huge plot of land. Those who had sold her the land were amazed and stunned by her cunning ruse, yet they had to abide by the deal they had struck with her.

'So it was that this lady took possession of all this territory in Africa. On her plot of land, a horse's head was discovered. This head, along with the movements and noises of the birds in the sky, they interpreted as prophetic signs that the city which they were about to found would be full of warriors who would excel themselves in the pursuit of arms. The lady immediately sent all over for workmen and spent her wealth freely to pay for their labour. The place which she had built was a magnificent and mighty city called Carthage, the citadel and main fortress of which were called Byrsa, which means "cowhide".

'Just as she was beginning to build her city, she received news that her brother was coming after her and her followers for having made a fool of him and tricked him out of his treasure. She told his messengers that she had most definitely given the treasure to the king's men for them to take back to him, but that perhaps it was they who had stolen it and replaced it with worthless objects instead. It was possibly even the gods who had decided to metamorphose the treasure and stop the king from having it because of the sin he had committed in ordering her husband's murder. As for her brother's threats, she had faith that, with the help of the gods, she could defend herself against him. Elissa therefore assembled all her fellow Phoenicians together and told them that she wanted no one to stay with her against their will nor suffer any harm for her sake. If any or all of them wanted to return home, she would reward them for their hard work and let them go. They all replied with one voice that they would live and die by her side, and would never leave her even for a single day.

'The messengers departed and the lady worked as fast as she could to finish the city. Once it was completed, she established laws and rules for her people to live an honest and just existence. She conducted herself with such wisdom and prudence that her fame spread all over the world and talk of her was on everyone's lips. Thanks to her bold and courageous actions and her judicious rule, she became so renowned for her heroic qualities that her name was changed to Dido, which means "*virago*" in Latin: in other words, a woman who has the virtue and valour of a man. She lived a glorious life for many years, one which would have lasted even longer had Fortune not turned against her. As this goddess is wont to be envious of those she sees prosper, she concocted a bitter brew for Dido to drink, which I'll tell you about all in good time.'

47. About Opis, Queen of Crete.

'In very early times, Opis or Ops, who was regarded as a goddess and as the mother of all the gods, was famed for her good sense. The ancient history books tell us that she remained steadfast and prudent throughout her life, no matter whether Fortune was hostile or kind to her. This lady was the daughter of Uranus, a very powerful man from Greece, and of his wife Vesta. Humankind at that time being extremely primitive and ignorant, Opis married her brother Saturn, who was king of Crete. This king had a dream that his wife would give birth to a son who would kill him. In an attempt to cheat fate, he therefore ordered all his wife's sons to be put to death. The queen used her cleverness and cunning to save her three sons, Jupiter, Neptune and Pluto, and she was greatly honoured and praised for this prudent behaviour. Thanks to her own intelligence and to the prestige of her sons, who were thought to be deities because they were so much wiser than the men of that era who were very backwards, she won such fame and glory for herself in her own lifetime that her contemporaries foolishly mistook her for a goddess and called her mother of all the gods. The people thus erected temples to this lady and made sacrifices to her. Their ridiculous beliefs lasted for many years, even up until the heyday of the Roman empire, since the Romans continued to pay respectful homage to this goddess.'

48. About Lavinia, daughter of King Latinus.

'Lavinia, queen of the Laurentines, was similarly renowned for her good sense. Descended from the same Cretan king, Saturn, whom I've just mentioned, she was the daughter of King Latinus. She later wed Aeneas, although before her marriage she had been promised to Turnus, king of the Rutulians. Her father, who had been informed by an oracle that she should be given to a Trojan prince, kept putting off the wedding despite the fact that his wife, the queen, was very keen for it to take place. When Aeneas arrived in Italy, he requested King Latinus's permission to enter his territory. He was not only granted leave to do so but was immediately given Lavinia's hand in marriage. It was for this reason that Turnus declared war on Aeneas, a war which caused many deaths and in which Turnus himself was killed. Having secured the victory, Aeneas took Lavinia as his wife. She later bore him a son, even though he himself died whilst she was still pregnant. As her time grew near, she became very afraid that a man called Ascanius, Aeneas's elder son by another woman, would attempt to murder her child and usurp the throne. She therefore went off to give birth in the woods and named the newborn baby Julius Silvius. Vowing never to marry again, Lavinia conducted herself with exemplary good judgement in her widowhood and managed to keep the kingdom intact, thanks to her astuteness. She was able to win her stepson's affection and thus defuse any animosity on his part towards her or his stepbrother. Indeed, once he had finished building the city of Alba, Ascanius left to make his home there. Meanwhile, Lavinia ruled the country with supreme skill until her son came of age. This child's descendants were Romulus and Remus, who later founded the city of Rome. They in turn were the ancestors of all the noble princes who came after them.

'What more can I tell you, my dear Christine? It seems to me that I've cited sufficient evidence to make my point, having given enough examples and proofs to convince you that God has never criticized the female sex more than the male sex. My case is conclusive, as you have seen, and my two sisters here will go on to confirm this for you in their presentation of the facts. I think that I have fulfilled my task of constructing the enclosure walls of the City of Ladies, since they're all now ready and done. Let me give way to my two sisters: with their help and advice you'll soon complete the building work that remains.'

End of the First Part of the Book of the City of Ladies.

PART II

Here begins the Second Part of the Book of the City of Ladies *which recounts how and by whom the houses and buildings were constructed inside the enclosure walls and how the City was filled with inhabitants.*

1. *The first chapter tells of the ten Sibyls.*

After the first lady, whose name was Reason, had finished speaking, the second lady, called Rectitude, turned to me and said, 'My dear Christine, I mustn't hang back from performing my duty: together we must construct the houses and buildings inside the walls of the City of Ladies which my sister Reason has now put up. Take your tools and come with me. Don't hesitate to mix the mortar well in your inkpot and set to on the masonry work with great strokes of your pen. I'll keep you well supplied with materials. With the grace of God, we'll soon have put up the royal palaces and noble mansions for the glorious and illustrious ladies who will come to live in this city for evermore.'

On hearing this honourable lady's words, I, Christine, replied to her, saying, 'Most excellent lady, here I stand ready before you. I will obey your every command, for my only wish is to do your bidding.'

She then answered me, 'My dear friend, look at these beautiful gleaming stones, more precious than any others in the world, that I have quarried and cut ready for you to use in the building work. Have I stood idly by whilst you were toiling away so hard with Reason? You must now arrange them in the order that I shall give you, following the line that I have traced for you.

'Amongst the highest rank of ladies of great renown are the wise sibyls who were extraordinarily knowledgeable. According to the most authoritative sources, there were ten sibyls, though some maintain there were only nine. My dear Christine, take good note of all this: what greater gift of divine revelation did God ever bestow on any prophet, even the most beloved, than that which He granted to these noble ladies I'm talking about? Didn't He confer on them the holy spirit of prophecy which allowed them to speak and write so straightforwardly and clearly that it was as if they were recounting past and completed actions in the manner of a chronicle, rather than anticipating events that would happen in the future? They even spoke more plainly and in greater detail than any prophet about the coming of Christ, which happened a long time after their day. These ladies kept their virginity intact and their bodies unsullied for the whole of their lives. All ten of them were called Sibyl, but this shouldn't be taken to be a proper name. The word "sibyl" in fact means "one who is privy to the thoughts of God". They were all given this name because their prophecies were of such momentous events that they could only have known of them if they had had access to the mind of God Himself. It's therefore a title of office rather than the name of an individual. Though they were all born in different countries of the world and lived in different eras, they all foresaw great future events including, with particular clarity, the birth of Christ, as I've already mentioned. Moreover, all ten of them were pagans, not even of the Jewish faith.

'The first sibyl came from the land of Persia, and for this reason is called Persica. The second one was from Libya, hence she was known as Libica. The third, born in the temple of Apollo at Delphi, was therefore called Delphica. It was she who predicted the destruction of Troy long before it occurred and she to whom Ovid dedicated a few lines in one of his books. The fourth one was from Italy: her name was Cimeria. The fifth, born in Babylon, was called Herophile: she was the one who prophesied to the Greeks who had come to consult her that they would destroy both Troy and its citadel, Ilium, and that Homer would give an untruthful version of these events in his writings. She was also known as Erythrea, for that was the name of the island where she made her home and where her books were subsequently discovered. The sixth one came from the island of Samos, and was called Samia. The seventh was known as Cumana, because she was born in the Italian city of Cumae, in the region of Campania. The eighth was named Hellespontina, for she came from Hellespont on the plains of Troy: she flourished during the time of Cyrus and the famous author Solon. The ninth one, called Phrygica, was from Phrygia, and she not only spoke at length about the fall of many different kingdoms but also described in vivid detail the coming of the false prophet Antichrist. The tenth was called Tiburtina, also known as Albunea, whose writings are held in great esteem because she wrote about Jesus Christ most clearly. Despite the fact that these sibyls were all of pagan origin, each of them eventually repudiated this faith on the grounds that it was wrong to worship a multiplicity of gods, that there was only one true God, and that all idols were false.'

2. *About the sibyl Erythrea.*

'It is a fact that, of all the sibyls, Erythrea was the most far-sighted, for her exceptional, god-given talent allowed her to relate and foretell many future events so explicitly that her words seemed to be more like gospel than prophecy. At the request of the Greeks, she recounted in verse form their struggles, battles and eventual destruction of Troy with such clarity that the actual events themselves turned out to be just as she had described them. She also wrote a concise and true account of the Roman empire, the dominion of the Romans and their exploits, long before they all happened. Again, this reads more like a description of past actions than a prophecy about the future.

'Erythrea accomplished an even greater and more marvellous feat in her prediction and revelation of the secret of God's majesty, which is the mystery of the Holy Spirit and the incarnation of the Son of God in the womb of the Virgin Mary, a secret that the prophets had only revealed through the use of obscure figures and cryptic symbols. In her book, she had written "*Jesus Christos Theon nios soter*", which is Greek for "Jesus Christ, Son of God, our saviour". She went on to recount his life and works, his betrayal and capture, his humiliation and death, his resurrection, victory and ascension, as well as the descent of the Holy Spirit on the Apostles, and Jesus's return on the Day of Judgement. Once again, it was as if she had given a succinct account of the mysteries of the Christian faith rather than simply predicting what was to come.

'On the subject of the Day of Judgement, this is what Erythrea wrote: "On that terrible day, as a sign of judgement, the earth will sweat blood. Down from the heavens will come the Lord to judge the whole of humankind as the good and the evil appear before Him. Every soul will rejoin its body and every person will be judged according to their just deserts. Riches and false idols will be as nought. Fire will sweep over everything and all living creatures shall perish. Then, in their distress, the people will give themselves up to weeping, wailing and gnashing their teeth. The sun, moon and stars will grow dark, the mountains and the valleys will be flattened out, and the sea, the earth and all things here below will become as one. The trumpet of the heavens shall sound, calling the human race to judgement. A great terror will fall upon the world as all people bewail their sinfulness. The earth will be created anew as kings, princes and all others appear before the judge and are repaid that which each of them is due. Bolts of lightning will fall from the heavens and set fire to the depths of hell." The sibyl devotes twenty-seven lines to describing these events.

'According to Boccaccio and all the other eminent writers who have mentioned her, her great talents are ample proof that she was loved by God and that she should be honoured above all women except the Christian saints of paradise. She remained a virgin all her life and was also presumably free of all bodily impurity, for it is impossible that such bright knowledge of the future could ever shine in a tainted and sinful heart.'

3. About the sibyl Almathea.

'As I've already mentioned, the sibyl Almathea was born in the region of Campania, which is situated near Rome. This lady was similarly blessed with an exceptional gift of prophecy. According to some history books, she was born at the time of the destruction of Troy and lived up until the reign of Tarquin the Proud. Some called her Deiphebe. Though this lady lived to a ripe old age, she was a virgin all her life. Because of her great knowledge, certain poets claimed that she was loved by Phoebus, whom they called the god of wisdom, and believed that her learning and longevity were gifts from him. This should be interpreted to mean that she was loved by God for her chastity and purity, and that it was He, the radiant source of all wisdom, who lit up within her the light of prophecy which allowed her to predict and describe many future events. In addition, it is written of her that as she stood on the shore of Lake Avernus near Baiae, she received a most marvellous message of divine revelation which she wrote down in the verse which bears her name. Though this revelation is very ancient, it is still an extraordinary testament to the greatness and wisdom of this lady, as anyone who consults it and reads it will see. Some tales tell how she led Aeneas down into the underworld and brought him back out again.

'Almathea came to Rome, carrying nine of her books with her which she offered for sale to King Tarquin. However, since he refused to give her the price she was asking for, she burnt three of the books in front of him. The next day, she asked him for the same price as she had done for the nine books, even though there were now only six left. She informed him that if she didn't receive the sum she wanted, she would burn three more of the books there and then, and the remaining three the following day, whereupon King Tarquin paid her the original price she had requested. The books were kept in a safe place, for it was discovered that they gave a full account of all the deeds that the Romans would go on to accomplish in the future. Moreover, all the great events that subsequently occurred turned out to have been predicted in these books which were carefully stored away in the emperors' treasury and were consulted just as one would a divine oracle.

'So, take note, my sweet friend: see how God showed great favour on this woman, giving her the ability to counsel and advise not just one emperor in her own lifetime but, in a sense, all future Roman rulers, as well as to predict all that the empire itself would go on to accomplish. Indeed, I ask you, was there any man who ever did as much? Yet you, like a fool, used to be very unhappy about belonging to the same sex as creatures such as these, thinking that God despised women!

'Virgil devoted some lines to this sibyl in one of his books. Almathea ended her life in Sicily, where her tomb was kept on display for a very long time.'

4. *About several prophetesses.*

'Yet these ten ladies were not the only ones in the world to whom God granted His great gift of prophecy. Indeed, there have been many of them belonging to all the different religions that have ever existed. If you look at the Jewish faith, you will find many examples, such as Deborah, who was a prophetess at the time of the Judges of Israel. It was thanks to the foresight of this Deborah that God's chosen people were delivered out of the hands of the king of Canaan who had held them in subjection for twenty years.

'Likewise, the blessed Elizabeth, cousin of Our Lady, was no less of a prophet when she said to the glorious Virgin who had gone to visit her: "How is it that the Mother of Our Lord has come to me?" She couldn't have known that Mary had already conceived of the Holy Ghost if she hadn't been moved by the spirit of prophecy.

'This is also the case with Anna, the good Hebrew lady who lit the lamps of the temple. Didn't she too have the gift of prophecy just the same as the prophet Simeon, to whom Our Lady presented Jesus Christ at the altar of the temple on the Feast of Candlemas? The holy seer recognized Jesus as the saviour of the world and took him into his arms, declaring: *"Nunc dimittis"*.[1] As soon as the good lady Anna, who was going about her duty in the temple, saw the Virgin coming through the door with the child in her arms, she too realized intuitively who Jesus was and so knelt down before him to adore him, exclaiming out loud that he was the one who had come to save humankind.

'You'll find plenty of other examples of female prophets if you look carefully in the Jewish faith, as well as countless examples in the Christian religion, several of whom are saints. But let's put them to one side, because you could say that God showed them particular favour, and let's talk about some more pagan women instead.

'The Queen of Sheba was extremely learned and the Holy Scriptures tell how, on hearing about the wisdom of Solomon whose fame had spread far and wide, she conceived a great desire to see him. She therefore left her home in the most remote corner of the lands of the East and rode overland through Ethiopia and Egypt, journeyed along the shores of the Red Sea, and crossed the great deserts of Arabia. She was accompanied with great ceremony by a noble host of princes, lords, knights and ladies, and came laden with many treasures. Arriving at the city of Jerusalem, she went to meet the wise King Solomon in order to see for herself whether what the whole world was saying about him was true. Solomon received her with all honours, as was her due, and she stayed with him for a long while, testing his wisdom in many different areas. She asked him various questions and set him plenty of difficult and obscure riddles, to all of which Solomon answered so fully that she declared that his great wisdom could not have come from mere mortal intelligence but was a special gift from God Himself. This lady made him a present of various costly objects, amongst which were certain small trees which could be tapped for the balm which they gave. Solomon had these trees planted near a lake called Allefabter, giving instructions that they should be cultivated and looked after with great care. She also gave him several precious jewels.

'Some of the writings which describe the wisdom of this woman and her gift of prophecy tell the story of how, when she was in Jerusalem and taken by Solomon to look at the magnificent temple that he had built, she saw a long wooden beam laid across a dirty puddle which was being used as a plank to step over the mud. On seeing the beam, the lady stopped to adore it, saying: "This plank, which is at present being treated as a lowly object fit only to be trodden underfoot, will one day be honoured above all trees in the world and will be adorned with priceless stones from the treasuries of princes. On the wood of this tree will die the man by whose hand the Jewish faith will be destroyed." The Jews did not take her words in jest but carried the plank away to be buried in a place where they thought no one would ever find it. However, what God chooses to safeguard will be safeguarded: the Jews did not manage to prevent the plank from being found again at the time of the passion of Jesus Christ Our Lord. From this tree it is said that they made the cross on which Our Lord met his death and was martyred. Thus this lady's prophecy turned out to be true.'

5. *About Cassandra and Queen Basine, as well as more about Nicostrata.*

'That Nicostrata whom we discussed earlier was also a prophetess. As soon as she crossed the River Tiber and had climbed up on to Mount Palatine with her son Evander, of whom the history books make great mention, she prophesied that on that hill would be built the most famous city that had ever existed, one which would rule over all other earthly kingdoms. In order to be the first person to lay down a founding stone, she constructed a fortress there, as we have said before, and it was on this spot that Rome was founded and subsequently built.

'Likewise, wasn't the noble Trojan maiden Cassandra, daughter of King Priam of Troy and sister of the illustrious Hector, also a prophetess, she who was so learned that she knew all the arts? Having chosen never to take any man for her lord, no matter how high-born a prince he might be, this girl foresaw what would happen to the Trojans and was forever sunk in sorrow. The more she saw the glory of Troy flourish and prosper in the period before the conflict between the Trojans and the Greeks began, the more she wept, wailed and lamented. The sight of the city in all its wealth and magnificence, and of her brothers in all their splendour, especially the noble Hector who was so full of valour, made it impossible for Cassandra to keep to herself all the horror that was to come. On seeing the war break out, her grief intensified and she never left off crying, shrieking and imploring her father and brothers to make peace with the Greeks for heaven's sake, warning them that otherwise the war would destroy every one of them. But her words were all in vain for no one believed her. Moreover, since she refused to be silent but understandably gave full vent to her sorrow at all this destruction and killing, she was often beaten by her father and brothers who told her that she was mad. Yet she never let up for a moment: even if her life depended on it, she would never stop telling them about what was going to happen. In the end, in order to have some peace and to block out the incessant noise she made, they had to shut her up in a distant room far away from other people. However, it would have been better for them if they had believed her, because everything came to pass just as she had said. They eventually regretted what they had done, but by then it was too late.

'Likewise, weren't the prophecies of Queen Basine equally extraordinary, she who had been married to the king of Thuringia and then became the wife of Childeric, the fourth king of France, as the chronicles recall? The story goes that, on her wedding night, she persuaded King Childeric that if he kept himself chaste that night he would receive a marvellous vision. Thereupon she told him to get up and go to the bedroom window and to describe what he could see outside. The king did as she said and it seemed to him that he could see great beasts such as unicorns, leopards and lions coming and going in the palace. Turning round to the queen in terror, he asked her what it all meant. She replied that she would reveal the answer to him in the morning and reassured him that he had nothing to fear but should go back to the window again. This he did, and the second time he thought he saw fierce bears and enormous wolves which seemed to be attacking each other. The queen sent him back to the window a third time and he thought he could see dogs and other small creatures tearing each other to pieces. The king was so horrified and amazed at these things that the queen had to explain to him that the animals he had seen in his vision represented their descendants, the successive generations of French princes who would one day sit on the throne. The different types of animal symbolized what the temperament and behaviour of these various princes would be like.

'So, you can clearly see, my dear Christine, how often God has disclosed His secrets to the world through women.'

6. *About Antonia, who became empress of Constantinople.*

'It was no small secret which God revealed to Justinian, who later became emperor of Constantinople, by means of a woman's vision. This Justinian was keeper of the coffers and treasures of the Emperor Justin. One day, Justinian went out for a walk in the fields, taking with him for company the woman he loved, who was called Antonia. At noon, Justinian wanted to take a nap and so lay down under a tree to sleep with his head resting in his lady's lap. Whilst he was asleep, Antonia saw a great eagle hovering overhead which was stretching out its wings in an effort to protect Justinian's face from the heat of the sun. Being a wise woman, she knew exactly how to interpret this sign. When Justinian woke up, she spoke to him most sweetly, saying to him: "My dearest heart, I love you and have always loved you: being the master of my body and my affection, you know this full well. Since no lover who is so adored by his lady should refuse her anything she asked him, I want you to grant me a favour in return for my virginity and the love which you have received from me, a favour which may seem insignificant to you but which means a great deal to me." Justinian replied that she shouldn't be shy about making her request, since there was nothing he wouldn't give her that was in his power to give. She thus spoke up, "The favour which I ask from you is that when you are emperor, you will not scorn your lover, the poor Antonia, but will faithfully take her in marriage to be your honoured companion who will rule at your side. Please promise me this here and now." When Justinian heard these words, he burst out laughing, for he supposed that she was only joking. Thinking that it was impossible that he should ever become emperor, he vowed that he would not fail to marry her if he did. He swore to this by all the gods, for which she thanked him. As a token of this promise, she made him give her his ring in exchange for hers. She then said to him, "Justinian, believe me when I tell you that you *will* become emperor, and very soon." With that, they took their leave of each other.

'Not long afterwards, it so happened that, having gathered his army together for battle against the Persians, the Emperor Justin fell ill and died. The barons and princes met to choose a new emperor but were unable to come to an agreement. To spite each other, they decided to elect Justinian as emperor. Without a second thought, Justinian launched his army into a furious attack against the Persian enemy. He was triumphant in the battle and took the king of Persia prisoner, thus covering himself in glory and winning the spoils of victory. On his return to the palace, his lover Antonia did not hesitate but made her way in secret to where he sat on his throne surrounded by all the princes. Kneeling down before him, she told him that she was a maiden come to ask him for justice concerning a young man who had betrothed himself to her and exchanged rings with her. The emperor, who had no idea who she was, replied that if it was true that the young man was engaged to her, the law required him to keep his word. He would gladly rule in her favour, if she could prove her case. Antonia took the ring off her finger and held it out to him, exclaiming, "Noble emperor, I can certainly prove it with this ring. See if you recognize it." The emperor realized that he had condemned himself out of his own mouth but chose none the less to keep his promise. He therefore had Antonia taken to his apartments and decked in finery, whereupon he promptly married her.'

7. Christine addresses Lady Rectitude.

'My lady, the more evidence I see and hear which proves that women are innocent of everything that they have been accused of, the more obvious it is to me how in the wrong their accusers are. Yet I can't help myself from mentioning a custom which is quite common amongst men and even some women, which is that when wives are pregnant and give birth to a daughter, their husbands are very often unhappy and disgruntled that they didn't bear them a son. Their silly wives, who should be overjoyed that God has delivered them safely and should thank Him with all their hearts, are also upset because they see that their husbands are distressed. But why is it, my lady, that they are so displeased? Is it because girls are more trouble than boys or less loving and caring towards their parents than male children are?'

Rectitude replied, 'My dear friend, since you've asked me why this happens, I can assure you that those who upset themselves tend to do so out of ignorance and stupidity. However, the main reason why they are unhappy is because they worry how much it's going to cost them to marry off their daughters since they will have to pay for it out of their own pockets. Others, though, are dismayed because they're afraid of the danger that a young and innocent girl can be led astray by the wrong sort of people. Yet neither of these reasons stands up to scrutiny. As for being worried that their daughters will disgrace themselves, all the parents have to do is bring them up properly when they're little, with the mother setting them an example through her own respectable behaviour and good advice; though if the mother has lax morals, she will hardly be a fit example for the daughter to follow. Daughters should be kept on a tight rein away from bad company and taught to fear their parents because bringing infants and children up strictly helps to establish good conduct later in life. Likewise, on the question of the expense involved, I would say that if the parents, whatever social class they may be, looked carefully at what it costs them to set their sons up or to pay for them to study or learn a trade, let alone all the extra money which their sons spend on disreputable acquaintances and unnecessary luxuries, they would soon realize that sons are scarcely less of a financial burden than daughters. Not to mention all the terrible anguish and worry that many sons frequently inflict on their parents by getting into nasty fights and vicious brawls or by falling into depraved habits, all this to the shame of their parents and at their expense. To my mind, this far outweighs any distress that their daughters might cause them.

'See how many names you can cite of sons who actually looked after their aged parents with kindness and consideration, as they should do. Though one can find both past and present examples, they're rather thin on the ground and their assistance comes only at the last minute. What usually happens is that, when they're all grown up, having been treated like a god by their parents and having learnt a trade or studied thanks to their father's help, or become rich and affluent by some stroke of good fortune, if their father falls on hard times or into destitution, they'll turn their backs on him and be ashamed and embarrassed when they see him. If, on the other hand, the father is well off, they can't wait for him to die so that they can get their hands on his estate. God knows how many sons of great lords and wealthy men long for the death of their parents in order to inherit their lands and possessions. Petrarch definitely spoke the truth when he said: "O foolish man, you wish to have children but you can have no deadlier enemies than these. If you are poor, they will despise you and will pray for your death so as to be rid of you. If you are rich, they will pray for it all the more in order to grab your wealth." I don't mean to say that all sons are like this, but many of them are. Moreover, if they're married, God knows how insatiable they can be as they suck their mother and father dry to the extent that they wouldn't care if the poor old things starved to death as long as they can inherit the lot. What dreadful offspring! If their mothers are widowed, instead of comforting them and being a rod and staff to them in their old age, they pay them back terribly for all the love and devotion their mothers have spent on bringing them up. Bad children have the idea that everything should belong to them, so if their mothers don't give them all they want, they don't hesitate to pour down their curses upon them. Heaven knows what kind of respect this is to show one's mother! Worse still, some of them think nothing of taking their mothers to court and bringing a case against them. That's the reward that many parents get for having spent their whole lives putting their money to one side for the benefit of their children. Plenty of sons are like this, and it may be too that some daughters are of the same ilk. But if you look closely, I think you'll find that there are more unworthy sons than daughters.

'Even if all male children *were* dutiful, the fact remains that you see more daughters than sons keeping their mothers and fathers company. They not only visit them more often, but also comfort them and look after them more when they're old and infirm. The reason for this is that boys tend to go out and about in the world whereas girls tend to be retiring and stay closer to home, as you yourself can attest. Though your brothers are very loving and devoted sons, they have gone out into the world whilst you have stayed behind alone to take care of your dear mother and are the main comfort to her in her old age.[2] To sum up, I would say that those who are upset and unhappy at having daughters are completely deluded. Whilst we're on this subject, I'd like to tell you about several women mentioned amongst others in the history books who were very kind and caring towards their parents.'

8. *Here begins a series of daughters who loved their parents, the first of whom is Drypetina.*

'Drypetina, Queen of Laodicea, was very loving towards her father. She was the daughter of the great King Mithradates and was so devoted to him that she followed him into all his battles. This girl was extremely ugly, for she had two sets of teeth, a very severe deformity. However, she loved her father so much that she never left his side, in good times or in bad. Despite the fact that she was the queen and lady of a vast realm, which meant that she could have lived a safe and comfortable life in her own country, she preferred to share her father's sufferings and hardships whenever he went off to war. Even when he was defeated by the mighty Pompey, she still did not abandon him but looked after him with great care and dedication.'

9. About Hypsipyle.

'Hypsipyle placed herself in mortal danger in order to save her father, whose name was Thoas, King of Lemnos. When his subjects rebelled against him and were advancing on the palace in order to kill him, his daughter Hypsipyle promptly hid him in one of her trunks and dashed outside in an attempt to calm the people's rage. All her efforts were in vain: unable to find the king, though they had searched for him all over, they pointed their swords at Hypsipyle and threatened to kill her if she didn't tell them where he was. They also promised her that if she helped them, they would crown her as their queen and be obedient to her. Yet this good and loving daughter, though confronted with death, put more store by her father's life than by being queen and didn't waver for a second. She answered them most courageously, saying that he had undoubtedly long since fled the place. Because they failed to find the king and she managed to convince them so thoroughly that he had already gone, they eventually believed her and made her their queen. For a while, she reigned peaceably over them. However, having kept her father hidden away for some time, she became afraid that she might eventually be betrayed by some jealous courtier. She therefore let him out one night and, having given him plenty of money, sent him off overseas into safety. In the end, her disloyal subjects found out what she had done and deposed her. They would have killed Queen Hypsipyle too if some of them hadn't been moved to pity by her devotion.'

10. *About the virgin Claudine.*

'What a great mark of affection Claudine displayed to her father on his glorious return home from his heroic exploits and many victories in combat as he was being welcomed into Rome with a triumphal procession, that most magnificent of ceremonies and very highest of honours that could be bestowed on a prince who arrived back as the victor of some incredible battle. This Claudine's father, a supremely valiant prince of Rome, was receiving his accolades in the procession when he was suddenly attacked by another Roman lord, one who bore him ill will. His daughter Claudine, a virgin dedicated to the goddess Vesta or, as we would say, a nun who had entered a convent, had gone out into the streets with other ladies from her order to greet this prince, as was the custom. When she heard the clamour and learnt that her father had been set upon by his enemies, the great love she bore him made her put aside the shy, retiring manner that a consecrated virgin should normally adopt and forget any fear of danger. She immediately leapt out of the chariot in which she had been sitting with her companions and dashed through the crowd. She fearlessly thrust herself in front of the swords and blades that had been drawn against her father, seized the man nearest to him by the throat, and struggled to defend her father with all her might. The vast crowd soon intervened to break up the attack. The Romans, who were accustomed to paying tribute to any person who performed a deed worthy of their admiration, honoured this virgin very highly and praised her to the skies for what she had done.'

11. *About a woman who breastfed her mother in prison.*

'The history books tell of a woman from Rome who was equally loving towards her mother. It so happened that the mother was convicted of some crime which she had committed and was condemned to die in prison of thirst and starvation. Full of filial devotion, the daughter was so griefstricken by this sentence that she begged the jailers who were guarding her mother to be allowed to visit her every day until her death in order to help the poor woman endure her fate with patience. In short, she wept and pleaded with the jailers so much that they took pity on her and gave her the right to see her mother once a day. But before they let her in, they subjected her to a rigorous inspection to make sure that she wasn't bringing anything with her for her mother to eat. After a while, it seemed to the jailers that these visits had gone on for far longer than they had expected. Although the mother should have soon died of starvation, she continued somehow to stay alive. Since the only person who visited the prisoner was her daughter, whom they searched thoroughly before allowing into the cell, they were completely baffled as to how the condemned woman managed to survive. One day, the jailers spied on the mother and daughter when they were together and saw the poor girl, who had just recently given birth, offering her breasts to her mother to drink from until all the milk was gone. So it was that the daughter gave back to her mother in her old age what the mother had given her when she was an infant. The daughter's great affection for her mother and her extraordinary devotion to her touched the jailers so deeply that they informed the judges who, in turn, were moved by compassion to set the mother free and send her back home to her daughter.

'On the subject of a daughter's love for her father, we could cite the example of the good and wise Griselda, who later became the marchioness of Saluzzo. I'll tell you more about her great steadfastness, constancy and loyalty later on. It was her deep affection inspired by a faithful heart which made her take such good care of her poor father, Giannucolo, whom she looked after when he was old and sick with true dedication and humility whilst she was still an innocent maiden in the very flower of her youth. Toiling away by the sweat of her brow, she did her utmost to eke out a wretched living for the two of them. Happily, there are great numbers of wonderful daughters who show their parents such affection and devotion as this. Though they're only doing their duty, they none the less reap huge rewards for their soul. They also deserve the highest praise in this life, too, as do those sons who are equally loving.

'What more can I tell you? I could give you countless other examples of this kind, but these will do for now.'

12. *Here Rectitude explains that the houses of the city have been completed and that it is time they were filled with inhabitants.*

'My dearest friend, it seems to me that our building is well underway and that the City of Ladies now has plentiful housing all along its wide streets. The royal palaces are completed and the defence towers and keeps are now standing proud, tall enough to be seen from miles away. It's high time that we began to fill this city with people. It should not stand deserted or empty but should be full of illustrious ladies, as they alone are welcome here. How happy the inhabitants of our city will be! They will have no cause to fear being thrown out of their homes by enemy hordes, for this place has a special property which means that those who move into it will never be dispossessed. A new Realm of Femininia is at hand,[3] except that this one is so much more perfect than the previous one because the ladies who live here will have no need to leave their territory in order to breed the new generations of women who will inherit their realm down the ages. The ladies we're going to invite here will be sufficient in number to last for all time.

'Once we have filled the city with worthy citizens, my sister, Lady Justice, will come bringing with her the queen, a magnificent lady who surpasses all others, accompanied by a host of the noblest princesses. It is they who will occupy the finest buildings and will make their homes in the lofty towers. So it's all the more urgent that, when the queen comes, she should find the city full of excellent ladies ready to receive her with all honours as their supreme mistress and as the empress of their sex. What type of citizens shall we bring? Will they be dissolute women of ill repute? Most certainly not! They will all be valiant ladies of great renown, for we could wish for no worthier population nor more beautiful adornment to our city than such virtuous and honourable women as these. Come now, Christine, let's set out in search of our ladies.'

13. Christine asks Lady Rectitude if it's true what men and books
say about the institution of marriage being unbearable because
women are so impossible to live with. In her reply, Rectitude begins
by discussing the great love that women have for their husbands.

Whilst we were doing as Rectitude had said and were on our way to fetch the ladies we were looking for, I said to her as we walked along, 'My lady, you and Reason have conclusively replied to all the questions and queries that I was unable to answer for myself and I think that I'm now much better informed than I was before on these matters. Thanks to you two, I have discovered that women are more than capable of undertaking any task which requires physical strength or of learning any discipline which requires discernment and intelligence. However, I would now like to ask your opinion about something which is weighing very heavily on my mind. Is it true what so many men say and so many authors in their books claim about it being the fault of women and their shrewish, vengeful nagging that the married state is such a constant hell for men? There are plenty of people who maintain that this is the case, arguing that women care so little for their husbands and their company that there is nothing which irritates them more. In order to avoid this misery and these problems, many authors have advised men to be wise and not to marry at all, on the grounds that there are no women – or hardly any – who are faithful to their spouses. This view is even echoed in the *Letter of Valerius to Ruffinus* which quotes Theophrastus who, in his book, stated that no wise man would take a wife because women cause trouble, lack affection, and gossip incessantly. He also says that if a man gets married thinking that he'll be well looked after and well cared for if he falls ill, he'd be much better off being attended by a loyal servant, who would also cost him a lot less too. If the wife falls ill, on the other hand, he'll be all anxious and will feel obliged not to leave her side. Theophrastus came out with much more in this vein, but I won't go into it any further. My dear lady, if such things are true, it would seem that these faults are so awful that they cancel out completely whatever good qualities or virtues a woman might have.'

Rectitude replied, 'My dear Christine, as you yourself said earlier on this subject, it's certainly easy to win your case when there's no one to argue against you. But believe me when I tell you that the books which put forward these ideas were definitely not written by women. Indeed, I have no doubt that if one wanted to write a new book on the question of marriage by gathering information based on the facts, one would come up with a very different set of views. My dear friend, as you yourself know, there are so many wives who lead a wretched existence bound in marriage to a brutish husband who makes them suffer greater penance than if they were enslaved by Saracens. Oh God, how many fine and decent women have been viciously beaten for no good reason, heaped with insults, obscenities and curses, and subjected to all manner of burdens and indignities, without uttering even a murmur of protest. Not to mention all those wives who are laden down with lots of tiny mouths to feed and lie starving to death in penury whilst their husbands are either out visiting places of depravity or living it up in town or in taverns. All that wives such as these get for supper when their husbands come home is a good hiding. I ask you, am I telling lies? Haven't you ever seen any of your neighbours being treated in this way?'

I replied, 'Yes, my lady. I've seen many women treated like this and I felt sorry for them.'

'I can well believe it. As for those husbands who are anxious when their wives fall ill, I ask you, my dear friend, do you know of any? Without going into further detail, let me tell you that all this rubbish that has ever been said and written about wives is just a string of falsehoods tied together. It is the husband who is the master of the wife, and not the other way round. A man would never allow himself to be dominated by a woman. However, let me assure you that not all marriages are like this. There are some married couples who love each other, are faithful to each other, and live together in peace: in these cases it is both spouses who are sensible, kind and gentle. Though there are bad husbands, there are also some who are decent, honourable and wise. The women who have the good fortune to marry them should thank God for giving them so much happiness here on this earth. You yourself can attest to this since you couldn't have wished for a better husband than you had. In your opinion, he surpassed all other men in kindness, gentleness, loyalty and affection, and you will never stop grieving for his death in your heart. Whilst it's undeniable that there are many fine women who are badly treated by their contrary husbands, it's also true to say that some wives *are* wilful and unreasonable. Indeed, if I claimed that all wives were paragons of virtue, I would quite rightly be accused of being a liar. However, these women are in the minority. Anyway, I'd rather not discuss such women because they're like creatures who go totally against their nature.

'Talking about good wives instead, let's go back to what that Theophrastus, whom you mentioned earlier, said about a sick man being as well looked after and as faithfully attended by a servant as by a wife. You see countless good and loyal wives who serve their husbands in sickness or in health with as much loving care as if they were gods! I don't think you're going to find many servants like that. Since we're on this subject, I'll now give you some examples of wives who adored their husbands and were utterly devoted to them. Now, thank the Lord, we can come back to our city with a fine host of decent and respectable ladies whom we can invite inside. Here is the noble Queen Hypsicratea, who was once wife of the mighty King Mithradates. Because she belongs to such ancient times and is of such inestimable worth, she shall be the first to take her place in the magnificent palace which has been prepared for her.'

14. *About Queen Hypsicratea.*

'How could anyone show more love for another person than the beautiful Hypsicratea did for her husband, she who was so kind and loyal? This lady was the wife of the great King Mithradates who ruled over lands where twenty-four different languages were spoken. Despite the fact that this king was the most powerful on earth, the Romans waged a terrible war on him. In all the time that he was engaged in his lengthy and arduous battles, his good wife never left him, no matter where he went. As was the barbarian custom, this king also had several concubines. However, this noble lady bore her husband such a deep love that she refused to let him go anywhere without her and frequently went off with him into battle. Though the fate of the kingdom was at stake and the threat of death at the hands of the Romans ever present, she travelled everywhere with him to far-off places and strange lands, crossing seas and perilous deserts and never once failing to be his faithful companion at his side. Her affection for him was so strong that she deemed that no man could possibly serve her lord with such perfect loyalty as she could.

'So, contrary to what the philosopher Theophrastus says on the subject, this lady was well aware that kings and princes can often have disloyal servants who serve them badly. Therefore, like the faithful lady she was, she devoted herself to ensuring that her lord's every possible need was met. Though she had to endure many hardships, she followed him through thick and thin. Since it was impractical for her to wear women's clothing in these conditions, and it was thought improper that the wife of such a great king and warrior should be seen at his side in battle, she cut off her finest womanly attribute, her long, golden hair, in order to disguise herself as a man. Neither did she give a thought to protecting her complexion, for she strapped on a helmet and her face soon grew dirty from all the sweat and dust. Her lovely, graceful body she clad in armour and weighed down with a coat of chainmail. She took off all her precious rings and costly jewellery and instead roughened her hands from carrying heavy axes and spears, as well as a bow and arrows. Round her waist she wore no elegant girdle but a sword. Because of the great love and loyalty she bore her husband, this lady so thoroughly adapted herself to her new surroundings that her charming and delicate young body, which was made for softer and more pleasurable living, was transformed into that of a strong and powerfully built knight-in-arms. Listen to what Boccaccio says in his version of the story: "Is there anything that love cannot accomplish? Here we see this lady, who was used to the finer things in life such as a soft bed and every possible comfort, choosing of her own free will to make herself as tough and rugged as any man, journeying over hill and dale, travelling by day and night, bedding down in deserts and forests often on the hard ground, in perpetual fear of the enemy and surrounded on all sides by wild beasts and serpents." Yet all this seemed agreeable to her as long as she could be at her husband's side to comfort and advise him, seeing to his every need.

'Later on, after having suffered many great hardships together, her husband was cruelly defeated by Pompey, a prince of the Roman army, and had to take flight. Though he was abandoned by all his men, his wife alone stayed with him, following him as he fled across mountains and valleys and through many dark and dangerous places. On the point of despair at having been deserted and forsaken by all his friends, the king was comforted by his faithful wife who gently encouraged him to hope for better days to come. Even when they were at their lowest ebb, she still made every effort to bring him good cheer and to lift his spirits by finding the right words to dispel his sadness and by inventing some amusing and distracting games for them to play together. By means of these things and her great kindness, she brought him such consolation that no matter how downcast or dejected he was, or how much suffering he had to bear, she found a way to make him forget his unhappiness. He was often moved to say that he didn't feel like he was in exile but rather as if he were at home in his palace having a delightful time with his devoted wife.'

15. *About the Empress Triaria.*

'Another lady who can be likened to Queen Hypsicratea for the similar circumstances in which she found herself and for the great affection which she bore her husband was the noble Empress Triaria, wife of Lucius Vitellius, Emperor of Rome. This lady loved him so deeply that she followed him everywhere, dressed like a knight, riding next to him at all times and fighting with great courage and valour.

'In the course of the war for control of the empire, which he was waging against Vespasian, the emperor besieged the city of the Volscians and managed to slip into it at night, launching a ruthless attack on the sleeping inhabitants. The noble lady Triaria, who had been following her husband every step of the way, did not now hold back. Instead, in order to ensure her husband's victory, she armed herself to the teeth and engaged in fierce combat at his side all along the streets, rushing here and there through the darkness. Feeling neither fear nor terror, she fought so hard that she distinguished herself above all others in the battle, accomplishing many extraordinary feats. Boccaccio comments that she thus clearly showed how much she loved her lord, and he expresses his approval of the bond between husband and wife which others have seen fit to criticize so heavily.'

16. *More about Queen Artemisia.*

'On the subject of ladies who bore a great love for their husbands, which they were not loath to display through their actions, we must once more cite that noble lady Artemisia, Queen of Caria. As we said before, after she had followed him into many battles, she lost her husband, King Mausolus, which was a terrible blow that left her utterly distraught and griefstricken. Just as she had shown throughout his life how much she loved him, she was determined to do no less at his death. Once she had completed all the funeral rites which were customary for a king, she had his body burnt on a huge pyre in front of a great assembly of princes and barons. She herself gathered together his ashes which she washed with her tears and placed in a golden vessel. It seemed to her that there was no reason why the remains of the person she had loved so deeply should have any other sepulchre than that of the heart and body in which this love had first taken root. She therefore mixed his ashes with some liquid and drank them down, little by little, over a period of time until she had swallowed every last drop.

'Having performed these rites, Artemisia none the less wanted to create a sepulchre for her husband which would preserve his memory for ever. She spared no expense as she sent for a number of craftsmen who were extremely skilled at planning and building great monuments. Their names were Scopas, Bryaxis, Timotheus and Leochares, all of whom were supremely gifted architects. The queen told them that she wished to create a sepulchre for her lord, King Mausolus, which would be the most splendid tomb of any prince or king and so magnificent that her husband's name would never die. They replied that they would gladly undertake the task. Artemisia ordered vast quantities of marble and jasper of many different colours to be provided, as well as all the other materials which they would need. The monument which these craftsmen constructed outside the walls of Halicarnassus, the capital city of Caria, was a huge building of exquisitely sculpted marble. Square in shape, it was 64 feet wide with walls 140 feet high. Even more spectacular still were the thirty great marble columns on which it rested. The four craftsmen, who were each responsible for one of the four sides, had outdone each other in their efforts to create a shrine which not only commemorated the name of him to whom it was dedicated but also attested to their great architectural genius. A fifth craftsman, by the name of Ytheron, was brought in to finish off the sepulchre with a great pyramid, which thus increased the height of the building by forty steps. After him came a sixth craftsman, Pythius, who carved a marble statue of a chariot which was placed on the very top of the pyramid.

'This monument was so extraordinary that it became known as one of the seven wonders of the world. Since it had been built for King Mausolus, it took its name from him and was called a "mausoleum". According to Boccaccio, because it was the most wonderful sepulchre that had ever been created for any prince or king, all other royal tombs thereafter were known as mausoleums. Thus it was that Artemisia's actions displayed and symbolized the true love that she felt for her noble husband, a love which lasted as long as she lived.'

17. *About Argia, daughter of King Adrastus.*

'Who could dare to claim that women have little love for their spouses when they consider the example of the lady Argia, daughter of Adrastus, King of Argos, who dearly loved her husband Polynices? This Polynices, who was married to Argia, was locked in a struggle with his brother Eteocles for control of the great kingdom of Thebes which, according to certain agreements they had drawn up between them, rightfully belonged to him. However, since Eteocles wanted to seize the entire kingdom for himself, his brother Polynices declared war on him, backed by his father-in-law King Adrastus and all the latter's troops. But the tide of fortune turned against Polynices: he and his brother killed each other in combat and all the troops were wiped out except for King Adrastus, the only one of the three princes who survived.

'On hearing that her husband had been killed in the battle, Argia ran out of the royal palace and left the city accompanied by all the other ladies of Argos. Boccaccio describes what she did next in the following words: "The noble lady Argia learnt that the dead body of her husband, Polynices, was lying unburied alongside the corpses of all the common soldiers who had also been killed. With a grieving heart, she stripped off her royal robes and finery and turned her back on the comforts and elegance of her luxurious quarters. Her great love and burning desire made her put aside all feminine weakness and sensibility as she set out for the site where the battle had taken place. The journey took several days but she didn't fear being attacked by treacherous enemies nor did she grow weary from the great distance involved or from the intense heat of the sun. When she arrived at the battlefield, she remained unperturbed by the sight of all the wild beasts and enormous birds which had been attracted by the dead bodies. Nor was she frightened by the evil spirits which some foolish people claim hover round men's corpses. What is even more astonishing," says Boccaccio, "is that she took no notice of an edict that King Creon had issued which forbade anyone, on pain of death, to go looking for the bodies or to bury them, an edict which applied to all the dead men without exception." However, Argia had not gone all that way just to obey Creon's edict, so, as night began to fall, she set about her business at the battlefield. Driven by her terrible grief and undaunted by the dreadful stench which rose up from the corpses, she began straightaway to examine each body one after the other in her search for the man she loved. Working by the light of a burning torch which she held in her hand, she did not stop until she recognized her beloved husband and found what she was looking for. Boccaccio exclaims, "What extraordinary love and utter devotion this woman showed!" Her husband's face, all blackened and discoloured, was half eaten away by the rust of his helmet and terribly decayed. It was all spattered with blood, coated with dust, and encrusted with filth. Yet, out of the deep love she bore him, she managed to identify him even though he was barely recognizable. Neither the stench of his body nor the foulness of his face could stop her from covering him in kisses and hugging him to her breast. She showed no concern for King Creon's edict as she shouted out, "Alas! Alas! I've found the one I loved!", and wept copious tears. After having kissed him several times on the mouth to check if there was any sign of life in him, she washed his rotting limbs with her tears as she called out for him again and again, sobbing, moaning and crying all the while. In order to perform the last and saddest rite of all, she burnt his body on a pyre and devotedly gathered up his ashes in a golden vessel. When she had done all this, she resolved to risk her life to avenge her husband's death. She and the many other ladies who helped her were so determined that they managed to capture the city and break through the walls, putting all those inside to death.'

18. *About the noble lady Agrippina.*

'A woman who deserves to be ranked amongst all the other splendid ladies who were greatly devoted to their husbands was the good and faithful Agrippina, daughter of Marcus Agrippa and of Julia, daughter of the Emperor Octavian who was ruler of the entire world. This honourable lady was given in marriage to Germanicus, a very noble and fine prince, full of wisdom, who dedicated himself to the welfare of the people of Rome. Unfortunately, Tiberius, a man of evil ways who was emperor at that time, grew envious of the lady Agrippina's husband, Germanicus, because of his good reputation and the love that everyone bore him, and had him attacked and murdered. Agrippina, his devoted wife, was so anguished at Germanicus's death that she too wanted to be killed. She did all she could to bring this about, screaming such terrible curses at Tiberius that he had her beaten, tortured and thrown into prison. Her grief at the loss of her husband was so great that she preferred to die rather than live, and decided to refuse all food and drink. When Tiberius heard about Agrippina's resolve, he was determined to force-feed her in order to prolong torturing her. But his efforts were all in vain. Though he tried to make her swallow food, she showed him that even if he had the power to put a person to death, he did not have the power to keep someone alive against their will, for this was how she died.'

19. *Christine addresses Rectitude, who replies to her with several examples, telling her about the noble lady Julia, daughter of Julius Caesar and wife of the prince Pompey.*

As Lady Rectitude was recounting these things to me, I spoke up, saying: 'My lady, it certainly seems to me that it is a great honour to the female sex to hear the stories of so many virtuous women. Amongst all their other qualities, it must be particularly gratifying for everyone to see that women are capable of such tremendous affection in marriage. Matheolus and all those other scribblers who have been driven by envy to utter such lies about women should keep their mouths shut and go back to sleep! However, my lady, I've just remembered something that the philosopher Theophrastus, whom I mentioned earlier, said about women hating their husbands when they're old and despising men who are scholars or clerks. He claimed that it is impossible to reconcile all the attention that you have to give to a woman with the time needed to study books.'

Rectitude replied, 'Come now, Christine, hold your tongue! I can immediately find plenty of examples which contradict these opinions and disprove them completely.

'In her time, Julia was the noblest of Roman ladies, being the daughter of Julius Caesar who later became emperor, and of Cornelia, his wife, who were both descended from Aeneas and Venus of Troy. She was married to the great warrior, Pompey. According to Boccaccio, this Pompey, though now elderly and decrepit, was at the height of his glory. He had spent his life defeating kings, deposing them and choosing their successors, subjugating countries to his will and destroying pirates, earning the respect of Rome and of the rulers of all other nations, as well as conquering new territories on both land and sea, all thanks to his extraordinary prowess. Despite the fact that his wife, the great lady Julia, was still a very young woman, she loved her husband so deeply and so truly that she met her death in a very unusual way. It so happened that, one day, Pompey went to make a sacrifice, as was the custom in those times, in order to thank the gods for the marvellous victories that he had won. During the ritual, Pompey was holding on to one side of the slaughtered animal as it was being laid on the altar, when his robes became splattered with blood from the creature's wound. He therefore took off the robe which he was wearing and sent one of his servants back to the house with it to fetch him a fresh, clean one.

'As luck would have it, the servant who was carrying the robe ran into Julia, Pompey's wife, who saw her lord's clothing all covered in blood. Knowing that those who distinguished themselves in Rome were often the target of the envy of others who attacked and sometimes killed them, the dramatic sight of her husband's blood convinced her that some ill must have befallen him. She was seized by a great pain in her heart as if she had suddenly lost all will to live. Being pregnant at the time, she fell to the floor in a faint, all colour drained from her body and her eyes turned up in their sockets. It all happened so quickly that there was no time to give her any help or to allay her fears before she expired. As would be expected, her death was a devastating blow to her husband. Yet it was not only a source of anguish to him and to the Romans, but to the whole world as well at that time. If she and her child had lived, the bitter war which broke out between Julius Caesar and Pompey, a war which had dreadful consequences in every country of the world, would never have taken place.'

20. *About the noble lady Tertia Aemilia.*

'Neither did the kind and beautiful Tertia Aemilia, wife of Scipio Africanus the Elder, love her husband any less for his being old. She was also an extremely prudent and virtuous lady. Though she was still young and lovely, her husband was already an old man. None the less, he used to sleep with one of her servants, a handmaiden of hers, on such a regular basis that his wife eventually found out. Despite the hurt she felt, she didn't give way to her pangs of jealousy but acted wisely, betraying no sign to her husband or to anybody else that she had discovered what was going on. She chose not to say anything about it to him because she thought that it would be improper to criticize such a great man as he. It was even more unthinkable to disclose it to a third party, for that would diminish and undermine the reputation of this fine man and would cast a slur on his character, he who had conquered so many kingdoms and empires. So the good lady continued to love, serve and honour him just as much as before. On his death, she gave the woman her freedom and married her off to a free man.'

I, Christine, replied: 'Now that you mention it, my lady, it occurs to me that I've definitely seen other women act like this. No matter what it is they find out, they carry on loving their husbands and being pleasant to them, even helping and looking after the women their husbands make pregnant, despite the fact that their husbands are so disloyal to them. In particular, I've heard about a lady from Brittany, the countess of Coëmen, who died recently whilst still in the flower of her youth: she was the loveliest of women and acted just like this with exemplary kindness and loyalty.'

21. *About Xanthippe, wife of the philosopher Socrates.*

'The honourable lady Xanthippe was a very wise and virtuous woman who married the great philosopher Socrates. Though he was already very old and spent more time poring over his books than buying his wife little treats and presents, the good lady never stopped loving him. Indeed, she thought so highly of his extraordinary wisdom, as well as his great goodness and steadfastness, that she loved him very deeply and took enormous pride in him. When the brave and noble Xanthippe learnt that the Athenians had sentenced her husband to death for having attacked their practice of worshipping idols and for claiming that there was only one god whom they should honour and serve, she was unable to control her emotions. Rushing out into the street with her hair all undone and racked with sobbing, she fought her way into the palace where her husband was being held and found him surrounded by the treacherous judges who were already handing him the cup of poison that would end his life. She came into the room just as Socrates had raised the cup to his lips and was about to drink the poison, whereupon she dashed it from his hands and spilt all the liquid on to the floor. Socrates chided her for this and tried to comfort her by telling her to have patience. Unable to do anything to prevent his death, she gave full vent to her sorrow, crying, "What a crime and a great loss it is to kill such a good man! What a sin and an injustice!" Socrates kept on trying to console her, explaining that it was better to be wrongfully put to death than to have deserved one's punishment. So he died, but throughout the rest of her life his loving wife never stopped grieving for him in her heart.'

22. About Pompeia Paulina, Seneca's wife.

'Despite being very old and totally preoccupied with his studies, the wise philosopher Seneca was greatly loved by his young and beautiful wife, who was called Pompeia Paulina. This noble lady's only thoughts were of serving her husband and of creating a tranquil place for him to work, for she loved him dearly and with great loyalty. When she learnt that the tyrant, the Emperor Nero, who had been Seneca's pupil, had sentenced his old teacher to bleed to death in a bath, she went out of her mind with anguish. Wanting to die along with her husband, she went and screamed obscenities at Nero in order to make him punish her in the same way. All her efforts were in vain, but she was so struck down with grief at her husband's death that she only outlived him by a short time.'

I, Christine, interrupted Rectitude, saying, 'Most worthy lady, your words have certainly made me think of many other examples of young and beautiful women who adored their husbands even though they were old and ugly. In my own lifetime, I've seen plenty of women who cherished their lords and were loyal and loving towards them for the whole of their lives. One such noble lady, the daughter of one of the great barons of Brittany, was given in marriage to the valiant Constable of France, my lord Bertrand du Guesclin. Though he was old and physically very ugly whilst this lady was in the flower of her youth, she none the less set greater store by his virtuous qualities than by his appearance, loving him so deeply that she grieved for his death as long as she lived. I could cite many other similar cases but I'll leave it there for now.'

Rectitude replied, 'I can well believe it. I'll now tell you more about women who were devoted to their husbands.'

23. *About the noble Sulpicia.*

'Sulpicia was the wife of Lentulus Cruscellio, a Roman nobleman, who clearly showed just how much she loved her husband. The judges of Rome sentenced him to spend the rest of his life in exile and poverty for certain crimes of which he had been accused. Despite being a very wealthy Roman lady who could have carried on living in the lap of luxury, surrounded by every comfort, the devoted Sulpicia preferred to follow her husband into penury and banishment rather than lead a pampered existence without him. She thus decided to give up all her inheritance and possessions and leave her native land. Her family put her under close guard but she managed to give them the slip by disguising herself and going off to join her husband.'

I, Christine, said, 'Yes, my lady, it occurs to me from what you've been saying about these women that I too have seen similar cases amongst my contemporaries. There are some I've known whose husbands have fallen ill with leprosy and had to be isolated from the world and sent to a leper colony. Their honourable wives have refused to leave them, preferring to go and look after them in their sickness and to respect the marriage vows they have sworn rather than stay behind in their comfortable houses without their husbands. Right now I know of one woman, a kind, young and lovely person, whose husband is suspected of having this illness. Though her parents are advising and urging her to leave him and live with them, she has told them that if he is taken to a doctor and found to have the disease, which will mean that he will have to be sent away, she intends to go with him. Her parents have had to agree to let him be seen by a doctor.

'Likewise, I know of other women, though I'll not give you their names because they might not want me to, whose husbands are so despicable and degenerate in their ways that the wives' parents wish they were dead and try everything they can to persuade their daughters to leave their dreadful husbands and to live with them instead. Yet these women do not abandon their husbands, preferring to be beaten and badly fed, to go penniless and be treated like drudges by them, saying to their family, "Since you chose him for me, I intend to live and die at his side." Such things are everyday occurrences, but no one remarks upon it.'

24. *About several ladies who, together, saved their husbands from execution.*

'Along with all these ladies who dearly loved their husbands, I want to tell you about one particular group of women. It so happened that, after Jason had gone to Colchis to win the Golden Fleece, some of the knights he had brought with him, who were originally from a town in Greece called Orchomenos, decided to leave their native land and settle in another Greek city by the name of Lacedaemonia. They were welcomed with great honour, as much for their noble lineage as for their great wealth. There they married various high-born girls of the city. They increased their fortune and status so rapidly and became so swollen with pride that they decided to plot against the rulers of the city and to seize power for themselves. However, their plans were discovered and they were thrown into prison and sentenced to death. Their wives were devastated by what had happened and they gathered together as if to meet in mourning, though in fact it was to see if they could find a way to save their husbands.

'In the end, they agreed amongst themselves that they would all dress up one night in their oldest clothes, wrapping their faces in cloaks so as not to be recognized. They then went off to the prison dressed like this and, with tears in their eyes, bribed the guards with gifts and promised rewards to let them see their husbands. Once they were alone with them, they made their husbands put on their clothes whilst they took the ones that the men had been wearing. They then sent their husbands out and the guards mistook them for the women leaving to go home. On the day that the prisoners were due to be killed, the jailers came to take them to the place of execution. When it was discovered that it was the wives of the condemned men, everyone was amazed by their clever trick and sang their praises. The townspeople took pity on their daughters, all of whom were spared. Thus these brave ladies saved their husbands from death.'

25. *Christine speaks to Lady Rectitude about those who claim that women cannot keep a secret. In her reply, Rectitude talks about Portia, Cato's daughter.*

'My lady, I am now totally convinced of what I have often seen for myself: many women of both the past and the present have clearly shown their husbands how much they love them and are devoted to them. That's why I'm so puzzled by a saying which is very common amongst men, including Master Jean de Meun in his *Romance of the Rose*, as well as other writers, that a man should avoid telling a woman anything which he wants kept secret because women are incapable of keeping their mouths shut.'

Rectitude replied, 'My dear friend, as you are aware, not all women are necessarily very wise and neither are all men. Therefore, if a man has any sense, he should judge for himself if his wife is trustworthy and well-meaning before he tells her anything in confidence, because it could have dangerous consequences. Any man who knows that his wife is dependable, careful and discreet can rest assured that there is no other creature in the world whom he can trust more implicitly nor on whom he can rely so completely.

'On the question of whether women are as indiscreet as some maintain, we also come back to the issue of wives who loved their husbands. The noble Brutus of Rome, who was married to Portia, certainly did not subscribe to this opinion. This fine lady, Portia, was the daughter of Cato the Younger, the nephew of Cato the Elder. Knowing how wise and virtuous she was, her husband did not hesitate to tell her that he and Cassius, another Roman nobleman, planned to kill Julius Caesar in the senate. However, foreseeing that this deed would have terrible repercussions, the sensible lady did her best to dissuade her husband from carrying out his plan. She was so disturbed by the thought of what he intended to do that she was unable to sleep at all that night. The next morning, as Brutus left the bedroom to go off and execute his plan, in a desperate attempt to stop him, Portia seized a barber's razorblade as if to clip her fingernails with it and dropped it on the floor. She then reached down to pick it up again and deliberately dug it deep into her hand. Horrified by the sight of her wound, her ladies screamed so loudly that Brutus turned back. When he saw how she had cut herself, he scolded her and told her that it was a barber's job to use the razor, not hers. She replied that she hadn't acted as stupidly as he might think: she had done it on purpose in order to find out how to kill herself, should any harm come to him after he had carried out his plan. Still refusing to change his mind, Brutus left the house. Soon after, he and Cassius together killed Julius Caesar. They were sent into exile for what they had done and Brutus was subsequently murdered, even though he had already been banished from Rome. When his wife, Portia, learnt of his death, she was so distraught that she had no further desire to live. Since all the sharp instruments and knives had been taken away from her, because it was obvious what she intended to do, she went over to the fire and swallowed some live coals instead. The noble Portia thus killed herself by burning her insides, truly the strangest death that anyone has ever suffered.'

26. On the same subject: about the noble lady Curia.

'I'll give you some more examples which refute what those men say about women being unable to keep secrets, examples which are also part of the series of wives who bore a great love for their husbands.

'Curia, a noble lady of Rome, who was as wise as she was loving, showed exemplary loyalty and devotion towards her husband, Quintus Lucretius. He and a group of other men were condemned to death for a certain crime of which they had been accused. Fortunately, they got wind of the fact that a warrant was out for their arrest and they all had time to make their escape. For fear of being discovered, they went to hide in some caves lived in by wild beasts, although even there they didn't dare make a proper shelter for themselves. Lucretius was the only one who, instead, heeded his wife's sensible advice and decided not to budge from his bedroom. When the men who were searching for him burst into the chamber, his wife wrapped her arms around him in bed and managed to hide him so convincingly that they didn't realize he was there. She found a cunning hideaway for him in between the walls of

the bedroom and none of her servants nor anyone else ever found him.
She also cleverly covered her tracks by running up and down the streets,
in and out of temples and churches, dressed in rags and with her hair
all unkempt and face streaked with tears, wringing her hands as if she
had lost her mind from grief. She rushed around searching everywhere
for someone who might tell her what had happened to her husband or
where he had gone, saying that wherever he was, she wanted to join him
in exile and share his hardships. She put on such a convincing act that
nobody ever guessed the truth. This was how she saved her husband
and consoled him in his terrible distress. In short, she was able to deliver
him from both exile and death.'

27. More on this subject.

'Now that we've started to discuss examples which disprove what certain
men have said about women being unable to hold their tongues, I could
certainly give you countless more examples but will limit myself to just
one.

'At the time when the mighty Emperor Nero ruled over Rome, there
was a group of men who thought that they would be doing the city a
great service if they killed the emperor because of all the terrible atrocities
and outrages he was committing. They decided to plot against him and
to plan how best to assassinate him. These men met at the house of a
woman whom they trusted so implicitly that they didn't worry about
discussing their plot in front of her. One night, when they had made up
their minds that they were going to execute their plan the next day, they
were eating at this lady's house but didn't watch carefully enough what
they were saying. Unfortunately, they were spied on by someone who
wanted to ingratiate himself with the emperor and so went straight to
Nero to tell him exactly what he had overheard. The conspirators had
scarcely left the woman's house when the emperor's officers arrived at
her door. Finding none of the men there, they took the woman to the
emperor, who questioned her at great length about the plot. However,
Nero was unable to make her tell him who the men were or even admit
that she knew anything about it either by promising her rewards or by

submitting her to prolonged torture. She thus proved herself to be extremely loyal and trustworthy.'

28. *Proof against those who claim that only an idiot takes his wife's advice or puts his trust in her. Christine asks some questions to which Rectitude replies.*

'My lady, having heard your arguments and seen for myself how sensible and dependable women are, I'm amazed that some people claim that only a stupid idiot listens to his wife and trusts her advice.'

Rectitude replied, 'I pointed out to you earlier that not all women are wise. However, those men who do have responsible, trustworthy wives are fools if they refuse to put their faith in them. You can see this from what I've just told you: if Brutus had let Portia persuade him not to assassinate Julius Caesar, he himself would not have been killed and he could have avoided causing all the harm that was subsequently done. Whilst we're on this subject, I'll tell you about certain other men who suffered the consequences of not listening to their spouses. Afterwards, I'll go on to give you some examples where the husbands did well to take their wives' advice.

'If Julius Caesar, whom we've just mentioned, had trusted his sensible and intelligent wife, who had seen various signs foretelling her husband's assassination and had a terrible dream about it the night before, which made her do everything she could to try to stop him from going to the senate that day, he would not have gone and met his death.

'The same can be said of Pompey, who first married Julia, daughter of Julius Caesar, as I told you before, and then took as his second wife another noble lady, by the name of Cornelia. Going back to what we were talking about earlier, this lady loved her husband so dearly that she refused to leave him, no matter what misfortune befell him. Even when he was forced to escape by sea after having been defeated in battle by Julius Caesar, this good lady Cornelia went with him and faced every danger at his side. When Pompey arrived at the kingdom of Egypt, the treacherous King Ptolemy pretended that he was glad to receive him, sending his people ahead to welcome Pompey although in fact their mission was to kill him. These people told Pompey to get back on board ship and leave everybody else ashore so as to lighten the vessel of its load and thus manoeuvre it more easily into port. Pompey was happy to comply with their wishes but his loyal wife tried to dissuade him from separating himself from all his men by doing so. Seeing that he wasn't going to change his mind, she tried to jump back on to the ship with him because she suspected deep down that something was amiss. However, he wouldn't allow her to do so and had to have her held back by force. That was the point at which all this lady's sorrow began, a sorrow which was to haunt her all her life. No sooner had her husband sailed only a short way out than, having never taken her eyes off him for a second, she saw him being killed by the traitors on board. She was so distraught that she would have thrown herself into the sea if she hadn't been restrained.

'Likewise, the same sort of misfortune struck the worthy Hector of Troy. The night before he was killed, his wife Andromache had a most extraordinary dream which told her that if Hector went into battle the next day he would surely lose his life. Horrified by what she took to be not simply a nightmare but a true prophecy,[4] this lady went down on her knees and begged her husband with hands joined together in supplication not to join the fighting that day, even bringing their two lovely children before him in her arms. However, he took no notice of her words, thinking that he would bring irreparable dishonour on himself if he allowed a woman's advice to stop him from going into combat. Neither was he moved by his mother's and father's entreaties after Andromache had asked them to intercede on her behalf. It thus all happened exactly as she had said and it would have been better for Hector if he had listened to her because he was killed by Achilles in battle.

'I could give you endless other examples of men who came to harm in various ways for not deigning to take their good wives' sensible advice. However, those who met a bad end because they dismissed what their wives had to say have only themselves to blame.'

29. *About various men who did well to trust their wives' advice.*

'I'll give you some examples of men who came to good because they did what their wives advised them to do. These should suffice as proof, although I could cite you so many cases that my testimony would be endless! What I have to tell you also backs up what I said earlier about ladies who were prudent and reliable.

'The Emperor Justinian, whom I mentioned to you before, had a baron who was his companion-in-arms and whom he loved as dearly as himself. This fine, brave knight was called Belisarius. The emperor had him appointed commander-in-chief of his knights and invited him to sit at his table where he was served as royally as Justinian himself. In short, the emperor showed him so much favour that the other barons grew extremely envious of him. They therefore informed the emperor that Belisarius intended to assassinate him and seize control of the empire for himself. The emperor believed their words all too readily and, in order to find a covert way of having Belisarius killed, he ordered him to lead an attack against a people called the Vandals who were so fierce that no one had yet defeated them. On receiving this order, Belisarius understood only too well that the emperor would never have given him this task if he had not fallen heavily out of favour and lost his good will. He was so devastated when he realized this that he was unable to do anything but go back to his house.

'When his wife Antonia, who was the emperor's sister, saw her husband stretched out on his bed, lying there pale and preoccupied and with tears in his eyes, her heart went out to him and she wouldn't let him be until he had told her why he was in such distress. Once she heard what had happened, this clever lady pretended to be very joyful and consoled him, saying, "What, is that all that's on your mind? Don't be upset!" It's important to remember that, at that time, the Christian faith was still very new because, being a Christian, the good Antonia said to her husband, "Have faith in Jesus Christ who died on the cross, and he will help you to perform your duty. If those who are jealous of you want to hurt you with their falsehoods, let your virtuous actions prove them all liars and cheats. Don't dismiss what I say, but take my advice and put your trust in the living God and I promise you that you will be victorious. However, be careful not to show that you are at all apprehensive about this mission, and make sure that you appear to be happy and delighted to do it, not downcast in any way. This is what we'll do: we'll gather your troops together as quickly as possible. See to it that no one knows what direction you're heading for and that you have plenty of ships standing by. Then, split your army into two halves. As swiftly and as stealthily as you can, lead your half off to Africa and launch an immediate assault on the enemy. I'll take the other half and we'll come in from the sea and attack them from the rear. Whilst they're busy fighting with you, we'll head for the towns and cities behind them, setting fire to everything and killing everyone in sight. We'll soon destroy the lot of them." Belisarius wisely took his wife's advice and did exactly as she said, organizing his expedition so well that he crushed the enemy completely and took the king of the Vandals as his prisoner. It was all due to his wife's sound advice, not to mention her cleverness and bravery, that he won a great victory which made the emperor love him even more than before.

'It so happened that Belisarius lost the emperor's favour a second time, once again due to the false reports of the jealous barons. On this occasion, he was completely stripped of his military rank but his wife comforted him and told him to take heart. The emperor himself was eventually deposed by these barons, whereupon Belisarius took his wife's advice and did everything in his power to fight to reinstate the ruler on his throne, even though he had suffered a great wrong at the emperor's hands. Thus the emperor discovered how loyal his knight was and how treacherous the others were, all thanks to this astute lady's intelligence and good counsel.

'Likewise, King Alexander did not scorn the wise words uttered by his wife, the queen, who was the daughter of Darius, king of the Persians. Racked with intense pain, Alexander realized that he had been poisoned by his disloyal servants and was on the verge of throwing himself into the river to end his torment when his wife came up to him. Though she was stricken with grief, she began to comfort him, advising him to go home and lie down on his bed where he could talk with his barons and give his last orders, as befitted an emperor of his stature. His honour would be greatly diminished if, after his death, it was said of him that he had given in to a lack of composure. He took his wife's advice and gave his orders, just as she had told him to do.'

30. *Christine talks about all the good that women have brought into the world, both now and in the past.*

'My lady, though I can see that women have brought countless good things into the world, these men still claim that they have brought only evil.'

Rectitude replied, 'My sweet friend, you can tell by what I've already explained to you that the opposite of what they say is true. No man can match the great services that women have done and continue to do for humanity. I proved this to you by the examples of those noble ladies who invented different arts and sciences. However, if what I've said about the earthly benefits that they have brought is not enough for you, let me tell you about the spiritual benefits. How can men be so ungrateful as to forget that it is thanks to a woman, the Virgin Mary, as I pointed out earlier, that the gates of paradise have been opened to them and that God has taken human form? What greater good could one ask for? And who could forget all the good things that mothers do for their sons and wives for their husbands? I beg them at least not to forget these gifts which are spiritual blessings. Let's look at the ancient faith of the Jews: if you take the story of Moses, to whom God gave the written laws of the Hebrews, you'll find that it was a woman who saved him from death, this holy prophet who was to be the source of so much good, as I'll now go on to tell you.

'At the time when the Jews were taken into captivity by the kings of Egypt, it was prophesied that one day a Hebrew man would be born who would deliver the people of Israel from slavery. When the noble lord Moses was born, his mother was unable to look after him and was forced to put him into a little wicker basket and to send him down the river. As God willed it – for He always saves those whom He wants to save – Thermutis, the daughter of King Pharaoh, was wandering along the riverbank just as the basket was floating by. She immediately had it pulled out of the water to see what was inside. As soon as she saw that it was a baby, the most beautiful child that was ever seen, she was overjoyed. She had him looked after and brought him up as her own son. Since he was miraculously unable to be fed by a woman who was not of his own faith, Thermutis brought in a Hebrew wet nurse to feed him. When he became an adult, Moses was chosen by God as the one to receive His laws. Moses also delivered the Jews out of the hands of the Egyptians, crossing the Red Sea and becoming the leader and ruler of the children of Israel. So it was thanks to the woman who saved Moses that such good came to the Jews.'

31. *About Judith, the noble widow.*

'Judith, the noble widow, saved the people of Israel from destruction at the time when Nebuchadnezzar II sent Holofernes to rule over the Jews, having conquered the land of Egypt. This Holofernes and his great army were besieging the Jews inside the city and had already inflicted so much damage on them that they could scarcely hold out much longer. He had cut off their water supply, and their stocks of food were almost exhausted. Despairing of being able to withstand much more, the Jews were on the point of being defeated by Holofernes and were in total dismay. They began to say their prayers, beseeching God to have mercy on His people and to prevent them from falling into the clutches of the enemy. God heard their prayers and, just as He would later save the human race by a woman, so He chose on this occasion to send a woman to their rescue.

'In the city lived a noble and valiant lady called Judith, who was a young and lovely woman of exemplary virtue and chastity. She took pity on the people in their distress and prayed to God day and night to save them. Inspired by God, in whom she had placed her trust, Judith hatched a daring plan. One night, commending herself to the Lord's care, she left the city accompanied only by one of her maid servants and headed for Holofernes's camp. When the soldiers who were on sentry duty saw in the moonlight how beautiful she was, they took her straight to Holofernes, who was delighted to receive such a dazzling woman. He made her sit down beside him and was soon entranced by her intelligence, proud bearing and beauty. The more he gazed at her, the more he burned with desire for her. She, who had other ideas, offered up a silent prayer to God to beg for His help in her endeavours, and managed to string Holofernes along with little promises until she could find the right moment. Three nights later, Holofernes threw a banquet for his barons and drank very heavily. Sated with food and drink, he couldn't wait any longer to sleep with the Hebrew woman so he sent for her to come to him, which she did. When he told her what he wanted, she was ready to do as he wished on condition that, for the sake of propriety, he made all his men leave his tent. He should then get into bed first, to be joined by Judith at midnight when everyone else was asleep. Holofernes accepted her terms. The good lady then began to pray, begging God to give her the necessary strength and courage in her trembling woman's heart to rid her people of this foul tyrant.

'When Judith thought that Holofernes would have fallen asleep, she and her maid servant crept up to the opening of his tent and stood listening. Hearing him sound asleep, the lady exclaimed, "Let's do it now, for God is with us!" She went inside and fearlessly grabbed hold of his sword that was hanging by the bed and drew it out of its scabbard. Using all her strength to lift the blade, she cut off Holofernes's head without making a sound. With the head wrapped in her skirts, she ran back to the city as fast as she could. Having returned to the gates without meeting any opposition, she called out, "Come and open up, for God is with us!" Once she was back inside, you can't imagine how overjoyed they all were at what she had done. In the morning, they impaled the head on a spike and stuck it on top of the city walls. They then threw on their armour and mounted a bold and swift attack on the enemy who were still sleeping, never once suspecting that this might happen. The enemy rushed to their leader's tent to wake him up and to get him out of bed as quickly as possible, but they were horrified to find him slain. The Jews took them all prisoner and killed every last one. Thus the people of Israel were delivered out of the hands of Holofernes by Judith, that valiant woman whose praises shall be sung for ever in Holy Scripture.'

32. *About Queen Esther.*

'On another occasion, God chose the wise and noble Queen Esther to rescue His people from the king, Ahasuerus, who had placed them in captivity. This Ahasuerus was the most powerful of all rulers and controlled many different kingdoms. He was a pagan and had enslaved the Jews. In each of his kingdoms, he sent out a search for the highest-born maidens who were also the loveliest and most accomplished, being determined to take the one he liked best for his wife. Amongst those brought before him was God's beloved Esther, a wise and noble Hebrew maiden who was as lovely as she was virtuous. Since she pleased the king more than any of the others, he chose her for his bride. He loved her so dearly that he couldn't refuse her anything she asked for.

'Some time later, one of his treacherous courtiers, a flatterer named Haman, roused the king's anger against the Jews to the point where the king gave an order that they should be arrested and killed wherever they were to be found. Queen Esther was totally unaware of this, for if she had known she would have been devastated to learn that her people were being treated with such cruelty. However, Mordecai, the leader of the Jews who was one of her uncles, told her what was happening and begged her to do something immediately because the king's orders would very soon be executed. The queen was deeply disturbed to discover all this. She therefore dressed herself up in her finest clothes and pretended to be going out with her ladies for a walk, choosing a garden which she knew the king could see from his windows. Passing by his quarters on her return, she saw the king at the window and so, as if it were the most natural thing in the world, she sank down to her knees and greeted him by prostrating herself before him. The king was so struck by this display of humility and so delighted by her dazzling beauty that he called out to her, saying that whatever she asked him for, he would not refuse her. The lady replied that she wanted nothing other than to invite him to dine with her in her rooms and asked that he bring Haman with him. He answered that he would gladly do so. He dined with her three days in a row, and was so captivated by her elegance and dignity, her charm and beauty, that he urged her once again to ask him any favour she wished. She threw herself at his feet and burst into tears, begging him to take pity on her people and not to dishonour her, after having shown her such distinction, by putting all her kin and countrymen to death. Full of rage, the king replied, "But, my lady, who has dared to do such a thing?", to which she answered, "My lord, it is none other than your chief minister, Haman, who is sitting right here."

'To cut a long story short, the king repealed his order and Haman, who had concocted the whole thing out of envy, was arrested and hanged for his sins. Mordecai, the queen's uncle, was made chief minister in his place. The Jews were freed and given the highest and most honourable status of all races in the land. Thus, as in the case of Judith, God elected a woman to save His people. But don't think that these two were the only ladies in Holy Scripture whom God chose to deliver the Jews. There were many other women whom I haven't time to discuss, like that Deborah I've already mentioned, who also rescued the people from slavery, as did these others.'

33. About the Sabine women.

'I could give you many examples of pagan women of antiquity who saved their countries, towns or cities. However, I'll limit myself to two important instances with which to prove my point.

'After the foundation of Rome by Romulus and Remus, Romulus filled the city with as many knights and soldiers as he could collect together after the numerous victories he had won. He was most anxious to obtain wives for these men in order that they would have heirs who would reign over the city in the years to come. However, he was unsure how to go about finding women for himself and his companions to marry, as the kings, princes and people in the surrounding country were reluctant to give them their daughters or to establish any links with them because they considered them to be too reckless, uncivilized and unreliable a race. For this reason, Romulus had to devise a cunning plan. He had it announced throughout the land that a tournament of jousting would take place and he invited all the kings, princes and citizens to come and bring their ladies and daughters to watch the entertainment provided by the foreign knights. On the day of the festivities, a vast crowd gathered on all sides, for a large number of ladies and maidens had come to watch the sport. Amongst them was the daughter of the Sabine king, a charming and beautiful girl, accompanied by all the other ladies and girls of her country whom she had brought along. The games took place outside the city walls, on a plain at the foot of a hill, with the ladies seated high up in rows. The knights outdid each other in their feats and exploits, for the sight of these lovely ladies inspired them to great deeds of bravery and daring. To keep my story brief, after they had been fighting for a while, Romulus decided that it was time to execute his plan and so took out a great ivory horn on which he gave a loud blast. At this sound, which was a signal for them to act, the knights stopped their jousting and ran towards the ladies. Romulus snatched the king's daughter, with whom he was already smitten, whilst the other knights each took the one they wanted. Forcing the ladies to get up on to their horses, the Romans galloped off towards the city and bolted the gates firmly behind them. Outside, the women's fathers and kinsmen let out great cries of grief, as did the ladies themselves who had been abducted, but their weeping was totally in vain. Romulus married his lady with great ceremony, and all the other knights did likewise.

'This event caused a terrible war to break out. As soon as he could, the Sabine king gathered a great army together to attack the Romans. However, it was not easy to defeat them as they were such experts in battle. The war had already lasted five years when, one day, the two sides prepared to meet in full strength on the battlefield and it was obvious that there was going to be an appalling massacre with enormous loss of life. The Romans had already left the city gates in huge numbers when the queen called all the ladies of Rome to meet together in a temple. This wise and beautiful young woman addressed them, saying: "Honourable Sabine ladies, sisters and companions, you all know only too well how we were abducted by our husbands and how this has caused a war between our fathers and kinsmen on the one side and our husbands on the other. There is no way that this deadly conflict can continue or even come to an end, without it being to our detriment, no matter who has the final victory. If we lose our husbands, whom we quite rightly adore now that we have borne them children, we shall be broken-hearted and devastated to see our babies deprived of their fathers. If, on the other hand, our husbands are victorious and our fathers and kinsmen are killed, we will surely deeply regret that all this conflict happened because of us. What is done is done and cannot now be undone. In my view, we need to find some way to bring this war to a peaceful end. If you decide to take my advice and follow my lead in what I'm going to do, I think that we'll be able to bring this about." Hearing her words, the other ladies replied with one voice that they would do as she said and would obey her instructions.

'The queen therefore undid her hair and took off her shoes, as did all the other ladies. Those who had babies picked them up in their arms and carried them with them. In addition, there was a whole host of children, as well as pregnant women. The queen walked at the head of this touching procession and they all headed straight for the battlefield just as the two armies were lining up. They took up their position in between the opposing sets of troops, making it impossible for the knights to attack each other without first running into the women. The queen and all the other ladies fell to their knees and shouted out, "Dear fathers and kinsmen, beloved husbands: for God's sake, make peace! If not, we are prepared to die trampled underfoot by your horses." Seeing their wives and children in tears, the knights were astonished and dismayed: there was certainly no way that they would run at them. The women's fathers were similarly moved to compassion at the sight of their daughters in this terrible state. The two sides looked at each other and, out of pity for the women who were humbly begging them to desist, their hatred turned to proper filial love. Sabines and Romans alike were forced to throw down their weapons as they rushed to embrace each other and make peace. Romulus led his father-in-law, the king of the Sabines, into the city and received him and his whole army with great honour. Thus, thanks to the good sense and bravery of the queen and her ladies, the Romans and the Sabines were prevented from massacring each other.'

34. *About Veturia.*

'Veturia, a noblewoman of Rome, was the mother of a very illustrious
Roman citizen called Marcius. He was a man of tremendous virtue and
astuteness, as well as being quick-witted and intelligent, valiant and brave.
This fine knight, Veturia's son, was sent by the Romans at the head of
a great army to attack the Coriolans. He defeated the enemy and seized
from them the fortress of the Volscians. In recognition of this victory
over the Coriolans, he was henceforth known as Coriolanus. He was
held in such high esteem for this exploit that he ended up controlling
the whole of Rome. However, since it is very dangerous to let one person
be solely responsible for the government of an entire people, the Romans
eventually rose up against him and sent him into exile, banishing him
from the city. Yet he avenged himself perfectly on them by going over
to those whom he had previously defeated and inciting them to rebel
against the Romans. Making him their captain, the Coriolans marched
in huge numbers on Rome, leaving a trail of destruction behind them.
Seeing the danger that they were in and fearing that they too would be
destroyed, the Romans sent various messengers to the Coriolans to
broker peace. However, Marcius refused to listen to them. Other del-
egations were sent, but still to no avail as Marcius continued to wreak
havoc. The Romans then sent their bishops and priests, all decked
in their robes of office, who humbly beseeched him to stop. Yet all
their efforts too were in vain. In desperation, the Romans asked the
noble ladies of the city to go and see the honourable lady Veturia,
Marcius's mother, and implore her to intercede with her son and make
him cease his hostilities. The good lady Veturia left the city, accompanied by all these ladies, and the procession of women headed over
towards Marcius. Like the dutiful and compassionate son he was, he
dismounted from his horse as soon as he heard she was coming and
went to greet her, receiving her with all due humility. Though she wished
to plead with him to make peace, he replied that it was not proper that
a mother should beg her son but should command him instead. The
noble lady thus took him back with her to the city and, thanks to her,
the Romans were saved from harm on this occasion. She alone was able

to do what Rome's most prominent citizens had been unable to achieve.'

35. *About Clotilde, Queen of France.*

'On the subject of the marvellous benefits that women have brought in the spiritual domain, which I was telling you about earlier, wasn't it Clotilde, daughter of the king of Burgundy and wife of the mighty Clovis, King of France, who first brought Christianity to the French monarchy and disseminated this religion amongst its princes and kings? What greater good than this could anyone ever do? Being enlightened with the faith and like the good Christian she was, this holy lady did not stop begging and pleading with her lord to receive the word of God and be baptized. Though he persistently refused to do so, this lady never left off praying to God, with tears, fasts and acts of devotion, to shine the light of faith into her husband's heart. She prayed to Him so fervently that eventually Our Lord took pity on her anguish. God chose to inspire Clovis at the moment when he was locked in battle against the king of the Alemanni and it seemed as though he was on the point of being defeated. The king looked up towards heaven and called out to God in his terrible distress: "Almighty God, whom my wife worships and adores, come to my aid in this struggle and I promise you that I will receive your holy faith." No sooner had Clovis uttered these words than the tide of the battle went his way and he was totally victorious. He gave thanks to God and, on his return, he was baptized along with all his barons and the rest of his people, to the immense joy and relief of both himself and his wife. From that day onwards, thanks to the prayers of Queen Clotilde, that good and saintly lady, the grace of God became so widespread throughout the land that the faith of the French has never once faltered since. Nor has there ever been a French king who was a heretic, thank God, which is more than can be said for certain kings and emperors. This redounds greatly to their glory and it is for this reason that the kings of France are known as "most Christian".

'If I were to recount to you all the great gifts that women have brought, it would take up far too many pages. However, whilst we're still talking about spiritual matters, there were many martyrs who were looked after, sheltered and hidden by lowly women, widows and honest townswomen, about whom I'll tell you more later. If you read these martyrs' legends, you will find that God was happy for them all, or at least the vast majority, to be comforted by women in their torments and sufferings. What am I saying? It's not just them: the Apostles too, as well as Saint Paul and the others, even Jesus Christ himself, were fed and cared for by women.

'As for the French, who quite rightly have great reverence for the body of my lord Saint Denis, who first brought Christianity to France, aren't they beholden to a woman for the fact that they now possess this body, as well as those of his blessed companions Saints Rusticus and Eleutherius? The tyrant who had them beheaded ordered their bodies to be thrown in the Seine. Those who were entrusted with this mission put the bodies into a sack to carry them to the river. These men were staying at the house of an honest widow called Catulla who got them drunk and took the holy bodies out of the sacks, replacing them with the carcasses of dead pigs. She then buried the blessed martyrs with as much dignity as she could in her house, leaving an inscription over them so that they could be identified at a future date. Many years later, it was again a woman, my lady Saint Genevieve, who erected a chapel in their honour on this site until Dagobert, the good king of France, founded the church which still stands there today.'

36. Against those who claim that it is not good for women to be educated.

After hearing these words I, Christine, said, 'My lady, I can clearly see that much good has been brought into the world by women. Even if some wicked women have done evil things, it still seems to me that this is far outweighed by all the good that other women have done and continue to do. This is particularly true of those who are wise and well educated in either the arts or the sciences, whom we mentioned before. That's why I'm all the more amazed at the opinion of some men who state that they are completely opposed to their daughters, wives or other female relatives engaging in study, for fear that their morals will be corrupted.'

Rectitude replied, 'This should prove to you that not all men's arguments are based on reason, and that these men in particular are wrong. There are absolutely no grounds for assuming that knowledge of moral disciplines, which actually inculcate virtue, would have a morally corrupting effect. Indeed, there's no doubt whatsoever that such forms of knowledge correct one's vices and improve one's morals. How could anyone possibly think that by studying good lessons and advice one will be any the worse for it? This view is completely unthinkable and untenable. I'm not saying that it's a good idea for men or women to study sorcery or any other type of forbidden science, since the Holy Church did not ban people from practising them for nothing. However, it's just that it's not true to say that women will be corrupted by knowing what's right and proper.

'Quintus Hortensius, who was a great rhetorician and a fine orator of Rome, did not subscribe to this opinion. He had a daughter named Hortensia, whom he loved dearly for her keen wits. He educated her himself, teaching her the science of rhetoric in which, states Boccaccio, she so excelled that she not only resembled her father in her intelligence, agile memory and excellent diction, but in fact surpassed him in her marvellous eloquence and command of oratory. On the subject of what we said before about all the benefits that women have brought, the good that this lady did is especially worthy of note. It was at the time when a triumvirate ruled over Rome that this Hortensia decided to take up the cause of women, thus performing a task which no man dared to do. As Rome was in great financial straits, it was proposed to levy certain charges on women and, in particular, to put a tax on their valuables. This Hortensia spoke so persuasively that she was listened to as attentively as if it had been her father speaking, and won her case.

'If we discuss more recent times, rather than going back to ancient history, Giovanni Andrea, the famous legist who taught at Bologna nearly sixty years ago, similarly opposed the view that women should not be educated. He gave his beloved daughter Novella, a fine and lovely girl, such a good education and detailed knowledge of law that, when he was busy with other tasks which prevented him from lecturing to his students, he could send his daughter in his place to read to them from his professorial chair. In order not to distract the audience by her beauty, Novella had a little curtain put up in front of her. Thus she lightened her father's load and relieved him of some of his duties. In his devotion to her, he chose to preserve her name for posterity by writing an important commentary on a legal text which he named *La Novella* in her honour.

'Therefore, it is not all men, especially not the most intelligent, who agree with the view that it is a bad idea to educate women. However, it's true that those who are not very clever come out with this opinion because they don't want women to know more than they do. Your own father, who was a great astrologer and philosopher, did not believe that knowledge of the sciences reduced a woman's worth. Indeed, as you know, it gave him great pleasure to see you take so readily to studying the arts. Rather, it was because your mother, as a woman, held the view that you should spend your time spinning like the other girls, that you did not receive a more advanced or detailed initiation into the sciences. But, as that proverb which we've already had occasion to quote says, "What is in our nature cannot be taken away." Despite your mother's opposition, you did manage to glean some grains of knowledge from your studies, thanks to your own natural inclination for learning. It's obvious to me that you do not esteem yourself any less for having this knowledge: in fact, you seem to treasure it, and quite rightly so.'

I, Christine, then replied, 'Without a doubt, what you're saying, my lady, is as true as the Lord's Prayer itself.'

37. *Christine addresses Rectitude, who gives examples to contradict those who claim that few women are chaste, beginning with Susanna.*

'As far as I can see, my lady, all forms of goodness and virtue can be found in the female sex. So why is it that these men say that so few women are chaste? If this were true, all their other qualities would be worthless, because chastity is the supreme virtue in a woman. Yet, hearing what you've just said, the truth would seem to be very different from what they claim.'

Rectitude answered, 'The complete opposite is true, as I've told you before and as you yourself already know. I could keep telling you more on this subject until the end of time itself! The Holy Scripture mentions so many excellent and chaste ladies who preferred to die rather than lose their chastity, bodily integrity and good conscience. One such lady was the virtuous and lovely Susanna, wife of Joachim, who was a very rich and influential member of the Jewish race. As this honest lady was walking in her garden one day, she was approached by two old men, corrupt priests, who tried to tempt her into sin. Seeing that she completely rejected their advances and that their pleas were getting them nowhere, they threatened to denounce her in court for having been found with a young man. On hearing their threats, and knowing that the punishment for an adulterous woman was to be stoned, she exclaimed, "I am caught on all sides, for if I refuse to do what these men want, my body shall be put to death. But, if I give in to their demands, I shall be committing a sin in the eyes of the Creator. However, I would rather be innocent and suffer death than risk rousing God's anger by sinning." Susanna therefore screamed out loud and the other members of her household came running. To cut a long story short, the corrupt priests managed to convince the court with their false testimony and Susanna was sentenced to death. Yet God, who always looks after His own, opened the mouth of the prophet Daniel, who was just a small child in his mother's arms: when the boy saw Susanna being led to her punishment, followed by a great crowd of people who were all weeping, he cried out that the innocent woman had been wrongfully accused. She was taken back to the court where the corrupt priests were properly cross-examined and found guilty by their own confessions. The blameless Susanna was saved and it was they who were punished instead.'

38. About Sarah.

'The twentieth chapter of the first book of the Bible tells of the chastity and virtue of Sarah. This lady was the wife of Abraham, the great patriarch. Many good things are said about this lady in Holy Scripture, but I can't go into them all here. None the less, we can cite her chastity as an example of what we were saying before about the large numbers of beautiful women who remained pure. Sarah was so astonishingly lovely that she outshone all other ladies of her time. She was lusted after by many princes but remained faithful and ignored them all. Amongst those who were after her was King Pharaoh, who forcibly stole her from her husband. However, thanks to her great virtue, which surpassed even her beauty, she was shown such grace by Our Lord, who loved her dearly, that she was protected from all taint. God tormented Pharaoh and all his household by afflicting their bodies with dreadful diseases and torturing their consciences with terrible visions. The king was unable to lay a finger on Sarah and thus had to let her go.'

39. *About Rebecca.*

'The good and honest lady Rebecca, wife of Isaac the patriarch, Jacob's father, was no less beautiful or pure than Sarah. The Holy Scripture sings her praises very highly for her many qualities, and she is mentioned in chapter 24 of the first book of the Bible. Being upright, decent and honourable, this lady was a model of chastity to all those women who saw her. Moreover, she behaved with such extraordinary humility and modesty towards her husband that she didn't seem like a noblewoman at all. For this reason, the good Isaac revered her greatly and cherished her most dearly. However, her exemplary purity and goodness earned her more than just the affection of her husband. God Himself deemed her to be so deserving of His love and favour that, when she was old and infertile, He nevertheless sent her twins, Jacob and Esau, from whom all the tribes of Israel were descended.'

40. *About Ruth.*

'I could tell you much more about the fine, untainted women mentioned in the Holy Scripture, but I'll have to keep my comments brief. Ruth, another noble lady, was the ancestor of the prophet David. She was extremely chaste, both in marriage and in widowhood, being greatly attached to her husband. This was apparent when, on his death, she left her people and her native land to go and spend the rest of her days with the Jews, the race to which her husband had belonged. She even went to make her home with her mother-in-law. In short, this worthy lady was so decent and virtuous that a whole book in the Bible was devoted to her and her life, in which all these things are recounted.'

41. *About Penelope, Ulysses's wife.*

'You can find many examples in books of pagan women who were righteous and honourable. Penelope, wife of the prince Ulysses, was a very virtuous lady: amongst her other qualities, she was particularly prized for her chastity. Several history books mention her in detail. This lady conducted herself most sensibly the whole time that her husband was away at the siege of Troy, which lasted ten years. Despite the fact that she was courted by various kings and princes for her great beauty, she refused to listen to a single word they said. She was not only extremely wise and prudent, but also very moral and pious. After the destruction of Troy, she waited yet another ten years for her husband, even though he was thought to have perished at sea, where he had faced many dangers. On his return, he found her assailed by a king who was attracted by her extraordinary virtue and purity to the point of wanting to force her to marry him. Disguised as a pilgrim, her husband made enquiries about her and was delighted to hear nothing but good reports. He was also overjoyed to find that his son Telemachus, who had only been a small child when he left, was now a young man.'

I, Christine, then said, 'My lady, from what you've told me, these ladies were no less chaste for all their attractiveness, whereas lots of men claim that it is hard to find a lovely woman who is also pure.'

Rectitude replied, 'Those who say this are telling it all wrong: there always have been and there always will be women who are just as spotless as they are beautiful.'

42. *Against those who assert that there are very few chaste and attractive women: the example of Mariamme.*

'Mariamme, a Hebrew woman, was the daughter of King Aristobulus. She was so lovely that, at the time, it was thought not only that she surpassed all other women in beauty, but also that she was more of a godlike and heavenly creature than a mere mortal woman. Her portrait was painted and sent to Mark Antony, King of Egypt, who, when he saw how lovely she was, declared that she must be the daughter of the god Jupiter himself, for he could not believe that this lady could be the child of any ordinary human being. Despite the fact that many great princes and kings were tempted by her stunning looks to try to seduce her, Mariamme resisted them all, thanks to her great virtue and tremendous courage, which only increased her fine reputation further. This was all the more to her credit considering that she was very unhappily married to Herod Antipater, king of the Jews. He was a terribly cruel man who had earlier had her own brother killed. For this reason, and for other atrocities which he committed, she bore him nothing but hatred. However, she never stopped being a faithful and honourable wife for all that, even when she found out that he had decreed that she should be put to death immediately if he died before she did, so that after him no one else would enjoy her great beauty.'

43. *More on this subject: the example of Antonia, wife of Drusus Tiberius.*

'It's often said that it's very hard for a beautiful woman to keep herself inviolate and to fend off the attentions of young men and courtiers who are eager to have affairs: it's like being in the midst of flames without getting burnt. The virtuous Antonia, wife of Drusus Tiberius, who was the brother of the Emperor Nero, was one such woman who knew how to defend herself. Whilst she was still a dazzlingly beautiful woman in the bloom of youth, this noble lady was plunged into grief by the loss of her husband, Tiberius, whom Nero poisoned to death. Having resolved to live a chaste life as a widow and never to marry again, this lady respected this vow for as long as she lived and was more highly commended for her exemplary virtue than any other pagan woman. Boccaccio states that she was especially deserving of praise considering that she lived at court surrounded by handsome, elegant and attractive young men who led an indolent and hedonistic existence. She spent her life free of criticism for even the least little hint of immoderation. Boccaccio goes on to say that Antonia was particularly worthy of acclaim, being not only a young and supremely beautiful woman but also the daughter of Mark Antony, a man who lived an extremely dissolute and disreputable life. Despite the dreadful behaviour she could see all around her, she preserved her chastity intact throughout her life, right up until she died of old age. Never once was she burnt by the flames of sensuality.

'I could find you many other such examples of chaste and beautiful women who lived a worldly existence at court, constantly prey to the attentions of young men. Even today, you can be sure that there are plenty of women like this, no matter what wagging tongues may say to the contrary. This is just as well, for it seems to me that at no other time in history have there ever been as many gossips as there are nowadays, nor so many men who are constantly ready to slander women without reason. I can't help wondering whether if all the lovely, innocent ladies of the past whom I've just mentioned to you were living now, they would be roundly attacked by envious tongues, as opposed to receiving the kind of praise which their contemporaries lavished on them in antiquity.

'To come back to what we were saying about virtuous, untainted women who led an honest existence, despite the fact that they frequented those who were extremely worldly, Valerius discusses the noble Sulpicia, an extraordinarily beautiful lady who, of all the women in Rome, was none the less considered to be the most chaste.'

44. *In order to contradict those who claim that women want to be raped, here begins a series of examples, the first of which is Lucretia.*

I, Christine, then said, 'My lady, I fully believe what you say and I'm sure that there are many beautiful women who are upright, decent and fully able to protect themselves from the traps laid by seducers. It therefore angers and upsets me when men claim that women want to be raped and that, even though a woman may verbally rebuff a man, she won't in fact mind it if he does force himself upon her. I can scarcely believe that it could give women any pleasure to be treated in such a vile way.'

Rectitude replied, 'My dear friend, you can be sure that women who are chaste and lead a moral existence would find no pleasure in being raped. On the contrary, they think that it is the worst thing that could possibly happen to them. There are several examples, such as that of Lucretia, which prove that this is definitely the case. Lucretia, a high-born lady of Rome and, indeed, the most virtuous of all Roman women, was married to a nobleman called Tarquinius Collatinus. Unfortunately, Tarquin the Proud, son of King Tarquin, was deeply smitten with the great Lucretia. Having seen with his own eyes how supremely chaste she was, he didn't dare approach her directly. Despairing of being able to persuade her with bribes and entreaties, he plotted how to win her by trickery. He therefore pretended to be a close friend of her husband's, which meant that he was able to come and go as he pleased in her house. One day, when he knew that her husband was absent, he was welcomed most honourably by his noble hostess, as befitted a guest whom she took to be her husband's great friend. That night, Tarquin, who had other ideas, scared Lucretia out of her wits when he broke into her bedroom. In short, having made her numerous promises of gifts and presents if she would do what he wanted, he saw that pleading with her was getting him nowhere. He therefore pulled out his sword and threatened to kill her if she made a sound or refused to give herself to him. She told him to go ahead and kill her because she preferred to die rather than submit to his advances. When he realized that his threats were all in vain, Tarquin came up with another despicable ruse, declaring that he would let it be known publicly that he had found her with one of her servants. To cut a long story short, the thought that he would do such a thing so appalled her that she finally gave in to him.

'Yet Lucretia was unable to bear this awful offence with resignation. When morning came, she went to find her husband, father and close relatives, who were all the most prominent citizens of Rome. With great sobs and moans, she confessed to them the deed that had been perpetrated on her. As her husband and family were trying to comfort her in her terrible distress, she drew out a knife from under her gown, saying: "Though I can absolve myself of sin and prove myself innocent this way, I can't get rid of my suffering and pain: henceforth no woman need live in shame and dishonour because of what has been done to me." With these words, she plunged the knife deep into her breast and immediately fell down dead in front of her husband and his friends. Like madmen, they all rushed after Tarquin. The whole of Rome was incensed by what had happened: they deposed the king and would have killed his son if they had caught him. After that, Rome never had another king. Some say that because of the outrage done to Lucretia, a law was passed which sentenced to death any man who raped a woman, a law which is moral, fitting and just.'

45. On this same subject: the example of the queen of the Galatians.

'The story of the noble queen of the Galatians, wife of King Ortiagon, is an apt example to illustrate this argument. During the time that Rome was engaged in its great conquests of foreign lands, the king of the Galatians and his wife were taken prisoner by the Romans. During their captivity, one of the generals of the Roman army who was keeping them prisoner became infatuated with the noble queen, who was not only beautiful and modest but also virtuous and chaste. He pleaded with her at great length and tried to bribe her with gifts, but, seeing that his entreaties were having no effect, he forced himself upon her. The queen was so distressed by this outrage that she couldn't stop thinking about how to avenge herself upon him. She therefore bided her time and hid her feelings until the right moment came. When the ransom arrived which would free the king and herself, the lady insisted that the money should be handed over in her presence to the general who was holding them captive. She advised him to weigh the gold to make sure that he was being given the right amount and not being cheated. Whilst he was busy checking the ransom money and when none of his men were present, the lady picked up a knife, slit his throat and killed him. She then cut off his head and, without a hint of remorse, took it to show her husband, telling him exactly what had happened to her and how she had taken her revenge.'

46. Still on this same subject: the examples of the Sicambrians, and of several virgins.

'I can give you examples of many married women who were unable to bear their anguish at being raped. I could also tell you as much again about widows and virgins. Hyppo, a Greek woman, was kidnapped by the sailors and pirates who were enemies of her country. As she was a very beautiful woman, they made her all sorts of advances. Seeing that she was unable either to escape or to avoid being raped, Hyppo was so horrified and dismayed at this prospect that she preferred to die. She therefore threw herself overboard and was drowned.

'Likewise, during one of their raids on Rome, the Sicambrians (or the Franks, as they're now known) attacked the city with a huge army and a great host of people. Thinking that they would succeed in destroying the city, the Sicambrians had brought their wives and children along with them. However, the battle suddenly turned against them. When their wives realized this, they agreed that they would rather die defending their honour than be defiled, for they were well aware that, as was then the custom, they were very likely to be raped, every last one of them. They therefore barricaded themselves behind their carts and chariots and took up arms against the Romans. They defended themselves as best they could, killing many of the enemy. Yet, in the end, almost all of them were slaughtered. Those who were still alive begged the Romans on bended knees to spare them from dishonour and to allow them to spend the rest of their days serving in the temple of the Vestal Virgins. On hearing that their request would not be granted, they all decided to kill themselves rather than be raped.

'Likewise, on the subject of virgins, there was Virginia, the noble Roman maiden, whom the corrupt judge Claudius tried to win first by trickery and then by force when he realized that pleading with her was useless. Though she was only a very young girl, she thought it preferable to kill herself than to be taken against her will.

'Likewise, there was a city in Lombardy whose lord was killed by the enemy. The lord's daughters, who were very beautiful girls, were so convinced they would be raped that they found a very unusual way to defend themselves, for which they should be applauded. They took raw chicken meat and tucked it between their breasts. The meat soon went off in the heat and so, when the enemy approached them, they smelt the stench and left them alone, saying: "My God, these Lombard women really stink!" Thanks to their foul smell, these women kept themselves very fragrant.'

47. *Proofs to refute the view that women are lacking in constancy: Christine asks questions, to which Rectitude replies with various examples of emperors who were unreliable and inconsistent.*

'My lady, the women you've been talking about were certainly extremely steadfast, resolute and faithful. Could one say as much of even the strongest men who ever lived? Yet, of all the vices that men, and especially authors, accuse women of possessing, they are unanimous that the female sex is unstable and fickle, frivolous, flighty and weak-minded, as impressionable as children and completely lacking in resolution. Are men therefore so unwavering that it is utterly unheard of for them to vacillate, given that they criticize women for being so unreliable and changeable? If, in fact, they themselves are lacking in constancy, it's totally unacceptable for them to accuse others of having the same failing or to insist that others should possess a virtue which they themselves do not.'

Rectitude's reply was, 'My dear sweet friend, haven't you heard the common saying that fools are very quick to spot the mote in their neighbour's eye but slow to see the beam in their own?[5] I'll show you just how unreasonable it is for men to criticize women for being inconstant and capricious. Their argument goes like this. First, they all assume that women are by nature weak. Then, having accused women of weakness, they presumably think themselves to be constant, or at least that women are not as constant as they are. Yet it's undeniable that they expect far greater constancy from women than they themselves can muster. Though they consider themselves to be so strong and to be made of such noble stuff, they're unable to stop themselves from falling prey to some awful vices and failings. Nor is this by any means always out of ignorance. Indeed, it's often down to deliberate bad intentions, because they're well aware that they're committing a sin. But they then excuse themselves, saying that to err is to be human. However, should a woman fall into error, usually thanks to a man's incessant scheming, lo and behold, they declare this to be due to women's innate weakness and inconstancy. Considering that they think women are so feeble, they should, rightly speaking, show greater tolerance of female frailty and not accuse women of dreadful sins that they consider to be only minor peccadilloes when they themselves are guilty of them. For there is no law, no written text, which says that they are allowed to sin more than women, or that their vices are any more excusable. None the less, they in fact give themselves such moral authority that, far from letting women get away with anything, they fall over themselves to impute to the female sex all manner of crimes and offences. Neither do they give women any credit for being strong and steadfast in the face of such awful criticisms. So, whatever the argument is, men have it both ways and always turn out to be in the right. You yourself have discussed this at length in your *Letter of the God of Love*.

'You asked me earlier whether men are so upright and worthy that they are justified in accusing others of inconstancy. I would say that if you examine human history from antiquity up to the present day, taking evidence from books and from both what you have seen with your own eyes in the past and what you can still see all around you today, and looking at men not just from the lower or uneducated classes but also from the upper classes, you can judge for yourself what perfection, strength and constancy they've displayed! This is the case with the vast majority of men, though there are some, thank heavens, who are wise, strong and steadfast.

'If you want me to give you examples of male inconstancy from the recent and distant past, since men persist in attacking women for this failing as if their own hearts were never subject to instability or change, just look at the behaviour of the most powerful princes and the most eminent men, in whom these are more dangerous faults than in others. Not to mention how many emperors are guilty of these things! I ask you, was the mind of a woman ever as weak, fearful, pathetic and frivolous as that of the Emperor Claudius? He was so unstable that whatever he ordered one minute, he reversed the next. It was impossible to take him at his word and he agreed with anything anybody said. In a fit of mad cruelty, he had his wife killed, and then, that night, he asked why she wasn't coming to bed! To those of his friends whom he had beheaded, he sent word that they should come and play with him! He was so lacking in courage that he lived in a constant state of fear and was unable to trust anyone. What can I tell you? Every kind of moral and mental debility was to be found in this atrocious emperor. But why am I just talking about this particular one? Was he the only ruler to sit on the imperial throne who was prey to such weakness? Was the Emperor Tiberius any better? Wasn't he more guilty of inconstancy, changeability and immorality than any woman has ever been?'

48. *About Nero.*

'Whilst we're on the subject of emperors, what about Nero? It was glaringly obvious just how unstable and weak he was. Initially he was very laudable and made an effort to please everyone. Soon, however, his lechery, cruelty and greed knew no bounds. The better to indulge his vices, he would often arm himself at night and go off with his partners in crime to seek out places of depravity and corruption, amusing himself by running round town gratifying his obscene desires. As a pretext for committing his foul deeds, Nero would bump into people in the street and, if they said anything, he would attack them and kill them. He broke into taverns and brothels and raped women, on one occasion narrowly escaping death at the hands of a man whose wife he had raped. He organized lewd bathing parties and feasts that lasted all night. He would order first one thing and then another, as his capricious fancies took him. Nero indulged in all sorts of carnal pleasures, excesses and perversions, and there were no limits to his arrogance and extravagance. He loved those who were wicked and persecuted those who were virtuous. He was complicit in the murder of his father and he later had his own mother killed. When she was dead, he ordered her body to be opened up so that he could see where he had been conceived. Seeing her like that, Nero declared that she had once been a truly beautiful woman. He killed Octavia, his first wife, who was a fine lady, and took a second one, whom he loved at first but then had her murdered as well. He also ordered the death of Claudia, who had been the wife of his predecessor, since she refused to marry him. Nero similarly had his stepson killed when he was not yet seven years old purely because it was said of the boy that, when he was at play, his behaviour was obviously that of the son of an emperor.

'Nero's teacher Seneca, the noble philosopher, was also put to death by the emperor's orders, for he was unable to contain his shame at what was going on before his very eyes. Nero poisoned his prefect by pretending to give him a cure for his toothache. Likewise, he gave poisoned food and drink to the noblest of his princes and to the most venerable and illustrious of his barons, who exercised a great deal of power. Not only did he murder his aunt and seize all her wealth, but he also destroyed all the most notable families of Rome and drove them into exile, killing all their children in the process. He trained a ferocious Egyptian man to eat human flesh so that he could feed him living victims to devour. What can I tell you? It would be impossible to relate all his appalling crimes or the full extent of his foul wickedness. To cap it all, he set Rome on fire and let it burn for six whole days and nights. Many people died in this terrible catastrophe, whilst he stood singing on his tower, watching the inferno rage through the city and taking enormous delight in the beauty of the flames. At his dinner table, he had Saints Peter and Paul beheaded, as well as many other martyrs. For fourteen years he continued in this fashion until the Romans could finally take no more and rebelled against him. In his despair, he took his own life.'

49. *About the Emperor Galba, as well as others.*

'What I've told you about the terrible wickedness and weakness of Nero may seem exceptional to you, but I can assure you that the emperor who succeeded him, Galba, would have been almost as bad as Nero had he lived longer. His cruelty was insatiable and, amongst all his other vices, he was so changeable that he was incapable of settling upon a course of action or of sticking by a decision. One minute he would be giving full vent to his brutality and the next minute he would be totally malleable and unable to dispense justice. He was not only reckless, jealous and suspicious, having little love for his princes and knights, but also cowardly, fearful and, above all, rapacious. His reign only lasted six months, for he was killed in order to put an end to his atrocities.

'However, Otho, the emperor who came after Galba, was not much of an improvement either. Indeed, despite what's said about women being self-obsessed, this emperor was so prissy and fussy about his appearance that he was truly the most ineffectual creature who ever lived. He was so indolent that all he ever thought about was his comfort. He was an inveterate thief who squandered his money and overindulged himself. Moreover, he was a cheat, a lecher and a base traitor who respected no one and possessed every weakness going. After having been defeated by his enemies, he met his end by committing suicide after only three months on the throne.

'Vitellius, who followed Otho, was even worse, being full of every sin imaginable. I don't know what more I can tell you. Don't take me for a liar, but read the stories of these emperors' lives for yourself. You'll soon see how few of them were actually upright, decent and consistent, considering how many of them there actually were. The virtuous ones were Julius Caesar, Octavian, the Emperors Trajan and Titus. But believe me, for every good one you'll find ten bad ones.

'By the same token, I could tell you about the popes and other men of the Holy Church who, of all people, should be as close to perfection as possible. When Christianity was in its infancy, such men were truly saintly. Yet ever since Constantine started making huge donations to the Church and endowing it with enormous wealth, holiness has fallen by the wayside: you only have to read the annals and chronicles which recount these churchmen's deeds to see this. Moreover, if you think that this was true in the past but that things have now improved, you can judge for yourself whether any of the estates in society are mending their ways or whether any of our temporal or spiritual leaders are displaying constancy and firmness in their words and actions. As this is clearly not the case, I'll say no more about it. So I'm baffled as to why men talk about the inconstancy and fickleness of women. How can men dare to open their mouths when they see that the conduct of those who govern them – who are certainly not women! – is marked by instability and hesitation, just like that of children, and that the resolutions and agreements they come up with in their counsels are rarely put into effect.

'To sum up on the question of inconstancy or vacillation: this failing consists of nothing other than acting contrary to what reason commands us to do, because reason teaches all rational beings to do good. When a man or a woman lets sensuality block out the light of reason, this is weakness and inconstancy. The worse the sin or vice in which a person indulges, the more his or her frailty grows, because the light of reason is increasingly dimmed. Thus, from what the history books tell us and from what, in my opinion, experience too would seem to confirm, although the philosophers and other writers go on about the unreliability of the female sex, you would never find even a handful of women who were anything like as perverse as these vast numbers of men.

'The worst women to be found in any text are Athaliah and her mother Jezebel, both queens of Jerusalem, who persecuted the people of Israel. In addition to them, there's Brunhilde, Queen of France, and one or two others. But just look at the wickedness of Judas, who so cruelly betrayed his excellent master, whose apostle he had been, and who had shown him such kindness. Not to mention the harsh and brutal Jews and the people of Israel who put Jesus to death out of envy, as well as committing the vicious murders of several holy prophets who came before Jesus's time, some of whom they stoned to death and others whose heads they smashed to pieces. Don't forget Julian the Apostate, whose terrible perversity led some to call him one of the antichrists, nor Denis, the foul tyrant of Sicily, whose life was so despicable that it's too disgusting to read about. And what about all the countless wicked kings from all over the world, the faithless emperors, the heretical popes and other impious prelates who were consumed with greed, as well as all the antichrists who are yet to come? You'll soon see that men would do better to hold their tongues. Women should praise the Lord and be thankful that He placed their precious souls in female vessels. I'll leave this subject there for now. However, in order to refute the opinion of those who claim that womankind is inconstant, I'll give you a few examples of some women who were paragons of steadfastness and whose stories are most uplifting and delightful to hear.'

50. *About Griselda, the marchioness of Saluzzo, a woman of unfailing virtue.*

'The story goes that there was once a marquis of Saluzzo called Gualtieri, who was unmarried. He was a handsome and very worthy man, though rather eccentric in his ways. His barons kept advising and urging him to marry in order to have heirs. Having held out for a long time against doing as they recommended, he eventually agreed to take a wife, on condition that they promised to accept whichever woman he chose to marry. His barons consented to this and swore an oath on it.

'From time to time, this marquis used to go off hunting animals and birds. In the countryside near his castle lay a small village where, amongst all the other impoverished peasants living there, dwelt a poor, sick, old man whose name was Giannucolo. This fine man, who had been a good and honest person all his life, had a daughter by the name of Griselda, who was eighteen years of age. She served her father with great diligence and earned a living for the two of them by spinning wool. The marquis, who usually passed by their house, had often noticed the girl's sober behaviour and virtuous habits. Moreover, she was very lovely in her appearance, all of which disposed him well towards her.

'After Gualtieri had promised his barons that he would definitely take a wife, he went to tell them to gather together on a certain day for his wedding, giving the order that all the ladies should also be present. He had great preparations made and, on the appointed day, when his knights and ladies were assembled before him, he had them all ride out on horseback to accompany him as he went to fetch his bride. He then headed straight for Giannucolo's house, where he came across Griselda. She was carrying a pitcher of water on her head, for she had just come back from the well. He asked her where Giannucolo was, whereupon she knelt down in front of him and told him that her father was inside. "Go and bring him to me," he ordered her. When the good man emerged from the house, the marquis informed him that he was there to take his daughter in marriage. Giannucolo replied that he was happy for the marquis to do as he wished. The ladies went into the little house to dress the bride and deck her out in the richest finery, as befitted the rank of a marquis, draping her in the robes and jewels that Gualtieri had prepared for her. He then led her away to be married in his palace. To cut a long story short, this lady behaved with such courtesy towards everyone, both the nobles of all ranks and the common people, that they loved her with great affection. She treated each of them on exactly the right level and was thus able to please them all. As was her duty, she served her husband well and loved him dearly.

That year, the marchioness gave birth to a daughter, an event which was received with great joy. However, when the child was old enough to be weaned, the marquis decided to test Griselda's constancy and patience. He therefore told her that, since the barons were unhappy for a child of her base lineage to reign over them, this meant that the girl would have to be put to death. Hearing these words, which would strike grief into the heart of any mother, Griselda replied that the child was his daughter and that he should do with her as he pleased. He had the child placed into the care of one of his squires, whilst he maintained his pretence that the man had come to take her away to be killed. In fact, she was taken in secret to Bologna, to the house of the countess of Panago, the marquis's sister, who looked after the child and brought her up. Though Griselda was convinced that her daughter had been killed, she gave no sign or hint that she was distressed. Another year later, the marchioness became pregnant again and had a beautiful son, whose birth was greeted with great rejoicing. Yet the marquis wanted to test

Griselda a second time and so he told her that this child too would have to be put to death to appease his barons and his men. The lady answered that, if it was not enough that the boy should die, she too would be prepared to lay down her life, if that was what he wanted. Griselda gave up her son to the same squire, just as she had done with her daughter, without revealing the least trace of sorrow. Neither did she say anything to the squire himself, other than begging him to make sure that he buried the child properly after having killed him so that wild beasts and birds could not devour his tender flesh. Throughout all this terrible suffering, Griselda's facial expression remained unchanged.

'Unfortunately, the marquis didn't stop there, but wanted to put her even further to the test. They had been together twelve years, during which time the honourable lady had conducted herself so well that this should have been ample proof of her constancy. However, one day, the marquis called her to his chamber and informed her that he was having trouble with his men and his subjects who were extremely unhappy at having the daughter of Giannucolo as their sovereign lady and were thus threatening to overthrow him because of her. In order to pacify them, she would have to be sent back to her father in the same state as she had been when she left home. He would then take a second wife of nobler birth. Hearing these words, which must have caused her great anguish, Griselda replied, "My lord, I've long been haunted by the thought that it is impossible to reconcile your nobility and splendour with my poverty. Neither have I ever felt myself to be worthy of being your mistress, let alone your wife. I'm ready to return right now to my father's house, where I shall live out my old age. As for the dowry which you have ordered me to take back with me, I am as aware as you are that when you came to fetch me outside my father's house, you had me completely undressed and put into the robes which I wore to go away with you. Apart from that, all I had for a dowry were my loyalty, honour, love, respect and poverty. It's therefore only fitting that I give you back the goods you gave me. So here is the dress, which I'm now taking off, and here is the ring with which you married me. I also leave with you all the other jewels, rings, clothes and ornaments which I wore to make myself beautiful in the bridal chamber. Naked I was when I left my father's house and naked I shall be when I return. It's just that it seems improper to me that this womb, which once bore your two children, should be seen naked in public. So, if you have no objection, I beg you to compensate me for the virginity which I brought into this palace and which I cannot take back with me, by allowing me just one slip to cover up the womb of the former marchioness, your wife." The marquis could barely contain his tears of compassion, but he none the less managed to control his emotions and, as he left the room, he ordered her to be given a single undergarment.

'In the presence of all the knights and ladies, Griselda had to take off her clothes and shoes and remove all her jewellery until she was left with just the slip on. Since word had soon spread that the marquis wanted to send his wife away, every man and woman came running to the palace, sickened with grief at this news. Griselda, bareheaded, barefoot and naked except for her slip, was put on to a horse. Accompanied by the barons, knights and ladies, all of whom were weeping and cursing the marquis as they lamented the loss of his wonderful wife, Griselda still didn't shed a single tear. She was taken to her father's house, where the old man had never once doubted that the day would come when his lord would tire of having made such a poor marriage. Hearing all the noise, he came out to greet his daughter, bringing her the ragged old dress that he had kept for her all that time, which he helped her put on without showing the least sign of unhappiness. So it was that Griselda went back to living with her father in great poverty and lowliness, serving him as she used to do and never once betraying a hint of sorrow or regret. Indeed, she used to console her father in his distress at seeing his daughter fall from such high distinction into such desperate wretchedness.

'When the marquis felt that he had tested his loyal wife long enough, he sent word to his sister that she should make her way to his palace with a noble company of lords and ladies, bringing with her the two children, but taking care not to let anyone know that they were his. He informed his barons and subjects that he wished to remarry, taking as his wife a young girl of noble birth whose guardian was his sister. On the day when his sister was due to arrive, he assembled together in the palace a fine host of knights, ladies and high-born people. A magnificent feast was also made ready. He then sent for Griselda, saying to her,

"Griselda, the girl that I'm going to marry will be here tomorrow and I'm determined that my sister and all her noble company should be given a fine and fitting welcome. Since you know my ways and are familiar with all the rooms and chambers, I want you to be in charge of making the arrangements and to give all the instructions to the household. You are to make sure that each person is properly received according to their rank, especially my bride-to-be, and that everything is organized as it should be." Griselda replied that she would gladly do his bidding. The next day, the guests were greeted with great ceremony on their arrival. Despite her ragged dress, Griselda wasn't put off from going up to the girl whom she thought was to be the new bride. With a smile on her face, she curtseyed to her and uttered these humble words: "My lady, you are most welcome." She greeted her son and the whole of the rest of the company in turn in a similarly gracious fashion. Though she was dressed like a pauper, it was obvious from the way she held herself that she was in fact a very honourable lady of great virtue. The newcomers were amazed that such fine speech and such a noble bearing should be cloaked in wretched garments like those she had on. Griselda had taken excellent care of the preparations and nothing was out of place. Yet she was so fascinated by the girl and boy that she was unable to tear herself away from their side, and kept gazing in deep admiration at their beauty.

'The marquis had made everything ready as if he were really going to marry the girl. When it was time for the mass to begin, he called Griselda over to him and, in front of everybody, said: "Griselda, what do you think of my new bride? Isn't she lovely and innocent?" She replied, with great dignity, "Certainly, my lord, no lovelier or more innocent creature was ever seen. However, I would like to ask a favour of you, in all good faith. I beg you to spare her the torments and trials with which you have tested me, for she is so young and delicately brought up that she would be unable to endure what your previous wife has done." On hearing Griselda's words, the marquis realized just how steadfast, constant and faithful she was, and was astounded by her virtue. He took pity on her for having had to bear the lengthy suffering that he had imposed on her when she had done nothing to deserve such treatment. In the presence of everyone, he spoke up, saying, "Griselda, your trials are at an end, for your steadfastness and loyalty, your fidelity and affection, your obedience and humility towards me have all now been proven. I truly believe that there is no man on earth who ever found a greater love in marriage through putting his wife to all the tests that I have put you to." The marquis then went up to her and hugged her tight. He covered her in kisses and declared, "You alone are my wife and I'll never want to take another. This girl whom you took for my bride is in fact our daughter, and this boy is your son. Let everyone here present know that what I have done has been to test my wife, not to criticize her. I didn't have the children killed after all, but ordered them to be brought up by my sister in Bologna, for here they are." The marchioness fainted from happiness at hearing her lord's words. When she regained consciousness, she took her children in her arms and bathed them with tears of delight. Without a doubt, her heart was filled with gladness and all those who were there wept with joy and compassion. Griselda was more highly exalted than ever before and she was decked once again in the finest array. This was followed by tremendous rejoicing as the lady's praises were sung to the skies. She and her husband lived together in peace and happiness for another twenty years. The marquis, who had previously neglected her father, Giannucolo, invited him to court and treated him with great reverence. Their children both made excellent marriages. After the marquis's death, his son succeeded him, with the full support of the barons.'

51. *About Florence of Rome.*

'If Griselda, the marchioness of Saluzzo, was a model of fortitude and constancy, the noble Florence, Empress of Rome, was certainly her equal. As the story goes in the *Miracles de Notre Dame*, Florence endured terrible adversity with extraordinary patience. This lady was even more virtuous and chaste than she was beautiful. Since her husband had to embark on a long journey to wage a great war, he consigned both his wife and the reins of power over to his brother's care. However, no sooner had the emperor set off than his brother succumbed to the devil's temptation and began to lust after his sister-in-law, Florence. In short, he made such persistent advances to her, threatening to use force if she didn't give in to his pleas to sleep with him, that she was obliged to lock him up in a tower. There he remained a prisoner until the emperor returned. When news reached Florence of her husband's imminent arrival, she released her brother-in-law so that he could go and greet the emperor, for she did not wish her husband to find out how disloyal his brother had been. She never once dreamt that her would-be seducer would speak ill of her. Yet, when he met up with the emperor, the brother told the worst possible slanders about Florence, accusing her of the most appalling sins and claiming that she had locked him up in order to gratify her lustful desires more easily. Taking his brother at his word, the emperor sent his men on ahead and ordered them to kill his wife as soon as they arrived, giving no explanation for their actions. He couldn't bear to lay his eyes on his wife again, nor even to find her still alive. When she found out what had transpired, she was dumbfounded. However, she managed to persuade the men who had been sent to kill her to let her escape and go off in disguise.

'This noble lady went on to have many strange adventures until, one day, she was given the task of looking after the child of a great prince. This prince's brother became inflamed with love for her. But, out of spite at seeing her reject all his entreaties, he killed the little child as it lay next to her in bed, for he hoped to ruin her this way. The empress bore all these terrible hardships with great patience and unfailing courage. As she was being led out to her execution for having supposedly killed the child, the lord and lady, who knew how virtuous and honest she was in her ways, took pity on her. Since they had no desire to see her killed, they made her leave the country. She lived a dreadfully poor existence in exile, but still remained as patient as ever, being utterly devoted to Christ and his sweet mother. One night, after having said her prayers, she fell asleep in an orchard. In her sleep, she had a vision of the Holy Virgin, who told her to gather a certain herb which grew beneath where her head lay, and to use this herb to earn her living because it would cure any disease.

'After a while, the lady had cured so many sick people with this herb that her fame spread far and wide. Then, according to God's will, the prince's brother, who had murdered the child, fell desperately ill with epilepsy. The lady was thus sent for to cure him. When she came up to him, she told him that he could clearly see that God was beating him with His scourges. If he made a public confession of his sins, he would be cured, for no other remedy would save him. Feeling enormous contrition, the man confessed his appalling wickedness, explaining that he was the one who had killed the child and had laid the blame on the good lady who looked after it. The prince was devastated by this news and wanted to bring the full force of justice down on his brother. However, the virtuous lady pleaded with him and managed to reconcile him to his brother, whom she then cured. In accordance with God's commandment, she thus rendered good to him from whom she had received only evil.

'Not long after, the emperor's brother, on whose account Florence had been exiled, developed a terrible case of leprosy which infected his entire body. As the news had spread everywhere about this woman who could cure any illness, the emperor sent for Florence. However, he was unaware of her true identity as he believed his wife to be long since dead. When she appeared at her brother-in-law's side, she told him that he would have to confess his sin in public or else he wouldn't get better. Though he held out for some time against doing so, he eventually admitted that he had concocted the whole despicable plot against the empress, who was completely innocent, and that he realized God was punishing him for this sin. On hearing this, the emperor was so distraught at the idea that he had wrongfully put his wife to death that he wanted to kill his brother. However, the good lady remonstrated with him and succeeded in calming the emperor's anger towards the sick man. Thus, thanks to her patience, Florence regained her position and was happy once more, to the great joy of the emperor and everyone else.'

52. About the wife of Bernabo the Genoese.

'On the subject of women who were steadfast and wise, we can recount a story which Boccaccio tells in his *Decameron*. One time, in Paris, a group of Lombard and Italian merchants sat eating supper together. They touched on many things in their conversation and soon fell to talking about their wives. One of the merchants, a Genoese named

Bernabo, began to sing the praises of his wife, lauding her beauty, good sense and, above all her other virtues, her exemplary chastity. In the assembled company was a disreputable man by the name of Ambrose, who retorted that Bernabo was a fool to commend his wife so highly for her virtue. He declared that there wasn't a woman alive who was so unyielding that she wouldn't finally give in to a man who tried to win her over with promises, sweet talk and presents. At these words, a great quarrel broke out between the two men. They ended up by making a wager of 5,000 florins: Bernabo bet that Ambrose would be unable to seduce his wife no matter how hard he tried, whilst Ambrose bet the opposite, claiming that he would bring Bernabo incontrovertible proof of his success. The others did all they could to prevent them from placing these bets, but to no avail.

'Ambrose lost no time in taking his leave and setting off for Genoa. On his arrival, he made enquiries about the habits and reputation of Bernabo's wife. In short, he heard such good reports of her that he despaired of winning his bet and bitterly regretted having been so foolish. However, since he was extremely unwilling to lose his 5,000 florins, he hit upon a cunning plan. He struck up a conversation with an impoverished old woman living in the lady's house, whom he then bribed with all sorts of gifts and promises until she agreed to carry a trunk, in which he would be hiding, into the lady's bedchamber. The old woman told the mistress of the house that the trunk contained some precious belongings which had been placed in her safekeeping. Since some thieves had already tried to steal it from her, she asked her if she could put it in the mistress's bedroom for a short while until the rightful owners returned. The lady replied that she would be happy to help her out. Ambrose, who had hidden in the trunk, spied on the lady at night and managed to catch sight of her naked body. He also stole from her a finely embroidered belt and purse that she herself had made. He then crept back into the trunk so silently that neither the lady nor the daughter who shared her bed heard a thing. After he had spent three nights in the trunk, the old woman came back to fetch it.

'Ambrose felt immensely pleased with what he had managed to achieve. He reported back to the lady's husband in front of the whole company of merchants, announcing that he had slept with the lady who had satisfied his every desire. First of all, he described the layout of the bedroom and the pictures that were hanging on the walls. Next, Ambrose showed Bernabo the purse and belt, which he immediately recognized as his wife's, and claimed that they were presents from the lady. As his final proof, he discussed the lady's naked body in minute detail, even down to a bright red birthmark under her left breast. The husband was totally convinced by these proofs and was understandably very distressed. None the less, he paid Ambrose the 5,000 florins in full and left for Genoa as soon as he could. Before he arrived, he sent word to one of his servants, a man who looked after his household and whom he trusted implicitly. In this message, Bernabo told his servant that he wanted him to kill his wife, describing to him exactly how he should perform the deed but failing to give him any explanation why. On receiving these orders, the servant asked the lady to ride out with him on the pretext that he was taking her to meet her husband. The lady set off with a glad heart, never doubting for a minute what the servant had told her. No sooner had they entered a wood than the servant informed her that he was under orders from her husband to kill her. However, this virtuous and beautiful lady soon managed to persuade him to let her go, on condition that she fled the country.

'Having made her escape, she travelled to a little town and succeeded in buying some men's clothes from a kind lady who lived there. She cut off her hair and disguised herself as a young man. She then continued on her way until she entered the service of a rich Catalan gentleman called Señor Ferant, who had come ashore at a port to refresh himself. She served him so well that he was absolutely delighted with her, telling himself that he had never had such a fine attendant. The lady called herself Sagurat da Finoli. When Señor Ferant went back on board ship, Sagurat went with him, and they sailed away to Alexandria. There he bought some falcons and some magnificent horses. Together with these purchases, they set off to visit the sultan of Babylon, who was a close friend of Señor Ferant's. After they had been there for some time, the sultan noticed how attentive Sagurat was towards his master and how handsome and poised he was. He was so impressed by him that he asked Señor Ferant to part with him, for he wished to make Sagurat his chief steward. Though Señor Ferant was very reluctant to let Sagurat go, he gave his consent. To cut a long story short, Sagurat served the sultan with such assiduity and performed his duties so well that his master placed his trust in no one else but him and put Sagurat in control of all his affairs.

'It so happened that, in one of the towns in the sultan's domain, a great fair was due to take place which attracted merchants from all over the world. The sultan ordered Sagurat to go and oversee the smooth running of the fair, and to look after his master's interests there. As God willed it, amongst the other Italians arriving with jewels to sell, was the treacherous Ambrose, who had made a fortune from the money he had won off Bernabo. As befitted a great lord who was also the sultan's honoured representative in town, Sagurat was visited every day by the merchants, including Ambrose, who all brought him marvellous jewels to look at. Ambrose showed Sagurat a small casket full of precious gems, which also contained the little purse and belt that he had stolen. Sagurat recognized them straightaway and picked them up. He stared at them in amazement, for he couldn't imagine how on earth they came to be there. Ambrose, who hadn't thought about this episode for some time, began to smile. Seeing his mirth, Sagurat asked him, "My friend, do I take it that you're amused to see me so fascinated by this little purse, which is a woman's trinket? It's actually a very lovely piece." Ambrose replied, "My lord, the purse is yours if you wish to have it. I'm just laughing because I've remembered now how I came by it." "May God bring you every joy," said Sagurat, "if you tell me how you obtained it." "By my faith," answered Ambrose, "a beautiful lady gave it to me as a present after I had spent the night with her. It also helped me win a wager of 5,000 florins which I had made with her idiot of a husband, a man by the name of Bernabo, who had bet that I would never so much as lay a finger on her. The wretched man killed his wife, though he was much more deserving of a punishment than she was. Men should know full well that, since all women are weak-willed and can easily be won over, they should never put their trust in them."

'The lady finally understood why her husband had been so angry, which had always been unclear to her before. However, like the sensible and resolute woman she was, she gave no hint of what she knew, but decided to wait until the right time and place. Sagurat therefore pretended to be highly entertained by this story and told Ambrose that he was a very amusing companion. He wished to become close friends with Ambrose and urged him to stay in the country so that they could go into business together, for he would put plenty of money his way. Ambrose was delighted by this proposition, especially since Sagurat went so far as to fix him up with his own residence. In order to lure him even further into his trap, Sagurat gave Ambrose lots of money and appeared to be so devoted to him that he wouldn't leave his side. Moreover, he had Ambrose tell the sultan his clever tale to make him laugh. To get to the end of this story, after having heard about how Bernabo had sunk into destitution, not just because of the huge sum he had lost but also due to the great distress he had suffered, Sagurat managed to engage some Genoese merchants, who were in the country at that time, to fetch Bernabo, by order of the sultan. On Bernabo's arrival at the sultan's court, Sagurat immediately sent for Ambrose. He had already informed the sultan that Ambrose's boast about seducing the lady was a lie and had asked his master to punish Ambrose accordingly if the truth of the matter could be established. The sultan gave Sagurat his word on this.

'When Bernabo and Ambrose appeared before the sultan, Sagurat spoke up, saying: "Ambrose, it would please our lord the sultan, here present, if you would tell him once again that funny story about how you won 5,000 florins off Bernabo, here present, and how you managed to seduce his wife." The colour drained from Ambrose's face: even such a vile trickster as he could scarcely conceal the truth any longer, for he had been taken off guard by this sudden request. None the less, he recovered himself a little and replied, "My lord, there's surely no need for me to repeat the story, as Bernabo is already very familiar with it. I'm ashamed to have caused him such embarrassment." For his part, Bernabo was so full of humiliation and sorrow that he begged to be spared from hearing the tale again and asked for permission to leave. With a smile, Sagurat replied that he shouldn't go yet but should stay to listen to the story. Realizing that he could prevaricate no longer, Ambrose spoke up in a trembling voice and began to tell the tale just as he had already told it both to Bernabo and to Sagurat and the sultan. When Ambrose had finished speaking, Sagurat asked Bernabo if it was true what Ambrose had said, to which he answered that it most certainly was. "But," retorted Sagurat, "how can you be so sure that this man definitely did sleep with your wife? Even though he brought you various types of proof, are you so stupid that you don't know that there are many ways he could have found out by trickery what her body looked like, without ever having laid a hand on her? And it was for this reason that you had her killed? You're the one who should be put to death, because you didn't have sufficient proof!"

'Bernabo grew very frightened but Sagurat couldn't hold back any longer, for it seemed to him that the right moment had now come to speak out. He therefore said to Ambrose, "You treacherous, lying cheat! Tell the truth, the whole truth, before you have to be tortured to make you tell it! It's high time you set matters straight, because it's obvious from what you've been saying that you're lying through your teeth. I want you to know that the lady you've been boasting about having seduced isn't dead. In fact, she's not very far from here and she's ready to disprove your foul lies. You never once touched her, that's absolutely clear!" The great crowd of people who were gathered there, from the sultan's barons to the group of Lombard merchants, were astounded to hear these revelations. To cut a long story short, Ambrose was put under such pressure that he admitted in front of the sultan and everyone else exactly how he had cheated in order to win the 5,000 florins. Bernabo almost went out of his mind with grief when he heard this confession, for he was convinced that his wife was dead. However, the good lady went up to him and said, "What would you give, Bernabo, if I were to return your innocent wife to you, alive and well?" Bernabo replied that he would give everything he had. She then said to him, "Bernabo, my brother and my friend, don't you recognize her?" As Bernabo was too stunned to understand what was going on, she unbuttoned her shirt, saying to him, "Look, Bernabo, here I am, your faithful companion whom you wrongfully condemned to death." With tears of joy, they promptly fell into each other's arms. The sultan and everybody else were so amazed at what had happened that they couldn't praise the lady highly enough for showing such constancy and they lavished gifts upon her. She also received all of Ambrose's wealth, for he was sentenced by the sultan to suffer a painful death. After that, husband and wife went back to their own country.'

53. After Rectitude has finished talking about women who were steadfast, Christine asks her why it is that all these worthy ladies of the past didn't refute the men and books who slander the female sex. Rectitude gives her answer.

Such were the stories that Rectitude told me on this subject. Lack of space prevents me from going into detail on all the other examples she gave me, such as that of Leaena, a Greek woman, who refused to denounce two men who were friends of hers, preferring to bite off her own tongue in front of the judge in order to show him that no matter how much he tortured her he had no hope of extracting by force the information he wanted from her. Rectitude also told me about some other women who were so strong-willed that they chose to die from drinking poison rather than fail to uphold truth and decency. I then turned to her and said, 'My lady, you've clearly demonstrated to me just how consistent and steadfast women are, in addition to all their other virtues. Surely there's no man of whom it could be said that he was their equal in this respect? I'm therefore amazed that so many worthy women, especially those who were learned and educated enough to write fine books in elegant style, could have allowed men to come out with their slanders all this time without contradicting them, when they knew only too well how false these men's accusations were.'

Rectitude replied, 'My dear Christine, this is an easy problem to solve. You should realize from what I've already told you that the virtuous ladies I've discussed with you were each involved in different types of activity and didn't all work towards the same end. This task of constructing the city was reserved for you, not them. These women's works alone were enough to make people of sound judgement and keen intelligence appreciate the female sex fully without their having to write anything else. As for the fact that the men who attacked and criticized women haven't yet been challenged, let me tell you that there's a time and a place for everything in the eternal scheme of things. Just think how long God allowed heresies against His holy law to prosper, which meant that they were very hard to stamp out and would still be around today if they hadn't been disputed and crushed. There are many things which flourish without hindrance until the time comes to take issue with them and refute them.'

I, Christine, came back to her again, saying: 'My lady, you're quite right. Yet I'm convinced that there will be plenty of dissenting voices raised against this very text. They'll say that, though some women of the past or the present might be virtuous, this isn't the case with all of them, or even the vast majority.'

Rectitude answered, 'It's just not true to say that the vast majority aren't virtuous. This is clearly proven by what I've said to you before: experience tells us that anyone can see for themselves, on any day of the week, how pious and full of charity and goodness women are. Not to mention the fact that it isn't women who are responsible for all the endless crimes and atrocities that are committed in the world. It's hardly surprising if not every single one of them is virtuous. In the whole of Nineveh, which was a very large city with a huge population, there wasn't one good man to be found anywhere when Jonah the prophet was sent by God to destroy it if the people didn't repent of their sins. Nor was there a single decent man living in the city of Sodom, as became clear when Lot left the place to be consumed by fire sent down from the heavens. What's more, you shouldn't forget that, though Jesus Christ's company only comprised twelve men, there was still one who was evil. To think that men dare to say that all women should be virtuous or that those who aren't should be stoned! I would ask them to take a good look at themselves and then let he who is without sin cast the first stone. Moreover, to what kind of behaviour should they themselves aspire? I tell you, the day that all men attain perfection, women will follow their example.'

54. Christine asks Rectitude if it's true what certain men have said about how few women are faithful in love, and Rectitude gives her reply.

Going on to a different subject, I, Christine, spoke up once again and said, 'My lady, let's put such topics to one side and move on to something else. Departing a little from the kind of things we've been talking about up until now, I'd like to ask you a few questions. I hope you won't mind discussing these matters that I'd like to raise with you: although the subject itself relates to the laws of nature, it does somewhat overstep the bounds of rational behaviour.'

Rectitude's answer was, 'My friend, say what you like. The pupil who puts questions to his teacher in the spirit of enquiry shouldn't be reprimanded for touching on any subject whatsoever.'

'My lady, there's a kind of natural attraction at work on earth which draws men to women and women to men. This isn't a social law but an instinct of the flesh: stimulated by carnal desire, it makes the two sexes love each other in a wild and ardent way. Neither sex has any idea what it is that causes them to fall for each other like this, but they succumb in droves to this type of emotion, which is known as passionate love. Yet men often say that, despite all the protestations of fidelity that a woman in love may make, she not only flits from one lover to another but is also extraordinarily unfeeling, devious and false. They assert that this fickleness in women comes from their lack of moral character. Of all the various authors who have made such criticisms of women, Ovid is particularly virulent in his book, the *Art of Love*. Having attacked women for their lack of steadfastness in love, Ovid and all the others then go on to claim that they have written their books about the deceitful ways and sinfulness of women for the common good of all: their aim is to warn men about women's wiles and to teach them how to avoid them, just as if women were snakes hidden in the grass. So, my dear lady, please tell me what the truth of the matter is.'

Rectitude replied, 'My dear Christine, as for what they say about women being underhanded, I'm not sure what more I can tell you. You yourself have tackled this issue at length, when you refuted Ovid, along with all the others, in your *Letter of the God of Love* and the *Letters on the Romance of the Rose*. However, getting back to what you said about these men's claims to be writing for the common good, I'll prove to you that this is definitely not the case. Here's why: you can't define something as being for the common good of a city, country or any other community of people, if it doesn't contribute to the universal good of all. Women as well as men must derive equal benefit from it. Something which is done with the aim of privileging only one section of the population is called a private or an individual good, not a common good. Moreover, something which is done for the good of some but to the detriment of others is not simply a private or an individual good. In fact, it constitutes a type of injury done to one party in order to benefit the other: it thus only profits the second party at the expense of the first. Such writers don't speak to women in order to teach them to beware the traps laid for them by men, even though it's undeniable that men very often deceive women by their false appearances and cunning ruses. Besides, it's beyond doubt that women count as God's creatures and are human beings just as men are. They're not a different race or a strange breed, which might justify their being excluded from receiving moral teachings. I can thus only conclude that if these authors were really writing for the common good, they would warn women against the snares set by men as well as advising men to watch out for women.

'Let's leave these issues for now and go back to your earlier question. What I told you before about those examples of women whose devotion endured until the day they died obviously wasn't sufficient proof for you that, far from being as inconstant or as fickle in love as these writers maintain, the female sex is in fact extremely steadfast in matters of the heart. The first example I'll give you is that of the noble Dido, Queen of Carthage. I've already described her great determination to you, though you yourself have also mentioned her elsewhere in your own writings.'

55. *On the subject of women's constancy in love: the example of Dido, Queen of Carthage.*

'As I mentioned to you before, Dido, Queen of Carthage, ruled gloriously over her city and led a peaceful and happy existence until the chance arrival of Aeneas on her shores. He had fled Troy after the city had been destroyed and was the princely leader of a great host of Trojans. Having survived terrible storms and shipwrecks, his food supplies had run out and he had lost huge numbers of his men. Penniless and tired of drifting aimlessly at sea, all he wanted was to find some peace. In his search for a place to stop, he had arrived at the port of Carthage. Unwilling to come ashore without having first been given leave to do so, he sent a messenger to the queen to request her permission to bring his ships into harbour. The noble queen, who was as courteous as she was courageous, knew very well that the Trojans had the finest reputation of any nation in the world and that Aeneas was a member of the Trojan royal family. She therefore not only gave him leave to land, but even went down to the sea in person, with a company of illustrious barons, ladies and maidens, in order to greet him herself and receive him and his people with all honours. Dido then invited him back to the city and treated him with great ceremony and lavish hospitality. Why make a long story of it? Aeneas was made to feel so comfortable and pampered during his stay in Carthage that he could scarcely remember all the hardships that he had suffered. He and Dido spent so much time together that eventually Love, who is all too skilled in the art of ensnaring hearts, made them fall in love with each other.

'However, as would soon become obvious, Dido was much more enamoured of Aeneas than he was of her. He gave Dido his word that he would marry no other woman but her and would love her for ever. None the less, he still abandoned her after all she had done not only to restore him to good health and to make him a rich man again but also to repair his ships and make them seaworthy once more, restocking them with provisions and loading them up with riches and treasure. All the wealth she possessed, Dido heaped on the man who had stolen her heart. Yet, unbeknownst to her, he slipped away in his ships like a thief in the night and thus repaid her most handsomely for all her hospitality! The wretched Dido was so devastated by his departure that she lost all interest in life and joy, consumed as she was by her passion for Aeneas. In the end, having uttered many regrets, she threw herself on a great pyre that she had prepared beforehand. Others say that she killed herself with Aeneas's own sword. Thus it was that the noble Queen Dido met her end, she who had been so exalted above all other women in her time.'

56. *About Medea in love.*

'Medea, the supremely learned daughter of the king of Colchis, bore an undying, passionate love for Jason. This Jason was a Greek knight who distinguished himself through his military prowess. He had heard that on the island of Colchis, which lay within Medea's father's domain, there was a marvellous ram with a golden fleece that was protected by strange enchantments. Although the task of winning this ram's fleece seemed to be an impossible one, it had nevertheless been prophesied that a knight would one day succeed in obtaining it. Jason, who was constantly looking for ways to increase his fame, heard this story and immediately left Greece with a great army, for he was determined to prove himself in this task. On Jason's arrival in the land of Colchis, the king told him that the magic protecting the Golden Fleece was so strong that there was no way that it could be won through the use of arms and that mere military prowess was futile. Since many knights had already died in the attempt, Jason should think twice before throwing his life away in such a swift and careless fashion. Jason replied that he wouldn't now give up on the task, even if it meant his death. The king's daughter, Medea, was so struck by Jason's good looks, royal lineage and impressive reputation that she thought he would make a good match for her. In her desire to show her love for him, she resolved to save him from death, for she felt such compassion that she couldn't bear to see a knight like him come to any harm. She thus freely engaged him in lengthy conversations and, in short, taught him various charms and spells which she knew would help him succeed in his quest for the Golden Fleece. In return, Jason promised to take no other woman but her for his wife, swearing that he would love her for evermore. However, Jason broke his word. After everything had gone just as he had planned, he left Medea for another woman. She, who would have let herself be torn limb from limb rather than play such a false trick on him, fell into utter despair. Never in her life did she experience happiness or joy again.'

17. About Thisbe.

'As you well know, in his book *Metamorphoses*, Ovid tells the following story. In the city of Babylon there lived two rich and noble citizens who were such close neighbours that the walls of their two houses adjoined each other. The two men each had a child, the most beautiful and delightful infants you ever saw. One of them had a son named Pyramus, and the other a daughter called Thisbe. These two children, who were innocent creatures only seven years of age, were already so devoted to each other that they were inseparable. In the mornings, they could hardly wait to get up and have breakfast in their respective houses before being allowed out to play with the other children and to spend time in each other's company. Not a day went by when Pyramus and Thisbe weren't to be seen busy together at their games. This went on as they grew older and, with each passing year, the flame of their passion burned ever more fiercely. Unfortunately, they spent so much time with one another that they drew attention to themselves and aroused people's suspicions. When Thisbe's mother heard what people were saying, she had her daughter locked in her rooms and declared in no uncertain terms that she would keep her away from Pyramus. The two children were so upset at Thisbe's confinement that they burst into floods of tears, for it seemed to them that it was more than they could bear to be prevented from seeing each other. Yet, though they had to endure this separation for a long time, their feelings for one another were not in the least weakened or diminished by it. Indeed, despite being kept apart, their love grew all the stronger over the years until they reached the age of fifteen.

'As fate would have it, Thisbe was crying alone in her room one day, her mind totally given over to thoughts of Pyramus, as she stood staring at the wall which divided the two palaces. In a tearful voice, she cried out, "O cruel stone wall, you cause me and my loved one such suffering that, if you had any compassion at all, you would crack a little so that I could at least catch a glimpse of my beloved." No sooner had she spoken than she happened to glance down at a corner of the wall and noticed that there was indeed a crack, through which she could see the light coming from the room on the other side. She therefore picked away at this crack with the buckle of her belt, for she had no other tool to hand, working away at the wall until the buckle passed right through to where Pyramus would see it, which is exactly what happened.

'Using the belt as a signal to attract each other's attention, the two lovers managed to talk together through the crack in the wall, exchanging their bitter laments. In the end, their love proved so much for them that they made a secret pact to run away from their parents one night. They would then meet up again outside the city walls near a fountain which stood under a white mulberry tree, a spot where they had played together as children. Thisbe, whose love was the stronger, was the first to reach the appointed place. Whilst she stood waiting for her lover, she was suddenly frightened by the roar of a lion which was headed towards the fountain for a drink. As she ran to hide herself in a nearby bush, she dropped a white veil that she had been wearing. The lion found the veil and vomited on to it the remains of some animals that it had eaten. Pyramus arrived on the scene before Thisbe dared to emerge from the bush and, catching sight of the veil in the moonlight, he could see that it was covered with gore. Convinced that his beloved had been devoured, he was so distraught that he killed himself with his own sword. As he lay there dying, Thisbe came out from her hiding place and found him in this sad state. Seeing the veil that he was still clutching to his breast, she guessed what had caused this tragic accident and, in her terrible anguish, she too lost all will to live. Once she realized that there was no life left in her lover's body, she let out great cries of grief and promptly killed herself with the same sword.'

58. *About Hero.*

'The young noblewoman Hero was no less enamoured of Leander than Thisbe was of Pyramus. In order to protect Hero's good name, Leander preferred to keep their love a secret and risk his own life rather than make it obvious to all and sundry that he was seeing her. He therefore adopted the habit of visiting his lady as often as he could by sneaking out of bed when everyone else was asleep. He would then go off alone to swim across a wide stretch of sea known as the Hellespont until he reached a castle called Abydos, which lay on the opposite side. He knew that Hero would be waiting for him in the castle, watching from a window. During the dark winter months, she would hold up a burning torch in one of the windows in order to help guide his way towards her.

'The two lovers used this method for their assignations for a number of years. However, Fortune grew envious of their happiness and decided to cast them down. One winter time, the sea was whipped up into huge, terrifying waves by fierce storms which lasted for many days. The two lovers became frustrated at this endless delay in being able to meet up and they cursed the wind and bad weather for not dying down. In the end, Leander could no longer contain his desire to see Hero, for he had seen her torch at the window and had taken this as a sign that she wanted him to come to her. Despite the awful danger to which he was about to expose himself, he thought that he would be guilty of faithlessness if he didn't go. But, alas, the wretched girl was simply afraid that he might try to come over and would gladly have done everything in her power to stop him from putting himself at such risk. She had only lit the torch in case he decided to try and see her after all. Fate was against Leander that night: the minute he started to swim, he was unable to battle against the current and was swept so far out to sea that he drowned. Poor Hero, who knew in her heart of hearts that something was amiss, couldn't stop crying. At daybreak, she went back to the window where she had stood all night, for she had been unable to sleep or even rest. When she saw the corpse of her beloved floating by on the waves, she threw herself into the sea, for she no longer had any interest in living. She thus died from loving too much, since she drowned with her arms wrapped round Leander's dead body.'

59. *About Ghismonda, daughter of the prince of Salerno.*

'In his *Decameron*, Boccaccio tells the story of a man called Tancredi, who was prince of Salerno. This prince had a beautiful daughter, a gracious, intelligent and refined girl by the name of Ghismonda. The father loved his daughter with such fervour that he couldn't bear to be away from her side and was thus extremely reluctant to allow her to marry, despite the pressure on him to do so. In the end, she was given in marriage to the count of Campania. However, she didn't remain a wife for very long because her husband died soon after they were married. Her father therefore took her back to live with him, determined not to let her marry a second time. Though she was the apple of her old father's eye, the lady herself felt that her youth and beauty were not yet over and that she wanted to continue living life to the full. Yet she didn't dare go against her father's wishes despite the fact that, quite understandably, she had no wish to waste the best years of her life without a husband.

'Spending much of her time at her father's side as he held court in his great hall, she started to notice that one young squire stood out from the many other gentlemen of the household. Compared to all these knights and noblemen, this man seemed to her to be more handsome and more refined and to have such excellent qualities that she thought him well worthy of her affection. In short, she was so impressed by his fine character that she decided that she would take him as her lover, for she wished to enjoy the remainder of her youth and give full rein to her passions. She none the less took her time before revealing her intentions to him. Seated at her father's table every day, she watched him closely in order to observe his behaviour and conduct. In fact, the more she saw of this man, whose name was Guiscardo, the more perfect he seemed to her in every way.

'Fully satisfied with what she had seen, she sent for him one day and said to him, "Guiscardo, my dear friend, my faith in your integrity, loyalty and honesty has convinced me to share some of my secret thoughts with you, thoughts which I can't disclose to anybody else. However, before I say anything to you, I want you to swear that you will never reveal these words to another living soul." Guiscardo replied, "My lady, have no fear: I shall never pass on anything you say to me to a third person. You have my word of honour upon it." Ghismonda then continued, "Guiscardo, I want you to know that I am strongly attracted to a certain gentleman and would like him to become my paramour. However, as it's very difficult for me to speak with him and I have no one to convey my thoughts to him, I would like you to act as our go-between. So you can see, Guiscardo, just how much I trust you above all others, because I'm making you responsible for protecting my good name." In response, Guiscardo sank to his knees, saying, "My lady, knowing that you are far too respectable and discerning ever to act in an improper way, I thank you most humbly for having decided to entrust your secret thoughts to me and no one else. My dearest lady, you can command me to do whatever you please, safe in the knowledge that my mind and body are entirely at your disposal. Moreover, I would be happy to offer my humble services to the man who is fortunate enough to be loved by such a worthy lady as yourself, for he is truly the object of a most honourable and noble passion." Having put him to the test and heard him give such a pleasing reply, Ghismonda took him by the hand and declared, "My dear Guiscardo, I must tell you that it is you I've chosen to be my one true love and on whom I want to lavish my affection. Your noble character and admirable qualities have convinced me that you are more than deserving of such a courtly relationship." The young man was overjoyed at her words and expressed his grateful thanks.

'To keep the tale brief, their love flourished for a long time without being discovered. However, Fortune became so jealous of their happiness that she could no longer bear to let the two lovers experience such pleasure. She thus decided to turn their joy into sorrow, and in the most extraordinary way. One summer's day, whilst Ghismonda was strolling in the garden with her ladies, her father, who was only happy when he was near her, went up to see if she was in her bedroom so that they could have a little *tête-à-tête*. Finding no one around but seeing all the windows closed and the bedcurtains drawn, he assumed that she was taking a nap and didn't want to wake her. He therefore lay down on a sofa and promptly fell sound asleep. When Ghismonda felt that she had spent long enough in the garden, she went up to her bedroom and lay down on her bed, explaining that she wanted to rest. She made all her ladies leave the room and close the door behind them. Neither she nor any of them had noticed that her father was there. Thinking that she was now alone, she got up from her bed and went to fetch Guiscardo, who was hiding in a dressing room, and led him into her chamber. They began to talk behind the bedcurtains, as freely as if no one else were present, and woke up the prince who soon realized that a man was in bed with his daughter. He was so horrified by this discovery that he had to restrain himself from confronting her on the spot, which would have brought instant disgrace upon her. He therefore stayed in the bedroom long enough to recognize her lover's voice before managing to slip out without them noticing.

'When the couple had finished making love, Guiscardo took his leave of the lady. The prince, who had ordered Guiscardo's arrest, had him taken prisoner and thrown into the dungeons. He then went up to speak to his daughter. With tears in his eyes and pain written all over his face, he said to her, "Ghismonda, I thought that in you I had the most beautiful, intelligent and virtuous daughter in the world. I'm thus all the more shocked because I never would have imagined that this was not the case. If I hadn't seen you with my own eyes, no one could possibly have persuaded me that you would lie with a man outside the bonds of marriage. However, as it's now quite clear to me how things stand, my disillusionment will haunt me for the rest of my old age; indeed, until the very day I die. What's made me most angry is that I used to think that you had a finer character than any other woman alive. Now I'm convinced of the total opposite when I see that the man you have chosen as your lover is amongst the lowest in my household. If you were absolutely determined to do this, you could at least have picked a worthier lover than Guiscardo from my host of courtiers. He's going to pay dearly for all the distress he's caused me. I tell you now that I'm going to have him put to death. I'd do the same to you too if my foolish devotion to you, surely the greatest that any father ever felt for a daughter, didn't stop me from doing so."

'As you can imagine, Ghismonda was horrified when she realized that her father had found out the thing that she had wanted above all else to be kept secret. Yet, what most cut her to the quick was the thought that her father had threatened to kill her lover. Though she would have preferred to die there and then, she gathered her wits together and put on a brave face. Without shedding a single tear, and despite her resolve to end her own life, she answered him, "Father, Fortune has obviously willed you to discover my secret, which I would have preferred to have kept hidden from you at all costs. I know I have no right to ask you for anything; however, if I thought I could win a reprieve from you for my lover by offering you my life instead of his, I'd beg you to kill me rather than him. I haven't any intention of asking your forgiveness if you're determined to carry out your threat against him, since I would have no further reason for living. You can be sure that by killing him, you will thus put an end to my life as well. As for being so upset by what you have found out, you have no one to blame but yourself. Given that you're a creature of flesh and blood, didn't you realize that you had a daughter who was made not of iron and stone, but of exactly the same material as yourself? Despite your age, you shouldn't have forgotten what it's like to be young and to live a life of luxury and pleasure, with all the temptations that such an existence places in one's way. Moreover, since you made it clear to me that you were totally against my remarrying, I fell in love with this man because I knew I was still young and capable of feeling passion. Neither did I give myself to him without having first devoted a great deal of thought to the matter. Indeed, I observed his behaviour most carefully and found him to be more generously endowed with every possible virtue than any other member of your court. You should know this only too well, for it was you who educated him. And what does nobility consist of, if not virtue? It doesn't depend on one's blood and ancestry. So you have no right to say that I picked the lowliest man of your household. Nor do you have any reason to be as angry with us as you claim to be, given that you yourself are at fault. However, if you're dead set on inflicting this terrible punishment on us, you shouldn't take it out on him, because it would be sinful and unjust to do so. Rather, you should punish me, for it was I who declared myself to him, not vice versa. Besides, just how do you think he should have reacted to my declaration? It would certainly have been very churlish on his part to refuse such a high-born lady. You should pardon him for his misdeed, not me!"

'The prince took his leave of Ghismonda at this point, but without being in the least better disposed towards Guiscardo. In fact, he had him killed the very next day, ordering that his heart should be ripped out of his chest. He then placed this heart in a golden cup and sent it with a cryptic message to his daughter. In this message, he told her that with the present that he was sending her he hoped to bring her joy from the thing that she most loved in the world, as a reward for having brought him such joy from the thing that he had cherished most in life. When the messenger saw Ghismonda, he gave her the present and repeated to her exactly what he had been told to say. Taking the cup, she lifted the lid and soon recognized what was inside. Though she was griefstricken, she succeeded in controlling her feelings and, without a flicker of emotion, replied, "My friend, please tell the prince that he has at least got one thing right: he has given this heart a most fitting sepulchre, for only gold and precious jewels would have been good enough for it." She then bent down towards the heart and kissed it, murmuring through her tears, "O sweetest of hearts, in which all my joy was entrusted, a curse be on him for his cruelty in forcing me to see you like this before my very eyes: if ever I wanted to gaze upon you in the past, I could always do so with the eyes of my soul. By a tragic twist of fate, your noble life has now come to an end. Yet, the wishes of wicked Fortune have been thwarted, for your enemy has in fact given you exactly the kind of sepulchre that you richly deserved. O dearest heart, it's more than fitting that I, who loved you so much, should perform the last rites for you by washing you down with my tears. I'll not fail you in this. Neither would it be right if your soul were ever separated from mine: my spirit will shortly be there to keep yours company. Once again, treacherous Fortune's plans have been foiled, she who has done you such harm. It's a boon that my cruel father has sent you to me so that I may pay my final respects to you. I can thus speak to you one last time before I depart this life and my spirit flies off to be at your spirit's side.

I know that, for both of us, this is our most fervent wish." With these and many other touching words, which would have moved anyone who heard them to tears, Ghismonda wept so heavily that it was as if two abundant streams were flowing out of her eyes into the cup. She gave no sobs or cries, but murmured quietly to the heart as she covered it in kisses.

'The ladies and maidens who were there with her were all utterly amazed at this sight. They knew nothing about what had happened and had no idea why she was so desperately upset. Out of sympathy with their mistress, they too burst into tears and made every effort to comfort her. Yet, it was all in vain. Even her most intimate companions could get no answer from her about why she was in such a state of anguish. When Ghismonda was at last exhausted from her grieving and could weep no more, she said, "O beloved heart, my duty towards you is now done. All that is left for me to do is to send my soul on its way to rejoin yours." So saying, she stood up and went over to a cupboard, taking out a small phial in which she had dissolved some poisonous herbs in water, in case she should ever need them. First pouring the liquid into the cup which contained the heart, she then swallowed the whole lot without a moment's hesitation and went to lie down on her bed to wait for death, wrapping her arms tightly round the cup. As soon as the ladies realized that she was in her death throes, they were horrified. They therefore ran to call her father, who had gone out for a walk to try to forget his unhappiness for a while. When he arrived at her bedside, the poison had already flooded her veins. Full of sorrow at this tragic sight, and bitterly regretting what he had done, he wept copious tears as he spoke tender words to her in a desperate attempt to console her. Though she could barely speak, his daughter answered, "Tancredi, save your tears for another. They have no place here and I have no desire whatsoever to see them. You're like a serpent that bites a man to death and then weeps for what it's done. Wouldn't it have been better for you if you had allowed your wretched daughter to enjoy her secret love affair with a worthy man rather than have to watch the sad spectacle of her death by your cruel hand, which thus means that what was supposed to be kept a secret has now been revealed to all?" With these last words, her heart finally gave out, the cup still clasped in her hands. Her despicable old father soon died of grief. Thus it was that Ghismonda, daughter of the prince of Salerno, ended her days.'

60. *About Lisabetta, and other women in love.*

'In his *Decameron*, Boccaccio also tells the story of a young girl called Lisabetta, who came from the Italian city of Messina. This girl had three brothers who were so avaricious that they delayed marrying her off for as long as possible. These brothers had a servant who looked after all their affairs, a good-looking and attractive young man who had been brought up in their father's household since he was a boy. He and Lisabetta spent such a lot of time together that they eventually fell in love with each other. While it lasted, their relationship brought them both much happiness. However, in the end, her brothers realized what was going on and took it as a terrible affront. They didn't make a public outcry about it, for fear of bringing disgrace on their sister, but decided instead to put the man to death. One day, they took the young man, whose name was Lorenzo, to visit one of their properties with them. No sooner had they arrived at this place than they killed him in the garden and buried his body amongst the trees. On their return to Messina, they made out that Lorenzo had been sent away on a long trip to see to some business of theirs.

'Lisabetta, in her deep devotion to the young man, was distraught at being deprived of her lover's company and felt sick at heart, for she suspected that something was amiss. Unable to contain her feelings any longer, she couldn't stop herself from asking one of her brothers where Lorenzo had gone to. Her brother answered her very abruptly, "What's it to you where he is? If you ever mention his name again, you'll be in trouble!" Convinced that her brothers had found out about her and Lorenzo, Lisabetta was no longer in any doubt that they had done away with him. In private, the poor girl was totally overwhelmed by her sorrow and, at night, unable to sleep, she shed bitter tears as she lamented the loss of her lover. In the end, she became ill from all her grieving. Using her illness as a pretext, she asked her brothers to allow her to spend some time visiting one of their properties that lay outside the city walls.

As soon as she received their permission, she guessed instinctively what had happened and went off by herself to the garden where Lorenzo was buried. She searched all around until she saw where the earth had recently been turned over to make a grave. Using a spade she had brought with her, she dug up the earth and succeeded in finding the body. As she held his corpse in her arms, her grief and distress knew no bounds.

'Realizing that she would be found out if she stayed there too long, she covered up the body once more with earth and took only Lorenzo's head, which her brothers had cut off. When she had finished showering the head with kisses, she wrapped it in a beautiful veil and placed it in the bottom of one of those big pots used for growing herbs. She then planted the top of the pot with some lovely cuttings of a delightful, sweet-smelling herb called basil, which she then carried back with her to town. She was so attached to this pot that she couldn't tear herself away from the windowsill on which she had placed it, and would water it, day and night, with nothing but her tears. Despite what some men say about women having short memories, her grief wasn't over in a matter of days, but rather seemed to increase with time. The basil itself grew thick and strong from the rich compost on which it fed. In short, Lisabetta paid such constant attention to the pot that some of her neighbours began to notice that she was forever weeping at her window and went to inform her brothers. They then spied on her and watched her in the full flood of her grieving. Totally baffled as to why she was behaving in this way, they stole the pot from her, which caused her even greater distress when she was unable to find it the next day. She begged them with all her heart to give her back the pot, promising them that they could have her share of the family inheritance if they did so. In her bitter lament, she cried out, "Alas! How unlucky I am to be the sister of such cruel brothers as these! They're so against my having any pleasure that they won't even give me back my wretched pot of basil. It means nothing to them, but it's all I want from them by way of a dowry. Alas, what a terrible injury they've done me!" The poor girl fell into such a state of anguish that she became seriously ill and had to take to her bed. During her illness, the only thing she asked for was her pot, refusing everything else that was offered to her. In the end, she died a pitiful death because of it. To prove to you that I'm not telling lies, a song was written about her and her pot after she died, a song which is still sung today.

'What can I tell you? I could give you endless examples of women who loved with a mad passion like this and who were faithful to the bitter end. Boccaccio recounts the story of another woman, whose husband made her eat the heart of her lover, and who then refused ever to eat again.[6] The same thing happened to the dame de Fayel, who was in love with the châtelain de Coucy. The châtelaine de Vergi likewise died of a broken heart, as did Isolde, who was so utterly devoted to Tristan. Deianira, who loved Hercules, also killed herself when he died. So there is no doubt that a faithful woman who gives her heart to another is capable of great ardour, despite the fact that there are some women who do lack constancy.

'However, these sad examples, along with all the other ones that I could tell you, are not intended to encourage women to launch themselves on the perilous and treacherous sea of passionate love. This is because such liaisons always have a tragic ending and the woman invariably loses out in terms of her health, status, reputation and, most important of all, her soul. Those women who are sensible and wise would do well to avoid embarking on affairs like this and not to waste any time on listening to men who are always looking for ways of leading them into such traps.'

61. *About Juno, and some other famous ladies.*

'I've now told you about a great number of the ladies who are mentioned in the history books. However, as I've no intention of discussing every single one, because we'd never get to the end of it, I think that these will have to do as evidence to refute the views of those men you have cited. I'll finish by recounting to you the stories of some women who were famous more for the extraordinary things which happened to them than for their exemplary virtues.

'According to what the poets say in their erroneous pagan fables, Juno was the daughter of Saturn and Opis. This Juno was the most famous of all pagan women, though this was due more to her good fortune than to her own merits. She was both the sister and the wife of Jupiter, who was known as the ruler of the gods. Juno and her husband enjoyed a life of such extraordinary affluence and prosperity that she was dubbed the goddess of wealth. The Samians, who obtained a statue of Juno after her death, attributed their particularly good luck to her. They also maintained that she governed the institution of marriage and answered the prayers of women who invoked her help. Everywhere, temples, altars and games were dedicated to her, and priests made sacrifices in her name. She was long held in esteem by both the Greeks and the Carthaginians. Her statue was later taken to the Capitol in Rome and placed next to that of her husband in the temple of Jupiter. Here she was worshipped for many years by the Romans, who ruled over the entire world and performed various different rituals in her honour.

'Likewise, Europa, the daughter of Agenor of Phoenicia, was also very famous. This was thanks to Jupiter, who fell in love with her and named one third of the world after her. Indeed, there are many countries, cities and towns which bear the name of a woman, amongst which we can cite England, so-called because of a lady by the name of Angela.

'Likewise, Jocasta, Queen of Thebes, was renowned for her terrible misfortune. By a tragic accident of fate, she married her own son after he had killed his father, though neither mother nor son was aware of the blood tie between them. She witnessed not just her son's appalling despair when he found out the truth of the matter, but also the deaths of their two children who later killed each other.

'Likewise Medusa (or the Gorgon) was famed for her great beauty. She was the daughter of the wealthy King Phorcys, whose vast kingdom was surrounded by sea on all sides. The ancient accounts of Medusa say that she was so incredibly beautiful that she surpassed all other women. What's even more extraordinary and almost supernatural, she had such a charming gaze, coupled with her lovely face, body and long curly blonde tresses, that she held any mortal creature who glanced at her transfixed by her look. It was for this reason that the fables said she turned people to stone.

'Helen, wife of Menelaus, King of Lacedaemonia, and daughter of Tyndareos, King of Sparta, and his wife Leda, was also renowned for her amazing beauty. The history books claim that she was the most stunning woman who ever lived, over and above all the other beautiful women ever mentioned, because it was she who caused the destruction of the city of Troy when she was abducted by Paris. For this reason, too, the poets believed that she was the daughter of the god Jupiter himself.

'Likewise, Polyxena, the youngest daughter of King Priam, was the loveliest maiden ever described in any historical account. Polyxena proved that she was not only beautiful but also extremely steadfast and resolute when she accepted her sad fate with dignity. Just before she was beheaded over the tomb of Achilles, she declared that she preferred to die rather than be taken into slavery. I could tell you about many others, too, but lack of space prevents me.'

62. Christine addresses Rectitude who, in her reply, refutes the view of those who claim that women use their charms to attract men.

I, Christine, then said, 'My lady, you were quite right before when you said that passionate love was like a perilous sea. From what I've seen, women with any sense should do everything they can to avoid it, for they only come to great harm. Yet, those women who want to look lovely by dressing elegantly come in for a lot of criticism, because it's said that they only do so in order to attract attention from men.'

Rectitude answered, 'My dear Christine, it's not my business to try and find excuses for those women who are too fussy and obsessive about their appearance, for this is no small failing in a person. Wearing clothes that aren't fitting to one's station in life is particularly reprehensible. However, whilst I've no intention of condoning such a vice, neither do I want anyone to think that they have the right to lay more blame than is strictly necessary on those who make themselves beautiful in this way. I can assure you that not all women who do this are interested in seducing men. Some people, not just women but also men, have a legitimate taste and natural bent for taking pleasure in pretty things and expensive, elaborate clothes, as well as in cleanliness and fine array. If it is in their nature to behave like this, it's very difficult for them to resist, though it would be greatly to their credit if they did. Wasn't it written of Saint Bartholomew the Apostle, a man of high birth, that he spent his whole life draped in fringed robes of silk which were hemmed with precious stones, despite the fact that Our Lord preached poverty? Though such behaviour is usually rather pretentious and ostentatious, Saint Bartholomew can't be said to have committed any sin because it was in his nature to wear expensive clothes. Even so, some do say that it was for this reason that Our Lord was content for Bartholomew to be martyred by being flayed alive. My reason for telling you these things is to show you that it's wrong for any mortal creature to judge another's appearance; God alone has the right to judge us. I'll now give you some examples on this subject.'

63. *About the Roman woman Claudia.*

'Both Boccaccio and Valerius tell the story of how Claudia, a Roman noblewoman, used to delight in wearing lovely clothes and was obsessed with making herself beautiful. Because she was more concerned about her appearance than any other lady in Rome, some people began to have doubts about her chastity, thinking that she had compromised her reputation. In the fifteenth year of the Second Punic War, a statue of the great goddess Pessinus, whom they believed to be the mother of all the gods, was being brought to Rome. All the noble ladies of the city gathered to greet the arrival of the statue, which had been loaded on to a ship to be taken up the Tiber. However, despite the sailors' best efforts, they were unable to bring the vessel into the harbour. Claudia, who was well aware that her behaviour had been misconstrued because of her appearance, knelt down before the statue and prayed out loud to the goddess. She declared that the goddess should know that her chastity was intact and her purity unsullied and so should grant her the favour of letting her pull the ship into port all by herself. Trusting in her virtue, Claudia took off her belt and tied it to the rails of the vessel. To everyone's amazement, she then towed it in as easily as if all the sailors in the world were rowing it to shore.

'I'm telling you this story not because I believe for a minute that this statue, which the foolish pagans took to be a goddess, could actually have the power to answer Claudia's prayer, but to demonstrate to you that though this woman was very solicitous about her appearance, she was none the less chaste for all that. She thus proved that her belief in her own virtue would help her, for it was this that came to her aid, not the hand of any goddess.'

64. *Rectitude explains that some women are loved more for their virtue than others are for their attractiveness.*

'Even supposing that the reason women put such efforts into making themselves beautiful and seductive, elegant and alluring, *were* because they wanted to attract male attention, I'll prove to you that this does not necessarily mean that men who are decent and sensible are going to fall more quickly or more heavily for them. On the contrary, those men who value integrity are more readily attracted to women who are virtuous, honest and modest, and love them more deeply, even if they are less glamorous than flirts such as these. Now, some might retort that, since it's a bad thing to appeal to men in the first place, it would be better if those women who used their virtue and modesty to catch men's eyes didn't in fact possess such qualities at all. However, this argument is utterly worthless: one shouldn't refrain from cultivating things which are good and useful just because some idiots use them unwisely. Everybody should do their duty by acting well, no matter what happens.

'I'll now give you some examples which prove that many women have been loved for their upright and moral behaviour. Most notably, I could tell you about various saints of paradise whom men lusted after specifically for their purity. This is also what happened to Lucretia, whose rape I recounted to you earlier. It was because of her exemplary virtue, not simply her beauty, that Tarquin fell for her. One night, her husband was at supper in the company of some other knights, one of whom was this Tarquin who subsequently raped her. Each of them started to talk about his wife, claiming that his was the most virtuous of them all. In order to find out whose wife was the worthiest of this accolade, they rode off to call on each of their houses in turn. Those wives whom they found busy at some honest task or other were held in the greatest esteem. Of all the women, Lucretia was deemed to be the one who was spending her time in the most commendable way. Like the highly respectable and sober woman she was, Lucretia wore a plain gown as she sat with the other ladies of her household busily working wool and conversing on moral subjects. The king's son, Tarquin, who had accompanied Lucretia's husband, was so impressed by her integrity, her simple and laudable conduct, as well as her modest bearing, that he conceived a burning desire for her and began to hatch the wicked plan which he would later execute.'

65. *About Queen Blanche, mother of Saint Louis, and other honest and decent ladies who were loved for their virtue.*

'Similarly, the most noble Blanche, Queen of France and mother of Saint Louis, was loved by the count of Champagne for her great wisdom, prudence, purity and kindness. This good lady reproached the count for having risen up against the king, Saint Louis, admonishing him for how he had acted in return for all the good things that her son had done for him. On hearing her wise words, he gazed with rapt attention at Queen Blanche and was captivated by her great virtue and respectability, despite the fact that she had long since passed the flower of her youth. The count was so suddenly overcome with love for her that he didn't know what to do. He would rather have died than declare his feelings to her, for he knew that she was far too honourable to answer his pleas. From that day forth, he would suffer terribly because of this fervent passion that had taken hold of him. None the less, the count managed to reply to her reproaches, stating that she should have no fear that he would ever wage war on the king, for he would always be a loyal subject to him. Moreover, she could be sure that not just his mind and body, but everything he owned, were entirely at her disposal. From that moment on, he adored her for the rest of his life, even though he had little hope of ever seeing his passion requited. He gave expression to his feelings of longing by writing poetry in which he sang his lady's praises most beautifully. These lovely poems were later set to music and made into delightful songs. The count had the texts inscribed on the walls of his great halls in both Provins and Troyes, where they can still be seen to this day. I could go on to tell you about many other women like this.'

I, Christine, added, 'Indeed, my lady, I myself have seen examples of such ladies with my own eyes. I know some wise and virtuous ladies who have confided their displeasure to me at finding themselves more desired once their youth and beauty had faded than when they were at their peak. These ladies said to me, "Good God, what can it be? Do these men see some foolish hint of encouragement in my face which might lead them to think that I would actually give in to their wicked desires?" Thanks to what you've just said, I can now see that it was their great virtue which won them these admirers. This also goes against the views of those who say that no decent woman who wishes to remain chaste will ever be courted or propositioned against her will.'

66. *Christine addresses Rectitude who, in her reply, refutes the opinion of those who claim that women are by nature mean.*

'I'm not sure what more to ask you, my lady, as all my questions have been answered. It seems to me that you've completely disproved the slanders which so many men have come out with against women. As far as I can see, it's even untrue what they so often say about avarice being the most prevalent of all the female vices.'

Rectitude replied, 'My dear friend, I can assure you that avarice is no more inherent in women than it is in men. Indeed, there would appear to be fewer avaricious women than men: as God knows and as you yourself can attest, the terrible evil that is so rampant in the world as a result of men's avarice is far greater than that which comes from women who possess this failing. However, as I pointed out to you before, the fool is all too ready to spot his neighbour's misdeed even though he is blind to his own great crimes.

'Just because women take pleasure in storing up cloth, thread, and all the other little items that are indispensable to a household, they earn themselves a reputation for being avaricious. Believe me, there are many, if not countless, women who, if they enjoyed great wealth, would not think twice about giving rewards and making generous gifts to those whom they thought would spend the money wisely. On the other hand, a woman who is poor is necessarily obliged to watch her pennies. In general, women are kept so short of money that they tend to hang on to the little they have because they know how hard it is to lay their hands on any more. Some people even go so far as to accuse women of being avaricious if they complain to their wayward husbands who are extravagant spendthrifts and beg them to be more careful with their money. Women like this know only too well how, thanks to the husband's foolish squandering, the whole household has to go without, and they and their poor children suffer as a result. This doesn't mean that such women are grasping or avaricious; on the contrary, it's a sign of their great prudence. Of course, I'm only referring to those wives who are discreet about admonishing their husbands. Otherwise this can cause great rows in marriage when the husband doesn't take too kindly to being criticized and ends up attacking his wife for something which is actually to her credit. As proof that this vice is not as common in women as some might say, just look at all the almsgiving that they eagerly perform. God knows how many prisoners, both in the past and still today, even those locked away in Saracen countries, have been comforted and helped out by women who were ready to give them money, not to mention how many poor people, impoverished gentlefolk and others they've also supported.'

I, Christine, then said, 'In fact, my lady, what you've just said reminds me of all the honourable ladies that I've seen making discreet displays of generosity, as far as their means allowed them. I know some of my female contemporaries take far greater delight in saying, "Here, take this" to someone who can put the money to good use than any miser ever did in grabbing some cash and hoarding it away in his coffers. I've no idea why men go around saying that women are avaricious. Although it's said that Alexander was famous for his generosity, I can tell you that I've seen little evidence for this!'

Rectitude burst out laughing and replied, 'My friend, the ladies of Rome were certainly not found wanting when the city was so heavily depleted by war that all the public funds to pay for troops were exhausted. The Romans were extremely hard pressed to find ways to raise money for the enormous army which they desperately needed. Out of their own great generosity, the ladies of Rome, including the widows, put all their jewellery and everything of value that they owned into a pile, which they then freely donated to the princes of the city. These ladies were very highly praised for their unselfish action. Their jewels were later returned to them, as was only right, for it was thanks to them that Rome's fortunes were restored.'

67. *About a generous and wealthy woman named Busa.*

'On the subject of women's largesse, the *Faits des Romains* mentions the rich lady Busa (or Paulina), who was a most honourable person. She lived in the land of Apulia at the time when Hannibal was laying waste to Rome with fire and sword, pillaging the whole country and slaughtering vast numbers of the population. After the terrible rout at Cannae, where Hannibal won a great victory, many of the wounded Romans who had survived the battle made their escape. This good lady Busa took in as many of these men as she could, lodging up to 10,000 of them in her various houses. Being extremely wealthy, she paid for them all to be looked after at her own expense. Thanks to her money, they received such good care and treatment that they were able to return to Rome and take up their arms once more. She was warmly applauded for this charitable deed. Believe me, Christine, I have an endless fund of stories about the generosity, altruism and liberality of women.

'Indeed, without going too far back into the past, amongst all the other examples of unselfish women of your own time whom I could tell you about, you shouldn't forget the wonderfully generous Marguerite de la Rivière, who is still alive today. This lady, who was the wife of the late lord, Bureau de la Rivière, First Chamberlain to King Charles the Wise, has always been unfailingly thoughtful, courteous and kind. She was once attending a splendid ball in Paris hosted by the duke of Anjou, who later became king of Sicily, to which a great company of noble ladies, knights and gentlemen, all dressed in their finery, had been invited. As this lovely young lady was looking round at all the splendid knights who were present, she noticed that one particular man was missing, a famous and excellent soldier by the name of my lord Amanieu de Pommiers, who was still living at that time. Though he was far too old for her to have known him personally, she remembered him for his brave and virtuous reputation. In her view, such a magnificent gathering could only be embellished by the presence of a fine and notable person like him, no matter how old he was. She went round all the guests asking if any of them knew why this knight wasn't there and eventually discovered that he was being held prisoner at the Châtelet because of a debt of 500 francs that he had run up travelling to fight in tournaments. "Well," the noble lady declared, "this whole kingdom should hang its head in shame for letting such a man as he spend even an hour in prison because of a debt!", whereupon she took off the beautiful and costly gold chaplet that she was wearing on her head and picked up a garland of periwinkle flowers with which to adorn her blonde hair instead. She handed the piece of jewellery to a messenger, saying, "Go and give this chaplet in payment for what he owes, so that he may come and join us once he has been released." The lady's orders were followed to the letter, and she was greatly commended for her action.'

68. *About the princesses and ladies of France.*

Once again I, Christine, interjected, 'My lady, now that you've reminded me of this woman of my own day and have started talking about the ladies of France, as well as those who have made their homes here, I would like you to tell me what you think of such women. Do you consider some of them to be worthy of inclusion in our city? Are they any less deserving of a place than foreign women?'

Rectitude replied, 'Certainly, Christine, I can assure you that there are many virtuous ladies among their number whom I'd be delighted to invite to become our citizens.

'First of all, we wouldn't refuse entry to the noble queen of France, Isabeau of Bavaria, who, by the grace of God, is now reigning over us. She has neither a shred of cruelty or greed in her body nor a single evil trait, for she is full of kindness and benevolence towards her subjects.

'No less worthy of praise is the young duchess of Berry, a wise, beautiful and gentle lady married to the Duke John, son of King John of France and brother of the late king, Charles the Wise. This honourable duchess conducts herself with such sobriety and discretion, even though she's still only a very young woman, that everybody commends her highly for her exemplary behaviour.

'What can I say about the duchess of Orleans, daughter of the late duke of Milan and wife of the Duke Louis, son of Charles the Wise, King of France? Could any lady be more prudent than she is? It's plain for all to see that she is not only steadfast and constant, but also very loving towards her husband and a fine example to her children. Moreover, she is astute in her affairs, fair-minded with everyone, sober in her bearing and endowed with every possible virtue.

'And what of the duchess of Burgundy, wife of the Duke John, son of Philip, who was himself son of the late King John of France? Isn't she also a fine lady, loyal to her husband, kind-hearted and well-disposed towards others, morally impeccable, and with no failing whatsoever?

'The countess of Clermont, daughter of the duke of Berry by his first wife, who is married to Count John of Clermont, son and heir of the duke of Bourbon, is everything that a noble princess should be in terms of her deep affection for her husband and her excellent upbringing in every respect, not to mention her beauty, wisdom and goodness. Her virtues shine all the more brightly thanks to her noble conduct and fine bearing.

'Amongst these ladies, there is one of whom you're particularly fond and to whom you're indebted as much for her own good qualities as for the kindness and affection you have received from her: this is the noble duchess of Holland and countess of Hainault, daughter of the late Duke Philip of Burgundy and sister of the present duke. Shouldn't this lady take her place amongst the ranks of the very finest ladies for her faithfulness, prudence and circumspection in her affairs, as well as her selflessness and extreme devotion to God? In a word, she is goodness itself.

'Doesn't the duchess of Bourbon also deserve to be commemorated for posterity alongside these other illustrious princesses, given that she is such an honourable lady, worthy of praise in every respect?

'What can I tell you? It would take me for ever to list the good qualities of all these ladies!

'The countess of Saint-Pol, daughter of the duke of Bar and first cousin to the king of France,[7] also merits a place amongst these fine ladies, for she is kind and beautiful, noble and virtuous.

'Likewise, another lady to whom you're devoted, Anne, daughter of the late count of La Marche and sister of the present duke, who is married to Louis of Bavaria, brother of the queen of France, would not disgrace this company of splendid ladies whose praises should be sung to the skies. Both God and the whole world are witness to her excellent qualities.

'Despite what the slanderers may say, there's a positively infinite number of countesses, baronesses, ladies, maidens, bourgeoises and women of every estate who are honourable and distinguished. God be praised for keeping them all in virtue, and may He inspire those who are less than perfect to mend their ways. You must have no doubts about this, for I can assure you that it's the absolute truth, no matter what those who defame women out of envy might say to the contrary.'

I, Christine, then replied, 'My lady, it certainly gives me great pleasure to hear you say this.'

She then turned to me and said, 'My dear friend, it seems to me that I've now completed my task in the construction of the City of Ladies. I've not only built all the lovely palaces and splendid houses and mansions for you, but also filled them almost to overflowing with a vast number of wonderful ladies from all different ranks of society. My sister Justice will now come forward to put the finishing touches to the city, and I will say no more.'

69. Christine addresses princesses and all other ladies.

'Most excellent, upstanding and worthy princesses of France and other countries, as well as all you ladies, maidens, and women of every estate, you who have ever in the past loved, or do presently love, or who will in the future love virtuous and moral conduct: raise your heads and rejoice in your new city. With God's help, it is now nearly complete, being resplendent with buildings and almost entirely filled with inhabitants. Thanks be to God for having led me through this difficult labour of learning in my desire to build an honourable and permanent place for you to dwell inside the walls of this city which will last for all eternity. I have come this far in the hope of being able to finish this task with the help of Lady Justice, who has promised me that she won't rest until she and I have done all we can to complete the city and shut its gates. So, pray for me, my worthy ladies!'

End of the Second Part of the Book of the City of Ladies.

PART III

Here begins the Third Part of the Book of the City of Ladies, *which explains how and by whom the high turrets of the towers were finished off, and which noble ladies were chosen to dwell in the great palaces and lofty keeps.*

1. *The first chapter recounts how Justice brought the Queen of Heaven to live in the City of Ladies.*

Lady Justice came to me in all her glory and said, 'In my opinion, Christine, you have indeed done your very best to bring your task to fruition. With my sisters' help, you've made a fine job of building the City of Ladies. It's now time for me to add the finishing touches, as I promised you I would. I shall bring you a most noble queen, she who is blessed amongst all women, to dwell here with her fine company. She will govern and rule over the city and will fill it with the great host of ladies who belong to her court and household. I can see that the palaces and splendid mansions have now been decorated and made ready and that the streets are all covered with flowers to celebrate the arrival of both the queen and her retinue of most worthy and excellent ladies.

'So let all princesses, ladies and women of every rank come forth to receive, with honour and reverence, she who is not only their queen, but also reigns with supreme authority over all earthly powers, second only to her one begotten son whom she conceived of the Holy Spirit, and who is the son of God the Father. It's truly fitting that a gathering of the whole of womankind should beg this revered, noble and magnificent princess to deign to join their number and to live amongst them in their city here below. Nor will she despise them for their lowliness in comparison with her own greatness. There is no doubt that she, in her humility, which surpasses that of all other women, coupled with her goodness, which is greater than that even of the angels, will not refuse to live in the City of Ladies. She will reside in the highest palace of all, one that my sister Rectitude has already prepared for her, and which is entirely made up of glory and praise.

'Let every woman now come forward and say, with me, "We greet you, O Queen of Heaven, with an *Ave Maria*, the same greeting that the Angel of the Annunciation made to you and which gives you more pleasure than any other form of address. The whole of womankind now implores you to agree to live in their midst. Extend your grace and pity to them by acting as their protectress, shield and defender against all attacks from their enemies and the world at large. Let them drink deep from the fountain of virtues which flows from you and may they quench their thirst so fully that they learn to abhor all forms of vice and sin. Please come to us, O Celestial Queen, Temple of God, Cell and Cloister of the Holy Spirit, Dwelling-place of the Trinity, Joy of the Angels, Light and Guide of those who stray, and Hope of all True Believers. O my lady, who could dare even to think, let alone utter, the idea that women are vile, seeing how exalted you are! Even if the rest of womankind were evil, the light of your goodness shines out so brightly that it puts all wickedness into the shade. Since God decided to take a member of the female sex as His bride and to choose you, most excellent lady, because of your great worth, all men should not only desist from attacking women but should hold them in the highest esteem." '

The Virgin replied, 'Justice, my son's dearly beloved, I will gladly come to live amongst these women, who are my sisters and friends, and I will take my place at their side. This is because Reason, Rectitude, you Justice and even Nature, have all persuaded me to do so. Women serve, honour and praise me without end, thus I am now and ever shall be the head of the female sex. God Himself always wished this to be so and it was predestined and ordained by the Holy Trinity.'

Flanked by all the other women who fell to their knees and bowed their heads, Justice replied, 'My lady, may you be praised and honoured for all eternity. Save us, Our Lady, and intercede on our behalf with your son who refuses you nothing.'

2. *About Our Lady's sisters and Mary Magdalene.*

'Behold, the Empress who is unparalleled in splendour is now living amongst us, despite all the slanders that prattling men have come out with. Next to her should be placed her blessed sisters and Mary Magdalene, for they stayed by her side at the foot of the cross during her son's passion. What great devotion and unfailing love these women showed by never once abandoning the Son of God in life or in death, even when all the apostles had rejected and forsaken him! You can see just how much God values women's love, even though there are those who claim that it is such a paltry thing, for He sparked a flame in the hearts of both the Magdalene and these other ladies that caused them to reveal their burning devotion, a devotion which He so warmly appreciated.'

3. *About Saint Catherine.*

'The ladies whom we shall invite to form the company of the blessed Queen of Heaven, who is Empress and Princess of the City of Ladies, are blessed virgins and holy women. We shall thus prove that God loves the female sex by showing that He endowed women, just as He did men, with the strength and fortitude needed to suffer terrible martyrdoms in defence of His holy faith, despite the fact that these women were only tender, young creatures. The whole of womankind can benefit from hearing about the lives of ladies such as these, whose heads are crowned with glory, for the lessons which they impart are more edifying than any others. It is for this reason that they will be the most revered inhabitants of the city.

'The most eminent of these exemplary women is Saint Catherine, who was the daughter of King Costus of Alexandria. Though this worthy maiden was only eighteen years old when she inherited her father's lands, she conducted both her private life and her public affairs with great discernment. She was a Christian and had refused to marry, preferring to devote herself entirely to God. One day, the Emperor Maxentius came to Alexandria in order to perform an important sacrifice as part of a great ceremony in honour of the pagan gods. Catherine, who was at home in her palace, could hear the bellowing of the animals which were being prepared for the ritual slaughter as well as the loud clamour of music. She sent word to find out what was going on and was told that the emperor had already arrived at the temple to make the sacrifice. No sooner had she heard this than she went up to the emperor and began to speak to him most eloquently about the error of his ways. Being well versed in both theology and the sciences, Catherine used philosophical arguments to prove that there was only one God, the Creator of all things, and that He alone should be worshipped. When the Emperor Maxentius heard this beautiful and noble maiden speak with such extraordinary authority, he didn't know what to say but could only gaze deeply at her in amazement. He sent for the wisest men that could be found in the whole of the land of Egypt, a country which was famous for the brilliance of its philosophers, fifty of whom were eventually brought to his court. However, once they realized why they had been summoned, they were extremely unhappy, saying that it was foolish of the emperor to have gone to all the trouble of bringing them from so far away simply to argue against a girl.

'To keep my tale brief, when the day of the debate arrived, the blessed Catherine blinded them with so many arguments that they were all convinced by what she said and were unable to answer her questions. The emperor was very angered by this and made all sorts of threats to them, but to no avail. By the grace of God, every one of them was won over by the virgin's holy words and became converted to Christianity. In his rage, the emperor sentenced all the philosophers to be burnt to death. The saintly virgin comforted them during their martyrdom, assuring them that they would be received into everlasting glory and praying to God to keep them strong in their faith. It was thus thanks to her that they took their place among the ranks of the blessed martyrs. God revealed His miraculous workings through them, for the fire destroyed neither their bodies nor their clothes: even after they had perished in the flames, not a single hair on their heads had been singed and their faces looked as though they were still alive. The tyrant Maxentius, who was inflamed with desire for the beautiful, holy Catherine, began to pay court to her in an attempt to persuade her to do his bidding. However, when he saw that he was getting nowhere with her, his pleas turned to threats and then to torture. He inflicted a cruel beating on her before throwing her into prison, with the express order that she was to be placed in solitary confinement for twelve days, at the end of which time he hoped to have starved her into submission. Yet the angels of the Lord went to her and gave her succour. When the twelve days were up, she was brought before the emperor once more. Seeing that she was even healthier and lovelier than ever, he was convinced that someone must have been visiting her in secret. He therefore ordered all the prison guards to be tortured. However, Catherine took pity on them and swore to Maxentius that the only comfort she had received came from God Himself. At a loss as to how to inflict an even crueller torture on her than before, the emperor took his prefect's advice and had wheels made which were fitted with razorblades. These wheels ground against each other in such a way that anything caught between them was torn to shreds. The emperor had Catherine stripped and forced her to lie between the wheels, yet she never once left off worshipping God with her hands clasped in prayer. The angels came down and smashed up the wheels, killing all the torturers standing nearby in the process.

'When the emperor's wife learnt about all the miracles that God was performing on Catherine's behalf, she converted to Christianity and criticized her husband for his conduct. She went to visit the holy virgin in her cell and begged her to pray to God for her sake. Because of this, the emperor had his wife tortured and her breasts cut off, whereupon the virgin said to her, "Most noble queen, don't be afraid of these tortures, for today you shall be received into neverending joy." The tyrant ordered his wife to be beheaded, at which sight huge numbers of his subjects converted. He asked Catherine to become his wife but when he realized that she was turning a deaf ear to all his pleas, he finally condemned her to be decapitated as well. In her prayers, she invoked the grace of God for all those who would remember her martyrdom and who would call out to her for help in their time of suffering. A voice came down from heaven saying that her prayer had been granted. As her martyrdom came to an end, milk, rather than blood, poured forth from her body. The angels took her saintly corpse and carried it to be buried on Mount Sinai, which was twenty days' journey away from

Alexandria. God performed many miracles at her tomb, which lack of space prevents me from recounting: suffice to say that, from this tomb, flowed an oil which cured many illnesses. The Lord then punished the Emperor Maxentius in the most horrible ways.'

4. About Saint Margaret.

'Neither should we forget the holy virgin Saint Margaret, whose legend is very well known. Born of noble parents in Antioch, she was introduced to Christianity by her nurse when she was only very young. To show her humility, she went out every day to look after her nurse's sheep. Olybrius, the emperor's prefect, caught sight of her once as he passed by. He became inflamed with love for Margaret and asked for her to be brought to him. To cut a long story short, she confessed to him that she was a Christian and refused to submit to his advances. He therefore had her severely beaten and thrown into prison. In her cell, she could feel herself subject to temptation and so called on God to let her see clearly exactly what it was that was pursuing her with such evil intent. To her horror, a foul dragon appeared which then swallowed her up. However, on making the sign of the cross, she broke out through its stomach. Next, in a corner of the cell, she glimpsed a figure that was as black as an Ethiopian. Margaret showed no fear as she threw herself upon the apparition and hurled it to the ground. She then placed her foot on its throat until it cried out for mercy, whereupon the cell was instantly filled with light and Margaret was comforted by angels. She was then taken once again before Olybrius who, when he saw that his threats were having no effect, ordered even more brutal tortures to be inflicted on her. However, God sent His angel down to destroy all the instruments of torture and the virgin escaped unscathed. At this sight, a whole host of onlookers converted. When the base tyrant realized what was happening, he sentenced Margaret to be beheaded. Before she died, she offered up a prayer for all those who would remember her martyrdom and would invoke her name in their hour of need, especially pregnant women and those in labour. The angel of the Lord came and told her that her prayer had been heard: she could now go to claim her palm of victory in the name of God. She proffered her neck to be decapitated and her soul was carried off to heaven by the angels.

'The villainous Olybrius also tortured and beheaded the blessed virgin Regina, a young girl only fifteen years of age. This was because she not only refused to give herself to him but also converted many people through her preaching.'

5. About Saint Lucy.

'Neither should the blessed virgin, Saint Lucy of Rome, be excluded from our litany. This virgin was kidnapped and taken captive by the barbarian king Aucejas. Back in his own country, he tried to take Lucy by force. She began to preach to him, managing by the grace of God to rid him of his evil intentions and to win him over by her excellent good sense. Proclaiming that she was a goddess, he installed her in his palace and treated her with great honour and respect. He provided her and her household with beautiful rooms and forbade anyone else from entering them for fear of disturbing her. She spent her time in constant fasting and prayer, leading a holy existence and beseeching God to shine the light of His faith down into her host's heart. Aucejas consulted her in all his affairs, and everything on which he took her advice turned out well for him. When he went off to war, he implored her to pray to her god for his sake. She said a blessing on him and, on his triumphant return, he declared that he wanted to adore her like a goddess and dedicate temples to her. Lucy told him not to do so on any account, for there was but one God who should be worshipped, whereas she was but a poor sinner.

'She lived in this holy state for twenty years until she received a vision from Our Lord telling her to return home to Rome where she would end her life as a martyr to the faith. When Lucy informed the king of her plans, he was deeply saddened and exclaimed, "Alas! If you leave me, my enemies will attack me and all my good fortune will disappear once you're gone from my side." But she answered him, "My lord, come with me and leave your earthly kingdom behind: God has chosen you to partake of a higher realm, one which will last for ever." At these words, the king abandoned everything to go off with the holy virgin, acting no longer as her sovereign but as her servant. Once they were in Rome, Lucy lost no time in revealing that she was a Christian. She was immediately taken prisoner and led off to be martyred. Aucejas was distraught at what had happened and ran to find her. He would gladly have attacked those who were torturing her but she forbade him at all costs from doing so. Weeping bitterly, he shouted out that only wicked people could do such an evil thing to a virgin of God. When he saw that they were about to decapitate the saintly maiden, he laid his head on the block next to hers and exclaimed, "I, too, am a Christian, and I offer my head to the living God, Jesus Christ, whom Lucy worships." Thus they were both beheaded and crowned in glory, along with twelve others who had also been converted by the blessed Lucy. Their joint feast day is celebrated on the seventh of the calends of July."[1]

6. *About the blessed virgin Martina.*

'We mustn't forget to mention the blessed virgin Martina, an extremely beautiful girl who was born of noble parents in Rome. The emperor wanted to make her marry him but she replied, "I am a Christian and have dedicated myself to the living God who delights in chastity of body and purity of heart. I adore only Him and to His care alone do I commend myself." Outraged by these words, the emperor had Martina taken to a temple where he tried to force her to worship the idols. Falling on her knees and raising her eyes towards the heavens, she clasped her hands together as she offered up a prayer to God. Immediately, the idols cracked and fell to the floor, the temple crumbled and all the priests who served the pagan gods were killed. The devil who was hidden in the chief idol screamed out loud and confessed that Martina was indeed the servant of God. In order to avenge the loss of his idols, the tyrannical emperor had Martina endure a cruel martyrdom but God appeared to her and comforted her. She prayed for those who were tormenting her and succeeded in converting them and many other people by her great virtue. When he saw this, the emperor became even more determined than before and he submitted Martina to tortures that were twice as brutal. However, her persecutors cried out that they could see God and His saints standing in front of her. They therefore begged for mercy and converted. Whilst she was deep in prayer on their behalf, a light shone down upon them and a voice from heaven was heard saying, "For the sake of my beloved Martina, I shall spare you." Seeing that they had indeed gone over to the Christian faith, the prefect shouted at them, "You fools! You've been tricked by this sorceress Martina!" Their fearless reply came, "It's you who have been deceived by the devil which possesses you, because you don't even recognize your own Creator." In his rage, the emperor ordered them to be hanged and flayed alive. They all praised God as they received their martyrdom with joy.

Next, the emperor had Martina stripped naked. She had such lily-white skin that the onlookers were all dazzled by her incredible beauty and the emperor burnt with desire for her. He made many threats to her and, as she refused to give in to him, he had her flesh cut to ribbons. From her wounds poured milk instead of blood and a delicious scent emanated from her body. His anger grew ever greater as he ordered her to be tied down flat on the floor between four posts, telling his torturers to smash her limbs. They beat her until they were completely exhausted, since God wanted to keep her alive a little longer in order for her to inspire everyone present to convert, including those who were persecuting her. Indeed, the torturers all cried out, "Your Majesty, we can't continue with this because angels are beating us with chains!" More men were brought in to punish Martina but they promptly fell down dead, much to the astonishment of the emperor, who was at his wits' end. None the less, he then had Martina spreadeagled on the ground and her body set on fire with burning oil. Never once did she leave off singing the glories of God as a delightful scent poured out of her mouth. When the torturers grew tired of inflicting these sufferings upon her, they threw her into a dark dungeon. The emperor's cousin, Elagabalus, who went to spy on Martina in her cell, saw her surrounded by angels and seated on a magnificent throne. The whole room itself was bathed in a brilliant light and was filled with the sound of melodious singing. Martina held up a golden tablet on which was written "O sweet Lord, Jesus Christ, praised be your works through your blessed saints". Elagabalus was so stunned by what he had seen that he went to tell the emperor, who retorted that his cousin had been taken in by Martina's sorcery. The next day, when the tyrant had her brought out again, everyone was amazed to see that her body was completely whole once more, and many of those present converted on the spot.

'The emperor took her back to the temple to make her sacrifice to the false gods. However, the devil who was lurking in one of the idols began to shriek, "Alas, alas! I give in!" The virgin ordered him to come out and reveal himself in all his foulness. Immediately there was a great roar of thunder and a bolt of lightning fell from the heavens, hurling the idol to the floor and burning the priests to death. The emperor then attacked Martina even more viciously than before, having her tied down and all her flesh torn off with iron pincers. Seeing that she was not yet dead but still kept praising God, he had her thrown to wild beasts for them to devour. A huge lion which hadn't eaten for three days came over to her and bowed down before her. It then lay down beside her like a little dog and began to lick her wounds. She extolled the glory of the Lord, saying, "Thanks be to God, for in His goodness He has calmed the ferocity of these savage beasts." The tyrant was so maddened by this spectacle that he gave the command for the lion to be taken back to its pit. To his horror, the lion reared up in rage and leapt out, killing his cousin Elagabalus. The emperor then ordered Martina to be burnt alive on an enormous fire. However, as she stood there joyfully in the midst of the flames, God sent a strong wind to spread the fire all around her, thus burning to death all those who were torturing her.

'The emperor commanded her beautiful long hair to be cut off, declaring that it was the source of all her magic powers. The virgin replied, "Just as you are taking away the hair that the Apostle calls the glory of a woman,[2] so the Lord will take away your kingdom and will persecute you until you suffer a terrible death in torment." He then ordered her to be locked up in a temple dedicated to his gods, and he himself secured the doors tight, marking them with his own seal. Three days later, he returned to find his gods lying smashed on the ground whilst the virgin, still alive and well, was seen playing with the angels. When the emperor asked her what she had done to his gods, she answered, "The glory of Jesus Christ has brought them down." At that point, he gave the command that her throat should be cut. A voice was then heard saying, "Martina, noble virgin, since you have fought the good fight in my name, come and join the saints in my kingdom and live in eternal joy with me." Thus the blessed Martina met her end. The bishop of Rome arrived with all his clergy to take the body away and give it a splendid burial in the church. That very same day, the emperor, whose name was Alexander, was afflicted with such searing pain that he bit himself all over in his agony and devoured his own flesh.'

7. About another Saint Lucy who was a virgin, as well as some other saints who were virgin-martyrs too.

'There was also another Saint Lucy, who came from the city of Syracuse. One day, as she was praying for her sick mother at the tomb of Saint Agatha, she received a vision of the saint surrounded by angels and adorned with precious jewels. Agatha said to her, "My sister Lucy, virgin dedicated to God, why are you asking me for what you yourself can do for your mother? I tell you here and now that, just as the city of Catania is exalted thanks to me, so will the city of Syracuse become famous thanks to you, for you have given Jesus Christ the priceless treasure of your virginity." Lucy stood up and her mother was cured. She gave up everything she had to God and ended her days as a martyr. One particular torture with which she was threatened by the judge who was persecuting her was to be taken to a house full of prostitutes where she would be raped, thus nullifying the vows she had sworn to her celestial bridegroom. To this threat, she replied, "The soul cannot be tainted if the mind does not give its consent. If you try to corrupt me by force, my chastity will be strengthened and my victory will be all the greater." The tyrant was determined to send Lucy to the brothel but she became so heavy that neither oxen nor any other beasts that they tied her to could pull her. Though they attached ropes to her feet in order to drag her, she remained as immovable as a mountain. As she was dying, she prophesied what would happen in the future to the Roman empire.

'Likewise, the glorious virgin Saint Benedicta, who was born in Rome, is equally deserving of our veneration. She was accompanied by twelve virgins whom she had converted to Christianity through her preaching.

In her desire to use her eloquence to increase the number of believers, she and her host of blessed virgins journeyed fearlessly across many lands, for God was with them. It was Our Lord's wish that they should be separated from each other in order that they might spread the word to as many countries as possible. Having introduced several different nations to Christianity, Benedicta ended her life holding the palm of martyrdom in her hand, just as did every one of her holy companions in turn.

'Likewise, no less perfect than Benedicta was Saint Fausta, a fourteen-year-old virgin. Because she refused to sacrifice to the gods, the Emperor Maximian ordered that she should be cut to pieces with an iron saw. Although the men entrusted with this task didn't stop sawing at her from the hour of terce to none,[3] they were unable to make even a scratch on her body. They therefore asked her, "What magic spell have you put on us to make all our lengthy efforts so futile?", whereupon Fausta began to preach to them. She told them about the Christian faith and soon succeeded in converting them. The emperor was infuriated by this and had her subjected to various other forms of torture, one of which consisted of banging a thousand nails into her head, which soon resembled a knight's helmet. None the less, she kept on praying for those who were persecuting her. The prefect himself was eventually converted once he saw the heavens open and beheld God sitting amongst His angels. As Fausta was being placed in a cauldron of boiling water, he cried out, "Holy servant of the Lord, don't go without me!" and jumped straight into the cauldron after her. When two other men whom she had converted saw this, they too leapt in. The water was bubbling away furiously but Fausta touched them all so that they felt no pain and said to them, "I am in your midst, just like the vine which bears fruit. As Our Lord says, 'Wherever several people are gathered together in my name, I am there in the middle of them.'" A voice was then heard exclaiming, "Come, holy spirits, your Father is calling you." At these words, their souls joyfully departed their bodies.'

8. *About Saint Justine and other virgins.*

'The holy virgin Justine, born in Antioch, was a young girl of extraordinary beauty who overcame the Devil. This demon, who had been conjured up by a necromancer, boasted that he would succeed in making Justine give herself to a man who was desperately in love with her and would not leave her alone. This was because Justine's would-be suitor had decided he would invoke the Devil's help, seeing that his promises and entreaties had had no effect on her. Yet it was all in vain, for the glorious Justine kept chasing away the Devil, no matter what different shapes he took to tempt her. In the end, the demon slunk off in defeat, having been totally vanquished by Justine. She then converted not only the man who had been pursuing her so relentlessly, but also the necromancer himself, whose name was Cyprian. Though he had led a wicked life, he became a better man afterwards thanks to her. Several other people were also converted by the signs of the Lord which He revealed through her. In the end, she departed this life as a martyr.

'Likewise, the blessed virgin Eulalia, born in Spain, was only twelve years old when she ran away from her parents. They had locked her up because she wouldn't stop talking about Jesus Christ. She escaped one night and went to cast down the idols in the pagan temples. She accused the judges who were persecuting the martyrs of acting in error, but insisted that she too wanted to die a martyr of the faith. Eulalia thus became one of the soldiers of Christ,[4] and underwent much suffering. Many people were converted by the signs which God made manifest through her.

'Likewise, another holy virgin, called Macra, was subjected to terrible torture in defence of the Christian faith. As part of her punishment, she had her breasts cut off. Later, as she lay in her prison cell, God sent her His angel to restore her to health. The next day the prefect was astounded at this sight, though he carried on persecuting her most cruelly. Eventually, she surrendered up her soul to God. Her body now lies near the city of Rheims.

'Likewise, the glorious virgin Saint Foy underwent martyrdom when she was only a young girl. She had to endure many torments but in the end the angel of the Lord came down to crown her in full view of everyone, bringing her a diadem encrusted with precious stones. God revealed His many mysteries through her, thus bringing about the conversion of scores of people.

'Likewise, when the blessed virgin Marciana saw that everyone was worshipping the false image of an idol, she picked it up and hurled it to the ground to smash it. For this action, she was beaten so hard that she was left for dead. That night, as Marciana lay locked in a cell, a corrupt priest crept in to try and rape her. By the grace of God, a huge wall suddenly rose up to stop him from getting anywhere near her. In the morning, many people saw the wall and were converted there and then. Marciana endured more terrible suffering but she never left off preaching in the name of Jesus Christ. She prayed to God to come and fetch her soul, at which point her martyrdom finally came to an end.

'Saint Euphemia was another martyr who had to endure appalling torments for Jesus's sake. This exceptionally lovely girl came from a very noble family. The governor Priscus used all sorts of threats to try and make her sacrifice to the idols and renounce Jesus Christ. However, the arguments she gave him against doing as he wished were so convincing that he didn't know how to answer her. In his fury at having been outwitted by a woman, he inflicted many cruel punishments upon her. Yet the more Euphemia's body was racked with pain, the more eloquent she became as words inspired by the Holy Spirit continued to pour out of her mouth. In the midst of her affliction, the angel of the Lord came down and not only destroyed the instruments of torture but also attacked those who had been tormenting her. With a face full of joy, she emerged unscathed from her suffering. The treacherous governor then had a huge furnace lit. When the flames leapt over 40 cubits into the air,[5] he had Euphemia thrown inside. From within the furnace, her delightful songs in praise of God were loud enough to be heard by everyone outside. When the fire died down, she emerged from the furnace as alive and well as before. Priscus grew angrier than ever and ordered red-hot pincers to be used to tear her limb from limb. However, those men who were supposed to perform this torture were so terrified that they didn't dare touch her and the pincers themselves fell to pieces in their hands. The brutal tyrant then had four lions and two other ferocious wild beasts brought in, but all they did was fall down before her and worship her.

In the end, the blessed virgin prayed to God to accept her soul, for her only desire was to be at His side. She thus died untouched by a single one of the animals.'

9. *About the virgin Theodosina, Saint Barbara, and Saint Dorothy.*

'Equally worthy of mention here is the blessed Theodosina, who showed such remarkable constancy in martyrdom. This extraordinarily beautiful girl, only eighteen years of age, was born of a very noble family. She used her fine intelligence to debate with Urban, a judge who was threatening her with persecution unless she renounced Jesus Christ. However, because she answered him with the words of God, he had her hung by her hair and given a severe beating. Yet still she reproached him, saying, "What a wretch is he who seeks to rule over others but is incapable of ruling himself. Woe betide him who thinks only of gorging himself with food and gives no thought to the starving. Shame on him who wants to be warm yet does not help clothe and comfort those who are dying of cold. Cursed be he who wishes to rest and yet forces others to work, who claims all things as his own when he has in fact received them from God, and who desires to be treated well by others but whose every action is wicked." Throughout her suffering, the virgin kept on coming out with other splendid words such as these. None the less, in her heart, she felt ashamed that her naked body was on display for everyone to see. God therefore sent a white cloud to cover her up completely from view. To Urban's increasing threats she replied, "You shall not take a single dish away from the celestial table that has been prepared for me." When he warned her that he meant to rob her of her virginity, she answered, "Your threats to defile me are all in vain because God dwells in the hearts of the pure." More incensed than ever, the judge had her thrown into the sea, weighed down with a heavy stone tied to her neck. However, she was kept afloat by the angels and she sang as they brought her back to shore. Theodosina then picked up the stone, which was heavier than she was, and carried it in her arms. Next the tyrant set two leopards on her, but all they did was dance around her in joy. In the end, Urban ran out of ideas and so had her beheaded, whereupon her soul visibly departed her body in the form of a pure white dove. That very night, she appeared to her parents wearing a priceless crown and shining more brightly than the sun, accompanied by a host of virgins. Holding a golden crucifix in her hand, she proclaimed to them, "Behold the glory that you wished to take away from me!", and straightaway they converted.

'Likewise, during the reign of the Emperor Maximian, the virtue of the blessed virgin Barbara, a high-born and supremely lovely girl, was in full flower. Because of her great beauty, her father locked her away in a tower, where she was divinely inspired to become a Christian. With no one else there to baptize her, Barbara took some water and christened herself in the name of the Father, the Son and the Holy Ghost. Though her father wanted her to make an advantageous marriage, she held out for as long as she could against complying with his wishes. Eventually she had to admit to him that she had become a Christian and had dedicated her virginity to God. On hearing this, her father was ready to kill her, but she managed to escape from him. Determined that she should die, her father set off after her and finally tracked down his daughter with the help of a shepherd who gave away her whereabouts. This shepherd was soon scorched to death for his pains, along with his flock. Her father took her before the prefect and there she was subjected to appalling tortures and hung upside down by her feet, all because she had disobeyed his orders. She kept saying to him, "You wretch, can't you see that your tortures are having no effect on me?" Boiling with anger, he had her breasts cut off and then dragged her around the town to display her mutilated body. Yet still she never let up singing God's praises. However, because she was ashamed that everyone would see her naked, virginal body, the Lord sent down His angel to heal her wounds and to drape her from head to foot in a white robe. When they deemed that her humiliation had gone on long enough, they took her back before the prefect, who flew into a rage at seeing her completely restored to health and her face shining like a star. He had new torments inflicted on her until even the torturers themselves grew tired of persecuting her. Finally, the prefect became so livid that he couldn't bear the sight of her any longer and ordered her to be taken away and decapitated. She began to pray, beseeching God to help those who would call on

Him for her sake in remembrance of her martyrdom. When she had finished praying, a voice was heard saying, "Come, my dearly beloved daughter. Come and rest in your Father's kingdom and receive your crown. All that you have requested will be granted." At the top of the mountain which was chosen as her place of execution, her wicked father himself cut off her head. On his way back down again, a bolt of lightning fell from the heavens and burnt him to a cinder.

'Likewise, the blessed virgin Dorothy of Cappadocia also underwent much suffering. Having refused to take any mortal man as her husband, Dorothy kept talking incessantly about her bridegroom Jesus Christ. As she was being taken off to be beheaded, a lawyer by the name of Theophilus mocked her by saying that once she was reunited with her bridegroom she should be sure to send him some roses and apples from her husband's garden. Dorothy replied that she would certainly do so. No sooner was her martyrdom over than a beautiful little child, about four years old, appeared with a small basket full of the most exquisite roses and the most mouthwatering and delicious-smelling apples. He came up to Theophilus and told him that it was Dorothy who had sent these gifts to him. As it was still winter time, being the month of February, Theophilus was so amazed by this sight that he immediately converted. He too later died a martyr's death for the sake of Jesus Christ.

'If I were to tell you about all the holy virgins who are now living in heaven thanks to their constancy in the face of torture, such as Saints Cecilia, Agnes, Agatha, and countless others, it would really take far too long. You only have to look in the *Miroir historial*, which contains many of these stories, to find out all about these other saints. However, I will tell you about Saint Christine, not simply because she's your patron saint, but also because she was a particularly splendid example of a virgin-martyr. I won't omit any of the details, for hers is a most beautiful and inspiring story.'

10. *About the life of Saint Christine the virgin.*

'The blessed virgin Saint Christine came from the city of Tyre. She was the daughter of Urban, governor of the city. Because of her great beauty, her father kept her locked up in a tower along with twelve other maidens. Despite the fact that he had built a pretty little oratory next to her bedroom for her to worship the pagan gods, she had already been inspired to adopt the Christian faith from the tender age of twelve and would have nothing to do with these idols. Her companions were most taken aback by this and they frequently urged her to offer up a sacrifice. Instead, she would take the incense as if to worship the gods but would then kneel down in front of a window which faced east, look up towards the heavens and pay homage to the eternal glory of the Lord. She would then spend the rest of the night gazing at the stars from her window, moaning softly as she invoked God's name in her prayers and begging Him to come to her aid against her enemies. Though they could see that her heart was given up to Jesus Christ, her maidens would often kneel down in front of her, their hands clasped together, imploring her to revere her parents' gods rather than put her faith in some strange deity. They were afraid that, if the truth came out, both she and they would be put to death. Christine retorted that they had all been tricked by the Devil into worshipping a multiplicity of gods when there was in fact only one true God.

'When her father eventually discovered that she was refusing to venerate the idols, he was extremely alarmed and reproached her severely. She replied that she would gladly make a sacrifice to the ruler of the heavens. Thinking that she meant Jupiter, her father was delighted and rushed to kiss her. But she cried out to him, "Don't touch my mouth, for I want to offer myself untainted to the Lord", which pleased him even more. She then went back into her room and locked the door behind her. Going down on her knees, she burst into tears as she recited a devout prayer to God. The angel of the Lord came and comforted her, bringing white bread and meat for her to eat because she had gone three days without food.

'A short while after, as she was looking out from her window one day, she saw some poor Christians begging at the foot of her tower. Having nothing of her own to give them, Christine went and fetched her father's idols which were made of gold and silver. She then smashed them to bits and gave the broken pieces to the beggars below. When her father found out what she had done, he gave her a savage beating. She told him in no uncertain terms that he was wrong to glorify these false images, for there was but a single God, who was three in one, and He alone should be adored. She herself was devoted entirely to this God and would worship no other, even if her life were at stake. At these words, her father flew into a terrible rage and put her in chains. Before throwing her into prison, he had her scourged as she was being led through the town. Having decided to judge her himself, he had her brought before him the next morning and threatened her with all sorts of tortures if she refused to revere the idols. However, when he saw that neither his pleas nor his threats were having any effect on her, he ordered her to be stripped and spreadeagled, with her arms and legs tied down, and commanded twelve men to whip her until they were exhausted. He kept asking her if she had changed her mind, saying to her, "Daughter, it truly breaks my paternal heart to have to torture my own flesh and blood, but my duty to the gods means that I have no choice, for you have turned your back on them." The holy virgin replied, "Tyrant! You're fit only to be called the enemy of my happiness, not my father! Though you may inflict a harsh punishment on this flesh which you have created, you have no power to subject my spirit to any temptation whatsoever, for it has been created by my Father who lives in heaven and it is protected by Jesus Christ, my saviour." Her brutal father grew even more furious and brought in a wheel that he had had made. He tied the poor little child to it, lit a fire beneath her and threw great quantities of boiling oil on to her body. As the wheel turned, all her limbs were broken.

'God, the merciful Father, took pity on His servant. He commanded His angel to go down and break the wheel, put out the fire and deliver the virgin safe and sound. More than a thousand pitiless unbelievers who had been watching her suffer were killed, blaspheming against God as they died. Her father asked her, "Tell me, who taught you such black magic?", to which she replied, "Ruthless tyrant, didn't I make it plain to you that my Father, Jesus Christ, was the one who taught me to have patience and to uphold my faith in Him, the living God? Thanks to Him, I shall overcome every possible torture you can devise and, with the grace of God, I will resist all the assaults that the Devil may make on me." Despairing at having been defeated, her father threw Christine into a dark and gloomy dungeon. As she lay there contemplating God's mysteries, three brightly shining angels came to visit her, bringing her food to eat and words of comfort. Urban kept dreaming up different kinds of torture to inflict on his daughter, for he was at his wits' end how to deal with her. He finally became so angry that he decided to get rid of her once and for all by tying a great stone around her neck and throwing her into the sea. However, just as she was being tipped into the waves, the angels took hold of her and carried her off across the water with them. She raised her eyes to heaven and offered up a prayer to Jesus Christ, begging him to baptize her using the sea water as the holy sacrament, for her sole desire was to be christened. Jesus Christ himself came down with a whole host of angels and baptized her with his own name, calling her Christine. He then crowned her and placed a bright star on her head before leading her back to dry land. That night, Urban was tormented by the Devil and died.

'The blessed Christine, whom God wanted to receive in heaven as a martyr, as was also her own most fervent wish, was taken back to the prison by her tormentors. The second judge, whose name was Dyon, knew all about what had already been done to her and ordered her to be brought before him. The sight of her beauty quickened his heart with desire, but when his honeyed words clearly failed to have any effect on her, he decided to subject her to new tortures. He had a huge cauldron of oil and pitch heated up over a great fire, into which she was thrown head first and prodded by four men wielding iron hooks. The holy virgin kept on singing sweet hymns in praise of God as she mocked her torturers by saying that they would be punished in hell. Realizing that his efforts were all in vain, the cruel judge had her suspended by her long, golden hair in front of the whole town. Women rushed up to her in tears, full of pity at seeing such a tender young creature being so ill treated. The women said to the judge, "Brutal tyrant, you're more ferocious than a wild beast. How can any man have it in his heart to be

so violent towards a lovely, innocent girl like this?" As they were about
to attack him, the judge grew so afraid that he said to Christine, "My
friend, don't suffer this torture any longer. Come with me, we'll go
together and worship the supreme god who has helped sustain you
through all this." Although by "supreme god" he meant Jupiter, she
understood something quite different. She therefore replied, "You've
convinced me to do as you say." He had her cut down and taken to the
temple, with a huge crowd of people following on behind. Having
brought her before the idols, Dyon thought that Christine would bow
down and worship them. Instead, she knelt down, raised her eyes to
heaven and said a prayer to God. She then stood up, turned towards
the idol and exclaimed, "In the name of Jesus Christ, I order the evil
spirit that lives inside this idol to come out now!" No sooner had she
uttered these words than the Devil himself appeared with a deafening
and terrifying roar. Everyone was so horrified that they all fell to the
floor. When the judge picked himself up, he said to Christine, "Our
almighty god has been moved by your words: he has taken pity on you
and come out to see his creature for himself." She was furious at this
and attacked him fiercely for being so blind that he couldn't even
recognize the hand of God at work. She then prayed to the Lord to cast
the idol down and turn it into dust, which is exactly what happened.
Thanks to the virgin's words and miraculous deeds, more than 3,000
men were converted. The terror-stricken judge said, "If the king finds
out the wrong that this Christine has perpetrated on our god, he'll have
me put to a horrible death." He went out of his mind with fear and died.

'A third judge, by the name of Julian, was then called in. He seized
Christine and boasted that he would definitely succeed in making her
worship the idols. However, no matter how hard he tried, he was unable
to move her from the spot where she stood. He therefore had a huge
fire lit all around her, in which she was tortured for three whole days.
Yet, throughout this time, sweet songs could be heard coming from the
flames. Her persecutors were absolutely terrified by these extraordinary
signs and went to tell Julian what they had seen. He thought he would
go mad with rage when Christine emerged completely unscathed after
the fire had died out. He therefore ordered serpents to be brought, and
Christine was set upon by two asps – a kind of snake that has a terribly

poisonous bite – as well as by two enormous adders. However, the
snakes just fell at her feet with their heads bowed and did her no harm
whatsoever. Next, two horrible vipers were let loose, but they simply
hung off her breasts and licked her. Christine looked up to the heavens
and exclaimed, "Lord God, Jesus Christ, thanks be to you for exalting
me with your holy powers so that these vicious serpents can recognize
your splendour in me." Despite these marvels, Julian would not stop
there but shouted over to the man who looked after the snakes, "Has
Christine cast a spell on you too which prevents you from making the
snakes attack her?" Fearful of what the judge might do to him, the man
tried to excite the snakes into striking Christine, but they just turned on
him instead and bit him to death. As everyone was too afraid of the
serpents to go near them, Christine commanded them in the name of
God to return whence they came without harming anyone, which they
did. She brought the dead man back to life, who immediately fell down
at her feet and became a Christian. The judge, who was too blinded by
the Devil to see that these were the workings of God, said to Christine,
"We've had quite enough of your witchcraft!" In her fury, she answered
him, "If your eyes could see God's powers, you would surely believe in
them." Livid with rage, he had her breasts torn off, whereupon milk
rather than blood poured forth from her wounds. As she wouldn't stop
calling out Jesus Christ's name, he had her tongue cut out too. Yet she
then spoke even more clearly and eloquently than before as she talked
of holy matters and blessed God, thanking Him for the favour He had
shown her. She began to pray to Him, asking to take her place at His
side once the crown of her martyrdom was completed.

'A voice from heaven was heard saying, "Pure, innocent Christine,
the heavens are open to you and the everlasting kingdom is ready to
welcome you. The whole company of saints is praying to God on your
behalf: ever since you were a child, you have steadfastly upheld the name
of Jesus Christ." Lauding God, she lifted her gaze towards heaven. The
voice spoke again, "My beloved daughter Christine, my chosen one,
come and accept the eternal crown and palm. Take the reward that you
deserve for having spent your life as a martyr glorifying my name." When
the evil Julian heard this voice, he reproached the torturers for not
having removed enough of Christine's tongue, telling them to cut it so

close that she would be unable to converse with her lord Jesus. They cut off the whole of her tongue, right down to the root, but she spat out these remains into the tyrant's face and blinded him in one eye. Speaking just as easily as ever, she exclaimed, "Tyrant, what was the point of your removing my tongue so that I couldn't praise God when my spirit will praise Him for evermore whilst yours is damned for all eternity? It's only fitting that my tongue should have blinded you, since you didn't believe my words in the first place." So saying, Christine could already see Jesus Christ seated at his Father's right hand as her martyrdom came to an end from two arrows that were shot at her, one in her side and the other near her heart. A relative of hers, whom she had converted, buried her saintly body and wrote down her magnificent legend.'

I exclaimed, 'O blessed Christine, worthy virgin exalted by God, and most triumphant and glorious martyr! Since the Lord chose to confer on you the crown of sainthood, I beg you to pray for me, a poor sinner who bears your name. O most merciful lady, please intercede on my behalf as my patron saint. See how delighted I am to recount your holy legend and include it in my book, showing my great devotion to you by leaving nothing out. If you please, pray also for the whole of womankind, in the hope that your saintly life will inspire all women to make a good end. Amen.'

Justice continued, 'What more can I tell you, my dear friend, to swell the number of inhabitants of our city? Let Saint Ursula come forward with her great host of blessed virgins, more than eleven thousand in total, all of whom were beheaded for the sake of Jesus Christ. Having been sent off to be married, they arrived in a country full of unbelievers who tried to force them to renounce Christianity. They all preferred to die rather than abjure their faith in Jesus Christ, their Saviour.'

11. *About several saints who saw their children being martyred in front of them.*

'What in the world is more tender than a mother towards her child? What greater pain is there than that felt in a mother's heart when she sees her child suffer? Yet, in my view, faith is an even greater thing, as was shown by the many valiant women who, for the love of Our Lord Jesus Christ, gave up their own children to be martyred. One such woman was the blessed Felicity, who saw all seven of her beautiful children being tortured in front of her. This fine mother comforted her little ones and urged them to have patience and to remain steadfast in their faith: in her devotion to God, she had put aside all maternal feelings for her own flesh and blood. After she had allowed every one of them to be sacrificed, she chose to suffer the same fate and so died a martyr's death.

'Likewise, this was also the case of the blessed Julitta, who had a son named Cyricus. Just as she gave her son nourishment for his body, so she gave him nourishment for his soul by thoroughly immersing him in the tenets of the Christian faith. Though he was just a young child, he never succumbed to the efforts made by his persecutors to force him to renounce the name of Jesus Christ. Indeed, as he was being tortured, he kept crying out as loud as he could in his little high-pitched voice, "I am a Christian, I am a Christian, and I give thanks to you, Lord God!" He spoke as eloquently as any forty-year-old man would have done. His loving mother comforted him before she too in turn underwent terrible torments. She never left off praising God and reassuring the other martyrs by telling them not to be afraid but to turn their minds towards the celestial joy that awaited them.

'Likewise, what could we say about the constancy and fortitude displayed by the blessed Blandina? She watched her beloved fifteen-year-old daughter being tortured and martyred before her very eyes. She consoled her child most joyfully and afterwards went to face her own martyrdom with a heart as glad as that of any bride going to meet her bridegroom. Blandina was subjected to so many different torments that her persecutors wore themselves out from their efforts. She was placed on a gridiron and roasted, before being torn to pieces with iron pincers. Yet she still kept on glorifying God, right up until the moment she died.'

12. *About Saint Marina the virgin.*

'There are so many stories that could be told about virgin-martyrs as well as other women who took religious orders or who displayed their saintliness in different ways. I'll tell you about two such women in particular, because their legends are very inspiring and they also prove what we've been saying about the constancy of women.

'A layman had a young daughter called Marina, whom he placed in the care of one of his relatives when he took holy orders and went off to devote himself to God. However, his thoughts were naturally still drawn to her and his anxiety about her welfare preyed heavily on his mind. He became so preoccupied that the abbot eventually asked him what it was that was causing him such distress. He explained that he was deeply concerned about a son of his left behind in the outside world and whom he was unable to put out of his thoughts. The abbot told him to fetch his son and bring him back to the monastery with him. In order for her to stay with her father, the young maiden was made to dress like a novice. She learnt to keep up this pretence and adhered perfectly to the rigours of her new life, growing ever more saintly with each passing day. Her father, who had given her a truly devout upbringing, died when she was eighteen years old. Henceforth, she lived alone in his cell, leading such a holy existence that the abbot and all the other monks were full of praise for her piety. None of them suspected that she was, in fact, a woman.

'About three miles away from the monastery lay a town where a market was regularly held. The monks frequently had to go to the market to buy their necessary supplies. Sometimes in winter when their business kept them overnight, they would take lodgings in town. Marina, who was known as Brother Marinus, often had to take her turn and spend the night at a certain inn where they usually stayed. It so happened that the innkeeper's daughter became pregnant. Under pressure from her parents to tell them who the father was, she accused Brother Marinus. Her parents went to complain to the abbot, who was deeply upset by this news and called Marinus in to see him. Since the holy virgin preferred to take the blame rather than prove her innocence by revealing that she was a woman, she fell weeping to her knees and said, "Father, I have sinned. Pray for me and I will do penance." The abbot was so angry that he had Marinus beaten and thrown out of the monastery, forbidding him ever to return. In penance, Marinus lay down on the ground in front of the gate and begged for a scrap of bread to eat from the other monks. The innkeeper's daughter gave birth to a son whom her mother then left with Marinus as he lay outside the monastery. The virgin took the child and fed him with the pieces of bread that she received from people as they went inside, bringing the boy up as if he were her own son. After a while, the monks took pity on Marinus and begged the abbot to show mercy on him and allow him back in. They had great difficulty in persuading him to do so, even though Marinus had already spent five years doing penance. On his return to the monastery, the abbot gave Marinus all the dirtiest and most unpleasant tasks to do, making him fetch the water for washing and cleaning and forcing him to see to everyone's needs. The holy virgin carried out all these jobs most willingly and with great humility.

'Some time later, she fell asleep in Jesus Christ. When the monks told the abbot, he said to them, "You can clearly see that his sin was so great that he was not forgiven. Wash his body all the same, but bury him well outside the monastery walls." However, once they undressed him and discovered that he was in fact a woman, they began to beat themselves and wail in dismay. They were horrified to see the terrible wrong that they had done to such a holy and innocent creature, and they were all amazed by her extraordinary saintliness. No sooner was the abbot informed than he rushed to Marina's cell. He burst into tears as he fell down at her feet, beating his breast and begging for mercy and forgiveness. Afterwards, he gave the order for her to be buried in a chapel inside the church. The monks all gathered round the tomb, including a certain monk who had lost his sight in one eye. As he bent down to kiss the body and pay his respects, his sight was immediately restored. That same day, the girl who had given birth to the baby went out of her mind and confessed her sin. She too was taken before the holy body and soon recovered her senses. Many other miracles occurred on this site, and still do today.'

13. *About the blessed virgin Euphrosyna.*

'Similarly, in Alexandria, lived a virgin named Euphrosyna whose father, Paphnutius, was a very wealthy man. God had granted him a daughter in answer to all the prayers which he had requested from a holy abbot and a community of monks which lay nearby. When this girl came of age, her father wanted to marry her off. However, because she had dedicated herself to God and wished to preserve her virginity, she ran away from home disguised as a man. She asked to be admitted into this monastery, making them believe that she was a youth from the emperor's court who devoutly wished to take orders. Seeing the boy's great fervour, the abbot was delighted to let him in. When Paphnutius realized that his beloved daughter was missing, he fell into despair. In order to find some comfort, he went to the abbot and poured out his heart to him, begging him and the whole community of monks to appeal to God for news of her. The abbot tried to reassure Paphnutius by saying that he couldn't believe that God would have answered his prayers and given him a daughter whom He would then allow to perish. He and his monks spent a long time praying on the father's behalf.

'Seeing the worthy man come back to the monastery day after day to try to alleviate his suffering at having received no news of his daughter, the abbot eventually said to him, "I truly believe that your daughter cannot have come to any harm: if she had, God would somehow have let us know it. We have here amongst us a pious young man who has come from the emperor's court. God has shown him such favour that whoever speaks to him is greatly comforted by his words. You could go and talk with him, if you wished." Paphnutius asked him to arrange such a meeting straightaway. The abbot then led him to see his daughter, whom he failed to recognize. She, however, recognized him instantly. Tears welled up in her eyes and she had to turn her head away from him as if she were finishing a prayer. Because of the harsh regime of abstinence which she followed, her fresh young complexion had already faded. A few moments later, she spoke to her father and cheered him immensely by saying that his daughter was serving God and living in a safe place. She also reassured him that, before he died, he would definitely see her again and would once more delight in her company. Thinking that the boy knew all this thanks to divine inspiration, the father felt much better. As he took his leave, he told the abbot that ever since he had lost his daughter, he had never known such peace of mind: "By God's grace, I'm as happy as if I had actually found my daughter." On his departure, he commended himself to the abbot and to the monks' prayers. It wasn't long before he started to come back time and time again to visit the holy man, for the only happiness he knew was when the two of them were in conversation.

'This state of affairs went on for a long time. The daughter, who called herself Brother Smaragdus, had spent thirty-eight years in her cell when God decided to call her to Him. She thus fell very ill. The good Paphnutius was very upset at this news and rushed to his side. Seeing that Smaragdus was on his deathbed, he began to cry out to him, "Alas! What about all the comforting words and the promises you gave me that I would see my daughter again?" Smaragdus later died in God's arms when the father was absent. In his hand, he clasped a letter which none of the monks could remove from his fingers. Everyone in the monastery, including the abbot, tried to do so but failed. At this point, the father came in, weeping and wailing at the loss of his dear friend, the only person who had ever consoled him. As he approached the body to kiss it, in front of everyone the hand opened and gave him the letter. He took it and read inside that she was his daughter and that no one else but him should prepare her body for burial. He, the abbot and all the other monks were astounded by these revelations and couldn't praise her highly enough for her devout constancy and determination. Her father was so moved by pity and relief at the thought that she had led such a holy life that his tears increased twofold. He sold everything he owned in order to join the monastery, where he eventually ended his days.

'Now that I've told you about several virgins, I'll go on to talk about some other holy ladies, all of whom suffered a glorious martyrdom.'

14. *About the blessed lady Anastasia.*

'At the time of the great persecutions in Rome during the reign of Diocletian, there lived a very patrician lady named Anastasia, who was one of the richest and most influential women in the city. This lady was full of heartfelt compassion at seeing a constant stream of blessed Christian martyrs being subjected to torture. Every day, she would disguise herself as a pauper and go off accompanied by a young girl to visit the martyrs in their cells and try to comfort them with costly wines, foods and whatever else she could find. She washed and dressed their wounds and anointed them with precious ointments. She carried on like this until her activities were reported to Publius, a Roman nobleman who wanted to marry her. Angered by this news, he put her under such close surveillance that she no longer dared to leave her house. Amongst the other martyrs detained in prison was Saint Chrysogonus, a most worthy man who had endured horrific tortures and had been greatly sustained by all the gifts brought by the holy lady Anastasia on her visits. Using a kind Christian lady as an intermediary, this saintly man sent Anastasia a series of letters in which he counselled her to have patience. She sent similar letters back to him, thanks to the same helpful lady. In the end, it was God's wish that Publius, the man who had placed her under strict guard, should pass away. The noble Anastasia thus sold everything she owned and devoted herself entirely to visiting the martyrs and bringing them succour, gathering round her a large company of Christian ladies and maidens.

'Amongst these women were three virgins, Anastasia's intimate companions, who were all sisters from a very distinguished family. One of the sisters was called Agape, another Chionia, and the third Irene. Having found out that these three virgins had become Christians, the emperor sent for them and promised them great gifts and advantageous marriages if they would renounce Jesus Christ. When they took no notice of his offer, he had them beaten and thrown into a horrible prison. Here they were visited by their saintly friend Anastasia, who never left their side day or night. She prayed to God that He would keep her alive until her wealth ran out so that she could continue to do these charitable works.

The emperor informed his prefect, Dulcitius, that all the Christians who were being held in the cells should be subjected to torture until they agreed to worship the pagan idols. The prefect thus ordered all the prisoners to be brought before him, including the three blessed sisters.

'When the wicked prefect laid his eyes on the three girls, he was greatly smitten with their beauty. In secret, he tried to cajole them with promises into letting him have his pleasure with them, in exchange for their freedom. Because they rebuffed all his advances, Dulcitius put one of his servants in charge of them and ordered him to escort the girls to his house, convinced that one way or another he would win them over. At nightfall, he set off alone without a lantern to the house where the three sisters had been taken. Hearing their voices as they sang God's praises through the night, he began to make his way towards them. As he passed through the room where all the kitchen implements were hanging up, he was so blinded by the lustful thoughts that the Devil had inspired in him that he hugged and kissed each pot in turn, thinking that he was with the three virgins. He gave himself up completely to his pleasures until he was exhausted. In the morning, he went outside to meet up with his men who were waiting for him. However, as soon as they saw him, they fled in terror, taking him for a devil because he was covered from head to foot in dirt, grease and soot, and his clothes were all torn and hanging off him in shreds. He was utterly baffled to see them all running away and couldn't understand why they were refusing to have anything to do with him. As everyone who came across him walking down the street made fun of him, he decided to go straight to the emperor to complain about being ridiculed as he passed by. On arriving at the palace, where some people were waiting that morning for an audience, he was immediately set upon. Whilst one person hit him with a stick, another pushed him from behind, saying, "Shove off, you filthy pig, you're stinking the place out!", and yet another spat in his face, much to the amusement of the crowd. In his shock at being treated like this, he almost went out of his mind, for the Devil had closed his eyes so tightly that he was unable to realize what a state he was in. Burning with shame, he made his way back home.

'He was replaced by another judge who had the three sisters brought before him and tried to force them to worship the idols. Seeing their adamant refusal to comply with his wishes, he ordered them to be stripped and beaten. Yet no matter how hard his men tried, they were unable to undress the girls: their clothes had become so firmly stuck to their skin that they couldn't be removed. The judge then had them thrown into a raging fire, but this did them no harm at all. None the less, the three sisters prayed to God to let them die, if He so pleased, and they ended their days as glorious martyrs. In order to show that they had died of their own free will, the fire didn't burn either a single hair of their heads or a scrap of their clothing. When the flames died down, their bodies were found to be completely intact, with their hands joined in prayer and their faces as fresh as if they were merely asleep. The blessed Anastasia took care of their bodies and buried them.'

15. About the blessed Theodota.

'Anastasia had another faithful companion, a lady by the name of Theodota, who had three young sons. Because she had declined to marry the Count Leucatius and had refused to worship the idols, Theodota was subjected to various types of torture. Thinking that they would break her will by appealing to her maternal instincts, they persecuted one of her sons. Yet the strength of her faith was greater than that of her earthly ties, for she comforted the boy, saying, "My son, don't fear these torments, for it is thanks to them that you will go to heaven." As she lay in prison, a son of the Devil came to try and seduce her but he immediately began to have a terrible nosebleed. He shouted out that there was a young man in the cell with her who had punched him in the face, whereupon she was taken off to be tortured once more. In the end, she and her three children died, glorifying God's holy name as their spirits departed their bodies. The worthy Anastasia buried them all.

'Having spent so much time helping the martyrs, the blessed Anastasia was herself eventually arrested and thus prevented from going to visit God's saints. In prison, she was deprived of all food and drink. Yet, because she had taken such excellent care of God's blessed martyrs and had assuaged their hunger, the good Lord decided that He would not let her suffer. He therefore sent down to Anastasia the soul of her saintly companion Theodota, who was bathed in a dazzling light. Setting out a table laden with delicious things for Anastasia to eat, Theodota kept her friend company for the whole thirty days that she had been condemned to go without food. Although it had been assumed that by the end of this time she would have died of hunger, she emerged alive and well, much to the prefect's dismay when he saw her standing before him. Since many people were converted at the sight of this miracle, the prefect had Anastasia placed on board a ship with various wrongdoers who had been sentenced to death. Once they were out on the open sea, the sailors followed the orders they had been given and scuttled the ship before taking off in a different vessel. The blessed Theodota appeared to Anastasia and the other prisoners and led them across the sea for a day and a night, as safely as if they had been on dry land. She eventually brought them to the island of Palmaria, where there were many bishops and holy men who had been sent into exile. They were greeted with great rejoicing and all gave thanks to God. Those who had been saved with Anastasia were baptized and became Christians. When news of what had happened later reached the emperor, he sent for all the men, women and children on the island, who were more than three hundred in number, and had every one of them tortured to death. Even the blessed Anastasia, who engaged in lengthy debates with the emperor, was subjected to torture and finally received her martyr's crown.'

16. *About the noble and holy Nathalia.*

'Nathalia was the noble wife of Adrian, leader of Emperor Maximian's army. She herself had secretly adopted Christianity during the time when the first Christians were being persecuted but she discovered that her husband, Adrian, on whose behalf she was forever praying to God, had suddenly converted at the sight of the martyrs being tortured and had praised the name of Jesus Christ. The emperor was so enraged by this news that he had thrown Adrian into a dank and gloomy dungeon. The blessed lady was overjoyed at her husband's conversion and went directly to his cell to console him and to beg him not to turn back now that he was on the right road. She kissed the bonds that held him fast and wept tears of compassion and joy. Enjoining him not to regret the loss of transient, earthly pleasures, she urged him to concentrate his mind instead on the infinite glory that awaited him. This holy lady stayed at her husband's side for a long time that day, offering words of solace both to him and to all the other martyrs, and praying to God that she too would soon be of their number. She implored the others to keep up her husband's morale, for she was afraid that his faith might waver once he was put to torture. Nathalia went to see Adrian every day, saying comforting things to him and encouraging him all the time to remain steadfast. Because she and several other ladies paid such frequent visits to the martyrs, the emperor forbade women from going into the cells. But Nathalia simply disguised herself as a man and was there on the day when her husband received his last torment. Binding his wounds and kissing his bloody body, she wept tears of devotion and beseeched him to pray to God for her sake. Thus the blessed Adrian met his end and she buried his body with all due ceremony. She took one of his hands that had been cut off and wrapped it up carefully to keep as a holy relic.

'Because this pious lady came from such a noble family and was so beautiful and wealthy, she found herself under great pressure to remarry after her husband's death. She thus threw herself into her prayers, begging God to deliver her out of the hands of those who were trying to force her to take another husband. One night, Adrian appeared to her whilst she was sleeping. As he comforted her, he told her that she should go to Constantinople and bury the bodies of the many martyrs that were being killed there. She did exactly as he said and performed this holy service for some time, visiting the blessed martyrs in their cells. Her husband then appeared to her a second time, saying, "My sister and my friend, handmaiden of Jesus Christ, come into the everlasting glory, for Our Lord is calling you." No sooner had she woken from her sleep than she passed away.'

17. *About Saint Afra, a repentant prostitute who turned to God.*

'Afra was a prostitute who converted to Christianity. She was brought before the judge, who said to her, "As if it weren't enough for you to sin with your body, you go and commit an error of faith by worshipping a foreign god! Sacrifice to our gods and they will pardon you." Afra replied, "I will sacrifice to my Lord, Jesus Christ, who came down to earth for the sake of sinners. It says in his Gospel that a female sinner washed his feet with her tears and was forgiven. He didn't despise either prostitutes or sinful publicans,[6] but rather allowed them to sit and eat with him." The judge retorted, "If you don't agree to make a sacrifice, you'll never see any of your clients again, nor will you receive any more presents from them." She answered, "I will never again accept a tainted gift. As for those that I did wrongfully receive, I've asked poor people to take them away and to pray for my soul." The judge sentenced Afra to be burnt to death for having refused to worship the gods. As she was being put into the fire, she glorified God, saying, "O Lord Almighty, Jesus Christ, you who call all sinners to repent, please accept my martyrdom in this hour of my passion and deliver me from the everlasting fire by means of this earthly fire that has been prepared for my mortal body." As the flames leapt up around her, she cried out, "Lord Jesus Christ, please receive me, a poor sinful woman martyred in your holy name, you who made a single sacrifice of yourself for the whole world. You were a righteous man nailed to a cross for the sake of all those who were immoral, a good man who died for the wicked, a blessed man for the damned, a gentle man for the cruel, an innocent and pure man for the corrupt. To you I offer the sacrifice of my body, you who live and reign with the Father and the Holy Ghost for ever and ever." Thus the blessed Afra ended her days, on whose behalf Our Lord later performed many miracles.'

18. *Justice talks about several noble ladies who served the Apostles and other saints and gave them shelter.*

'My dear friend Christine, what more can I tell you on this subject? I could go on recounting an infinite number of such stories to you. Because you said before that you were so astonished at the amount of criticism that writers have heaped on women, I can assure you that no matter what you've read in the works of pagan authors, I think you'll find few negative comments on women in holy legends, in stories of Jesus Christ and his apostles, and even in lives of the saints. If you look at such texts, what you will find instead are countless instances of women who were endowed by God with extraordinary constancy and virtue. What great acts of kindness women have unstintingly and diligently performed for the servants of God! What exemplary charity and devotion they have shown them! So much hospitality and so many other kindnesses are surely not things to be taken lightly. Even if certain foolish men want to dismiss them as insignificant, it is undeniable that, according to our faith, such acts are the rungs on the ladders that lead to heaven.

'We can cite the example of Drusiana, a noble widow, who took Saint John the Evangelist into her home, where she served him and prepared his meals. Saint John returned from exile, much to the delight of the people of the city who came out to greet him, just as Drusiana's dead body was being lowered into the ground. She had died from grief at his lengthy absence. The neighbours said to him, "John, here lies Drusiana, the lady who was such a kind hostess to you and who died because you stayed away so long. She'll never serve you again." At this, Saint John exclaimed, "Rise up, Drusiana! Go home and get my food ready for me!", whereupon she was brought back from the dead.

'Likewise, we could mention the worthy Susanna, a noblewoman from the city of Limoges. She was the first person to give shelter to Saint Martial, who had been sent by Saint Peter to convert the French. This lady showed him every kindness.

'Likewise, the same can be said of Maximilla, that excellent lady who cut Saint Andrew down from the cross and buried him, thus putting her own life in danger.

'Likewise, the holy virgin Ephigenia was a devoted follower of Saint Matthew the Evangelist, whom she served. After his death, she built a church dedicated to him.

'Likewise, there was another fine lady whose pure love for Saint Paul the Apostle was so great that she went everywhere with him and served him most diligently.

'Likewise, at the time of the apostles, lived a noble queen by the name of Helen – not the mother of Constantine, but the queen of Adiabene – who went to Jerusalem. The city was desperately short of food because of a famine that was raging all around. When Helen learnt that Our Lord's saints, who had come to Jerusalem to preach to and convert the people, were dying of hunger, she bought enough food to keep them well supplied until the famine was over.

'Likewise, when they were taking out Saint Paul to be beheaded on Nero's orders, an honourable lady by the name of Plautilla, who used to look after the saint, came up to him shedding bitter tears. Saint Paul asked her for the veil that she was wearing on her head. As she handed it to him, some wicked people who were standing nearby mocked her, saying more fool her for giving up such a pretty object. Saint Paul used the veil to blindfold himself. Later, after his death, the angels gave the blood-stained veil back to her, which she then kept as a precious relic. Saint Paul appeared to her and said that, for having done him this service on earth, he would do her a service in heaven by praying for her soul. I could tell you about many other cases like this.

'Basilissa was a noble lady full of the virtue of charity. She was married to Saint Julian. On their wedding night, they made a pact that they would both preserve their virginity. It's impossible to measure the full extent of this virgin's saintliness or the vast numbers of women and maidens who were saved by her holy teachings and encouraged to lead a devout existence. In short, her exemplary charity won her such divine favour that Our Lord spoke to her in person when she was on her deathbed.

'My dear Christine, I'm not sure what more to say to you. I could tell you endless stories about women of all different social ranks, whether virgins, wives or widows, whose wonderful strength and constancy revealed how God was working through them. Let what I have said be enough. It seems to me that I have well and truly acquitted myself of my task, which was to complete the high turrets of your city and to fill it up with illustrious ladies, just as I promised. These final examples will act as the gates and portcullises of our city. Although I haven't cited the names of every single holy lady who has ever lived, or is still living, or is indeed yet to come, for it would be impossible for me to do so, they can all none the less take their place in this City of Ladies, about which we can say: *"Gloriosa dicta sunt de te, civitas Dei."*[7] I'm therefore handing it over to you now that it is finished and the gates are closed and locked, just as I said I would. Adieu, and may the peace of God remain with you always!'

19. *The end of the book: Christine addresses all women.*

'Most honourable ladies, praise be to God: the construction of our city is finally at an end. All of you who love virtue, glory and a fine reputation can now be lodged in great splendour inside its walls, not just women of the past but also those of the present and the future, for this city has been founded and built to accommodate all deserving women. My dearest ladies, the human heart is naturally filled with joy when it sees that it has triumphed in a particular endeavour and has defeated its enemies. From this moment on, my ladies, you have every reason to rejoice – in a suitably devout and respectable manner – at seeing the completion of this new city. It will not only shelter you all, or rather those of you who have proved yourselves to be worthy, but will also defend and protect you against your attackers and assailants, provided you look after it well. For you can see that it is made of virtuous material which shines so brightly that you can gaze at your reflections in it, especially the lofty turrets that were built in this final part of the book, as well as the passages which are relevant to you in the other two parts. My beloved ladies, I beg you not to abuse this new legacy like those arrogant fools who swell up with pride when they see themselves prosper and their wealth increase. Rather, you should follow the example of your queen, the noble Virgin.

On hearing that she was to receive the supreme honour of becoming the mother of the Son of God, her humility grew all the greater as she offered herself up to the Lord as His handmaiden. Thus, my ladies, since it is true that the more virtuous someone is, the more this makes them meek and mild, this city should make you conduct yourselves in a moral fashion and encourage you to be meritorious and forbearing.

'As for you ladies who are married, don't despair at being so downtrodden by your husbands, for it's not necessarily the best thing in the world to be free. This is proven by what the angel of the Lord said to Esdras: "Those who used their free will fell into sin, turned their backs on God and corrupted the righteous; for this reason they were destroyed."[8] Those wives whose husbands are loving and kind, good-natured and wise, should praise the Lord. This is no small boon but one of the greatest blessings in the world that any woman can receive. Such wives should serve their husbands with devotion, and should love and cherish them with a faithful heart, as is their duty, living in peace with them and praying to God to keep them safe and sound. Those wives whose husbands are neither good nor bad should none the less thank the Lord that they're not any worse. They should make every effort to moderate their husbands' unruly behaviour and to strive for a peaceable existence with them according to their social condition. Those wives with husbands who are wayward, sinful and cruel should do their best to tolerate them. They should try to overcome their husbands' wickedness and lead them back to a more reasonable and respectable path, if they possibly can. Even if their husbands are so steeped in sin that all their efforts come to nothing, these women's souls will at least have benefited greatly from having shown such patience. Moreover, everyone will praise them for it and will be on their side.

'So, my ladies, be humble and long-suffering and the grace of God will be magnified in you. You will be covered in glory and be granted the kingdom of heaven. It was Saint Gregory who said that patience is the key to paradise and the way of Jesus Christ. You should all resolve to rid yourselves henceforth of silly and irrational ideas, petty jealousies, stubbornness, contemptuous talk or scandalous behaviour, all of which are things that twist the mind and make a person unstable. Besides, such ways are extremely unhealthy and unseemly in a woman.

'As for you girls who are young virginal maidens, be pure and modest, timid and steadfast, for the wicked have set their snares to catch you. Keep your gaze directed downwards, say few words, and be cautious in everything you do. Arm yourselves with strength and virtue against the deceitful ways of seducers and avoid their company.

'As for you widowed ladies, be respectable in the way you dress, speak and hold yourselves. Be devout in your words and deeds, prudent in the way you run your affairs, and patient, strong and resilient in the face of suffering and aggravation, for you will have sore need of such qualities. Be unassuming in your temperament, speech and bearing, and be charitable in your actions.

'In short, all you women, whether of high, middle or low social rank, should be especially alert and on your guard against those who seek to attack your honour and your virtue. My ladies, see how these men assail you on all sides and accuse you of every vice imaginable. Prove them all wrong by showing how principled you are and refute the criticisms they make of you by behaving morally. Act in such a way that you can say, like the Psalmist, "The evil done by the wicked will fall on their own heads."⁹ Drive back these treacherous liars who use nothing but tricks and honeyed words to steal from you that which you should keep safe above all else: your chastity and your glorious good name. O my ladies, fly, fly from the passionate love with which they try to tempt you! For God's sake, fly from it!¹⁰ No good can come to you of it. Rather, you can be sure that though it may seem to be superficially attractive, it can only be to your harm in the end. This is always the case, so don't think otherwise. My dear ladies, remember how these men accuse you of being weak, flighty and easily led, and yet still use the most convoluted, outlandish and bizarre methods they can think of to trap you, just as one would a wild animal. Fly, fly from them, my ladies! Have nothing to do with such men beneath whose smiling looks a lethal venom is concealed, one which will poison you to death. Instead, my most honoured ladies, may it please you to pursue virtue and shun vice, thus increasing in number the inhabitants of our city. Let your hearts rejoice in doing good. I, your servant, commend myself to you. I beg the Lord to shine His grace upon me and to allow me to carry on devoting my life to His holy service here on earth. May He pardon my great faults and grant me everlasting joy when I die, and may He do likewise unto you. Amen.'

End of the Third and Final Part of the
Book of the City of Ladies.

NOTES

1. See Deuteronomy 17: 6.

2. *Antiphrasis* refers to a rhetorical and polemical practice of reading whereby a text is deliberately interpreted to mean the opposite of what it explicitly seems to say. In the *City of Ladies*, Christine thus chooses, at times, to read misogynists' criticisms of women as praise rather than condemnation.

3. Christine compares her rescue of women from the attacks of misogynist writers to the deliverance of the Jews from the slavery imposed on them by Pharaoh, King of Egypt. See II Kings 17: 7.

4. Christine here paraphrases Mary's reply to the Angel of the Annunciation. See Luke 1: 38.

5. The medieval view of woman as a flawed being, a kind of deformed male, *was* largely derived from Aristotle. In his view, menstruation in particular was a sign that the female sex did not match up to the physiological perfection of the male sex. However, *On the Secrets of Women*, which Christine quite rightly says was not written by Aristotle, takes these arguments about female physiology to extremes by claiming, amongst other things, that menstrual blood can seep out of the eyes, poison children and induce madness in dogs. See glossary.

6. Christine here refers to the medieval theological dispute on the interpretation of Genesis 1: 27, 'So God created man in his own image, in the image of God created he him; male and female created he them', and I Corinthians 11: 7, man 'is the image and glory of God: but the woman is the glory of the man'.

7. Christine here wrongly refers to Cato the Elder by the name of his great-grandson.

8. The denier, or silver penny, was introduced by the Carolingians in the eighth century and became the main unit of currency in medieval western Europe.

9. See Matthew 18: 2−4, Mark 9: 33−7 and Luke 9: 46−8.

10. The Latin proverb is *'fallere, flere, nere, statuit deus in muliere'*.

11. Martha and Mary's brother was called Lazarus. See John 11: 1−44.

12. See Luke 7: 12−15.

13. See Matthew 15: 22–8.
14. See John 4: 7–29.
15. See Luke 11: 27.
16. The seven liberal arts comprised the *trivium* (grammar, logic and rhetoric) and the *quadrivium* (arithmetic, geometry, music and astronomy).
17. See n. 16.
18. See Proverbs 31: 10–31.

PART II

1. These words are the beginning of Simeon's prayer to God to let him die in peace now that he has seen the Saviour. See Luke 2: 29.
2. Christine's brothers, Paolo and Aghinolfo, returned to Bologna after the deaths of her father and her husband to look after family property there.
3. In her original text, Christine uses the Old French neologism, '*Feminie*', meaning land of women, which is derived from *femina*, the Latin word for woman. This term, used to refer to the land of the Amazons, was coined by Benoit de Sainte-Maure, the twelfth-century French author of the *Roman de Troie*, a verse narrative about the Trojan war. I have followed Benoit's lead in translating '*Feminie*' by an equally made-up word in English which both refers to women and has an ending typical of the name of a country: 'Femininia'.
4. The classical theory of dreams was popularized in the Middle Ages by Macrobius's commentary on Cicero's *Somnium Scipionis*, which was written around AD 400. Macrobius divided dreams into five types, three of which are significant and two of which are insignificant. The *somnium* or enigmatic dream, the *visio* or prophetic vision, and the *oraculum* or oracular dream, all have a prophetic value for the dreamer. The *insomnium* or nightmare, and the *visum* (also referred to as the *phantasma*) or apparition, have no prophetic value as they have a purely physiological or psychological origin.
5. See Luke 6: 41 and Matthew 7: 3.
6. This is a reference to the wife of Guillaume de Roussillon (*Decameron* IV, ix).
7. Charles VI, King of France, was born in 1368 and reigned 1380–1422. He was married to Isabeau of Bavaria in 1385 and later suffered from periodic bouts of madness which eventually led the other royal princes, most notably his brother Louis, Duke of Orleans, and his nephew, John the Fearless, Duke of Burgundy, to battle for control of the French crown.

PART III

1. The calends are calculated as the number of days up to and including the first day of a particular month. The seventh of the calends of July is thus 25 June.

2. The apostle referred to is Saint Paul. See I Corinthians 11: 15.

3. In the Middle Ages, the monastic day was divided up into hours at which certain prayers were read, starting in the very early hours of the morning with matins or lauds, then followed by prime, terce, sext, none, vespers and compline. Terce corresponds roughly to 9 a.m. and none to 3 p.m. Saint Fausta was thus tortured for the best part of six hours.

4. Martyrs, and later monks too, were commonly known as 'soldiers of Christ', or *milites Christi*, for they were deemed to be engaged in the fight against the Devil.

5. A cubit is between 18 and 22 inches in length. The flames of the furnace into which Euphemia was thrown were thus about 60 feet high.

6. The term 'publican' means tax-gatherer, a profession which, along with that of the prostitute, was particularly despised by the Jews.

7. 'Glorious things are spoken of thee, O City of God' (Psalms 87:3). Christine is probably also alluding here to Saint Augustine's *City of God*, a highly influential text in the Middle Ages, which posited the need to found the Heavenly City on earth in the form of the Christian church.

8. See the Vulgate Old Testament, II Esdras 8: 56–8.

9. See Psalms 7: 16. The Psalmist himself is traditionally thought to be David.

10. Christine would seem here to be deliberately parodying Genius in the *Romance of the Rose*, who actively discourages men from having anything to do with women by comparing the female sex to snakes in the grass: 'Fly, fly, fly, fly, fly my children, I advise and admonish you frankly and without deceit to fly from such a creature' (Guillaume de Lorris and Jean de Meun, *The Romance of the Rose*, Frances Horgan, trans and ed., World's Classics (Oxford and New York: Oxford University Press, 1994), p. 256, ll. 16548–50).

GLOSSARY

This glossary is intended to provide a brief guide to the characters, places and books mentioned in the *City of Ladies* and a reference to the chapters where they appear. It is not an exhaustive index: places and characters which occur frequently and are too well known to need an explanation, such as Greece, Rome and Israel, and God, Jesus Christ and the Devil, have been omitted. Proper names are indexed as follows: in small capitals for the form in which they appear in the text; in small capitals in brackets where Christine herself gives an alternative form; and in upper and lower case in brackets for fuller or more commonly used forms. Given the lack of standardization of Greek and Roman names, I have generally followed the spelling adopted in the *Oxford Classical Dictionary*, 3rd edition. For French and Italian names, where there are no set conventions, I have followed customary usage: thus Philip the Bold, Petrarch, etc., have been anglicized, but Jean de Meun, Giovanni Andrea, etc., have been left in the original. For well-known texts cited directly by Christine, I have also followed customary usage: thus works such as the *Decameron* or the *Letter of the God of Love* are referred to by their usual English title, whereas others such as the *Miroir historial* or the *Problemata* have been kept in the original. Lesser known texts, whose Latin titles Christine herself translates into French, have been anglicized: for example, *On Philosophy*. For works not mentioned directly by Christine but on which information is provided in the glossary, titles have been given in the original throughout, accompanied by an anglicized equivalent only in those cases where an English translation of the text is available. Dates are given for historical characters, where known.

ABRAHAM: first of the Old Testament patriarchs and founder of the Hebrew nation; husband of Sarah. II.38.

ABSALOM: son of David, King of Israel, who was famed for his beauty. I.14.

ABYDOS: town on the Asiatic side of the Hellespont; home of Leander, not Hero as Christine erroneously suggests. II.58.

ACERBAS SYCHAEA: see SYCHAEUS.

ACHILLES: Greek hero in the Trojan war who was killed by Paris with the help of the god Apollo. I.19, II.28, II.61.

ADAM: the first man, from whose rib Eve was created. I.9.

ADELPHUS (Clodius Celsinus Adelphius): prefect of Rome in AD 351 and husband of Proba. I.29.

ADRASTUS: king of Argos, a city in the Peloponnese region of Greece; father-in-law of Polynices. II.17.

ADRIAN (Saint Adrian): (d. ?early 4th century AD) martyred husband of Saint Nathalia, usually believed to have been persecuted by Diocletian, not Maximian as Christine suggests. III.16.

AEËTES: king of Colchis and father of Medea. I.32.

AENEAS: son of Anchises and Venus; Trojan prince who abandoned his lover Dido and later married Lavinia, daughter of King Latinus. I.24, I.48, II.3, II.19, II.55.

AENEID: see VIRGIL.

AFRA, SAINT: (d. early 4th century AD) repentant prostitute of Augsburg who was martyred by the judge Gaius during the persecution of Diocletian. III.17.

AGAPE (Saint Agape): (d. early 4th century AD) virgin and martyr, companion of Saint Anastasia; one of three sisters who were killed in Thessalonica during the persecution of Diocletian. III.14.

AGATHA, SAINT: date uncertain, virgin and martyr who died in Catania, Sicily. III.7, III.9.

AGENOR: king of Phoenicia and father of Europa and Cadmus; ancestor of Dido's father. I.46, II.61.

AGNES, SAINT: (d. early 4th century AD) virgin and martyr killed in Rome. III.9.

AGRIPPINA (Vipsania Agrippina): (c. 14 BC–AD 33) Roman noblewoman, daughter of Marcus Agrippa and his first wife Attica; married to Germanicus. II.18.

AHASUERUS: (5th century BC) king of Persia and husband of Esther. Often identified by modern scholars with Xerxes I. II.32.

ALBA (Alba Longa): ancient city in the Albian hills in Latium, c. 20 km south-east of Rome. I.48. See ASCANIUS.

ALBUNEA: see SIBYLS.

ALEMANNI: confederation of Germanic tribes who attacked the Roman empire from the third century AD onwards. They were defeated by the Frankish king Clovis at the battle of Tolbiac in AD 496. II.35.

ALEXANDER (Marcus Aurelius Severus Alexander): Roman emperor who reigned AD 222–35, thought to have persecuted Saint Martina. III.6.

ALEXANDER THE GREAT: (356–323 BC) king of Macedon and pupil of Aristotle. Soldier and conqueror of most of the then known world. Married to Barsine (or Stateira), daughter of Darius, king of the Persians. I.14, I.19, II.29, II.66.

ALEXANDRIA: ancient capital and chief Mediterranean port of Egypt; one of the main centres of the Christian church in the third century AD. II.52, III.3, III.13.

ALLEFABTER, LAKE: the Dead Sea, known in antiquity as Lake Asphaltites. II.4.

ALMATHEA: see SIBYLS.

AMAZONIA: mythical female realm founded by the Amazons in Cappadocia. I.4, I.18, I.19. See also FEMININIA, REALM OF, and SCYTHIA.

AMAZONS (SCYTHIANS): mythical race of women warriors who were thought to have come from Scythia, in the region of the Caucasus. I.4, I.16, I.17, I.18, I.19, I.20.

AMBROSE: Lombard merchant (Decameron II, ix). II.52.

AMBROSE, SAINT: (AD 339–97) bishop of Milan. I.10. See also DOCTORS OF THE CHURCH.

ANASTASIA: (late 14th to ?early 15th century) Parisian manuscript illuminator known to Christine. I.41.

ANASTASIA (Saint Anastasia): (d. early 4th century AD) Roman noblewoman who comforted Christian martyrs; killed during the persecution of Diocletian at Sirmium, a city in the Roman province of Pannonia which lay south and west of the Danube. III.14, III.15.

ANCIENTS: Greek and Roman authors of classical Antiquity. I.30, I.41.

ANDREA, GIOVANNI: (1275–1347) professor and jurist at the University of Bologna; father of Novella. Author of the Novella super Decretalium, a commentary on canon law. II.36.

ANDREW, SAINT: (d. c. AD 60) the first apostle, traditionally thought to have proselytized in Greece and to have been crucified in Patras. III.18.

ANDROMACHE: wife of the Trojan prince Hector. II.28.

ANGELA: according to Christine, whose source for this information is unknown, the woman after whom England was named. II.61.

ANJOU, DUCHESS OF (Marie of Châtillon-Blois): (d. 1410) daughter of Jeanne of Brittany and Charles of Blois; married to Louis I, Duke of Anjou, in 1360. I.13.

ANJOU, DUKE OF (Louis I): (1339–84) son of King John II of France; became king of Sicily in 1380. II.67.

ANNA: Hebrew prophetess who recognized the infant Christ during the Presentation in the Temple. II.4.

ANNE (of Bourbon): (d. after 1406) daughter of John I of Bourbon, Count of La Marche; married to Louis of Bavaria in 1402. Her brother, Jacques II of Bourbon, succeeded his father in 1393. II.68.

ANNUNCIATION, ANGEL OF THE: according to Luke 1:26–38, it is the angel Gabriel who announces to the Virgin Mary that she will conceive of the Holy Spirit and give birth to the Saviour. III.1.

ANTICHRIST: name given in the Bible to the false prophet who will lead humankind astray with false miracles until defeated by the archangel Michael. Sometimes equated with Satan or one of his angels, or with humans such as the persecuting emperors Nero and Caligula. II.1, II.49.

ANTIOCH: city in Pisidia, Asia Minor; third biggest city in the Roman empire after Rome and Alexandria. III.4, III.8.

ANTIOPE: a queen of the Amazons. I.18.

ANTONIA: (6th century AD) wife of Belisarius, Justinian's bodyguard. Her correct name, which Christine slightly misspells, is Antonina. II.29.

ANTONIA: (end 1st century BC) younger daughter of Mark Antony and Octavia; wife of Drusus Tiberius. II.43.

ANTONIA: (6th century AD) former actress who married the Emperor Justinian; sister of Antonia, wife of Belisarius. Christine confuses her name with that of her sister: her correct name is Theodora. II.6.

APIS: Christine follows classical mythology in conflating two different characters: Osiris, an Egyptian god in the form of a bull who was married to his sister Isis; and Apis, a king of Argos who, according to legend, was the son of Jupiter and Niobe. I.36.

APOLLO (PHOEBUS): Greek sun-god, also associated with healing, prophecy, poetry and music. I.4, I.30, I.31, II.1, II.3.

APOSTLES: this term refers both to the twelve disciples whom Christ originally chose to spread his message to the world – which is Christine's meaning here – and, more generally, to those whom he later appointed to his apostolic mission. I.10, I.29, II.2, II.35, III.2, III.18.

ARABIA: name given to the whole of the Arabian peninsula in the ancient world; an important part of the trade route to the East. I.12, II.4.

ARACHNE: girl from Lydia, Asia Minor, who challenged the goddess Athene to a tapestry-weaving contest and was turned into a spider for her presumption. I.39.

ARCADIA: mountainous region in the central part of the Peloponnese. I.33. See
PALLAS.

ARCHELAOS: Macedonian king who reigned 413–399 BC. I.41.

ARGIA: daughter of Adrastus, King of Argos, and wife of Polynices. According
to legend, it was Polynices's sister Antigone, not Argia as Christine claims,
who went to rescue his dead body from the battlefield. II.17.

ARIARATHES (Ariarathes VI Epiphanes Philopater): (2nd century BC) king of
Cappadocia and husband of Berenice. I.25.

ARISTOBULUS (Aristobulus II): (2nd century BC) king of the Jews and grand-
father of Mariamme, not her father as Christine suggests. The correct name
of Mariamme's father is Alexander. II.42.

ARISTOTLE: (384–322 BC) Greek thinker and pupil of Plato in Athens, where
he later set up a school in which he taught philosophy. Regarded as the
supreme philosophical authority in the later Middle Ages. I.2, I.9, I.11, I.14,
I.30, I.38, I.43.

— *Categories*: treatise on logic. I.11.

— *Metaphysics*: name given to a series of treatises on the nature of being. I.2.

— *Problemata*: work on various topics, attributed to Aristotle. I.11.

ARMENIANS: inhabitants of Armenia, a mountainous region of Asia. I.20.

ARTEMISIA: Christine follows Boccaccio in conflating two different women of
the same name: the early fifth-century BC ruler of Halicarnassus who fought
with Xerxes, King of Persia, at the battle of Salamis; and the mid fourth-
century BC ruler of Caria who built a monument in memory of her husband
Mausolus. I.21, II.16.

ART OF LOVE: see OVID.

ASCANIUS: son of Aeneas by Creusa, daughter of Priam; traditionally thought
to have founded the ancient city of Alba Longa in Latium, *c.* 1152 BC.
I.48.

D'ASCOLI, CECCO (Francesco Stabili): (*c.* 1269–1327) Italian poet, astrologer
and alchemist who was burnt at the stake for heresy. I.9.

ASSYRIA: ancient kingdom situated in the Upper Tigris region of modern Iraq.
I.15.

ATHALIAH: the only queen to rule Judaea, she reigned 843–837 BC after killing
off her male rivals. II.49.

AUCEJAS: of doubtful existence and date unknown. Barbarian king thought to
have abducted Saint Lucy and eventually to have been converted by her.
III.5.

AUGUSTINE, SAINT: (AD 354–430) son of a pagan father and a Christian
mother (Saint Monica); bishop of Hippo in North Africa. I.2, I.10. See also
DOCTORS OF THE CHURCH.

AVERNUS, LAKE: lake next to the ancient city of Baiae, near Naples; traditionally thought to be the entrance to the underworld. II.3.

BABYLON: ancient city situated on the River Euphrates in modern Iraq. I.15, I.17, II.1, II.52, II.57.

BAIAE: see AVERNUS, LAKE.

BAR, DUKE OF (Robert): (d. 1411) father of Bonne of Bar, Countess of Saint-Pol. II.68.

BARBARA, SAINT: of doubtful existence and date unknown. According to one version of her legend, she was the daughter of a wealthy man named Dioscorus and was martyred at Nicomedia in Asia Minor by the Roman prefect Martinianus. One of the most popular saints in the Middle Ages. III.9.

BARTHOLOMEW, SAINT: (1st century AD) one of the Apostles, traditionally thought to have been martyred by being flayed alive. II.62.

BASILISSA (Saint Basilissa): (?4th century AD) Egyptian noblewoman chastely married to Saint Julian. Both are of doubtful existence but were thought to have been martyred. III.18.

BASINE: (5th century AD) wife of the Merovingian king Childeric I and mother of Clovis. II.5.

BELISARIUS: (AD 500–565) bodyguard and general of the Emperor Justinian; husband of Antonia. Defeated Gelimer, king of the Vandals, in AD 533–4. II.29.

BELUS: Phoenician king of Tyre and father of Dido. I.46.

BENEDICTA, SAINT: (?3rd century AD) daughter of a Roman senator. Instrumental in spreading Christianity, she was thought to have been martyred by her own father in Origny, France. III.7.

BERENICE: Christine follows Boccaccio in conflating two different characters: Laodice, the second-century BC sister of Mithradates Eupator, King of Pontus, who was married first to Ariarathes VI, King of Cappadocia, and then to Nicomedes, King of Bithynia; and Berenice, the third-century BC daughter of Ptolemy II, King of Egypt, and wife of Antiochus II, ruler of the Seleucid empire in Asia Minor. I.25.

BERNABO THE GENOESE: Lombard merchant (*Decameron* II, ix). II.52.

BERRY, DUCHESS OF (Jeanne of Boulogne and Auvergne): (d. 1423/4) second wife of John, Duke of Berry, whom she married in 1389. An important patron of the arts. II.68.

BLANCHE (of Castile): (1188–1252) daughter of Alphonse VIII of Castile and Eleanor of Aquitaine. Married to King Louis VIII of France in 1200 and became regent in 1226 during the minority of her son, the future Saint Louis (Louis IX). I.13, II.65.

BLANCHE (of Navarre): (d. 1398) daughter of Count Philip of Evreux, King of Navarre, and Jeanne of France. Married King Philip VI of France in 1349, not King John II as Christine erroneously states. I.13.

BLANDINA (Saint Blandina): (2nd century AD) slave converted to Christianity; thought to have been martyred in Lyons during the persecution of Marcus Aurelius. III.11.

BOCCACCIO (Giovanni Boccaccio): (1313–75) famous Tuscan author whose Latin text *De Claris Mulieribus* (*Concerning Famous Women*) (c. 1375) was one of Christine's main sources for the *City of Ladies*, though she never cites it by name. She may have read this text in an early fifteenth-century French translation, known as the *Des Cleres et Nobles Femmes*. I.28, I.29, I.30, I.34, I.37, I.39, I.41, II.2, II.14, II.15, II.16, II.17, II.19, II.36, II.43, II.52, II.59, II.60, II.63.

— *Decameron*: (c. 1350) Italian prose work comprising a hundred stories told by ten different narrators over ten days. II.52, II.59, II.60.

BOLOGNA: large town in northern Italy. II.50.

BOOK OF THE MUTATION OF FORTUNE: see CHRISTINE.

BOURBON, DUCHESS OF (Anne of Auvergne): (d. after 1416) married to Louis II, Duke of Bourbon, in 1371. II.68.

BOURBON, DUKE OF (Louis II): (1337–1410) husband of Anne of Auvergne and father of John of Clermont. II.68.

BRUNHILDE: (c. AD 545/50–613) Visigoth princess and wife of the Merovingian king Sigibert of Metz. She later married her own nephew, Merovech, the son of Sigibert's brother, Chilperic I. II.49.

BRUTUS (Marcus Junius Brutus): (c. 85–42 BC) Roman statesman and republican; principal assassin of Julius Caesar; husband of Portia. II.25, II.28.

BRYAXIS: (4th century BC) sculptor who worked on the Mausoleum at Halicarnassus. II.16.

BUCOLICS: see VIRGIL.

BURGUNDY, DUCHESS OF (Marguerite of Bavaria): (d. 1423) daughter of Albert of Bavaria, Count of Hainault; married to John the Fearless, Duke of Burgundy, in 1385. Both she and her husband were important patrons of Christine. II.68.

BUSA (PAULINA): a rich woman of Apulia, southern Italy, who gave shelter to the Roman army after the defeat at Cannae. II.67.

BYRSA: name of the citadel of Carthage. I.46.

CADMUS: Phoenician founder and first king of the city of Thebes in the Boeotian region of Greece. I.4.

CAMILLA: warrior-maiden and daughter of Metabus, king of the Volscians;

appears in the *Aeneid*, where she fights like an Amazon and is finally killed by a cowardly archer, Arruns. I.24.

CAMPANIA: region near Naples from which the Italian nobleman came who was briefly married to Ghismonda (*Decameron* IV, i). II.1, II.59.

CANAAN: biblical name for Palestine. The king of Canaan from whom Deborah freed the Jews was called Jabin. I.10, II.4.

CANDLEMAS: (2 February) traditional name for the Feast of the Purification of the Virgin, now known as the Feast of the Presentation in the Temple. So-called because when the prophet Simeon recognized Christ as the Saviour, he referred to him as a light sent to illuminate the Gentiles. II.4. See also SIMEON.

CANNAE: village in Apulia and site of Hannibal's victory over the Romans in 216 BC. II.67.

CAPPADOCIA: region of Asia Minor. I.25, III.9.

CARIA: mountainous region of south-west Asia Minor, the ancient capital of which was Halicarnassus. I.21, II.16.

CARMENTIS: see NICOSTRATA.

CARTHAGE, CARTHAGINIANS: Phoenician colony and its people on the coast of north-east Tunisia, traditionally thought to have been founded by Dido, which later became a Roman colony. I.46, II.54, II.55, II.61.

CASSANDRA: prophetess, daughter of Priam and Hecuba of Troy. II.5.

CASSIUS (Gaius Cassius Longinus): (1st century BC) Roman military leader who took part in the assassination of Julius Caesar. II.25.

CASTALIA: spring situated on Mount Parnassus, near Delphi; sacred haunt of Apollo and the Muses. I.30.

CATANIA: large town near the eastern coast of Sicily. III.7.

CATEGORIES: see ARISTOTLE.

CATHERINE, SAINT: (d. ?early 4th century AD) virgin and martyr, traditionally thought to have been persecuted by the Emperor Maxentius, whose cult flourished from the ninth century. One of the most popular saints in the Middle Ages. III.3.

CATO (THE ELDER) (Marcius Porcius Cato): (234–149 BC) Roman orator and censor who was thought in the Middle Ages to be the author of a collection of moral sayings. I.9.

CATO UTICENSIS (THE YOUNGER) (Marcius Porcius Cato): (95–46 BC) Roman statesman and father of Portia; great-grandson of Cato the Elder, not his nephew, as Christine erroneously states. I.10, II.25.

CATULLA: according to legend, pious Parisian matron who buried the bodies of Saint Denis and his companions after their martyrdom by Decius. II.35.

CECILIA, SAINT: (?3rd century AD) according to legend, virgin and martyr of Rome whose husband and brother-in-law were also martyred along with her.

Her cult flourished from the fifth century and she became one of the most popular saints in the Middle Ages. III.9.

CERES: ancient Italo-Roman corn-goddess whose daughter, Proserpina, was kidnapped by and then married to Pluto, god of the underworld. I.35, I.38, I.39.

CHALDAEANS: inhabitants of a region of Babylonia on the Persian Gulf who were famed for their knowledge of astrology. I.31.

CHAMPAGNE, COUNT OF (Thibaut IV): (1201–53) king of Navarre and a *trouvère* (lyric poet). Traditionally thought to have been an ardent admirer of Blanche of Castile, mother of Saint Louis. II.65.

CHARLES OF BLOIS, SAINT, DUKE OF BRITTANY: (*c.* 1319–64) younger son of Guy of Châtillon, Count of Blois, and Marguerite of Valois, sister of King Philip VI. Married to Jeanne, Countess of Penthièvre in 1337; father of Marie, Duchess of Anjou. Although Christine refers to him as a saint, he was not officially canonized, despite his reputation for piety and sanctity. I.13.

CHARLES IV (The Fair): (1294–1328) king of France and youngest son of Philip IV. Married three times: to Blanche of Artois (marriage annulled in 1322 following an adultery scandal); Marie of Luxembourg (d. 1324); and Jeanne of Evreux in 1325. I.13.

CHARLES V (THE WISE): (1338–80) son of John II and Bonne of Luxembourg; king of France who reigned 1364–80. Important patron of the arts and sciences who invited Christine's father Tommaso da Pizzano to his court. Subject of a biography, *Le Livre des Fais et des Bonnes Meurs du Sage Roy Charles V* (*The Book of the Deeds and Good Character of King Charles V the Wise*), commissioned from Christine by his brother Philip the Bold, which she completed in 1404. Held up as the epitome of the good king in all of Christine's political works. I.36, II.67, II.68.

CHÂTELET: ancient fortress in Paris which served as a prison in the Middle Ages. II.67.

CHILDERIC (Childeric I): (*c.* AD 436–82) Merovingian king of France; husband of Basine and father of Clovis. II.5.

CHILPERIC (Chilperic I): (*c.* AD 537–84) king of the Franks and husband of Fredegunde. I.13, I.23.

CHIONIA (Saint Chionia): (d. early 4th century AD) virgin and martyr, companion of Saint Anastasia; one of three sisters who were killed in Thessalonica during the persecution of Diocletian. III.14.

CHRISTINE (de Pizan): (*c.* 1364–1430) author and narrator of the *City of Ladies*, *passim*.

— *The Letter of Othea to Hector*: (*c.* 1400) courtesy book written for a young knight in the form of a commentary on episodes from classical mythology. I.17, I.36.

— *The Letter of the God of Love*: (1399) narrative poem attacking clerks and knights who slander women. II.47, II.54.

— *Letters on the Romance of the Rose*: (*c.* 1400–1402) correspondence about Jean de Meun's *Romance of the Rose* exchanged between Christine and members of the royal chancellery, Jean de Montreuil, Gontier and Pierre Col, who defended the text against her claim that it was immoral, obscene and anti-feminist. II.54.

— *The Book of the Mutation of Fortune*: (completed 1403) allegorical poem accounting for the role of Fortune throughout human history. I.17.

CHRISTINE, SAINT: Christine de Pizan follows tradition in conflating two martyrs of the same name: a Phoenician virgin from Tyre, of doubtful existence and date unknown; and a fourth-century AD Italian virgin from Bolsena in Tuscany. III.9, III.10.

CHRYSOGONUS, SAINT: (d. ?early 4th century AD) martyr of Aquileia, Italy, and spiritual guide of Saint Anastasia; traditionally thought to have been killed during the persecution of Diocletian. III.14.

CICERO (Marcus Tullius Cicero): (106–43 BC) Roman statesman, orator, philosopher and poet. An important authority on rhetoric for medieval writers. I.9.

CIMERIA: see SIBYLS.

CIRCE: sorceress, daughter of the sun-god Helios and the ocean-nymph Perse. I.32.

CLAUDIA (Claudia Antonia): (1st century AD) daughter of Claudius I and Aelia Paetina. Her husband, Faustus Cornelius Sulla, was killed by Nero. II.48.

CLAUDIA (Claudia Quinta): (3rd century BC) Roman woman famed for her chastity during the period of the Second Punic War. II.63.

CLAUDINE: (2nd century BC) daughter of Appius Claudius Pulcher, a Roman consul. II.10.

CLAUDIUS (Appius Claudius Crassus Inregillensis Sabinus): (5th century BC) Roman consul and decemvir who attempted to rape the maiden Virginia. II.46.

CLAUDIUS (Marcus Aurelius Claudius II Gothicus): Roman emperor who reigned AD 268–70 and was a contemporary of Zenobia. I.20.

CLAUDIUS (Tiberius Claudius Nero Germanicus): (10 BC–AD 54) ineffectual and unpredictable Roman emperor. II.47.

CLERMONT, COUNTESS OF (Marie of Berry): (d. 1434) daughter of John, Duke of Berry, by his first wife, Jeanne of Armagnac. Married to John, Count of Clermont, in 1400. II.68.

CLOELIA: (end 6th century BC) Roman girl given as hostage to Lars Porsenna, king of the Etruscan city of Clusium. I.26.

CLOTAR (Clotar II): (AD 584–629) son of Queen Fredegunde and King Chilperic. I.13, I.23.

CLOTILDE (Saint Clotilde): (5th to 6th century AD) daughter of Chilperic, King of Burgundy, and wife of Clovis. II.35.

CLOVIS (Clovis I): (c. AD 466–511) Merovingian king who founded the kingdom of the Franks; the first Christian king of France. II.35.

COËMEN, COUNTESS OF: according to Christine, a beautiful lady of Brittany who was renowned for her devotion to her husband. II.20.

COLCHIS: country at eastern end of the Black Sea, bounded on the north by the Caucasus. According to legend, home of Medea and the Golden Fleece. I.32, II.24, II.56.

CONSTANTINE I (Flavius Valerius Constantinus): (AD 272/3–337) Roman emperor who established Christianity as the religion of the Roman empire. II.49, III.18.

CONSTANTINOPLE: city founded by Constantine I on the site of Byzantium in AD 324. I.22, II.6, III.18.

CORIOLANS: Volscian inhabitants of the ancient town of Corioli in Latium. II.34.

CORIOLANUS: see MARCIUS.

CORNELIA: (1st century BC) daughter of Lucius Cornelius Cinna, a Roman consul; wife of Julius Caesar and mother of Julia. II.19.

CORNELIA: daughter of Quintus Caecilius Metellus Pius Scipio, a Roman consul; married first to Publius Licinius Crassus in 55 BC and then to Pompey in 52 BC. She accompanied Pompey to Egypt after he was defeated at Pharsalus by Julius Caesar in 48 BC. II.28.

CORNIFICIA: (1st century BC) well-educated daughter of Quintus Cornificius, the orator and poet who was a friend of Cicero. I.28.

CORNIFICIUS: (1st century BC) Roman orator and poet; brother of Cornificia. I.28.

COSTUS: (?4th century AD) king of Alexandria and father of Saint Catherine. III.3.

COUCY, CHÂTELAIN DE (Guy de Thourotte): (d. 1203) early *trouvère* who died whilst on crusade. Immortalized as a great tragic lover by the late thirteenth-century French author Jakemes in the *Roman du Castelain de Coucy et de la Dame de Fayel*. II.60.

CRATINUS: (2nd century BC) botanist, physician and painter; traditionally thought to have been the teacher of Irene. His correct name is Crateuas. I.41.

CREON: king of Thebes after the deaths of Eteocles and Polynices. II.17.

CUMAE: earliest Greek colony on the Italian mainland, situated c. 20 km north-east of Naples; home of the Cumaean Sibyl. II.1.

CUMANA: see SIBYLS.

CURIA (Turia): (1st century BC) virtuous and devoted wife of Quintus Lucretius Vespillo. II.26.

CYPRIAN (Saint Cyprian): (d. ?early 4th century AD) according to legend, necromancer from Antioch who was converted by Saint Justine and became a bishop. Traditionally thought to have been martyred in Nicomedia during the persecution of Diocletian. III.8.

CYRICUS (Saint Cyricus): (d. ?early 4th century AD) son of Saint Julitta, traditionally thought to have been martyred with his mother at Tarsus. III.11.

CYRUS (The Great): (6th century BC) founder of the Persian empire. I.17, II.1.

DAGOBERT (Dagobert I): (AD 608–38/9) son of Clotar II; Merovingian king of Austrasia who later became king of Neustria and Burgundy. Founded the church of Saint Denis in Paris c. AD 624. II.35.

DAMASCUS, FIELDS OF: according to Christine, who follows Boccaccio, the place from which God took the clay to make the body of Adam. This detail is not found in Genesis. I.9.

DANIEL: one of the five major prophets of the Old Testament. II.37.

DARIUS (Darius III): (4th century BC) king of Persia and father of Barsine (Stateira), Alexander the Great's wife. II.29.

DAVID: the second Old Testament king of Israel and a prophet. Traditionally venerated as the author of the Psalms. II.40, III.19.

DEBORAH: Old Testament prophetess and a judge of Israel. II.4, II.32.

DECAMERON: see BOCCACCIO.

DEIANIRA: wife of Hercules. According to legend, she unwittingly poisoned her husband by giving him a shirt soaked with the blood of a centaur, Nessus, whom he had killed for trying to abduct her. Nessus had claimed that the shirt would act as a love charm to win back her husband if he was ever unfaithful to her. II.60.

DEIPHEBE: see SIBYLS.

DELPHI: city south of Mount Parnassus famed for its oracle dedicated to the god Apollo. II.1.

DELPHICA: see SIBYLS.

DENIS (Dionysius I): (c. 430–367 BC) brutal and ruthless tyrant of Sicily. II.49.

DENIS, SAINT: (3rd century AD) patron saint of France. Bishop of Paris who was beheaded during the persecution of Decius. His cult flourished from the late fifth century. II.35.

DIANA: Italian goddess originally associated with woods and the moon; later identified in mythology with the Greek goddess Artemis, the virgin-huntress. I.41.

DIDO (ELISSA): Phoenician princess who founded the city of Carthage and who later fell tragically in love with the Trojan prince Aeneas. I.46, II.54, II.55.

DIOCLETIAN (Gaius Aurelius Valerius Diocletianus): Roman emperor who reigned AD 284–305; persecutor of Christians. III.14.

DIOMEDES: king of Argos and Greek hero in the Trojan war. On his return to Greece, his companions were turned into birds by Venus, not by Circe, as Christine implies. I.32.

DIONYSIUS: (1st century BC) according to Christine, who follows Boccaccio, a famous painter who was a contemporary of Marcia. I.41.

DOCTORS OF THE CHURCH: the great theologians of the early Church, four Greek and four Latin. The latter group, to which Christine is probably referring here, comprised Saints Ambrose, Augustine, Gregory the Great and Jerome. I.2.

DOROTHY, SAINT: (d. early 4th century AD) virgin and martyr traditionally thought to have been martyred in Caesarea, Cappadocia, during the persecution of Diocletian. III.9.

DRUSIANA: lady of Ephesus who, according to legend, sheltered Saint John the Evangelist in her house and was later raised by him from the dead. III.18.

DRUSUS TIBERIUS: (38 BC–AD 9) Roman general and husband of Antonia. Younger brother of the Emperor Tiberius, not Nero, as Christine erroneously suggests. She also confuses his name with that of his brother Tiberius: his correct name is Nero Claudius Drusus. II.43.

DRYPETINA: (2nd century BC) daughter of Mithradates Eupator; queen of Laodicea in Asia Minor. II.8.

DULCITIUS: according to legend, Roman prefect who tried to seduce the three sisters Agape, Chionia and Irene. III.14.

DYON: judge traditionally thought to have tormented Saint Christine. III.10.

EARTHLY PARADISE: the Garden of Eden from which Adam and Eve were expelled after the Fall. I.9.

ELAGABALUS (Marcus Aurelius Antoninus): Roman emperor who reigned AD 218–22; cousin of the Emperor Alexander who persecuted Saint Martina. III.6.

ELEUTHERIUS, SAINT: (3rd century AD) deacon and companion of Saint Denis in Paris who was beheaded during the persecution of Decius. II.35.

ELISSA: see DIDO.

ELIZABETH (Saint Elizabeth): cousin of the Virgin Mary and mother of John the Baptist. II.4.

EPHESUS: Ionian city on the coast of Asia Minor. I.16, I.41.

EPHIGENIA: according to legend, Egyptian woman who became a follower of Saint Matthew and built a church in his honour. III.18.

ERYTHREA: see SIBYLS.

ESAU: son of Isaac and brother of Jacob in the Old Testament. II.39.

ESDRAS (Ezra): Hebrew prophet and leader. III.19.

ESTHER: (5th century BC) Old Testament Jewish heroine and wife of Ahasuerus. II.32.

ETEOCLES: elder son of Oedipus and Jocasta; brother of Polynices with whom he fought for control of the city of Thebes. II.17.

ETHIOPIA: ancient empire of eastern Africa, also known as Abyssinia. I.12, I.15, II.5, III.4.

EULALIA (Saint Eulalia): (4th century AD) virgin and martyr born in Merida and killed in Barcelona by the judge Dacian. III.8.

EUPHEMIA, SAINT: (4th century AD) virgin and martyr persecuted and killed in Chalcedon by Priscus, governor of Bithynia. III.8.

EUPHROSYNA (Saint Euphrosyna): (?5th century AD) according to legend, a virgin of Alexandria who disguised herself as a monk (Brother Smaragdus). Her story is probably based on that of Saint Pelagia of Jerusalem, a fourth-century AD virgin and martyr. III.13. See also MARINA, SAINT.

EUROPA: daughter of King Agenor of Phoenicia; abducted by Jupiter, who had disguised himself as a bull. II.61.

EVANDER: son of Nicostrata and the god Hermes (Mercury). According to Roman legend, the first person to build a settlement on the site of the future city of Rome. II.5.

EVANGELISTS: the authors of the four Gospels, i.e. Matthew, Mark, Luke and John. 1.29, III.18.

EVE: the first woman, created from one of Adam's ribs; often cited by misogynist writers in the Middle Ages as the ultimate proof of women's inherent sinfulness and disobedience. I.9.

FAITS DES ROMAINS: (c. 1213) anonymous French compilation of tales of exemplary deeds from Roman history in the period up to Caesar. Extremely popular source for writers in the later Middle Ages. II.67.

FAUSTA, SAINT: (d. early 4th century AD) a fourteen-year-old virgin tortured by the magistrate Evilasius at Cyzicus in Pontus during the persecution of Diocletian, not Maximian as Christine suggests. III.7.

FAYEL, DAME DE: tragic heroine of a late thirteenth-century French romance. II.60. See COUCY, CHÂTELAIN DE.

FELICITY (Saint Felicity): (2nd century AD) according to legend, a martyr who was persecuted and killed in Rome, along with her seven sons, by the prefect Publius. III.11.

FEMININIA, REALM OF: another name for Amazonia. II.12.

FERANT, SEÑOR: Catalan merchant who befriended Sagurat da Finoli (*Decameron* II, ix). II.52.

FLORENCE OF ROME: according to legend, empress of Rome wrongfully condemned to death by her husband. II.51.

FORTUNE: personification often used in medieval literature to symbolize the capricious nature of human affairs. I.19, I.20, I.32, I.34, I.46, I.47, II.58, II.59.

FOY, SAINT: (late 3rd to early 4th century AD) virgin and martyr who died in Agen during the persecution of Dacian. III.8.

FREDEGUNDE: (d. AD 597) wife of Chilperic I and mother of Clotar II. I.13, I.23.

GAIA CIRILLA (Tanaquil): (late 7th to early 6th century BC) wife of the Roman king Tarquinius Priscus. I.45.

GALATIANS: a Celtic people who invaded Macedonia in 279 BC. II.45. See also ORTIAGON.

GALBA (Servius Sulpicius Galba): (3 BC–AD 69) Roman emperor, one of the three whose reigns only lasted a few months each in AD 69. II.49. See also OTHO and VITELLIUS.

GALLIENUS (Publius Licinius Egnatius Gallienus): Roman emperor who reigned AD 253–68 and was a contemporary of Zenobia. I.20.

GENEVIEVE, SAINT: (*c.* AD 420–512) patron saint of France. II.35.

GENOA: northern Italian city on the Tyrrhenian coast. II.52.

GEORGICS: see VIRGIL.

GERMANICUS (Germanicus Julius Caesar): (15/16 BC–AD *c.* 19) Roman general and husband of Agrippina. II.18.

GHISMONDA: daughter of Tancredi, Prince of Salerno (*Decameron* IV, i). II.59.

GIANNUCOLO: father of Griselda (*Decameron* X, x). II.11, II.50.

GOLDEN FLEECE: mythical ram guarded by a fierce dragon; object of the quest undertaken by Jason, leader of the Argonauts, at the behest of King Pelias of Iolcus who wanted to rid himself of Jason as legitimate heir to the Iolcan throne. I.32, II.24, II.56.

GORGON: I.34. See MEDUSA.

GREGORY, SAINT (Gregory the Great, Pope Gregory I): (*c.* AD 540–604) son of a senator, he became prefect of Rome and later pope, in AD 590. I.28, III.19. See also DOCTORS OF THE CHURCH.

GRISELDA: the long-suffering marchioness of Saluzzo (*Decameron* X, x). II.11, II.50, II.51.

GUALTIERI: marquis of Saluzzo and husband of Griselda (*Decameron* X, x). II.50.

GUESCLIN, BERTRAND DU: (*c.* 1320–80) Constable of France and famous knight during the Hundred Years War. Married to Jeanne of Laval, daughter of John of Laval, Lord of Châtillon, and Isabeau of Tinteniac, in 1374. II.22.

GUISCARDO: courtier to the prince of Salerno and lover of Ghismonda (*Decameron* IV, i). II.59.

HALICARNASSUS: Greek coastal city and capital of Caria; reputed to be one of the most spectacular cities in the ancient world. I.21.

HAMAN: (5th century BC) chief minister of Ahasuerus and would-be persecutor of the Jews. II.32.

HANNIBAL: (born 247 BC) Carthaginian general who attacked Rome in 218 BC. II.67. See also CANNAE.

HECTOR: son of Priam and Hecuba and husband of Andromache; greatest of the Trojan heroes during the war with Greece. I.19, II.5, II.28.

HECUBA: wife of Priam and queen of Troy. I.19.

HELEN (Helen of Troy): beautiful wife of King Menelaus of Sparta. Her abduction by the Trojan prince Paris caused the war between Greece and Troy. II.61.

HELEN, QUEEN OF ADIABENE: (1st century AD) ruler of the district of the two Zab rivers in northern Mesopotamia, Assyria; converted to Judaism and went to live in Jerusalem. III.18.

HELLESPONT: narrow strait dividing Europe from Asia, at the point where the waters of the Black Sea and the Sea of Marmara meet the Aegean; i.e. the modern Dardanelles. II.1, II.58.

HELLESPONTINA: see SIBYLS.

HERCULES: greatest of the Greek heroes and companion of Theseus; husband of Deianira. I.18, I.41, I.46, II.60.

HERO: beautiful priestess of Aphrodite at Sestus, on the opposite side of the Hellespont from Abydos, home of her lover Leander. II.58.

HEROD: (3rd century AD) son of Odenaethus and stepson of Zenobia. I.20.

HEROD ANTIPATER: (*c.* 73–4 BC) king of the Jews and governor of Galilee; husband of Mariamme. Christine mistakenly refers to him by the name of his father: he is traditionally known as Herod the Great. II.42.

HEROPHILE: see SIBYLS.

HIPPOLYTA: a queen of the Amazons who married Theseus. I.18.

HIPPOLYTUS: son of Hippolyta and Theseus. I.18.

HOLLAND, DUCHESS OF, AND COUNTESS OF HAINAULT (Marguerite of

Burgundy): daughter of Philip the Bold, Duke of Burgundy, and Marguerite, Countess of Flanders. Sister of John the Fearless and wife of William VI of Bavaria, who became duke of Holland in 1404. II.68.

HOLOFERNES: general of the Assyrian army who besieged the Jews and was killed by the Old Testament widow Judith. II.31.

HOMER: date uncertain. Greek poet traditionally regarded as the father of the epic; author of the *Iliad* and the *Odyssey*. I.29, II.1.

HORACE (Quintus Horatius Flaccus): (65–8 BC) Roman poet famous for his *Odes, Satires* and a treatise known as *On the Art of Poetry*. I.30.

HORTENSIA: Roman noblewoman and daughter of Quintus Hortensius Hortalus. In 42 BC, she pleaded successfully against the Triumvirate's proposal to levy a special tax on the property of wealthy women. II.36.

HYPPO: according to Christine, who follows Boccaccio, a Greek woman captured by pirates who drowned herself rather than be raped. II.46.

HYPSICRATEA: (2nd century BC) wife of Mithradates Eupator and queen of Pontus. II.13, II.14, II.15.

HYPSIPYLE: daughter of Thoas, King of Lemnos, who became queen after her father was deposed. II.9.

IDMONIUS OF COLOPHON: father of Arachne. I.39.

ILIUM: name of the citadel of Troy. II.1.

INACHOS: river-god and ancestor of the kings of Argos; father of Io (see ISIS). I.36.

INDIA, KING OF: according to legend, ruler who commissioned Saint Thomas to build a palace. I.7.

IRENE: (?2nd century BC) according to Christine, who follows Boccaccio, a Greek painter and pupil of the artist Cratinus. I.41.

IRENE (Saint Irene): (d. early 4th century AD) virgin and martyr, companion of Saint Anastasia; one of three sisters who were killed in Thessalonica during the persecution of Diocletian. III.14.

ISAAC: son of Abraham and an Old Testament patriarch. Husband of Rebecca and father of Jacob. II.39.

ISABEAU OF BAVARIA: (c. 1370–1435) Bavarian princess married to Charles VI, King of France, in 1385. II.68.

ISIS: Christine follows classical mythology in conflating two different characters: Isis, an Egyptian goddess and an important deity in the Roman world, who married her brother Osiris (Apis); and Io, daughter of Inachos, who was a priestess of Hera at Argos. Zeus fell in love with Io and turned her into a cow to protect her from Hera's jealousy. I.36, I.38.

ISOLDE: tragic heroine of a legend, first popularized in French in the twelfth century, whose doomed passion for Tristan, nephew of her husband, King Mark of Cornwall, leads to the lovers' deaths. II.60. See TRISTAN.

JACOB: son of Isaac and brother of Esau; an Old Testament patriarch. II.39.

JASON: prince of Thessaly and leader of the Argonauts. Conqueror of the Golden Fleece and lover of Medea. I.32, II.24, II.56.

JEAN DE MEUN: (1235/40–1305) learned clerk who translated many Latin texts. Best known as the author of the continuation of Guillaume de Lorris's *Romance of the Rose*. One of Christine's main targets in her critique of misogynist writers. See her *Letters on the Romance of the Rose*. II.25.

JEANNE (of Evreux): (d. 1371) third wife of King Charles IV of France. She was married in 1325 and widowed two years later. I.13.

JEZEBEL: apostate queen of Israel who incited her husband Ahab to worship the idol Baal and who persecuted the Old Testament prophet Elijah. II.49.

JOACHIM: rich Jew of Babylon and husband of Susanna. II.37.

JOCASTA: wife of King Laius of Thebes and mother of Oedipus, whom she later unwittingly married after he had killed his father. Their two sons were Eteocles and Polynices. II.61.

JOHN, COUNT OF CLERMONT: (1381–1434) son of Louis II of Bourbon and Anne of Auvergne; husband of Marie of Berry. II.68.

JOHN, DUKE OF BERRY: (1340–1416) son of John II of France and Bonne of Luxembourg; married to Jeanne of Armagnac in 1360 and then to Jeanne of Boulogne and Auvergne in 1389. Important patron of the arts. II.68.

JOHN, DUKE OF BURGUNDY (John the Fearless): (1371–1419) son of Philip the Bold, Duke of Burgundy; an important patron of Christine. II.68.

JOHN, KING OF FRANCE (John II, The Good): (1319–64) married to Bonne of Luxembourg in 1332. Christine erroneously implies that he, not his father, Philip VI, was the husband of Blanche of Navarre. I.13.

JOHN, SAINT (The Evangelist): (1st century AD) one of the Apostles and author of the Fourth Gospel. Traditionally also the author of the Book of Revelation which he wrote during his exile on the Greek island of Patmos during the persecution of the Emperor Domitian. III.18.

JONAH: Old Testament prophet who was called upon by God to go to Nineveh and preach repentance. II.53.

JUDAS (Iscariot): apostle who betrayed Jesus. II.49.

JUDITH: Jewish heroine who delivered her people by killing the Assyrian general Holofernes. II.31, II.32.

JULIA: (c. 73–55 BC) daughter of Julius Caesar and Cornelia; married to Pompey in 59 BC and died in childbirth, not in grief at her husband's supposed death as Christine suggests. II.19, II.28.

JULIA: (39 BC–AD 14) daughter of Octavian; third wife of Marcus Agrippa, whom she married in 21 BC; mother of Agrippina. II.18.

JULIAN: judge traditionally thought to have tormented Saint Christine. III.10.

JULIAN THE APOSTATE (Flavius Claudius Julianus): Roman emperor who reigned AD 361–3, called the Apostate because he renounced Christianity and attempted to restore the pagan gods. II.49.

JULIAN, SAINT: (d. ?early 4th century AD) husband of Basilissa. III.18.

JULITTA (Saint Julitta): (d. early 4th century AD) mother of Saint Cyricus, with whom she was traditionally thought to have been martyred in Tarsus. III.11.

JULIUS CAESAR (Gaius Julius Caesar): (c. 100–44 BC) Roman patrician, general and statesman; husband of Cornelia. After his defeat of Pompey, he became dictator, not emperor as Christine states. Later assassinated by Brutus and Cassius. II.19, II.25, II.28, II.49.

JULIUS SILVIUS (Silvius): son of Aeneas and Lavinia. I.48.

JUNO: early Italian goddess originally associated with women and childbirth; later identified in mythology with Hera, Greek goddess of the sky and wife of Zeus. II.61.

JUPITER: originally the Italian sky-god associated with rain, storms and thunder; later identified in mythology with the Greek god Zeus; husband and brother of Juno. I.15, I.36, I.41, I.46, I.47, II.42, II.61, III.10.

JUSTICE: third of the three Virtues who visit Christine. I.6, and Part III, *passim*.

JUSTIN: (6th century AD) eastern Roman emperor and adoptive uncle of Justinian. II.6.

JUSTINE, SAINT: (d. early 4th century AD) according to legend, virgin of Antioch who became an abbess. Traditionally thought to have been martyred in Nicomedia during the persecution of Diocletian. III.8.

JUSTINIAN (Flavius Petrus Sabbatius Justinianus): (AD 527–65) imperial body-guard later chosen as the successor of the Emperor Justin; husband of Antonia. II.6, II.29.

LACEDAEMONIA: name of the Peloponnesian region ruled by the city of Sparta. Christine uses it as a synonym for Sparta itself. I.21, II.24, II.61.

LAMPHETO: a queen of the Amazons. I.16.

LATINUS: king of Latium, husband of Queen Amata and father of Lavinia. I.48.

LAURENTINES: ancient people of Italy who inhabited the coast of Latium. I.48.

LAVINIA: daughter of King Latinus; she was originally betrothed to Turnus but later given in marriage to Aeneas. I.48.

LEAENA: (6th century BC) Greek courtesan and mistress of Harmodius who, with his accomplice Aristogiton, planned to assassinate the Athenian tyrant Hippias and his younger brother Hipparchus. II.53.

LEANDER: youth of Abydos in love with Hero. II.58.

LEDA: wife of Tyndareos, King of Sparta, and mother of Helen of Troy. According to legend, it was the god Zeus, disguised as a swan, who courted and impregnated her. II.61.

LEMNOS: island in the Aegean between Mount Athos and the Hellespont. II.9.

LENTULUS CRUSCELLIO (Lucius Cornelius Lentulus Crus): (1st century BC) Roman praetor proscribed by the Triumvirate after 43 BC; husband of Sulpicia. II.23.

LEOCHARES: (4th century BC) sculptor who worked on the Mausoleum at Halicarnassus. II.16.

LEONTIUM: (3rd century BC) Greek scholar who took issue with the philosopher Theophrastus. Christine does not mention that Leontium was reputed to be a harlot. I.30.

LETTER OF OTHEA TO HECTOR: see CHRISTINE.

LETTER OF THE GOD OF LOVE: see CHRISTINE.

LETTER OF VALERIUS TO RUFFINUS: (c. 1180) Latin tirade against marriage, inspired by Theophrastus, which comes from the De Nugis Curialium (Courtiers' Trifles) of Walter Map (1140–c. 1209), a member of the court of Henry II of England and later archdeacon of Oxford. As it was written under the pseudonym of Valerius, the text was frequently attributed in the Middle Ages to Valerius Maximus. II.13.

LETTERS ON THE ROMANCE OF THE ROSE: see CHRISTINE.

LEUCATIUS: (4th century AD) Roman prefect who courted Saint Theodota. III.15.

LIBICA: see SIBYLS.

LIBYA: traditionally, the coastal land west of Egypt, but often in the ancient and medieval worlds taken to represent the continent of Africa in its entirety. II.1.

LILIA: (5th century AD) mother of Theodoric, king of the Ostrogoths. I.22.

LISABETTA: girl from Messina whose brothers killed her lover (Decameron IV, v). II.60.

LOMBARDY: province of northern Italy. II.46, II.52.

LONGINUS (Cassius Longinus): (c. AD 213–73) eminent Greek rhetorician and philosopher who was a counsellor to Zenobia and her husband Odenaethus. I.20.

LORENZO: lover of Lisabetta (Decameron IV, v). II.60.

LOT: nephew of Abraham who settled in Sodom and was spared, along with his daughters, when the city was destroyed by God. II.53.

LOUIS, DUKE OF ORLEANS: (1372–1407) son of King Charles V of France;

married to Valentina Visconti in 1389. An important patron of Christine. II.68.

LOUIS OF BAVARIA (Louis the Bearded): (c. 1368–1447) brother of Isabeau of Bavaria, Queen of France. Married first to Anne of Bourbon in 1402 and then to Catherine of Alençon in 1413. II.68.

LOUIS, SAINT (Louis IX): (1214–70) crusader-king of France who came to the throne as a child in 1226 under the regency of his mother, Blanche of Castile. Canonized in 1297. I.13, II.65.

LUCIUS VITELLIUS: (1st century AD) Roman consul, not emperor as Christine, following Boccaccio, erroneously states. Husband of Triaria and father of the Emperor Vitellius. II.15.

LUCRETIA: (6th century BC) wife of Tarquinius Collatinus. According to legend, she was raped by Sextus, son of Tarquin the Proud, and subsequently committed suicide. II.44, II.64.

LUCY, SAINT (Luceja): of doubtful existence and date unknown. According to legend, a Roman virgin and martyr who converted Aucejas, her barbarian captor. III.5.

LUCY, SAINT: (d. early 4th century AD) virgin and martyr killed in Syracuse during the persecution of Diocletian. III.7.

MACEDONIANS: inhabitants of mountainous country situated between the Balkans and the Greek peninsula, whose most famous ruler was Alexander the Great. I.41.

MACRA (Saint Macra): (d. 3rd century AD) virgin and martyr whose body was traditionally thought to have been buried near Rheims. III.8.

MANTO: daughter of the seer Tiresias; lived in Thebes during the reign of Oedipus. I.31, I.32.

MANTUA: city in northern Italy near to which the poet Virgil was born. I.31.

MARCHE, COUNT OF LA (John of Bourbon): (d. 1393) husband of Catherine of Vendôme and father of Anne of Bourbon. II.68.

MARCHE, COUNTESS OF LA (Catherine of Vendôme): (d. 1411) married John of Bourbon, Count of La Marche, in 1364; mother of Anne of Bourbon. She inherited the lands of Vendôme and Castres on the death of her brother (before 1375). I.13.

MARCHES: province on Adriatic coast of Italy. I.9.

MARCIA: (1st century AD) Roman painter better known as Lala of Cyzicus. I.41.

MARCIANA (Saint Marciana): (d. early 4th century AD) virgin and martyr of Rusuccur traditionally thought to have been killed in Caesarea, Mauretania, during the persecution of Diocletian. III.8.

MARCIUS (CORIOLANUS) (Gnaeus Marcius Coriolanus): Roman aristocrat who captured the town of Corioli in 493 BC; son of Veturia. II.34.

MARCUS AGRIPPA (Marcus Vipsanius Agrippa): (c. 64–12 BC) Roman military leader, husband of Julia and father of Agrippina. II.18.

MARGARET, SAINT: date unknown. Virgin and martyr who probably existed only in pious fiction and whose cult flourished from the ninth century AD. One of the most popular saints in the Middle Ages. III.4.

MARIAMME: beautiful Hebrew woman married to Herod the Great in 37 BC. II.42. See HEROD ANTIPATER.

MARINA, SAINT: of doubtful existence and date unknown. Virgin traditionally thought to have been disguised as a monk (Brother Marinus) by her father Eugenius in order to smuggle her into a monastery. Very popular saint in the Middle Ages; her story was probably based on that of Saint Pelagia of Jerusalem, as Marina is a Latin translation of the Greek name Pelagia. III.12. See also EUPHROSYNA.

MARINUS, BROTHER: see MARINA, SAINT.

MARK ANTONY (Marcus Antonius): (c. 82–30 BC) Roman statesman and general, husband of Octavia and father of Antonia. Reputed to have led a dissolute youth, his most famous love affair was with the Egyptian queen Cleopatra, with whom he ruled Egypt for some years although he was never officially king. II.42, II.43.

MARPASIA: a queen of the Amazons. I.16.

MARTHA: woman of Bethany; sister of Lazarus the leper. I.10. See also MARY MAGDALENE.

MARTIAL, SAINT: (3rd century AD) bishop of Limoges who, according to legend, was sheltered by Susanna. III.18.

MARTINA: (Saint Martina) (?3rd century AD) virgin and martyr traditionally thought to have been persecuted by the Emperor Alexander. III.6.

MARY: Blessed Virgin and mother of Christ; elected by Christine and the three Virtues to be Queen of the City of Ladies. I.9, II.2, II.4, II.30, II.51, III.1, III.19.

MARY MAGDALENE: repentant prostitute and follower of Christ; Christine follows medieval tradition in confusing her with Mary, sister of Martha of Bethany. I.10, III.2.

MASSYLIA: region on the north African coast. I.46.

MATHEOLUS (Mathieu of Boulogne): author of the *Liber Lamentationum Matheoluli* (*The Book of the Lamentations of Matheolus*) (c. 1295), a satirical diatribe against wives and women in general. Christine probably read this text in the French translation known as the *Lamentations* (c. 1371–2), by Jean Le Fèvre de Ressons, an attorney at the Parliament of Paris and a poet. Le Fèvre wrote a refutation of Matheolus, the *Livre de Leesce*, which was circulated with copies of his translation. I.1, I.2, I.8, II.19.

MATTHEW, SAINT: (1st century AD) tax-collector chosen by Christ to become an apostle; one of the four Evangelists. III.18.

MAUSOLUS: king of Caria, who reigned 377–353 BC; husband of Artemisia who built the Mausoleum in his memory. I.21, II.16.

MAXENTIUS (Marcus Aurelius Valerius Maxentius): Roman emperor who reigned AD 307–12, traditionally thought to have persecuted Saint Catherine. In fact, he was renowned in antiquity for his tolerance of Christians. III.3.

MAXIMIAN (Marcus Aurelius Valerius Maximianus): (*c.* AD 250–310) Roman emperor who persecuted Christians. III.7, III.9, III.16.

MAXIMILLA: according to legend, Greek woman who took the body of Saint Andrew down from the cross. III.18.

MEDEA: sorceress, daughter of Aeëtes and Eidyia, not Perse as Christine erroneously states. Fell tragically in love with Jason, whom she helped to win the Golden Fleece. I.32, II.56.

MEDUSA (GORGON): beautiful girl transformed by Athene into a snake-haired monster who turned to stone anyone who looked at her directly; eventually killed by the Greek hero Perseus. II.61.

MENALIPPE: a queen of the Amazons who fought with Hippolyta against Hercules and Theseus. I.18.

MENELAUS: king of Sparta whose wife, Helen, was carried off to Troy by Paris. II.61.

MERCURY: Roman god of messages and commerce; later identified in mythology with the Greek god Hermes. I.33.

MEROË, ISLAND OF: ancient Nubian capital on a large spit of land on the east bank of the Nile. I.12.

MESOPOTAMIA: country in Asia Minor between the Rivers Tigris and Euphrates. I.20.

MESSINA: city on the north-east corner of Sicily. II.60.

METABUS: king of the Volscians and father of Camilla. I.24.

METAMORPHOSES: see OVID.

METAPHYSICS: see ARISTOTLE.

MICON: (5th century BC) Athenian painter and sculptor; father of Thamaris. I.41.

MILAN, DUKE OF (Gian Galeazzo Visconti): (1351–1402) married to Isabelle of France, daughter of John II of France and Bonne of Luxembourg, in 1360; father of Valentina Visconti, Duchess of Orleans. II.68.

MINERVA: Roman goddess of war, commerce and industry; later identified in mythology with Athene, the Greek goddess of wisdom. I.4, I.34, I.38, I.39. See also PALLAS.

MIRACLES DE NOTRE DAME: (finished *c.* 1227) popular collection of stories pertaining to the Virgin Mary written by Gautier de Coinci (*c.* 1177–1236), a Benedictine monk and author of other religious works. II.51.

MIROIR HISTORIAL: universal history, part of vast Latin encyclopedic work, the *Speculum Maius*, by Vincent of Beauvais (*c.* 1190–*c.* 1264), a Dominican friar and important scholar. Translated into French in 1333 by Jean de Vignay, a monk of the order of Saint-Jacques-du-Haut-Pas in Paris, for Jeanne of Burgundy, Queen of France. Christine's major source for Part III of the *City of Ladies*. III.9.

MITHRADATES (Mithradates V Euergetes): (152/1–120 BC) king of Pontus and father of Berenice (Laodice). I.25.

MITHRADATES (Mithradates VI Eupator Dionysius): (120–63 BC) king of Pontus, husband of Hysicratea and father of Drypetina. II.8, II.13, II.14.

MORDECAI: Jewish palace official at the court of King Ahasuerus; adoptive father of Esther, not her uncle, as Christine erroneously states. II.32.

MOSES: greatest leader of the Jews and their major law-giver, who rescued them from captivity in Egypt. II.30.

MUSES: the nine Greek goddesses who originally presided over music and poetry in general. A special province was later assigned to each of them: Calliope (epic poetry and eloquence), Clio (history), Erato (love poetry), Euterpe (flute-playing), Melpomene (tragedy), Polyhymnia (mimic art), Terpsichore (lyric poetry and dance), Thalia (comedy), and Urania (astronomy). I.30.

MYTILENE: one of the chief cities on the island of Lesbos off the coast of Asia Minor; birthplace of Sappho. I.30.

NATHALIA (Saint Nathalia): (4th century AD) noblewoman of Nicomedia and wife of Saint Adrian; killed in Argyopolis, near Constantinople. III.16.

NATURE: personification commonly used in medieval literature to symbolize the agent of God who creates all living things. I.8, I.9, I.14, I.27.

NEBUCHADNEZZAR II: king of Mesopotamia who reigned 605–562 BC and who subjugated and enslaved the Jews through his general, Holofernes. II.31.

NEPTUNE: Roman god of the sea; later identified with the Greek sea-god Poseidon. I.4, I.47.

NERO (Nero Claudius Caesar): (AD 37–68) Roman emperor who reigned AD 54–68. His many victims included his mother Agrippina and his tutor Seneca. II.22, II.27, II.43, II.48, II.49, III.18.

NICAULA: legendary empress of Arabia, Ethiopia, Egypt and the island of Meroë. I.12.

NICOSTRATA (CARMENTIS): according to legend, nymph and prophetess associated with divine incantation and poetry who taught the indigenous population of Latium to use writing and to whom a shrine was later erected at the Porta Carmentalis in Rome. Mother of Evander. I.33, I.37, I.38, II.5.

NIMROD: first great king mentioned in the Old Testament who ruled over a vast area of Assyria and Babylonia. I.15, I.31.

NINEVEH: ancient Assyrian city on east bank of the River Tigris; according to legend, named after King Ninus. I.15, II.53.

NINUS: king of Nineveh and Babylon and husband of Semiramis. I.15.

NINUS: son of Ninus and Semiramis. I.15.

NIOBE: queen of Thebes, daughter of Phoroneus and mother of Apis. I.36.

NOVELLA: (early 14th century) learned daughter of Giovanni Andrea of Bologna. II.36.

OCEAN: according to early Greek cosmology, the great river supposed to encircle the earth and into which all other streams and rivers flow. I.16.

OCTAVIA (Claudia Octavia): first wife of the Emperor Nero, whom she married in AD 53 and who divorced her in AD 62. II.48.

OCTAVIAN (Augustus or Gaius Julius Caesar Octavianus): (63 BC–AD 14) first emperor of Rome, adopted son of Julius Caesar and father of Julia. II.18, II.49.

ODENAETHUS (Septimius Odenaethus): (3rd century AD) king of Palmyria and husband of Zenobia. I.20.

ODOACER: first barbarian king of Italy who reigned 476–93 AD and was overthrown by Theodoric. I.22.

OEDIPUS: son of King Laius and Queen Jocasta of Thebes who unwittingly killed his father and married his mother. On discovering what he had done, he tore out his own eyes. I.31.

OLYBRIUS: Christine conflates two different characters of the same name: the prefect traditionally thought to have persecuted Saint Margaret; and the second-century AD proconsul who martyred Saint Regina. III.4.

OLYMPIAD: name given to ancient games which took place in the Peloponnesian city of Olympia. I.41.

ON PHILOSOPHY: unidentified text which, according to Christine, denigrates women. I.8.

ON THE SECRETS OF WOMEN: a thirteenth-century work on gynaecology often attributed in the later Middle Ages to Albert the Great (c. 1190–1280), a famous Swabian philosopher and theologian. I.9.

OPIS (OPS): Roman goddess of abundance and wife of Saturn. I.47, II.61.

ORCHOMENOS: principal city of the Greek region of Boeotia; later eclipsed by Thebes. II.24.

ORITHYIA: a queen of the Amazons. I.18, I.19.

ORLEANS, DUCHESS OF (Valentina Visconti): (d. 1408) daughter of the duke of Milan; married to Louis, Duke of Orleans, in 1389. II.68.

ORLEANS, DUKE OF (Philip of France): (d. 1375) fifth son of King Philip VI; married in 1344 to Blanche of France (1327–92), daughter of Jeanne of Evreux and Charles IV. I.13.

ORTIAGON: king of the Galatians whose wife killed the Roman general who had raped her. II.45.

OTHO (Marcus Salvius Otho): (AD 32–69) profligate Roman emperor overthrown by Vitellius after a reign of only a few months. II.49.

OVID (Publius Ovidius Naso): (43 BC–AD 17) Latin author exiled from Rome after he offended the Emperor Augustus, not castrated as Christine erroneously states. I.9, II.1, II.54, II.57.

— *Art of Love*: witty manual on the art of seduction. I.9, II.54.

— *Metamorphoses*: fifteen-book encyclopedia of legends about figures from classical mythology who changed their form; provided the chief subject-matter for medieval commentators on mythology. II.57.

— *Remedies of Love*: witty manual on the art of ending love affairs. I.9.

PALATINE, MOUNT: chief of the seven hills of Rome; traditionally thought to have been the site of the first Roman settlement. I.33, II.5.

PALLAS: ruler of Arcadia, a kingdom in the Peloponnese; father of Nicostrata. I.33.

PALLAS: surname of the Greek goddess Athene who was later identified with the Roman goddess Minerva. I.34, I.39.

PALMARIA: island in the Gulf of Genoa to which early Christians were frequently exiled. III.15.

PALMYRIA: city-state in Syria which, from the second century AD onwards, enjoyed the protection of successive Roman emperors. I.20.

PAMPHILE: Greek woman traditionally thought to have invented the art of growing and spinning silk. I.40.

PANAGO, COUNTESS OF: sister of Gualtieri, Marquis of Saluzzo (*Decameron* X, x). II.50.

PAPHNUTIUS: (?5th century AD) father of Saint Euphrosyna. III.13.

PARIS: son of Priam and Hecuba; abductor of Menelaus's wife, Helen. II.61.

PARNASSUS, MOUNT: sacred mountain in Greece, north of Delphi; home of Apollo and the Muses. I.30.

PAUL, SAINT (Saul): (d. c. AD 65) persecutor of Christians after Christ's crucifixion. Converted and became the chief apostle of the Gentiles; beheaded in Rome during the persecution of Nero. II.35, II.48, III.18.

PAULINA: see BUSA.

PENELOPE: wife of Ulysses who faithfully awaited her husband's return from Troy during his twenty years' absence. II.41.

PENTHESILEA: queen of the Amazons who came to the aid of Troy after the death of Hector. Killed by Achilles, not by his son Pyrrhus, as Christine erroneously states. I.18, I.19.

PERSE: ocean-nymph and mother of Circe, not of Medea, as Christine erroneously states. I.32.

PERSIA: country lying in the fold of the southern Zagros mountains, Asia Minor, which expanded into a vast empire under Cyrus the Great. I.17, II.1, II.6.

PERSICA: see SIBYLS.

PESSINUS: Phrygian mother-goddess whose name Christine confuses with the place in Asia Minor from which her statue was taken to Rome in 204 BC, during the Second Punic War. Her correct name is Cybele. II.63.

PETER, SAINT: (d. c. AD 64) leader of the Apostles, who was crucified in Rome during the persecution of Nero. I.10, II.48, III.18.

PETRARCH (Francesco Petrarca): (1304–74) important Tuscan humanist author who wrote in both Latin and Italian; probably knew Christine's father at the University of Bologna. The work to which Christine is alluding here is his monumental work about overcoming the vicissitudes of Fortune, the *De Remediis Utriusque Fortunae* (*Remedies for Fortune Fair and Foul*), finished c. 1366. II.7.

PHARAOH (Abimelech): king of Egypt who stole Sarah from her husband Abraham. II.38.

PHARAOH (?Rameses II): king of Egypt mentioned in Exodus who enslaved the Jews; father of Thermutis, who rescued Moses. I.3.

PHILIP, DUKE OF BURGUNDY (Philip the Bold): (1342–1404) fourth son of John II of France; married to Marguerite of Flanders in 1369; father of John the Fearless. II.68.

PHILIP, KING (Philip VI): (1293–1350) king of France who reigned 1328–50; husband of Blanche of Navarre and father of Philip, Duke of Orleans. I.13.

PHOEBUS: see APOLLO.

PHOENICIA: country forming a narrow strip along the coast of Syria. I.46, II.61.

PHORCYS: sea-deity and father of Medusa. II.61.

PHORONEUS: king of Argos and brother of Io (Isis). I.36.

PHRYGIA: region of north-west Asia Minor. II.1.

PHRYGICA: see SIBYLS.

PLATO: (427–347 BC) founder of Greek philosophy and teacher of Aristotle in Athens. I.2, I.30.

PLAUTILLA: according to legend, Christian woman who gave her veil to Saint Paul when he was being led to his death. III.18.

PLUTO: Greek god of the underworld. I.35, I.47.

POLYNICES: son of Oedipus and Jocasta; brother of Eteocles, husband of Argia, and son-in-law of Adrastus. II.16, II.17.

POLYXENA: daughter of Priam and Hecuba who was sacrificed by Achilles's son Pyrrhus on his father's tomb in order to appease his ghost and invoke favourable winds to send the Greek ships back to Greece. II.61.

POMMIERS, AMANIEU DE: (mid to late 14th century) Gascon lord who fought for Charles V against the English in the Hundred Years War. II.67.

POMPEIA PAULINA: (1st century AD) wife of Seneca. II.22.

POMPEY (Gnaeus Pompeius Magnus): (106–48 BC) Roman general and consul; elderly husband of Julia, and later of Cornelia. Defeated by Julius Caesar and killed in Egypt. II.8, II.14, II.19, II.28.

PORTIA: (d. 43/42 BC) daughter of Cato Uticensis; married to Brutus in 45 BC. II.25, II.28.

PRIAM: king of Troy. I.19, II.5, II.61.

PRISCUS: (4th century AD) governor of Bithynia traditionally thought to have arrested and martyred Saint Euphemia. III.8.

PROBA (Faltonia Betitia Proba): (4th century AD) Christian poetess and wife of Clodius Celsius Adelphius. Composed a lost epic on the civil war between Constantine II and Magnentius. I.29, I.30.

— Cento: (c. AD 360) text on the creation of the world and the life of Christ which reworked 694 verses from Virgil to demonstrate the parallels between his text and parts of the Old and New Testaments. Also the name of another text by Proba which supposedly reworked verses from Homer. I.29.

PROBLEMATA: see ARISTOTLE.

PROVERBS, BOOK OF: see SOLOMON.

PROVINS: town south-east of Paris. II.65.

PTOLEMIES: name of the Macedonian kings of Egypt. I.20.

PTOLEMY (Ptolemy XIII): (63–47 BC) younger brother of Cleopatra and king of Egypt at the time of the treacherous murder of Pompey. II.28.

PUBLIUS: (4th century AD) Roman nobleman who wanted to marry Saint Anastasia and to prohibit her visits to the Christian martyrs. III.14.

PYGMALION: king of Phoenicia and brother of Dido. I.46.

PYRAMUS: lover of Thisbe of Babylon. II.57, II.58.

PYRRHUS (Neoptolemus): son of Achilles and Deidamia; Greek hero in the Trojan war who killed Penthesilea and ordered the sacrifice of Polyxena. I.19.

PYTHIUS: (4th century BC) architect from Priene who designed the Mausoleum at Halicarnassus and created the statue of the chariot on top of the pyramid. II.16.

QUINTUS HORTENSIUS (Quintus Hortensius Hortalus): (114–50 BC) famous Roman orator who became consul after 69 BC; a colleague of Cicero; father of Hortensia. II.36.

QUINTUS LUCRETIUS (Quintus Lucretius Vespillo): Roman statesman who served as consul under Pompey in 48 BC and under Augustus in 19 BC; husband of Curia. II.26.

RAVENNA: Italian city on the Adriatic coast. I.22.

REASON: first of the three Virtues who visit Christine. Part I, *passim*.

REBECCA: wife of the patriarch Isaac; mother of Jacob and Esau. II.39.

RECTITUDE: second of the three Virtues who visit Christine. I.5, and Part II, *passim*.

REGINA (Saint Regina): (2nd century AD) virgin and martyr from Autun in Burgundy who was the daughter of a pagan, Clement. Persecuted by the proconsul Olybrius whom she refused to marry. III.4.

REMEDIES OF LOVE: see OVID.

REMUS: according to legend, he and his twin brother Romulus became founders of Rome. Killed by his brother in a quarrel over power. I.48, II.33.

RHEIMS: large town in north-east France. III.8.

RHODES: island in the eastern Mediterranean situated close to the coast of Asia Minor. I.21.

RIVIÈRE, BUREAU DE LA: (d. 1400) counsellor and First Chamberlain to Charles V, King of France. II.67.

RIVIÈRE, MARGUERITE DE LA: (d. after 1405) wife of Bureau de la Rivière. According to Christine, she paid off Amanieu de Pommiers's debt in order to release him from prison. II.67.

ROMANCE OF THE ROSE: famous 23,000-line allegorical poem about the pursuit of love. Begun by Guillaume de Lorris *c.* 1240 and continued by Jean de Meun *c.* 1275. I.2, II.25.

ROMULUS: twin brother of Remus and mythical founder of Rome. According to legend, he stole wives for his men from the Sabines, whom he had invited to Rome for a festival. I.48, II.33.

RUSTICUS, SAINT: (3rd century AD) priest and companion of Saint Denis in Paris who was beheaded during the persecution of Decius. II.35.

RUTH: Old Testament Moabite woman who looked after her Israelite mother-in-law, Naomi, after her husband's death. II.40.

RUTULIANS: people of ancient Italy living south-west of Rome, near the modern town of Anzio. I.48.

SABINES: people of ancient Italy who occupied the area north-east of Rome along the west side of the Tiber as far as the Apennine foothills. II.33.

SAGURAT DA FINOLI: alias used by the wife of Bernabo the Genoese (*Decameron* II, ix). II.52.

SAINT-POL, COUNTESS OF (Bonne of Bar): (d. after 1419) daughter of Robert, Duke of Bar, and Marie of France, daughter of King John II. Married to Valeran of Luxembourg, Count of Saint-Pol and Ligny. II.68.

SALAMIS: island near Athens; site of the sea battle at which the Persians were defeated by the Greeks in 480 BC. I.21.

SALERNO: town on the Mediterranean coast near Naples. I.59.

SALUZZO: town in Piedmont, north-west Italy. II.1, II.50, II.51.

SAMIA: see SIBYLS.

SAMOS, SAMIANS: a large Aegean island, and its inhabitants, close to the coast of Asia Minor. II.1, II.61.

SAMSON: one of the Old Testament Israelite judges, famed for his strength, who fought against the Philistines. I.18.

SAPOR (Sapor I): king of Persia who reigned AD 240–72 and was defeated by Zenobia and her husband. I.20.

SAPPHO: (born *c.* 612 BC) famous lyric poet from Mytilene on Lesbos, hailed in antiquity as the tenth Muse. Christine confuses her with Sophron, a fifth-century BC mime writer from Syracuse whose works Plato admired. I.30.

SARACENS: term used in the Middle Ages to denote the Muslims against whom the Crusaders fought for control of the Holy Land. II.13, II.66.

SARAH: strikingly beautiful wife of Abraham the patriarch, who was stolen from her husband by the Pharaoh, Abimelech. II.38, II.39.

SATURN: Roman god of abundance and husband of Opis; father of Jupiter. I.15, I.47, I.48, II.61.

SCIPIO AFRICANUS THE ELDER (Publius Cornelius Scipio Africanus Maior): (236–183 BC) Roman conqueror of Spain and victor of the Second Punic War; husband of Tertia Aemilia. II.20.

SCOPAS: (4th century BC) sculptor who worked on the Mausoleum at Halicarnassus. II.16.

SCYTHIA: homeland of the Amazons. I.16.

SECOND PUNIC WAR: war between Carthage and Rome, 218–201 BC. II.63.

SEMIRAMIS: according to legend, famous warrior-queen who built the city of Babylon with her husband Ninus. Thought to have married her own son Ninus to ensure her control over the succession to the throne. I.15.

SEMPRONIA: (2nd century BC) learned woman of Rome; daughter of Tiberius Sempronius Gracchus, a Roman censor. Married to Scipio Aemilianus Africanus Numantinus, a Roman soldier and statesman. I.42.

SENECA (Lucius Annaeus Seneca): (c. 4 BC–AD 65) Roman senator, orator and writer; tutor to the Emperor Nero, who later forced him to commit suicide. II.22, II.48.

SHEBA, QUEEN OF: ruler of the Sabeans of south-west Arabia who visited Solomon to test his reputation for wisdom. II.4.

SHINAR, PLAINS OF: area in Babylonia where, according to legend, the Tower of Babel was built. I.15.

SIBYLS: inspired prophetesses. The name originally referred to a single person but eventually became a generic term as the number of such prophetesses multiplied. Collections of their sayings, the *Sibylline Oracles*, were kept in various cities and officially consulted in Rome from 496 BC to AD 363. I.4, II.1, II.2.

CIMERIA: the Italian sibyl. II.1.

CUMANA (ALMATHEA or DEIPHEBE): the Cumaean sibyl. In Virgil's *Aeneid*, she led Aeneas into the underworld; she is traditionally thought to have presented her works for sale to Tarquin the Proud. II.1, II.3.

DELPHICA: the Delphian sibyl. II.1.

ERYTHREA (HEROPHILE): the Erythrean sibyl; traditionally thought in the Middle Ages to have prophesied the Last Judgement. II.1, II.2.

HELLESPONTINA: the Hellespontine sibyl. II.1.

LIBICA: the Libyan sibyl. II.1.

PERSICA: the Persian sibyl. II.1.

PHRYGICA: the Phrygian sibyl. II.1.

SAMIA: the Samian sibyl. II.1.

TIBURTINA (ALBUNEA): the Tiburtine sibyl. Mentioned in a passage of Virgil's fourth *Eclogue* which was interpreted in the Middle Ages as her prophecy to the Emperor Augustus of the coming of Christ, though this honour was also sometimes given to the Cumaean sibyl. II.1.

SICAMBRIANS (Cimbrians): Germanic tribe who invaded Italy in the second century BC and were defeated near Verona by Gaius Marius, a Roman consul. Those of the tribe who remained in northern Gaul were later assimilated into the Franks. II.46.

SICILY: large island in the western Mediterranean separated from Italy by the Straits of Messina. II.67.

SIMEON: aged prophet who recognized the infant Christ during the Presentation in the Temple. II.4.

SINAI, MOUNT: mountain in the desert between Egypt and Palestine, traditionally held to be sacred to God. According to legend, site of the tomb of Saint Catherine. III.3.

SMARAGDUS, BROTHER: see EUPHROSYNA.

SOCRATES: (469–399 BC) Greek philosopher and teacher of Plato; husband of Xanthippe. II.21.

SODOM: city of ill repute built on the plains of Jordan and destroyed by God. II.53.

SOLOMON: king of Israel who reigned 962–922 BC and was famed for his wisdom. Traditionally regarded as the author of the Book of Proverbs. I.43, I.44, I.45, II.4.

SOLON: (c. 640–c. 560 BC) Athenian politician and poet. II.1.

SOPOLIS: (1st century BC) according to Christine, who follows Boccaccio, a famous painter who was a contemporary of Marcia. I.41.

SPARTA: city in the Peloponnese. II.61.

SULPICIA: (1st century BC) Roman noblewoman whose husband, Lentulus Cruscellio, was proscribed by the Triumvirate. II.23.

SULPICIA: (3rd century BC) Roman noblewoman famed for her virtue; daughter of Servius Paterculus and wife of Quintus Fulvius Flaccus, a Roman consul; elected by the Romans to consecrate a statue of Venus Verticordia, goddess of chastity. II.43.

SUSANNA: virtuous Hebrew woman and wife of Joachim. II.37.

SUSANNA: (3rd century AD) noblewoman of Limoges who, according to legend, sheltered Saint Martial. III.18.

SYCHAEUS (ACERBAS SYCHAEA): husband of Dido. I.46.

SYNOPPE: a queen of the Amazons. I.16.

SYRACUSE: large town on the south-east coast of Sicily.

TANCREDI: prince of Salerno and father of Ghismonda (*Decameron* IV, i). II.59.

TARQUIN (Lucius Tarquinius Priscus): (616–579 BC) fifth king of Rome and husband of Gaia Cirilla. I.45.

TARQUIN (TARQUIN THE PROUD) (Lucius Tarquinius Superbus): (534–510 BC) traditionally, the last king of Rome and the ruler to whom the Cumaean sibyl is thought to have sold her books of prophecies. Father of Sextus. II.3, II.44.

TARQUIN: (6th century BC) according to legend, Roman nobleman who raped Lucretia. Christine confuses him with his father, Tarquin the Proud: his correct name is Sextus. II.44, II.64.

TARQUINIUS COLLATINUS (Lucius Tarquinius Collatinus): (6th century BC) great-nephew of Tarquinius Priscus and one of the founders of the Roman republic; husband of Lucretia. II.44.

TELEMACHUS: son of Ulysses and Penelope. II.41.

TERTIA AEMILIA: daughter of Lucius Aemilius Paullus, a Roman consul in 219 BC; wife of Scipio Africanus the Elder. II.20.

THAMARIS (Timarete): (5th century BC) Greek painter and daughter of Micon. I.41.

THAMIRIS: according to legend, a queen of the Amazons who defeated Cyrus, King of Persia. I.17.

THEBES: ancient city in the Boeotian region of Greece; according to legend, founded by Cadmus. I.4, I.31, II.17, II.61.

THEODORIC: son of Lilia; leader of the Ostrogoths sent by the eastern emperor Zeno to secure Italy from the barbarian king Odoacer, whom he defeated in AD 493. King of Italy who reigned AD 493–526. I.22.

THEODOSINA (Saint Theodosina or Theodosia): (d. early 4th century AD) virgin of Tyre traditionally thought to have been martyred in Caesarea, Palestine, by the judge and prefect Urban. III.9.

THEODOTA (Saint Theodota): (d. early 4th century AD) noblewoman of Nicaea who was martyred by the proconsul Nicetius during the persecution of Diocletian. III.15.

THEOPHILUS: (d. early 4th century AD) lawyer from Cappadocia traditionally thought to have been converted by Saint Dorothy. III.9.

THEOPHRASTUS: (c. 370–288 BC) Greek philosopher from Lesbos who took over from Aristotle as head of his school in Athens. Author of a lost work, the *Liber de nuptiis* (*Book on Marriage*), usually referred to as the *Aureolus* or 'Golden Book', which contained notable misogamous passages that were subsequently quoted by many medieval writers from Saint Jerome onwards. I.30, II.13, II.14, II.19. See also LETTER OF VALERIUS TO RUFFINUS.

THERMUTIS: daughter of Pharaoh who rescued Moses. II.30.

THESEUS: Greek hero and king of Athens; friend and companion of Hercules, and husband of Hippolyta. I.18.

THISBE: lover of Pyramus of Babylon. II.57, II.58.

THOAS: king of Lemnos and father of Hypsipyle. II.9.

THOMAS, SAINT: (1st century AD) one of the Apostles; traditionally thought to have spread Christianity as far as India. I.7.

THURINGIA, KING OF: (5th century AD) ruler of an area of eastern Germany which lay north of Bavaria and west of Saxony; first husband of Queen Basine. II.5.

TIBER, RIVER: large, fast-flowing river in central Italy; rises in the Apennines, cuts through Rome and enters the Mediterranean at Ostia, south-west of Rome. I.26, I.33, II.5, II.63.

TIBERIUS (Tiberius Claudius Nero Caesar): (42 BC–AD 37) adopted son of Augustus, Roman emperor whose reign ended in terror and tyranny. II.18, II.47.

TIBURTINA: see SIBYLS.

TIMOTHEUS: (4th century BC) sculptor who worked on the Mausoleum at Halicarnassus. II.16.

TIRESIAS: legendary seer of Thebes and father of Manto. I.31.

TITUS (Titus Flavius Vespasianus): Roman emperor who reigned AD 79–81. II.49.

TRAJAN (Marcus Ulpius Traianus): Roman emperor who reigned AD 98–117. II.49.

TRIARIA: (1st century AD) wife of Lucius Vitellius, a Roman consul. II.15.

TRISTAN: lover of Isolde and hero of tragic legend. II.60. See ISOLDE.

TRIUMVIRATE: Roman term for a board of three men in public office, usually elected by the people; the most famous triumvirate, established in 43 BC and comprising Mark Antony, Marcus Aemilius Lepidus and Octavian, assumed supreme authority over Rome. II.36.

TROS: king of Phrygia who founded the city of Troy. I.4.

TROY, TROJANS: ancient city in Asia Minor and its people who were besieged by the Greeks. I.4, I.19, I.32, II.1, II.2, II.3, II.5, II.19, II.28, II.41, II.55, II.61.

TROYES: town south-east of Paris. II.65.

TURNUS: king of the Rutulians and Aeneas's rival for the hand of Lavinia. I.24, I.48.

TYNDAREOS: king of Sparta; husband of Leda and father of Helen of Troy. II.61.

TYRE: city in Phoenicia. III.10.

ULYSSES (Odysseus): king of Ithaca and Greek hero in the Trojan war who was renowned for his cunning; husband of Penelope and father of Telemachus. I.32, II.41.

URANUS: according to Greek myth, father of Saturn and Opis. I.47.

URBAN: (4th century AD) judge and prefect of Caesarea in Palestine traditionally thought to have tormented Saint Theodosina. III.9.

URBAN: date unknown. Father of Saint Christine and governor of the city of Tyre. III.10.

URSULA, SAINT: (?4th century AD) traditionally thought to have been a British virgin and martyr who was killed in Cologne during the persecution of the Emperor Maximian. III.10.

VALERIAN (Publius Licinius Valerianus): Roman emperor who reigned AD 253–60; defeated by Sapor, King of Persia, in AD 260. I.20.

VALERIUS (Valerius Maximus): (1st century AD) Roman author during the reign of Tiberius who wrote a handbook of memorable deeds and sayings, the *Factorum ac Dictorum Memorabilium Libri*, which became an important source for political writers in the Middle Ages. II.13, II.43, II.63. See also LETTER OF VALERIUS TO RUFFINUS.

VANDALS: eastern Germanic barbarian race who overran the western Roman empire in the fifth to sixth century AD. II.29.

VENUS: originally an Italian deity of beauty; later identified in mythology with Aphrodite, Greek goddess of love. According to legend, she was the mother of Aeneas. II.19.

VERGI, CHÂTELAINE DE: heroine of eponymous thirteenth-century French romance, she died of a broken heart, thinking that her lover had betrayed her. II.60.

VESPASIAN (Titus Flavius Vespasianus): Roman emperor who reigned AD 69–79. II.15.

VESTA: Roman goddess of fire whose priestesses, the Vestal Virgins, took vows of absolute chastity. I.47, II.10, II.46.

VETURIA: (5th century BC) Roman noblewoman and mother of Marcius. II.34.

VIRGIL (Publius Vergilius Maro): (70–19 BC) Latin author whose works were highly influential in the Middle Ages. I.9, I.29, I.31, II.3.

— *Aeneid*: twelve-book epic of Aeneas's wanderings after the fall of Troy and up to his arrival in Italy and defeat of his rival, Turnus. I.29.

— *Bucolics (Eclogues)*: collection of pastoral poems. I.29.

— *Georgics*: didactic poem on the agricultural life. I.29.

VIRGINIA: (5th century BC) Roman maiden traditionally thought to have been killed by her father to save her from being raped by Claudius, although Christine states that she committed suicide. II.46.

VITELLIUS (AULUS VITELLIUS): son of Lucius Vitellius and Triaria; the third of the three Roman emperors who reigned in AD 69. II.49.

VOLSCIANS: people of ancient Italy who attacked Rome in the fifth century BC. I.24, II.15, II.34.

VULCAN: Roman god of fire and thunderbolts. I.34.

XANTHIPPE: (5th century BC) wife of Socrates. Although Christine represents her as a loving spouse, she was in fact traditionally renowned for her shrewishness. II.21.

XERXES (Xerxes I): king of Persia who reigned 485–465 BC and attacked Greece to avenge the defeat of his father, Darius I, at the battle of Marathon in 490 BC. I.21. See also AHASUERUS.

YTHERON: (4th century BC) architect who worked on the Mausoleum at Halicarnassus; his correct name is Satyrus. II.16.

ZENOBIA (Septimia): second wife of Odenaethus, King of Palmyria, who ruled the eastern empire in AD 262–7. I.20.

BIBLIOGRAPHY

This bibliography is intended to provide the interested general reader with suggestions for further study. The specialist looking for a more exhaustive list of secondary sources on the works of Christine de Pizan is encouraged to consult the following excellent bibliographies: Angus J. Kennedy, *Christine de Pizan: A Bibliographical Guide* (London: Grant & Cutler, 1984); Edith Yenal, *Christine de Pisan: A Bibliography of Writings By Her and About Her,* Scarecrow Author Bibliographies, no. 63 (Metuchen, N. J. and London: Scarecrow Press, 1989), second edition; and Angus J. Kennedy, *Christine de Pizan: A Bibliographical Guide: Supplement I* (London: Grant & Cutler, 1994). For primary texts, I have included translations in modern English, where available.

I. PRIMARY TEXTS BY CHRISTINE DE PIZAN

Curnow, Maureen Cheney, 'The *Livre de la Cité des Dames* of Christine de Pisan: a Critical Edition', 2 vols (unpublished Ph.D. dissertation, Vanderbilt University, 1975). See also Patrizia Caraffi and Earl Jeffrey Richards, eds., *La Città delle Dame* (Milano: Luni Editrice, 1997). Earl Jeffrey Richards, trans., *The Book of the City of Ladies* (London: Pan Books, 1983).

Fenster, Thelma S., and Erler, Mary Carpenter, eds. and trans., *Poems of Cupid, God of Love; Christine de Pizan's 'Epistre au dieu d'Amours' and 'Dit de la Rose'; Thomas Hoccleve's 'The Letter of Cupid'; George Sewell's 'The Proclamation of Cupid'* (Leiden: Brill, 1990).

Hicks, Eric, ed., Christine de Pisan, Jean Gerson, Jean de Montreuil, Gontier et Pierre Col, *Le Débat sur le Roman de la Rose,* Bibliothèque du XVe Siècle, 43 (Paris: Champion, 1977). Joseph L. Baird, and John R. Kane, eds. and trans., *La Querelle de la Rose: Letters and Documents,* University of North Carolina Studies in the Romance Languages and Literatures, 199 (Chapel Hill: University of North Carolina, Department of Romance Languages, 1978).

Kennedy, Angus J., and Varty, Kenneth, eds. and trans., *Ditié de Jehanne d'Arc*, Medium Aevum Monographs, New Series IX (Oxford: Society for the Study of Mediaeval Languages and Literatures, 1977).

Loukopoulos, Halina D., 'Classical Mythology in the Works of Christine de Pisan, with an Edition of *L'Epistre Othea* from the Manuscript Harley 4431' (unpublished Ph.D. dissertation, Wayne State University, 1977). Jane Chance, trans., *Christine de Pizan's Letter of Othea to Hector*, Focus Library of Medieval Women (Newburyport: Focus Information Group, 1990).

Solente, Suzanne, ed., *Le Livre de la Mutacion de Fortune*, 4 vols. (Paris: Picard, 1959–66). Translated extracts in Charity Cannon Willard, ed., *The Writings of Christine de Pizan* (New York: Persea Books, 1994).

— *Le Livre des Fais et des Bonnes Meurs du Sage Roy Charles V*, 2 vols. (Paris: Champion, 1936–40). Translated extracts in Willard, *The Writings of Christine de Pizan*.

Willard, Charity Cannon, and Hicks, Eric, eds., *Le Livre des Trois Vertus*, Bibliothèque du XVe siècle, 50 (Paris: Champion, 1989). Sarah Lawson, trans., *The Treasure of the City of Ladies, or, The Book of the Three Virtues* (Harmondsworth: Penguin, 1985); and Charity Cannon Willard, trans., *A Medieval Woman's Mirror of Honor: The Treasury of the City of Ladies* (New York: Persea Books, 1989).

2. PRIMARY TEXTS BY OTHER MEDIEVAL AUTHORS CITED IN THE INTRODUCTION

Augustine, Saint, *Concerning the City of God Against the Pagans*, Charles G. Osgood, ed. and trans. (Indianapolis and New York: The Library of Liberal Arts, 1956).

Blamires, Alcuin, ed., *Woman Defamed and Woman Defended: An Anthology of Medieval Texts* (Oxford: Clarendon Press, 1992).

Boccaccio, Giovanni, *De Claris Mulieribus*, Vittorio Zaccaria, ed., in *Tutte le Opere di Giovanni Boccaccio*, Vittore Branca, ed., vol. 10, I Classici Mondadori (Verona: Mondadori, 1970). *Concerning Famous Women*, Guido A. Guarino, trans. (London: George Allen & Unwin, 1964).

de Boer, C., ed., *'Ovide Moralisé': Poème du commencement du quatorzième siècle, publié d'après tous les manuscrits connus*, 5 vols. (Amsterdam: Johannes Müller, 1915–38).

Cazelles, Brigitte, trans., *The Lady as Saint: A Collection of French Hagiographic Romances of the Thirteenth Century* (Philadelphia: University of Pennsylvania Press, 1991).

Fiero, Gloria K., Pfeffer, Wendy, and Allain, Mathé, eds. and trans., *Three Medieval Views of Women: 'La Contenance des Fames', 'Le Bien des Fames', 'Le Blasme des Fames'* (New Haven and London: Yale University Press, 1989).

Guillaume de Lorris and Jean de Meun, *Le Roman de la Rose*, Félix Lecoy, ed., 3 vols., Classiques Français du Moyen Age (Paris: Champion, 1965–70). *The Romance of the Rose*, Frances Horgan, trans. and ed., World's Classics (Oxford: Oxford University Press, 1994).

Larrington, Carolyne, *Women and Writing in Medieval Europe: A Sourcebook* (London and New York: Routledge, 1995).

Roche-Mahdi, Sarah, ed. and trans., *Silence: A Thirteenth-Century French Romance*, (East Lansing: Colleagues Press, 1992).

Van Hamel, A.-G., ed., *Les Lamentations de Matheolus et le Livre de Leesce de Jehan le Fèvre, de Ressons*, 2 vols. (Paris: Emile Bouillon, 1892–1905). Translated extracts in Blamires, ed., *Woman Defamed and Woman Defended*, 177–97.

Vincent of Beauvais, *Speculum Quadruplex, sive Speculum Maius: Naturale – Doctrinale – Morale – Historiale*, 4 vols. (Graz: Akademische Druck, 1964–5, reprint of edition of 1624).

3. SECONDARY WORKS ON CHRISTINE DE PIZAN

Blanchard, Joël, 'Compilation and legitimation in the fifteenth century: *Le Livre de la Cité des Dames*' in Earl Jeffrey Richards *et al.*, eds., *Reinterpreting Christine de Pizan* (Athens, Georgia: University of Georgia Press, 1992), 228–49.

Brown-Grant, Rosalind, *Reading Beyond Gender: Christine de Pizan and the Moral Defence of Women* (Cambridge: Cambridge University Press, 1999).

Brownlee, Kevin, 'Martyrdom and the female voice: Saint Christine in the *Cité des Dames*' in Renate Blumenfeld-Kosinski and Timea Szell, eds., *Images of Sainthood in Medieval Europe* (Ithaca: Cornell University Press, 1991), 115–35.

Curnow, Maureen Cheney, ' "La pioche d'inquisicion": legal-judicial content and style in Christine de Pizan's *Livre de la Cité des Dames*' in Richards, *Reinterpreting Christine de Pizan*, 157–72.

Delany, Sheila, 'Rewriting woman good: gender and the anxiety of influence in two late-medieval texts' and ' "Mothers to think back through": Who are they? The ambiguous case of Christine de Pizan' in her *Medieval Literary Politics: Shapes of Ideology* (Manchester: Manchester University Press, 1990), 74–87 and 88–103 respectively.

Dulac, Liliane, 'Un mythe didactique chez Christine de Pizan: Sémiramis ou la veuve héroïque (du *De Claris Mulieribus* à la *Cité des Dames*)', *Mélanges de philologie romane offerts à Charles Camproux* (Montpellier: Centre d'Etudes Occitanes, 1978), 315–43.

Gottlieb, Beatrice, 'The problem of feminism in the fifteenth century' in Julius

Kirschner and Suzanne F. Wemple, eds., *Women of the Medieval World* (Oxford: Blackwell, 1985), 337–64.

Hindman, Sandra L., 'With ink and mortar: Christine de Pizan's *Cité des Dames*: an art essay', *Feminist Studies* 10 (1984), 457–84.

Kolve, V. A., 'The Annunciation to Christine: authorial empowerment in the *Book of the City of Ladies*' in Brendan Cassidy, ed., *Iconography at the Crossroads: Papers from the Colloquium Sponsored by the Index of Christian Art, Princeton University, 23–24 March 1990* (Princeton: Princeton University Press, 1993), 171–96.

McLeod, Enid, *The Order of the Rose: The Life and Ideas of Christine de Pizan* (London: Chatto & Windus, 1976).

McLeod, Glenda K., *Virtue and Venom: Catalogues of Women from Antiquity to the Renaissance* (Ann Arbor: University of Michigan Press, 1991).

Phillippy, Patricia A., 'Establishing authority: Boccaccio's *De Claris Mulieribus* and Christine de Pizan's *Cité des Dames*', *Romanic Review* 77 (1986), 167–93.

Quilligan, Maureen, *The Allegory of Female Authority: Christine de Pizan's Cité des Dames* (Ithaca and London: Cornell University Press, 1991).

Schibanoff, Susan, 'Taking the gold out of Egypt: the art of reading as a woman', in Elizabeth A. Flynn and Patrocinio P. Schweickart, eds., *Gender and Reading: Essays on Readers, Texts and Contexts* (Baltimore and London: Johns Hopkins University Press, 1986), 83–106.

Willard, Charity Cannon, *Christine de Pizan: Her Life and Works* (New York: Persea Books, 1984).

4. BACKGROUND WORKS

Blamires, Alcuin, *The Case for Women in Medieval Culture* (Oxford: Clarendon Press, 1997).

Bloch, R. Howard, 'Medieval misogyny', *Representations* 20 (1987), 1–24.

Bullough, Vern L., 'Medieval medical and scientific views of women', *Viator* 4 (1973), 485–501.

Dronke, Peter, *Women Writers of the Middle Ages* (Cambridge: Cambridge University Press, 1984).

Ferrante, Joan M., *Woman as Image in Medieval Literature: From the Twelfth Century to Dante* (New York: Columbia University Press, 1975).

Gaunt, Simon, *Gender and Genre in Medieval French Literature* (Cambridge: Cambridge University Press, 1995).

Gold, Penny Schine, *The Lady and the Virgin: Image, Attitude and Experience in Twelfth-Century France* (Chicago and London: University of Chicago Press, 1985).

Krueger, Roberta L., *Women Readers and the Ideology of Gender in Old French Verse Romance* (Cambridge: Cambridge University Press, 1993).

Lacy, Norris J., 'Fabliau women', *Romance Notes* 25 (1985), 318–27.

Maclean, Ian, *The Renaissance Notion of Woman: A Study in the Fortunes of Scholasticism and Medical Science in European Intellectual Life* (Cambridge: Cambridge University Press, 1980).

Marks, Elaine, and de Courtivron, Isabelle, *New French Feminisms: An Anthology* (New York: Harvester Wheatsheaf, 1981).

Moi, Toril, *Sexual/Textual Politics: Feminist Literary Theory* (London: Methuen, 1985).

Rigby, S.H., *English Society in the Later Middle Ages: Class, Status and Gender* (London: Macmillan, 1995).

Robertson, Elizabeth, 'The corporeality of female sanctity in *The Life of Saint Margaret*' in Blumenfeld-Kosinski and Szell, *Images of Sainthood in Medieval Europe*, 268–87.

Thomasset, Claude, 'The Nature of Woman' in Christiane Klapisch-Zuber, ed., *A History of Women: Silences of the Middle Ages* (Cambridge, Mass. and London: Belknap Press, 1992), 43–69.

Wilson, Katharina M., *Medieval Women Writers* (Manchester: Manchester University Press, 1984).

Wilson, Katharina M., and Makowski, Elizabeth M., *Wykked Wyves and the Woes of Marriage: Misogamous Literature from Juvenal to Chaucer* (Albany: State University of New York Press, 1990).

Woolf, Virginia, *A Room of One's Own* (Harmondsworth: Penguin, 1928).

Christine de Pizan's name can also be spelled 'Pisan', and readers should look under both spellings in reference sources, including the www.

PENGUIN ONLINE

READ MORE IN PENGUIN

In every corner of the world, on every subject under the sun, Penguin represents quality and variety – the very best in publishing today.

For complete information about books available from Penguin – including Puffins, Penguin Classics and Arkana – and how to order them, write to us at the appropriate address below. Please note that for copyright reasons the selection of books varies from country to country.

In the United Kingdom: Please write to *Dept. EP, Penguin Books Ltd, Bath Road, Harmondsworth, West Drayton, Middlesex UB7 0DA*

In the United States: Please write to *Consumer Services, Penguin Putnam Inc., 405 Murray Hill Parkway, East Rutherford, New Jersey 07073-2136.* VISA and MasterCard holders call 1-800-631-8571 to order Penguin titles

In Canada: Please write to *Penguin Books Canada Ltd, 10 Alcorn Avenue, Suite 300, Toronto, Ontario M4V 3B2*

In Australia: Please write to *Penguin Books Australia Ltd, 487 Maroondah Highway, Ringwood, Victoria 3134*

In New Zealand: Please write to *Penguin Books (NZ) Ltd, Private Bag 102902, North Shore Mail Centre, Auckland 10*

In India: Please write to *Penguin Books India Pvt Ltd, 11 Community Centre, Panchsheel Park, New Delhi 110017*

In the Netherlands: Please write to *Penguin Books Netherlands bv, Postbus 3507, NL-1001 AH Amsterdam*

In Germany: Please write to *Penguin Books Deutschland GmbH, Metzlerstrasse 26, 60594 Frankfurt am Main*

In Spain: Please write to *Penguin Books S. A., Bravo Murillo 19, 1°B, 28015 Madrid*

In Italy: Please write to *Penguin Italia s.r.l., Via Vittorio Emanuele 45/a, 20094 Corsico, Milano*

In France: Please write to *Penguin France, 12, Rue Prosper Ferradou, 31700 Blagnac*

In Japan: Please write to *Penguin Books Japan Ltd, Iidabashi KM-Bldg, 2-23-9 Koraku, Bunkyo-Ku, Tokyo 112-0004*

In South Africa: Please write to *Penguin Books South Africa (Pty) Ltd, P.O. Box 751093, Gardenview, 2047 Johannesburg*